LAWLESS

Jessie Keane was born rich. Then the family business went bust and she was left poor and struggling in dead-end jobs, so she knows both ends of the spectrum and tells it straight. Her fascination with London and the underworld led her to write the No.1 Heatseeker *Dirty Game*, followed by bestsellers *Black Widow*, *Scarlet Women*, *Jail Bird*, *The Make*, *Playing Dead*, *Nameless* and *Ruthless*. She now lives in Hampshire. You can reach Jessie on her website www.jessiekeane.com.

JESSIE KEANE

LAWLESS

PAN BOOKS

First published 2014 by Pan Books
an imprint of Pan Macmillan, a division of Macmillan Publishers Limited
Pan Macmillan, 20 New Wharf Road, London N1 9RR
Basingstoke and Oxford
Associated companies throughout the world
www.panmacmillan.com

ISBN 978-0-330-53865-7

3 5 7 9 8 6 4 2

A CIP catalogue record for this book is available from the British Library.

Typeset by Ellipsis Digital Limited, Glasgow
Printed and bound by CPI Group (UK) Ltd, Croydon, CR0 4YY

Visit **www.panmacmillan.com** to read more about all our books
and to buy them. You will also find features, author interviews and
news of any author events, and you can sign up for e-newsletters
so that you're always first to hear about our new releases.

With love to Cliff, as always.

ACKNOWLEDGEMENTS

To all those who have helped me along the way to this book, thank you. Special mentions go to Steve and Lynne Ottaway, Sue Kemish, Louise Marley and Karen and Paul, all good friends and supporters.

Big love and hugs to everyone on the Pan Macmillan team, particularly my fabulous editor Wayne Brookes, PR supergirl Katie James and Creative Director Geoff Duffield. Thanks too to my agent Jane Gregory.

For information on the Naples Camorra, I am grateful to Tom Behan for his excellent *See Naples and Die – The Camorra and Organised Crime*.

The release of Roy Orbison's album *I'm Still In Love With You* has been listed as 1974, 1975 and 1976, so I've employed a little artistic licence and taken it as 1974.

For information about the London underworld, thanks to all my usual sources. You know who you are.

AUTHOR'S NOTE

The Camorra is Naples' equivalent organization to the Mafia. It came into existence in the eighteenth century, about a hundred years before its Sicilian counterpart.

Now it is a huge political and economic force in southern Italy, and its tentacles stretch out even further, well beyond Italy's shores . . .

THE DARKE FAMILY

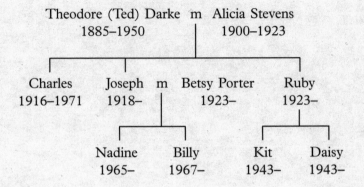

Theodore (Ted) Darke m Alicia Stevens
1885–1950   1900–1923

Charles   Joseph m Betsy Porter   Ruby
1916–1971   1918–   1923–   1923–

Nadine   Billy   Kit   Daisy
1965–   1967–   1943–   1943–

*'What's gone and what's past help
Should be past grief.'*

WILLIAM SHAKESPEARE
The Winter's Tale

PROLOGUE

1975

It happened one night as Reg drove Ruby Darke home to Marlow on the edge of the Thames. And really, was she even surprised? For weeks there had been such stress, such an atmosphere of dread surrounding her that the final thing, the last act in this horrible play, was almost a relief.

She was a strong woman. Tough in business, uncompromising, used to cutting deals and making her mark. After years of graft, she was now not only Ruby Darke the once-despised mixed-race child from the East End, she was also known as the Ice Queen of Retail, owner of the Darkes chain of department stores.

Ice Queen, she thought to herself. What a joke.

She had never felt as weary or as vulnerable as she did at this moment. Michael, her great love, had been murdered, Kit was in trouble – and now there was Thomas Knox who had come into her life and tipped her world upside-down, ruined everything. And these awful people, this merciless Italian clan who seemed intent on damaging the Darke family any way they could.

As the Mercedes turned into the drive leading up to her small Victorian villa, she sat up and stretched in anticipation.

A hot bath, a warm bed. She needed both, then she'd start to feel a bit better.

But . . . there should have been two men on the gate.

The thought sprang into her brain and with it Ruby felt a bolt of fright shoot from her feet right to the top of her head. The family was under threat, so Rob had been taking extreme measures to keep them all safe. Instead of leaving it to Reg, her chauffeur and minder, to protect her, he'd assigned two men to guard the gate . . .

But they weren't there.

'Reg . . . ?' she started, alarmed, her heartbeat quickening.

Reg said nothing. He kept driving.

Ruby reached forward and tapped his shoulder. 'There was no one on the gate. Where are they?'

Reg didn't answer. He brought the car to a halt outside Ruby's front door. In the white glare of the headlights she could see people moving about. But not Kit's people. These were men she recognized, with a shiver of foreboding.

She lunged across the seat and threw open the far door, getting ready to run. But someone blocked her path and leaned in. As the interior lights came on, she saw Fabio Danieri standing there grinning at her.

Then the other rear door opened, and Vittore Danieri got in and sat beside her. Ruby shrank back. Fabio got in too, so that she was caught, helpless, between the two of them.

'Good evening, Miss Darke,' said Vittore, turning his dark vulpine gaze on her.

Jesus, they were going to snatch her. They really were.

She thought of Kit, the son who still resented her, hated her for giving him up all those years ago. He had said he would try to forgive her, but he never had; she knew it. Now her heart clenched as the bitter realization hit her. If

2

they thought he would pay them even a single penny to get her back, they were mistaken. He wouldn't.

But maybe this wasn't a kidnap at all. Perhaps this was it, the end: perhaps they just intended to kill her, not bargain over her. As if reading her thoughts, Fabio drew out a knife and held it almost casually against her throat.

Panicking, straining away from him, terror gripping her, she could only think of Thomas's last angry words: that there could be bits of her daughter Daisy sent through the post to her, bits of Daisy's children if this feud with the Danieris wasn't brought under control. But he'd got it wrong. She realized that now.

It wouldn't be bits of Daisy, or her kids.

It would be bits of *her*.

'Now, Ruby Darke,' said Fabio. 'You choose. Where should I cut you first?'

1

Earlier in 1975

The late Michael Ward and Tito Danieri had been business partners, barely tolerating each other but rubbing along well enough as they poured their own money and a big government grant into the refurbishment of a group of derelict cotton warehouses in the Albert Docks. Now it was the evening of the launch, and all the VIPs were assembled there, cooing over an elaborate model of the projected finished article.

There would soon be designer shops, restaurants, a docklands railway – everything that was needed for smart young execs to live the 'café society'. Everyone was impressed. There were drinks, nibbles and hostesses shimmying around among the excited crowds, handing out smiles and nourishment.

It was a fun night, and Tito pressed a lot of flesh and charmed a lot of women with his bulky prosperous silverback looks, ice-blue eyes and dashing grey beard. Michael Ward – his business partner – of course, wasn't there, because Michael Ward was dead.

Tito gave the nod at around twelve-fifteen, and one of his boys hurried off to fetch his coat. He made his way outside into the damp night air with his three minders moving ahead of him. It had been a good night, he thought with satisfaction, puffing on a freshly lit Cohiba. And there would be more to come. He was a millionaire now, a situation that could be improved upon still further. Tito had big plans.

Sorry, Michael, you didn't live to see this, our night of triumph, he thought.

A shame, really, but they'd never got on. Tito's friendship with the Conservative peer Cornelius Bray – and other things – had grated on Michael Ward, who was firmly in businesswoman Ruby Darke's corner. And Ruby and Cornelius . . . well, there was bad blood there. Lots of it.

Suddenly there was someone standing right in front of Tito, between the boys and himself. He couldn't see a face, not even in the sickly sodium glare of the street lights. The face was covered. Tito's eyes widened in shock and his mouth opened to say, *What the fuck . . . ?*

But there was no time for that. A piercing, awful pain in his chest whipped the breath out of him, crushed any facility for speech.

Stabbed I've been stabbed what are they doing why are they such fucking fools . . .

He couldn't breathe, couldn't shout to his minders for help. His mouth drooped open further, the cigar falling to the ground in a small shower of sparks. Tito felt blackness descend like a thick curtain as his legs started to buckle beneath him.

'*Not smiling now, are you, Tito?*' the figure whispered, and then there was more pain, *unbelievable* pain, as something was yanked from his chest.

It was Miller's voice! It was him, that *cunt* Kit Miller! *Knife . . .*

He clawed at Kit, but he was already gone, running off

into the deeper shadows. Tito folded almost gracefully to the ground. He barely had time to hear the shouts as his boys realized what had happened, then he closed his eyes and died.

2

One of Tito's less experienced boys, one of the three who'd been with him at the Docklands launch, was sent to the favourite family-owned nightclub – which Tito had grandiosely named Tito's in his own honour – to find Vittore, Tito's brother, while the other two, each of them trembling with shock, said they would call on Tito's mother Bella, break the bad news. They'd had to leave the scene when the ambulance and the police came. What the fuck – it was too late to do anything for Tito, anyway.

It was gone one in the morning, and downstairs Tito's was quiet, a man tinkling away a bluesy few notes on a piano, the lighting low and drifts of cigarette smoke creating a drowsy miasma around the couples talking softly at the tables as the hostesses slowly circled them. Donato went through the main body of the club and straight upstairs. One of the boys was on the door there, and he took one look at pudgy Donato's face and let him through without a word.

Inside the flat it was less tasteful nightclub, more Roman orgy. There were chandeliers and Aubusson carpets, deep sofas and a roaring fire. Five men, all big faces from around Little Italy, were being fawned over by a mob of girls – all of them beautiful, all scarcely wearing a thing.

Everyone was laughing, drinks were being filled and

refilled. A fat swarthy-skinned man with his trousers pushed down was in a corner with a blonde woman between his legs, her mouth full of cock. Another man had a girl on his lap, squeezing a handful of naked tit. And another – ah, Jesus, there was Fabio! – he was lounging there with one of the women, a luscious nude brunette, nibbling at her neck, whispering in her ear.

Donato went straight over to him.

'Fabio!' said Donato. He was a cruel-eyed youngster, short, stocky, always up for a fight. Now, he looked like a kid who'd had his favourite toy snatched away. He looked like he was about to cry.

Fabio glanced up, still smiling, a curl of smoke coming from the cigarette held loosely in his hand. The voluptuous naked girl with him stared up at Tito's boy with dead-eyed disinterest. With Fabio distracted, she raised her glass and took a long drink of champagne.

'Donato?' asked Fabio, half-smiling, thinking that he'd fuck the girl very shortly. She'd be only too happy to open her legs for powerful Tito's handsome baby brother; they always were. Across the room was a large gilded mirror, and Fabio could see himself reflected in there: he'd been admiring himself all evening, his glossy black hair, his perfect nose, his olive skin. He was a very good-looking young man, and he *loved* mirrors.

'Is Vittore here?' asked Donato.

As if Fabio hadn't been hearing that all his life! Is Tito here? Is Vittore here? Always looking over Fabio's shoulder as they said it, searching for the older brothers, the ones that could be relied upon for good sense – never for Fabio, the youngest. It hurt him, every single time. Like it had hurt him when his mother and father took in his little sister, Bianca, a white-blonde miniature usurper, just three years old, who had instantly become the centre of his parents' universe. He'd been seven when that happened, and for him it had been a disaster. At least, before *she* came along he'd been the youngest, the baby of the family. After Bianca arrived on the scene, what was he? Not even that, not any more.

'Can you *see* Vittore here?' snapped Fabio. *Stupid cunt*.

'Fab, it's Tito . . .' Donato yanked out a chair and seemed to collapse into it. His face was bleached of colour. He looked like a man in turmoil.

'What about Tito?' asked Fabio impatiently when Donato said no more.

Donato's eyes came up and met Fabio's.

'He's fucking *dead*, Fab. He's *dead*.'

Fabio felt time freeze. He looked at Donato. There were actual *tears* making tracks down Donato's face now. Donato the hard nut. Not very bright. Not bright enough to see that he'd been made a patsy by two much smarter players, that was for sure. He was sitting there blubbering like a child.

'What . . .' Fab felt the smile, the one he had used to such effect on the girl – fuck knew what her name was – stall on his face. The smile stayed there, but the life had gone out of it. 'What did you say?'

'Tito's dead,' said Donato. And he told Fabio about it then, through sobs and hitches and gasps.

About halfway through, the girl got up. Fabio grabbed her arm. 'Where you going?' he asked.

'I . . .' she started.

Fabio yanked her back down.

'Ow!' she complained. People were turning, staring. Fabio still held her arm, crushing it.

'No, you *don't* run off and tell everyone the news like it's a freak show,' he said in a low voice. 'You stay here.'

'You're hurting—' she said.

'*You stay here*,' he said, and this time she remained silent. His returned his attention to Donato. He was thinking *Tito, dead? No. Not possible.*

Tito had been there all his life, an absolute and uncaring despot; ruling the roost after Papa went, with Vittore waiting in the wings, ready to take over when *his* turn came. Fabio's turn at being head of the family was *way* off. It had been set in stone for so long, this fact, that Fabio had almost come to accept it. Almost. He'd always known he'd have to attend two funerals before his turn came. Two graves to stand by, and then all hail King Fabio! He'd always thought that, even as a small boy.

'And where the fuck were *you* when all this was happening?' he asked.

'We were right there with him,' said Donato. 'Right there. This bastard came out of nowhere and did it.'

'Right in front of your eyes,' said Fabio.

'Yeah. Just like that.'

Fabio let go of the girl and stood up. He was nodding, his head bent. Then without warning he lashed out, grinding the glowing tip of the cigarette hard into Donato's cheek. Donato shrieked; so did the women in the room. The stink of scorched skin drifted up, and a faint repulsive sizzling. Everyone was suddenly on their feet, knocking chairs over, backing away, yelling and screaming. Donato was sobbing in agony. He had fallen to the floor and was holding his hands to his burned face.

'You were there when it happened? And you didn't *stop* it?' roared Fabio, leaning in and jabbing the glowing cigarette against Donato's face again, then again. Donato screamed.

One of the other men made as if to intervene. Fabio saw the movement and lifted his arm and pointed a rigid finger at him.

'I *really* wouldn't,' Fabio hissed. Then he turned to the room at large and shouted: 'Place is closed, folks. Everyone out *now.*'

No one moved. Everyone stared at the stricken Donato.

'*Off you fuck!*' yelled Fabio, full volume.

They started moving then, the women gathering up their clothes, grabbing handbags, edging away, their eyes still on him, the way you would keep your eyes on a dangerous animal that could turn and attack.

Fabio pressed the point harder: '*Get out of here! Show's over!*'

Slowly, everyone started to move toward the door. Fabio stood glowering until the last guest closed the door behind them, leaving him alone with the cowering Donato.

'You stupid *cunt,*' he said, and grabbed a heavy marble candlestick from a table and waded in.

Then, when he had seen to Donato, taught him a lesson he would never forget, Fabio went through to the office next door. With hands that shook with a mixture of excitement and terror, his knuckles sore and bloodstained, he phoned his brother Vittore. He didn't know what to do, but he knew that Vittore would. And the irony of this did not escape him.

3

This is a nightmare, thought Bella Danieri. She couldn't
believe that she wasn't asleep and dreaming this horror.
Her boy Tito was dead. In the small hours of that same
morning, she sat with Fabio and Vittore in her kitchen.
Maria had come in, briefly – she knew she wasn't welcome,
she was *never* welcome at any family occasion – and she'd
hugged Bella and said she was so sorry about Tito, was
there anything she could do?

'Go to bed,' said Bella, shrugging off her daughter-in-
law's embrace as if she were an annoying insect to be swatted
aside.

Maria stiffened, glanced at Vittore; he nodded and she
left the room. Presently they heard the door across the
hallway close loudly, and Bella slopped brandy into three
glasses.

'Who did it?' said Vittore into the sudden silence. 'That's
what I want to know.'

Fabio glanced at his older brother. 'He had a lot of
enemies.' *Even you, brother dear. And me. Neither of us could
wait for him to be out of the way, so that we could have our
turn.*

But he didn't say it; Vittore would flatten him if he did.
Instead, he sipped the brandy and stared at Mama Bella.
Earlier, when Vittore had confirmed the news, she had

sobbed and shrieked and clutched at her chest. Now she seemed calmer.

'I want to know the answer. Whoever did this is a *dead* man,' said Vittore.

Bella took a swig of the drink. It warmed her, but not enough to reach the chill that had settled over her soul as Vittore spoke. Vittore wanted revenge. He wanted to find who had killed Tito, and take vengeance on them. But that would place him, Vittore, her favourite boy, in danger. She didn't want that. She had just lost one son. She didn't want to lose another, most particularly not the one who was so precious to her.

'There is something I have to say to you both,' she told them.

'Oh? What is it, Mama?' asked Fabio.

Bella looked from one to the other. Vittore so masculine, so imposing; Fabio so handsome. Her boys. Then her eyes dropped to Fabio's grazed and bloody knuckles. She guessed that someone had paid for bringing bad news to Fabio; this was the way it worked in the Camorra.

'It could have been anyone who did this,' she said shakily. 'One of the establishment, someone Tito crossed over a business deal or a woman.'

'Tito crossed a lot of people,' agreed Fabio.

'It could have been Miller – Michael Ward's number one,' said Vittore. 'Maybe he believed we carried out the hit on his boss. That's a possibility.'

'Or it could have been any one of a dozen others,' said Bella tiredly, shaking her head. When her eyes met Vittore's again they were full of command. 'Now I'm telling you. *Both* of you. There will be no reprisals. I won't have more bloodshed.'

'But Miller—' said Vittore.

'*We don't know who did this*,' said Bella, steel in her voice.

'Mama—' started Vittore, coming to his feet.

'*No!*' Bella stood up too. The fists she rested on the table were shaking, but her eyes flashed with fire. 'I've lost one child this night, do you think I will risk another? I mean it, Vittore. *No reprisals.*'

Fabio drank down his brandy and eyed the two of them, staring at each other across the table.

'Swear to me,' said Bella.

'What . . . ?' Vittore was almost twitching with suppressed aggression.

'Swear it,' she repeated, glancing down at Fabio.

He shrugged. 'All right, Mama. If it means that much to you, I swear. No reprisals.'

Her gaze turned to Vittore. 'And you? Vittore?' she prompted.

He heaved a sigh. 'No reprisals, Mama. I swear, all right? I swear it.'

Bella nodded. After a second she sank back into her chair. Looked at her boys, her two remaining living sons, and asked herself, *Are they lying, to please me?*

She suspected they were. But she had done this much. She thought of Kit Miller, and *his* mother. There was one more thing she could do, to make sure that no other sons ended up on a mortuary slab. She'd had years of this, of the killing, the crooked deals, the stress and the lust for revenge, and she was tired of it all. Then her mind turned with soul-wrenching sadness to her daughter; this would break her heart.

'Someone ought to go in the morning and tell Bianca,' she said.

Vittore nodded. 'I'll do it,' he said.

4

'Blood will flow.'

Ruby Darke would never forget those words, coming down the phone line at her. It was like a witch's curse, she thought later, because blood *did* flow, oh yes indeed. But she didn't know, not then. She just picked up the phone, like you do, like thousands of people do, every day. They pick up, and *bang*. Their world changes for ever. ERNIE's snatched their premium bond numbers out of the pile. Or someone they kissed goodbye only an hour ago is dead, heart attack. The fates roll the dice, and we are all helpless pawns on the great game board of the uncaring universe.

Ruby didn't expect either good news or bad, not that day. But when she looked back, that was how it all started: with the phone

the witch's curse . . .

ringing in her Victorian villa in Marlow.

She was hurrying through the hall, the spring sunlight making pretty patterns as it shone through the stained-glass panels beside the front door. She threw a casual remark back at her daughter Daisy, who was in the kitchen with Nanny Jody, feeding Matthew and Luke, Daisy's year-old twins.

'Hello?' Ruby unclipped an earring, smiled her automatic professional smile.

She hadn't *genuinely* smiled since last November, not since Michael Ward had been found shot dead in an alleyway. She thought about him every day. Mourned him bitterly. Missed him so much. Even though she knew what he'd been, she'd loved him.

On the surface, Michael had been a businessman, giving generously to charities, stumping up for the Aberfan disaster, raising donations for the Hackney Road Queen Elizabeth Hospital for Children. But underneath the façade? He was a crook, the feared leader of one of the big organized gangs who 'ran' the streets of London, like the Krays had, and the Richardsons, the Regans, the Nashes and the Carters . . . Some of those gangs were off the scene now, and there were new developments: the Maltese were muscling in, the Mafia was cruising around, looking tasty, and then there was Tito Danieri's lot, his *camorristi*, who should have been sweating it out in Naples but were here instead, causing trouble. Ruby wanted no part of that world.

Ruby and Michael had been in their forties when they met, too old to be called boyfriend and girlfriend. But they'd been passionate, committed lovers and she felt she'd buried a part of herself when she'd lost him. Slowly, though, she was coming back to some semblance of normality, telling herself to get on with it, that life had to go on regardless how much it hurt.

In the aftermath of Mike's murder she'd ceased to care about the business – Darkes department stores, the chain she had built up from a single corner shop originally run by her dad – but now she was forcing herself to take up the reins again. As it had done so often in the past, work provided solace, kept her sane. Helped her to cope with her loss, just as it had when her twins were taken from her at birth.

She was lucky, she had to keep telling herself that. Against all odds, thirty years after she was separated from them, Daisy and Kit had come back into her life. Daisy, who'd been brought up by her biological father and his wife, had found it easier to forgive than Kit, who'd never known what it was to have a family. Even after he'd learned how she was forced to give him up, he couldn't stop blaming her for abandoning him. While everyone else had rallied round after Michael's death, Kit had kept his distance. That hurt her terribly.

Daisy, however, had been wonderful, as had Rob, Kit's second-in-command, and all her staff. There had been notes of sympathy from her workers at all the stores, and even from Michael's contacts and business associates, people she barely knew. Flowers from a man called Thomas Knox, and a note expressing his deepest sympathy. Then, a little later, a letter sent to her office, offering her help if she should ever need it, asking her to call him, asking if he could call her . . .

Ruby had quickly decided that she never would. She suspected that Knox, like Michael, operated on the precariously narrow line between big business and criminal activities, skirting between legit and not-so-kosher deals. Bad enough that Kit was following that same perilous path; all she wanted now was to escape that shadowy underworld. It was dark and it was dangerous. Look at what had happened to Michael. Wasn't that proof enough?

'Do you know a Thomas Knox?' she'd asked Rob one day. She could always talk to Rob, far more easily than she could talk to Kit. Rob was solid as a rock; he'd been her minder last year, when she'd had need of one. He'd saved her life.

'Knox? Sure. Hard man, a real face. He was at Michael's funeral – didn't you see him? Big guy. Fortyish. Blondish sort of hair. Why?'

'No reason,' said Ruby.

She was sure she *had* seen Knox there, watching her with hard blue eyes.

She kept the flowers – they were beautiful – but she binned the note, and the letter.

As she picked up the phone, Ruby's mind had already made the assumption that it would be something to do with her plan to roll out coffee shops across the Darkes chain. Shifting to professional mode, she forced herself to confront her reflection in the mirror above the telephone table. Lately, she had avoided mirrors. Now she looked and there she was: Ruby Darke, still battling away, still coping. She saw a woman of a certain age and mixed race, dark haired with café au lait skin. She was model-thin (maybe too thin, since Michael had gone and food had lost its appeal) and elegant. She was dressed in black, and pearls. Her features were delicate, and her straight, thick black hair was swept back into a neat chignon. She looked confident and wealthy. But her eyes, darkest brown with speckles of copper-gold, told the true story. The expression in them was anxious and miserable, full of sadness.

'Is that Ruby?' It was a female voice, accented – French or Italian? – with a hint of uncertainty.

'It is.' A little frown of puzzlement wrinkled Ruby's brow. 'Who is this?'

'I am Bella Danieri. Tito's mother.'

Ruby's false business smile dropped away. Italian, then. She'd heard the news about Tito, and how he'd died. Everyone had.

'I want you to come to his Requiem Mass,' said Bella. 'If you would.'

'Well I . . .'

'Please. I want you to come.' And Bella started reeling off the time, the place, the date.

Ruby paused, hearing but not wanting to, wondering how she could get out of this. She hadn't even *known* Tito, not really. He'd been an associate of Michael's, so she'd brushed up against him once or twice. She hadn't liked him. One look into those soulless eyes had told her all she needed or wanted to know about Tito Danieri. She had formed the strong impression that Michael had done his utmost to keep her out of Tito's way. So no, she didn't want to attend his funeral.

'I don't know . . .'

'Please, you must.' Bella's voice trembled. She stopped speaking. Then she seemed to gather her strength to go on. 'Please come. I have to talk to you. Or I tell you, blood will flow.'

And there it was. The witch's curse.

Blood will flow.

And God help them all, because it did.

5

There was something awesome about Bianca Danieri, with her straight fall of silvery white-blonde hair, her lily-pale skin and her turquoise-blue eyes. *And* she knew it. Exploited it, in fact. To emphasize the whiteness of her hair and skin, she *always* wore white. The woman in white, pale as the proverbial ghost; that was Bianca. Even her name meant 'white'. She could nail a room in one second flat, turn the attention of everyone in it directly to her.

Bianca was twenty-five years old and for the first time ever her brothers had trusted her enough – or Mama Bella had nagged them sufficiently – to run one of the just-about-to-launch new Danieri family discos. This one was in Southampton at the Back of the Walls, where the ancient city fortifications still stood. Not a prime site in London's West End like the ones the family already owned, oh no – not like Tito's, or Fellows or Goldie's; of course not. Bianca had to prove herself in the wasteland of the sticks first. Well, so what? Prove herself she would.

The disco was to be called Dante's – Bianca's own choice, she liked the idea of replicating an inferno in here – and the red, black and gold paint was still tacky and stinking the place out. The kitchens had been fitted over the past week, the black carpets (which wouldn't show the inevitable stains) were being laid today, then the furnishings were coming in. The sparks were in now, fiddling with the strobes. It was all hands to the pump.

'Hey, Cora, you listening?' said Bianca. 'Drayman's delivering at eleven, you sort him out, OK?'

Cora, a tall redhead who'd been running bars since before Bianca was born, nodded.

'And Tanya . . . where the hell's Tanya?'

While Cora was in charge of bar staff, Tanya was here to manage the waiters and waitresses, or rather 'hosts' and 'hostesses'. They would be working front-of-house, dressed in fetching little devil costumes, and red horns. Red wings had been discussed as an option, but Bianca had dismissed that idea. 'Take up too much room,' she said. 'You turn around, knock a punter's drink flying. Nah. Silly idea.'

'Tanya had a hot date last night, I heard,' said Claire, a tiny brunette already puffing on her twentieth cigarette of the day.

'I told her to get in early.'

Cora and Claire exchanged looks. They both knew that Tanya had been moonlighting at Nero's, a club in Portsmouth where the girls were all tricked out in dinky little togas. They also knew that if Bianca found out about this, she would grab Tanya by the throat and give her seven kinds of shit before kicking her smartly out the door. You didn't mess with Bianca.

'She'll be in soon,' said Cora loyally.

'She'd better be.' Bianca might look like a cool blonde angel, but she wasn't up for being taken for a mug, not now, not ever. She'd been adopted into a fierce immigrant family, and had absorbed their ways; she wouldn't take any shit. And it mattered so much to her that this went right. *So* much.

She was special and she knew it. Bella was always telling her so.

'We *chose* you out of all the little girls we could have brought home from the orphanage,' Bella would say.

Bianca had no memory of the orphanage. All she *did* remember was a blonde woman, smiling. One of the nuns or matrons or whatever they were called, no doubt. And Tito, cuddling her in the family kitchen, saying she was his little sister, his precious one – with Vittore looking on, uninterested, and Fabio looking furious. Oh – and a bead of blood, dripping from a blade of grass. Weird. She must have fallen over when she was small, cut herself perhaps. Something like that.

'Speak of the devil!' said Claire, as Tanya came in the door, looking washed out.

'Sorry,' she said quickly. 'Sorry I'm late.'

'What the fuck time d'you call this?' asked Bianca.

Tanya looked truculently up at the clock on the wall, brand new and still without its batteries, both hands stuck at the vertical.

'Twelve,' she said.

There was a brief, freezing silence.

'Don't even *think* about being bloody funny,' said Bianca. 'Carpet fitters are coming in today, and *they're* late too, so get on the sodding phone and hurry them up, *capisce*? And you keep an eye on them when they get here, I don't want to see any joins in awkward places, I want this to look the business.'

'And what will you be doing?' asked Tanya. It wasn't her job to balls around looking at *carpets*. She was supposed to be in charge of the waiting staff, wasn't she?

Bianca looked at her. 'You got a hangover?'

'A bit.'

'Then I'll make allowances. Not that it's anything to do with you, but I'll be interviewing doormen, if that's all right with you, Tanya?'

Tanya shrugged. *Sure.*

'OK, get on with it then, the lot of you. I'll be up in the office.'

Bianca went upstairs. Cora and Claire looked at Tanya.

'What?' she asked.

'You don't half push your luck,' said Claire. 'She ain't in the mood for fun and games.'

'She never flaming is,' said Cora.

'She's on edge with all the decorating and stuff going on. She wants the place to look right. Tito's trusted her with it, and she wants to impress him.' They all knew how Bianca worshipped her eldest brother, Tito. Claire took a long pull at her cigarette, then stubbed it out in a black ashtray on the bar. 'Let's get on then, shall we . . . ?'

Half an hour later, the carpet fitters arrived. And half an hour after that, Vittore Danieri showed up.

'Bianca here?' he asked the three women, who were pausing by the bar for a fag and a coffee.

Vittore had an authoritative way about him, like Bianca; he was big, blockish like Tito, robust and tough-looking and ugly with a hooked nose, receding black hair and bulging dark brown eyes. There was a stillness, a hardness about him – and he looked somehow *polished* like Tito too, in the way that rich guys did.

'Why hasn't he got a neck?' they'd joked between themselves when they first set eyes on him. Vittore's head was set low on his shoulders and it poked aggressively forward; he *didn't* seem to have a neck, it was true, but then he didn't seem to have a sense of humour either, so they maintained a show of respect in his presence.

'Bianca's upstairs,' said Tanya, her eyes catching his.

She thought of it as *turning on the headlights*. She turned them on now, gave him full beam, eyelashes fluttering, *You want some of this?* She knew he was married, but she didn't give a toss about that. Of course, she would prefer to have Tito, but Vittore would do. The family was loaded, and all the brothers – even that vain little tit Fabio who'd come down here once trying to chuck his weight about – had an aura of power that appealed to her.

'Right,' said Vittore, and passed by all three of them without a second glance.

'Shit,' said Tanya, shaking her head. 'Am I losing it, or what?'

'Girl, you never had it to lose,' laughed Cora.

'Yeah, funny,' said Tanya, and Claire gave a smirk.

'Come on,' sighed Claire. 'Work to do . . .'

Bianca wasn't particularly surprised to see Vittore show up unannounced. She was thrilled that Tito had entrusted her with the start-up of Dante's, after she had spent several years learning the business up in London; but she was under no illusions. He was expecting her to fail, to need bailing out at any moment.

She was used to this. With three older brothers, she was always the one standing on the sidelines, the one nobody consulted or enquired after, because she was a *girl* and in their eyes that made her something less than a man, someone less likely to get things properly done. She had kicked against it for most of her life, but it was *there*, always staring her in the face: the testosterone wall.

She might have been used to it, but that didn't mean she liked it, or accepted it. In fact, it enraged her. She knew she was capable, sensible, *tough* enough to run this place. When she put herself forward for it, her brothers been taken by surprise; it was obvious that they wanted to say no, but Mama had backed her. They all knew Mama was the boss, so Tito had said OK, why not? All the time expecting Bianca to make a bollocks of it.

And here it was, Vito checking up on her, proof that they thought her inadequate; a mere female and not even *one of them*. She was adopted, not *proper* Danieri blood.

She waited patiently for him to say the words: *Everything OK, Sis? Need a hand?*

Expecting – almost hoping – that she would say, *Yes, someone's giving me trouble, can you help me please, Vittore?*

She would rather *choke* than say any such thing. She was tough, through and through. She carried a .22 calibre gun in her handbag, she looked you straight in the eye and dared you to look back. She was Tito Danieri's little sister. She was Camorra.

'Vittore!' she greeted him warmly as she sat behind her desk, elbow-deep in paperwork. *Fucking* paperwork. 'What can I do for you?'

It's more what I can do for you, Sis. I'm here to help you out of whatever trouble it is you can't handle.

And all the while he'd be mocking her in his head, thinking, *Knew it. She can't cut it, not like us boys.*

Well, she was going to show them.

'Sis . . .' he hesitated. Vittore's face was somehow . . . changed. No confident sneer today, and his mouth looked tight, strained.

Bianca felt alarm spiral up through her core. Felt that soul-draining weakness that comes with the certainty that something nasty is coming, something *bad*.

'What is it?' she said, rising to her feet.

'No. *No.* Sit down, Bianca. This is bad news. I'm sorry.'

Bianca sank back into her seat. 'Is it Mama?' she asked, dry-mouthed.

He was shaking his head.

'It's Tito,' he said. 'It happened last night, when he was at the new place in Docklands.' Vittore swallowed hard, and Bianca was horrified to see that his eyes shone with tears. 'He's dead, Bianca. Tito's gone.'

6

'Are you sure about this?' Daisy asked her mother on the day of Tito's funeral.

'No, I'm not,' said Ruby. 'But I'm going.'

'Then I'll come with you,' said Daisy, her face looming up in the mirror at Ruby's shoulder.

Ruby glanced at her watch. Ten to eleven. She felt a shiver of apprehension run right through her. The sort of shiver that told your senses *Just don't, OK?* But she sent her daughter's reflection a smile. 'I'd rather you didn't. Stay here with the babies.'

Daisy's eyes, blue as cornflowers, stared into her mother's. She thought that Ruby'd had more than enough upsets over the past few months. She wished she wasn't being so damned *obstinate* about this. But then, Ruby was obstinate about nearly everything: Daisy supposed that was how she came to be such a success in life.

Could she look any less like me? wondered Daisy, watching her mother straighten her pearls in the hall mirror. It never failed to amaze and amuse her when she looked at Ruby. Daisy herself had the healthy tanned complexion, golden-blonde hair and robust build of a Valkyrie. There was certainly no question who Daisy's father was: she was every inch the daughter of big, blond Cornelius Bray. She looked *nothing* like exotic, dark-skinned Ruby – unlike her twin, Kit.

Daisy didn't even *sound* like her mother. Ruby's voice still held a hint of the East End she'd grown up in; when Daisy spoke it was with the beautifully rounded vowels of the Home Counties, as befitted the daughter of Lord and Lady Bray. But Lord Bray hadn't wanted to know about his dark-skinned son; Kit had been raised in a succession of uncaring state orphanages. And she had always felt so guilty about that.

In fact, Daisy felt that lately she passed her days *consumed* with guilt, not only about Kit but about her babies too. She loved her boys desperately, but being a stay-at-home mum had left her feeling restless, a little frustrated, a little *bored* even. Did that make her a failure as a mother? She felt that she was. And having abandoned her babies – and every waking minute spent away from them was torment – had she now compounded her failure by being a complete washout at her job?

'How's it going?' Ruby asked.

'Hm?'

'At the store.'

Shortly after Christmas, Daisy had asked her mother if she could perhaps work in the Darkes flagship Marble Arch store. Ruby had been surprised, but gratified. She had *dreamed* of her daughter following in her footsteps one day. But she insisted that if Daisy was going to work in the store, then she was going to have to learn the trade from the bottom up, just as she had. And Daisy had agreed, even though it wasn't what she'd envisaged. She'd pictured herself doing a little clerical work in Ruby's office, helping out Joan, her mother's PA. She liked Joan, who was a merry-eyed matron and kindness itself.

The trouble was, nothing had turned out the way she'd

imagined – least of all store work. And on top of that there was the agony of leaving the twins in Jody's care. Daisy felt shaky and near to tears, hyper-emotional every time she had to leave them. Plus she was still breastfeeding, which meant she had to express milk for their feeds, and wear pads inside her bra because her breasts leaked. Granted, the boys were gradually being weaned on to formula feed so she wouldn't have to do it that much longer, but each day it seemed more of a struggle. Maybe Simon, her ex, was right: maybe she *was* a bad mother. True to his usual form, Simon had flown into a rage when she'd told him she planned to start work in the store, accusing her of abandoning the boys. Much as she hated the thought of doing anything that would please him, it was so, so tempting to throw in the job.

'It's going OK, is it?' Ruby persisted. 'At the store?'

Daisy gave a smile. 'Oh yes. Great.'

Ruby studied her daughter's face; she suspected that Daisy was lying, probably to spare her feelings, to avoid worrying her when she had enough on her plate as it was.

I'm so lucky that I've found Daisy again. That she's here with me, she thought. All the pain she had been through over the years, all the anguish, was softened by Daisy's presence. Her relationship with Daisy, after almost three decades apart, had fallen almost easily into a comfortable, loving mode. But her relationship with Kit was never going to be so simple.

Ruby heaved a sudden sigh.

'What?' asked Daisy, watching her mother curiously.

'I was thinking about your brother,' said Ruby.

'Well, *he* won't be at the funeral, that's for sure. He hated Tito!' Daisy snorted. 'And you don't have to go either. Not if you really don't want to.'

But Ruby knew that was not true. She *did* have to be there. Because of Bella, Tito's mother. And because of the phone call.

Blood will flow.

What could Bella have meant by that? Was it a threat? Or a warning? Ruby shuddered to think of that voice on the phone, trembling yet full of determination.

She had no choice. She had to find out what Bella was talking about.

7

'Honey, wake up! Wake *up*!' squealed a voice in Kit's ear.

'Wha . . . ?' he groaned, deep in a dream where a woman jangling with gold smiled at him with flirtatious sea-green eyes.

An alarm was going off. Someone was shaking his shoulder.

Ah shit no. Lemme sleep. Let me go back to her . . .

'Wake UP!' shouted the female voice, shaking him harder.

Kit opened his eyes. A shadowed face was leaning over him, hair tickling his face. For a moment he thought it was *her.* But then he realized it wasn't. Felt the numb deadness crush him again. 'What the fuck . . . ?' he mumbled.

'It's ten o'clock. You said not to let you sleep past ten, remember?' said the girl, sounding annoyed.

Kit came properly awake. No, this wasn't Gilda. It was . . . damn. Couldn't remember her name. His head ached, he'd drunk too much last night and fallen into bed with her, one of the hostesses maybe? One of the dancers? Who knew? Who cared? He'd been in a club, drinking. Which club, he didn't know. His mouth was parched and sour, his eyes gritty.

Ten . . . Why had he asked her to wake him at ten? He couldn't even remember doing that, and he knew that was bad. This whole *drinking* thing was bad.

The alarm was still blaring away. He reached out, thumped the switch to *off.* Silence fell, except for the steady background hum of traffic out on the main road. And then it came back to him, all of it. Today was the day of the funeral. Today was the day that Tito Danieri got planted.

'Coffee,' she said, and slapped a mug down beside the alarm clock.

Kit pulled himself into a sitting position, rubbed his hands over his face. He looked at them, briefly. Both his palms bore pale ugly scars, but they were as much a part of him now as his teeth or his hair. He was used to them. Then he looked around the bedroom. It was flooded with light, fabulous and airy just like every other room in his house, which was a tall and fiendishly expensive Georgian place a stone's throw from Belgravia. No more poky bedsits for him: he'd made it. Or rather, *Michael* had made it, and then had made *him*. Once he would have been so thrilled with all this. His *own house*, after growing up in rat-hole council orphanages and then making his own way out on the streets. Now, he barely even cared.

He reached for the coffee.

'So what are your plans for today?' asked the girl, sitting there naked on the edge of the bed. She was pretty, blonde, but he still couldn't remember who the hell she was.

I have to stop this, he told himself. *The drinking. The women. Maybe after today, I'll be able to. Who knows?*

'Going out,' he said, wincing as scalding-hot and sour-tasting instant coffee scorched his lips. He put the mug down. Looked at her.

'Only I thought maybe we could spend some time together? I'm not on till eight.' Her tone was hopeful.

One of the dancers? Oh yeah. And her name is . . . Susie.

'Sorry, Susie,' he said. 'Busy.'

The girl's cheeks coloured. 'I'm not Susie,' she spat. 'My name's Alison.'

'Sure.'

'I just thought . . . after last night . . .' she said, her voice trailing off. She was wounded by his indifference. She looked at the man in the bed, so handsome, so well-muscled; he was like a hard-looking version of that famous actor, Omar Sharif. His skin was the colour of warm caramel, his face very still in repose, as noble and serene as an emperor's – but his eyes, unlike Omar's, were that fabulous, unexpected bright cornflower blue. She was already halfway in love with him, and he didn't even know her *name* . . . and now, looking at him, she didn't think he remembered that they had made love last night either. And maybe they hadn't. For sure, *she* had been making love: but now she could see, with painful clarity, that for Kit it had been anonymous, mindless sex.

Alison got off the bed. 'You know what? You're a bastard.'

'I'm sorry . . .'

'Yeah! Tell it to the fucking marines,' she said, and hurried off into the bathroom.

Kit sat there in the bed, alone, and thought of the day ahead.

The day of Tito's funeral.

Something to look forward to, after all.

8

'Well, Astorre, how are we going to get through this?' Bella Danieri asked the framed black-and-white photo of her late husband on the mantelpiece. No answer came. Of course it didn't. Astorre had been gone for ten years now, he didn't have to go through the excruciating pain of burying their eldest child, his favourite son, Tito. She was thankful for that.

Bella picked up the photograph and kissed the still, silent face. He'd been no looker, her Astorre. Bulging-eyed and over-excitable, Astorre had been a bruiser of a man, bludgeoning his way through life. He was *camorristi*, one of the much-feared Camorra, a powerful Naples urban underworld organization. And he'd been doing well in the city of his birth until the feud with Corvetto forced the Danieris out of the district of Villaricca.

Astorre had dragged himself and his Italian émigré family from those dangerous Naples gutters to the even meaner streets of London, pushing aside all those who would attempt to hold him back from enjoying his due: a comfortable life of crime.

He had achieved his goals too; he'd mixed with the best of the best. The resettled Danieris had dined with MPs, celebrities and minor aristocracy. Their eldest son Tito had taken over the reins after Astorre's passing, extending their

34

criminal empire still further. Tito had proved himself a skilled puppet-master, building on Astorre's talent for business, blackmail and subtle mayhem, ensuring that the family would always be safe. Too many people in high places stood to lose their easy life of privilege should the authorities ever bring trouble to the Danieri family door.

Bella stood and looked around at this room, stuffed full of the possessions accumulated over a lifetime. The Danieri family had thrived in exile. At first, of course, life had been a struggle, but now they owned this big townhouse with its many rooms, placed squarely and elegantly here in Little Italy, in the heart of Clerkenwell. They were safe, secure, among their own kind, and reasonably content with that.

Bella preferred to keep her family close, under her control. She didn't like Bianca being away so much, down on the south coast, but she kept her adopted daughter's room just as she left it, so that it was always ready for her return.

Why should her sons and her daughter find places of their own when there was this big house here, with plenty of space for them all? Of course, Tito had kept an apartment over one of the clubs – she didn't want to know about *that*, or about what he got up to when he was there, God forbid. Fabio, her youngest boy, still lived here with his Mama, and why not?

And Vittore!

Bella's lip curled. Her favourite boy, the middle son, had shocked and upset her by insisting on marrying that whore Maria. He'd been ready to break his mama's heart by moving out, setting up his own household with the slut.

Bella soon put a stop to *that*. She had cajoled, pleaded, cried, clutched at her chest. 'I am losing my son!' she wailed.

In the end, Vittore had relented, as she had known he would. Now Vittore and Maria had their own set of rooms

– lounge, kitchen, wine cellar, bathroom, bedroom, even their own little patch of garden – in the big family home, and there was no more talk of them moving out.

The rain battered against the window and Bella gazed out at the dark sky, the lashing rain. She sighed then, and cursed the weather in this country. In Napoli, sweet hot Napoli, people sat outside, sharing grappa with their neighbours and laughing at the problems of the world under a brilliant, scorching sun. Here, they huddled indoors even in the summer months, and the air was never dry, it was always damp, humid: everyone went out in raincoats to dodge the showers. But there could never be any going back for the family; she knew that. *This* had become their country, their home.

Once it had seemed that nothing could touch them here, nothing at all: and then *it* happened. Her son Tito, walking out of the renovated Docklands one night. An assassin, lying in wait, striking when it was least expected. A single thrust with a long, narrow blade, and her precious boy, her eldest, was dead.

With trembling fingers Bella placed her long-dead husband's picture back on the mantelpiece. She was so tired of it all: the fight, the struggle. Tired to death; all she wanted was *peace*. No reprisals, no beatings. She'd told the boys and she meant it. Tito was gone, *nothing* was going to bring him back. Let him rest.

Blinking back tears, she focused on her reflection in the mirror. Why not admit it? Her husband might have been no looker, but she wasn't either. Years of sophisticated company, high-end dinner parties, charity galas, and still she looked like what she was: an Italian peasant woman, her greying hair scraped back in a bun, her face a pallid network of wrinkles, her sallow complexion not flattered by the unadorned black dress she wore, her eyes stricken with grief.

'Mama?'

Bella turned. It was her Vittore. Her beloved boy. He too was showing signs of age: his hairline was receding, forming a widow's peak at the front. It gave him a sinister look, wolfish.

Vittore had always been her favourite, the one she had nursed at her breast for longest, the one she doted on the most. Now he was the eldest living boy and head of the family. He came forward, looking at his watch. It was nearly ten thirty. He kissed her dutifully on both cheeks, held her close for a moment, then pushed her back.

'*Finally* he comes to see his mother,' Bella sniffed.

'Shouldn't Bianca be here?' asked Vittore, ignoring her remark. He was used to such things.

Bella gave a shrug; Bianca was a law unto herself. She smiled faintly and patted his cheek. Vittore was her special one, that would never change.

She thought of the old English rhyme: *A boy's your son till he takes a wife, a girl's your daughter all your life*. Bella's heart clenched with pain as she thought how Vittore had gone against her wishes and wed Maria. She had *warned* him about dirty girls and their seductive ways, but what could you do? Men had their needs, and that bitch Maria had snared Vittore despite all Bella's efforts to prevent it.

But Bianca was completely hers. And she was proud of her. Bianca was intelligent, incisive – she was a true daughter of the Camorra. Bianca had adored Tito ever since she'd arrived on the scene, and her affection had been amply returned. It was Tito who had taught the girl how to shoot, how to do business.

'She said she would be here,' said Bella. 'Or maybe she'll go straight to the church.'

Vittore grunted a reply.

'Where is Fabby?' asked Bella, using her son's baby-name. Her youngest son was always off doing something or other, mostly things that were best not known about. She had no illusions about her family; she knew what her husband and then her sons had become. What her daughter might be, too, now that she was finally getting involved in the business. Still, she loved them and excused them so much. But today, Fabio should be *here*.

'Something to do with the funeral director,' lied Vittore.

There was no trouble with the undertaker. Vittore knew that because he had handled all the arrangements himself. Fabio was off somewhere, doing something he shouldn't. That was for sure. If he screwed up, today of all days, then Vittore promised himself he would kick Fabio's stupid arse from here to the moon. 'There were one or two things to be straightened out, that's all.'

The doorbell rang, and Vittore went to answer it. A moment later, he returned, followed by Bianca – dressed in black today, not her usual white. She embraced Bella, who started to cry.

'This is breaking my heart,' she said.

'I know, Mama. I know,' said Bianca.

Maria appeared in the doorway. Pretty, curvy, dark-haired. Bianca went and hugged her briefly.

Bella ignored her daughter-in-law. 'I don't want Fabby to be late,' she fretted. She was wondering whether she had done the right thing, phoning Ruby Darke. And she wondered whether the woman would even bother to show up.

'He won't be, Mama. Don't worry,' said Vittore.

Don't worry! Bella had spent her lifetime worrying over her family, trying to maintain an iron hold over them. She couldn't alter her ways. And now Tito was gone to join his father Astorre in heaven. In her mind's eye, Bella always pictured her Astorre as he'd been way back in the days when they'd been young, and still living in their proper home, their *true* home – Napoli.

9

Naples, 1925

Bella came out of the church feeling deliriously happy. She was blinking in the blaring sunlight, her laughter drowned out by noisy trumpeters as friends and family showered her and her new husband with rice. Bella beamed up at Astorre, her groom. Astorre Danieri had done the decent thing and married her, his childhood sweetheart, and she loved him dearly.

'Bellisima!' everyone yelled at the bride.

Bella was twenty years old and for the first time in her life she felt beautiful. Astorre was twenty, too – and Bella was already pregnant, having succumbed to Astorre in one of her father's olive groves and allowed him to lift her skirts and have her. Only once, it had happened – Bella always afterwards blamed the heat for her weakness that day, for why else would a good Catholic girl lie with a man unwed?

When she told Astorre of her condition, he shrugged. He'd half-expected this would happen: he was a stud – a stallion, the girls said of him in tones of admiration – and it came as no surprise to him that his arrow had found its mark. 'We'll marry,' he said, and went immediately to see her father.

Now here they were, husband and wife at last! Bella was so happy she thought she would burst.

But life was hard, even if she was newly married, and in

love. *In the dry baking heat of an Italian summer, with Vesuvius rumbling and smoking on the horizon, it was a difficult time to be pregnant, and Bella suffered badly from morning sickness. She struggled to keep the house nice while, as camorristi, both Astorre's father and then Astorre himself were drafted into the Fascist Party.*

Four years earlier, Benito Mussolini, the blacksmith's son from Romagna, had declared himself Il Duce and the leader of the Fascists. Astorre's father, a widower, became involved in political life, but Astorre contented himself with trading in the port, where there were good profits to be made on the sly with cigarettes and drugs and other lucrative contraband.

It was a risky time and Bella was full of fear for her new husband. Just the year before their wedding, there had been unrest on the streets, many deaths. Yes, the Fascists were in power, but that communist bastard Matteotti had accused them of poll-rigging. After he was shot for his trouble, Casalini, Mussolini's deputy, was gunned down in a retaliatory shooting.

'Be careful,' Astorre told his father Franco when at last he held his own first-born, Tito, safe in his arms. Bella'd had a bad time with both the pregnancy and the birth, but here was their reward. They had a son.

Astorre was concerned about his father. The communists were still causing trouble, targeting those in power, and Papa had made a particular enemy of one of the scum, Corvetto. A hard-nosed thug who had once been camorristi, Corvetto was a turncoat and a braggart. Papa knew secrets about the man, secrets the communist did not want known.

'No worries,' said his father. 'Il Duce has banned all the left-wing bastards now, they can't form parties any more.'

Astorre didn't believe that would make any difference. Nevertheless, he joined his father in politics.

And Bella worried all the more.

10

1975

'Put the money in here! Right here, cunt, don't you make one funny move or you're DEAD, you got me?'

The terrified female bank teller behind the smashed counter stared in horror at the men, four of them, big threatening blocks of muscle clad in balaclavas and boiler suits, each one wielding a pick handle.

Some of the customers were screaming. Moira Stanhope had seen her kids off to school this morning, come into work as usual, set up her position – it was just another day. And now, all hell had broken loose.

The noise of the screens being broken, the sudden impact of the men's entry into the bank, the shouting, the threats of violence, the bags being thrown across the glass-strewn counters, all conspired to make Moira and the two other tellers freeze, unable to function.

'NOW! You hear me? Get the money in the bag NOW!'

Moira started fumbling the cash into the bag. Such was the shock of this intrusion, she didn't even think to press the panic button that was connected straight to the nearest police station. The other tellers were doing the same as her, every one of them white with fear, moving like stuttering automatons.

Fabio Danieri watched with satisfaction, feeling so wired that he could barely keep still. Shout at anyone loud enough and they crumbled, anyone in the armed forces could tell you that. And sweet Jesus, could he shout. They *all* could, all his boys, all the little gang he'd grown up on the Clerkenwell streets with, they were swearing and screaming at the tellers, *Move! Do it! Hurry Up!*

And like dumb cattle the tellers were obeying, ladling the loot into the bags, pushing them back over the counter.

Piece of piss, thought Fabio.

Then they were leaving the building, hurrying out – not too fast – to the car where Derby their jockey sat at the wheel of the high-performance car, engine running. They whipped off their balaclavas as they went, piled in, and Derby was away, slowly at first, sedately, but soon . . .

'Holy fuck!' shouted Derby, his eyes glued to the rear-view mirror.

'What?' Fabio strained to see. A cop car was nudging in behind them.

'Shit,' he said. They had the bulging bags of cash stacked up around them. Quickly Fabio and the others started stripping off their boiler suits. Fabio was wearing jogging shorts and a black T-shirt under his. He could hear the bank's alarms going now.

'It's OK. No lights, no siren. Just a patrol car, it's nothing,' said Derby.

Then Fabio saw the customers running out of the bank, waving wildly to the occupants of the police car, pointing to the car stuffed with men and bags with Derby at the wheel.

'*Double* shit,' said Fabio. 'Hit it, Derby.'

Derby wasn't called that for nothing. Give him a few thou of stolen horsepower and he could outrun anything the filth could chuck at him. It was close, but they raced through the streets and finally Derby gave them the slip. The boys dumped the car and the bags in a coach depot car park, stashing the cash all over their bodies under their clothes. Then they split up – and *shit* here came the filth again, just as they were saying their farewells.

'Leg it!' said Fabio.

All the boys scattered.

'Oi! Stop right there, arsehole!' shouted one of the police, coming up fast at Fabio's rear.

Fabio had no intention of stopping. He took to his heels, hurling himself down an embankment straight into a huge patch of brambles. The copper – no doubt dreaming of promotion – followed.

Both men started swearing and wincing. Shit, those things *hurt*.

It was the death of a thousand cuts. Flesh tearing, blood dripping off him like raindrops, Fabio hauled himself out of the damned brambles, seeing the copper still in there, trapped, struggling, trying to break free. Fabio sped off as fast as he could. He found himself in what appeared to be a deserted storage depot, surrounded by lorries in for repair.

Exhausted, he ran to the nearest shed door, slid it open. He slipped inside and slumped down on the floor, sweating, bleeding, shaking with the force of the adrenaline pumping madly through his veins. Minutes passed. He got his breath back, and . . . then he heard it.

A police radio, crackling, coming closer.

Shit.

He had to get out of here. He had the cash stuffed down his underpants. He inched open the door. No one in sight, but they were *there*, he could hear the bastards.

Fabio slipped outside, looking around for a way out. Quickly he pulled himself up onto the low roof of the building and nearly messed himself when a policeman went straight by the door, talking into his radio. A couple of seconds earlier, and he'd have seen Fabio coming out.

But Fabio had been lucky. And he meant to stay that way. When he was sure the copper was out of sight, he jumped from the roof onto a wall, and then almost fell down onto the other side, which turned out to be a main road. A road he *knew*.

Thank you, God.

He grinned triumphantly then broke into an easy loping run, heading homeward. He was fit as well as handsome, he took care of himself. He was just a jogger now – so long as nobody looked too closely at the scrapes and the bloodstains, and the black top hid a lot of it anyway. All around him, bedlam was breaking out. Cop cars sped past, blue lights flashing, sirens wailing.

Fabio trotted on, knowing precisely where he was going. In fact, he was getting tired of this, getting away with things by the skin of his teeth, these little bank jobs. But he'd accumulated a good bit of stake money in the process. Soon he would start getting into something far more lucrative and less risky.

Fabio had been working on a plan. The smash-and-grabs at the banks had brought in cash, but he was making a name for himself and that was dangerous: it was time to quit while he was ahead. The drugs game was a much better bet. Friends in the trade had told him the figures, and they were mind-blowing. He could buy a load of coke in Colombia for three or four grand, then sell it on for thirty grand in the UK. What was not to like?

Furthermore, he had a ready market in the clubs his family already owned. He could get people in his pay circulating among the socialites, the carefree daddy's-little-rich-girls-out-on-the-town, and they could knock it out for a thousand pounds an ounce, netting him a clear thirty or forty grand profit on every deal.

Compared to that, bank jobs paid *peanuts*.

No need to enlighten Vittore as to this new status quo though. Big brother might think he owned the world now that Tito had gone off to run heaven, but Fabio liked having this secret, hugging it to himself. He would make a fucking fortune and it would all be *his*. No *way* was the family taking a share.

11

Kit was on his way out when he saw the woman. There must have been a smash on the road; the traffic was crawling in both directions. He sat at the wheel of his Bentley, grid-locked, and stared out at the God-awful weather. It had stopped raining for now, but it was still as cold as a witch's tit out there. He wondered when this bastard headache was going to let go. Occasionally he sipped out of the open bottle of Scotch on the seat beside him.

He was too drunk to drive, he knew that.

He didn't *care*.

Places to go, things to do kept turning over and over in his mind.

That was when he saw her. Traffic crawling along in the other direction, his own car going nowhere fast. And there was her face, in the back of a big black limousine – she was pale as ivory, with huge turquoise-blue eyes and . . . hadn't Marilyn Monroe said she had a body for sin? Well this woman had a mouth like that. Sensual, full-lipped, you could imagine her doing all sorts of things to you with that mouth. Her hair was so white it was almost silver, falling straight to her shoulders, a black veil pushed back from it. He couldn't see any lower, only that she was all in black and it drained the life out of her features. Drunk as he was, he still felt the swift urgent tug of sexual attraction.

Her head turned a little, and her eyes met his. She didn't look away, just returned his stare. This was no shrinking violet: her gaze was direct, intelligent. Then the traffic in her lane moved on, and she was gone. He turned in his seat, wanting to maintain the eye-contact, but that was it, folks: end of show. She was gone, off across the city, one more person moving around the vast metropolis.

He picked up the bottle again and drank.

This is a nightmare, thought Bianca.

Vittore had hired a trio of limos from the funeral directors. One, of course, for Mama and himself (he was her favourite, they *all* knew that), while Fabio would have a limo to himself, leaving Bianca to share with Maria, Vittore's poor doormat wife, who didn't comment but must surely notice that she had been relegated, separated from her husband by his overbearing mother, yet again.

Now the limousine Bianca and Maria were travelling in was stuck in the traffic, crawling along, prolonging the agony of this day. The other two limos, travelling behind the hearse, were lost to view. The driver had said he knew a better route to the church, and had turned the car around. He was sweating, the idiot, he didn't know the way at all. Now they were sitting, unmoving, in yet another line of cars.

Inch by inch, the car crept along. Bianca sat there like wood, gazing out at the matt dove-grey of the sky, thinking *This cannot be happening.*

But it was.

Today the family was saying its final farewell to Tito, who had been murdered in cold blood by some piece of scum – she *spat* on them, whoever they were.

Tito was dead.

She couldn't believe it, but it was true.

Her eldest brother, the one she'd loved so much, idolized, was dead and gone. She knew that it was mostly Tito's doing that she had been entrusted – at last – with Dante's. Vittore would never have entrusted her with any responsibility. Vittore had always seemed indifferent to her; he was secure in his position as Mama's firm favourite. As for Fabio, he had mocked the very idea.

'Bianca? What, you joking, Tito?' he'd laughed when the possibility of her running a club had first been broached.

All her life, Fabio had mocked her. Resented her. Cuffed her around the ear, punched her when Mama wasn't looking, because she was the interloper, the new baby, and she'd taken his privileged place.

Only Tito had loved her as a brother truly should, indulging her, showing her the noble old Italian ways, accepting her unstintingly into the family. He'd taught her everything, even how to shoot. She remembered how he'd taken her hunting rabbits on farmers' fields, and how she had treasured that time alone with him.

Now, her heart was broken. He was gone.

A sleek Bentley paused alongside the limo, heading in the other direction. Her eyes caught and held the stare of the man sitting behind the wheel. Even sunk deep in grief, she was arrested by how amazingly handsome he was: dark-skinned, black-haired. And his eyes were a startlingly clear bright blue – but they seemed full of some private pain.

Then the limo edged forward and the man slipped out of her line of sight. She turned to look back, but he was gone.

Maria was taking her hand, squeezing it. Bianca snapped back to the present, looked at her sister-in-law, the poor cow.

'He's in a better place, you know. Tito, I mean,' she said.

Bianca took her hand away.

A better place?

She knew that plenty of people would think Tito was destined for hell, particularly the one who'd killed him. And she wanted to know who that was; she was *desperate* to know who the bastard was who had robbed Tito of his life and brought such devastation on her family. Adopted or not, she had absorbed the culture she'd been taken into. She was a true child of the Camorra, and that was a proud and unforgiving heritage.

When she found out who was responsible, she would have her revenge.

She *swore* it.

12

It was freezing cold and windy as the mourners filed inside the church. Outside, some brave early daffodils were being tossed in the breeze and flattened into the muddy soil. It was scarcely warmer inside the building. The atmosphere was grim. The organist was playing a dirge, appropriately sad for a Requiem Mass.

Many had come to pay their respects, because they had to. The Danieris expected it. Tito might be gone, but there was still Vittore; there was still Fabio. Failure to attend would be noted, and frowned upon. Everyone knew that.

Loitering outside were a couple of plain-clothes policemen, noticed but ignored by the bulk of the mourners. The police had only recently released the body, and 'enquiries were ongoing' into Tito's murder. But so far no one had been arrested and everyone knew that the police wouldn't dig too deeply or trouble themselves too much: obviously it was another gangland killing, one of many that occurred every year around the city, nothing too remarkable.

Bastards, thought Bianca, walking up the aisle beside Maria, both of them curtsying and crossing themselves before the altar before joining Mama in the front pew.

'Where have you *been*?' demanded Bella of her daughter.

Bianca squeezed her mother's hand. 'Sorry. Traffic. Got held up.'

'Have you seen Fabio?'

'He's just arrived, we saw him as we came in. He's . . .' *Out there, unloading the coffin.*

Bianca couldn't bring herself to say the words. They choked her, cut off her breath. All the way here, she had felt sick with horror. Traffic slowing the cars down, holding her up, had been yet another twist to the torment, prolonging this when she just wanted it to be over.

She thought then, very briefly, of the man's face, the one in the car going in the other direction. Dark skin, blue eyes, something autocratic in his bearing . . .

'Fabio's a good boy,' said Bella.

Bianca came back to the here and now. Her mother was still talking about Fabio. 'Good', in her opinion, was pushing it. Fab had a certain laddish charm, but he couldn't pass a mirror without kissing it. 'Good' wasn't a word she would ever associate with him. He'd bullied her all her life, hated her on sight. He wasn't 'good' at all. But Mama Bella was nodding, affirming her opinion of her youngest son to herself.

She looks exhausted, Bianca thought, feeling the emotion of the day rise up and almost stifle her. She was glad of the thick black veil she now wore pulled down over her face, identical to her mother's. It hid the tears that spilled over and slid down her cheeks. She bit her lip so hard she almost drew blood.

Bianca glanced behind her, seeing the mourners shuffling inside. Among them she saw a tall dark-skinned woman moving near the rear of the church, her eyes downcast.

'What's *she* doing here?' asked Bianca, gulping back her tears.

Bella looked up, saw who Bianca was staring at, said nothing.

'Isn't that Ruby Darke?' said Bianca. 'The woman who runs the department stores? Did she know Tito? Oh wait – wasn't she involved with Michael Ward . . . ?'

Bianca fell silent. Ruby Darke was also the notorious Kit Miller's mother, and there were rumours circulating like Chinese whispers that Tito's death could have been a revenge killing for the death of Michael Ward. That pointed to Miller, who had been Ward's number one man. But these were merely rumours, unfounded, unsubstantiated. There was no proof, nothing positive to suggest they could be true.

'I asked her to come,' said Bella.

Bianca's head whipped round. She stared at her mother. 'You what? Why?'

'I have to talk to her.'

'Mama, you've taken leave of your senses,' said Bianca, shaking her head. 'You know what's being said . . .'

'Yes, I know. That's why I want to talk to her.'

'But—'

'Hush! Show some respect,' said Bella, her tone sharpening. She looked back. 'Ah, dear God, my boy, my poor boy . . .'

They were bringing in the coffin. The music swelled, the priest came forward in his ceremonial robes. Bianca, Bella and Maria rose to their feet along with the rest of the congregation as the pall-bearers came up the aisle, carrying their sad burden. Bianca felt her mother sway and she grasped her arm, held her steady. She felt as if her heart was being ripped, still beating, from her chest.

Ah, Tito . . .

She thought of Tito cuddling her in his arms when she was small, kissing her forehead, murmuring words of comfort. He'd taught her so much, shared the ways of the

Camorra with her. Her big brother, she'd loved him so. It crucified her that he had died, a man in his prime, with no wife, no children, to lament his passing.

Bianca watched the grim procession of pall-bearers pass by with the coffin. Vittore was there, giving solid support at the front, with the slighter Fabio immediately behind him, smartened up in a black suit, his almost girlishly good-looking face and hands marred by scratches and cuts. The mahogany coffin was covered in a luxuriant mass of red hothouse roses formed into the shape of a cross. The men moved slowly, placing their burden carefully on the dais while the priest looked on.

For Bianca the whole thing was torture. It was all she could do to watch as the coffin was sprinkled with holy water and then it was incensed. Prayers were said for Tito's soul and the choir sang 'On Eagle's Wings'. Then came the funeral Mass and absolution, with candles lit around the coffin.

And then they were all outside in the biting wind, gathered around the freshly dug grave. The elderly priest intoned his words of conclusion: 'May his soul and the souls of all the faithful departed through the mercy of God rest in peace.'

At last, it was over.

Having kept a tight grip on her mother throughout, Bianca could feel Bella trembling, shuddering with sobs. To bury one's own child must be agony. The crowds of mourners began to disperse, leaving only close family by the graveside. Then Bianca saw Ruby Darke again, standing alone some distance away from their silent little group.

'What the fuck's she doing here?' asked Fabio.

Bella stepped forward and slapped her youngest son's face. 'Shut up! You are in a place of worship, standing at your brother's grave,' she snapped.

Maria's eyes met Bianca's. Maria was mouse-like in the presence of her forceful mother-in-law. Bianca felt almost sorry for her sometimes, when she wasn't feeling scornful over Maria's lack of backbone. Bianca loved Mama, but she knew she could be manipulative, and Vittore was a sucker for her machinations. Maria, who was not bright, was no match for Bella. In Maria's place, Bianca would have given Bella a hell of a fight.

'Go now, all of you,' said Bella imperiously. 'I wish to talk to her alone.'

'Mama—' started Bianca.

'Go home. Go back to the house, Bianca. Make sure everything's ready for our guests.'

13

Seeing that Bella was now alone at the graveside, Ruby summoned her nerve and approached the older woman.

'Mrs Danieri?' she said hesitantly.

Bella nodded.

'You wanted to talk to me,' said Ruby.

'Yes. I did. Thank you for coming, Miss Darke.'

Ruby was wishing she hadn't. She hated this – standing in a damp, cold graveyard among strangers. She'd been glared at by Bella's children, and she was still wondering anxiously what this strange request, that peculiar telephone call, was all about.

Blood will flow.

She shivered anew to think of those words. Her eyes skimmed over the woman wearing the thick black veil, the shapeless clothes, then down at the coffin, lying there in the unfilled grave, the brass plate sullied by the first sprinklings of dirt.

'There have been rumours, Miss Darke,' said Bella.

Ruby wished that Bella Danieri would lift her veil, that she could see her face, judge her mood more clearly. In business and in life, she liked to know exactly what she was dealing with. Here, she felt she was flying blind.

'What rumours?' asked Ruby.

'Rumours that your son Kit could have been the one who killed my boy Tito.'

Ruby said nothing. Her heart was beating very fast: she wondered if she was about to be sick.

'And you know what I think?' Bella went on, then paused.

She's about to tell me that they're going to kill Kit, thought Ruby in horror.

But Bella's next words surprised her.

'I think *enough.* We – you and I – we're the matriarchs of our families. That's the word, isn't it? Matriarchs?'

Ruby had to swallow hard so that she could speak.

'Yes. That's the right word.'

But Ruby was thinking that she wasn't much of a matriarch. She had built a new relationship with her daughter – but barely any relationship at all with her son. To imagine that she could influence Kit in any way was madness. Just a few weeks ago, he had told her that Michael Ward, who had been like a father to him, had wanted him to try and patch things up with Ruby, to forgive her. That had been almost Michael's last wish on earth. So Kit had said he would try.

But he hadn't.

Kit was still cool to her, still as remote as ever.

She could hardly see Bella's eyes through the veil, but she could *feel* them, watching her face keenly. 'We have the power to stop this here,' said Bella. 'You and I.'

'I thought all Italian families cared about was revenge,' said Ruby.

'I'm too tired for revenge,' said Bella, and she sounded tired, too: old and exhausted.

'Do you believe these rumours?'

'Did I say I believed them?' Bella shrugged. 'Tito had many enemies, you know.'

Ruby said nothing, but she was chillingly aware of Bella's eyes on her, gauging her reaction. She was aware of what the Danieri family *was*. Michael had told her about the Camorra in Naples and how it had now come onto the streets of London. It was a brotherhood, a society, older than the Mafia which had its roots in Sicily. She didn't think for a minute that Bella was simply a sweet, doddering old woman. Like the rest of her kin, she could be lethal.

'You were close to Michael Ward,' said Bella.

'Yes,' said Ruby. 'I was.'

'He was married to my niece Serafina up until the time she died. She grew up here, and changed her name to Sheila. She wanted to "fit in", you see.'

'I know all that.'

'Then you came along. And I think he was happy with you.'

'I hope so.'

'But then he died too. Violently. Perhaps your boy Kit believed that Tito gave the order to kill Michael. That Vittore or Fabio carried out that order. And for that, for the death of the man who meant so much to him, perhaps your Kit sought revenge.'

Ruby said nothing. She was too frightened to speak. Terrified of saying the wrong thing, landing Kit in the shit. If what Bella said was right, then this wouldn't stop here.

Blood will flow.

Not Kit's, she thought. *Please not Kit's.*

'But you know the funny thing?' asked Bella.

Ruby shook her head dumbly.

'No, not funny. That's the wrong word. *Sad* is the right one, I think. My boys didn't do it. They didn't kill Michael.'

Ruby stared at the woman. Clearly, she was making excuses for Tito, Vittore and Fabio.

'You think I am fooling myself,' said Bella.

Ruby shook her head. 'I think you're protecting your sons.'

'I am *not* making a feeble attempt to cover their backs.' Bella pushed the veil back from her face, and Ruby felt shock at the sight of the poor woman's pudgy and wrinkled face, but Bella's eyes were hard as two black stones and they crackled with authority and intelligence. 'Tito thought he might give the word to Vittore and Fabio, but first they came to me. Tito wanted to do it, he said, but this was my late niece's husband, this was *blood*. So first he wanted to get my blessing. But I told him no. Under no circumstances. Miss Darke, none of my sons would go against their mama's wishes.'

'But . . .' Ruby floundered, searching for words. Her brain was spinning. She had believed the rumours, as much as anyone. She had believed that Tito killed Michael. She *knew* that Kit believed that too, and although it was never spoken about, she was quietly convinced that he had taken Tito's life in retaliation. But now . . .

Bella was saying that the rumours were wrong.

That *Kit* was wrong.

That he had, in fact, killed the wrong man.

So who *was* responsible? Who had taken Michael Ward, snatched the great love of her life, away from her?

She could feel Bella's eyes boring into hers. Ruby gulped hard; her mouth was very dry. 'So you're saying . . .' she started, then faltered to a halt.

'I am telling you, none of my sons killed Michael Ward,' said Bella with conviction. 'Not Tito, not Fabio, not Vittore. *None* of them did it.'

14

Naples, 1926

Baby Tito was nearly a year old when the volcano erupted with a staggering, ground-shaking roar. What followed that first hideous crackling boom *was a strange day, overcast and brooding – like the end of the world. Astorre was out walking the streets, going to see his friend Gilberto, watching the ash spew out of Vesuvius in huge belching clouds. It drifted over, fogging the streets of the city with fine grey powder.*

Astorre covered his mouth and thought with a prickle of dread of long-buried Pompeii and Herculaneum. He prayed that the volcano, forever smouldering on the edge of the city, should fall silent again soon. That was when he saw Gilberto rushing toward him through the drifting smog. Gilberto was panting, dishevelled, bathed in sweat and a film of gritty soot.

'Your father!' he gasped out, eyes wild, choking as he inhaled ash, clutching at Astorre.

Astorre's heart nearly stopped. 'What? What are you talking about?'

'He's been shot! Shot and killed.'

In dawning horror Astorre ran with his friend to the carabinieri station, and there he was, his beloved papa: laid out dead and mangled, torn horrifically apart by a hail of bullets. Astorre collapsed onto his father's chest, sobbing with grief.

Gilberto stayed with him, tried to comfort him. But it was impossible.

'This is Corvetto,' Astorre said in between his tears. His father's blood was staining Astorre's hands, his face, his clothes.

'How can—' asked Gilberto.

'I know!'

They left his father's corpse lying there, covered in blood and tears. Astorre stumbled out of the room as if he was drunk. Gilberto took Astorre's arm to steady him as they went out onto the powdered, noise-muffled streets. And there – there – walking along the other side of the road in the softly drifting grey veil of ash, his eyes on the two men as they came out of the police station, was Corvetto, walking among a phalanx of his men, well guarded, safe enough to sneer. Astorre surged forward. Gilberto grabbed him.

'Don't be a fool!' he said. 'You want to be laid out next to your father? There are too many of them. Be sensible, Astorre. Pick your time.'

Astorre knew Gilberto was making perfect sense. Standing there soaked in his father's blood, sick and dizzy with horror and loss, the nightmare miasma from the volcano fogging his sight, choking his throat and filling him with dread, he acknowledged that Gilberto was right. Astorre would wait, and when he was ready, when the timing was perfect, then he would have his revenge. He looked at Corvetto. Their eyes locked. Astorre lifted his arm and flicked his thumb against the underside of his teeth. Corvetto's smile died.

Like you will die, thought Astorre.

Corvetto had understood the gesture. It meant I am going to get you.

Corvetto walked on, surrounded by his heavies. For a moment, seeing Astorre Danieri there, he'd felt a chill, someone stepping on his grave. But he was safe; his guards were many and his home was a fortress. Astorre Danieri's father Franco had been a thorn in his side, needing removal. Now the deed was done. If necessary, he would apply the same remedy to the son, Astorre. Let him make his threats; it was Corvetto who had the power – not him.

15

1975

Minutes after she had spoken to Bella at the graveside, Ruby was getting into her car, thankful that it was all over. Her mind was churning over all that Bella had said. Big solid Rob was at the wheel of the Mercedes, Rob with the toffee-coloured hair and the sexy khaki-green eyes. She knew that Daisy thought he was gorgeous, and he was.

Her old chauffeur Ben had retired after Christmas, and Rob – the minder that Michael Ward had assigned to her months before his death – had taken over the job, with Kit's permission. Kit was Rob's boss now, Michael's successor, and she supposed it was generous of her son to spare Rob – who was after all Kit Miller's own personal attack dog, his own right hand – for this.

Ruby sighed. Thoughts of Rob always led on to thoughts of Kit, and to the Christmas just past, a dismal Christmas without Michael. She'd received many cards from her business associates, and her old friend Vi – as usual. Also as usual, she'd got one from her long-estranged brother Joe and his wife Betsy, written as always in Betsy's hand. A card at Christmas! That was all the contact she ever got from Joe these days, and he didn't even write the damned thing.

Of course she always sent one right back – she did that religiously, every year – but she sometimes wondered why she bothered, when it was clear that they were no more than strangers now. It went without saying that there had been no card from Kit – and no presents either. Not so much as a short visit to wish her well.

He promised Michael he was going to try to forgive me.

Didn't look as if he was trying very hard.

He wasn't trying at *all*.

'That was bloody awful,' she told Rob as she slid into the back seat.

Rob said nothing. Of course it was awful. It was a *funeral*.

'Let's go home,' she said.

'Holy *shit*,' said Rob, straightening in his seat, looking ahead.

'What? What is it?' Ruby craned her head to see. There were lines of cars parked up in front of them, there were people moving about on the pavement. She couldn't see anything past all that. She *could* see some of the Danieri family, standing beside a black limousine parked four spaces from her Mercedes.

'Over there,' said Rob, indicating the far side of the road.

More parked cars, people milling about, everyone dressed in the heavy black of mourning, and . . .

'Oh God!' she burst out.

Kit was walking across the road, moving toward one of the Danieri limousines. Bella's daughter Bianca had already departed, with her youngest son Fabio. But Vittore the eldest was still there, just getting into a limo with his mother.

'Fuck,' said Rob.

Ruby threw her door open. 'Stop him, Rob, will you? Quick!'

Rob was already out of the car, moving around the front of it. Ruby followed, her heart in her mouth. If Kit reached the Danieri party, there would be massive trouble. The situation was a tinderbox, ready to blow: one spark, and all Bella's efforts to defuse it would come to nothing.

Kit moved fast, even though he seemed to be weaving a little, unsteady. By the time Rob caught up with him, he was standing in front of the Danieri limousine.

'So that bastard Tito's planted at last,' said Kit loudly, with a laugh. 'And not a fucking *minute* too soon.'

A gasp went up from some of the remaining guests at Kit's words. They turned and stared at this crazed-looking interloper. Ruby hurried up; Rob quickly put himself in between Kit and Vittore. Bella, black-veiled, inscrutable, stood there unmoving. Vittore, blank-eyed with hate, looked like he wanted to do Kit extreme damage.

Kit was swaying on his feet. He was scruffy, unshaven, his tie askew, his shirt collar grubby.

'You're drunk,' Ruby realized, saying it aloud.

Kit turned his attention to her. 'Mother dear,' he said, as if seeing her there for the first time. 'Hello! I am, in fact, royally pissed. Because I've been celebrating the funeral of one of the worst *scumbags* ever to walk the earth.'

Vittore cursed in Italian, his tone vicious, his eyes murderous as they rested on Kit's grinning face.

For God's sake, Kit, what are you doing? Ruby wondered in panic.

'So here I am. Paying my respects to the dear departed,' he said, giggling like a lunatic.

'This is not the way to do things,' said Ruby.

'No?' Kit's eyes grew sharper as they met his mother's. 'And how would *you* know? You don't even *keep* your kids, do you, much less *bury* the bastards.'

Ruby felt a stab of pain at that.

Rob placed a hand on Kit's chest as he lurched forward.

'Mate,' said Rob in a low voice. 'You're drunk. Your

mum's right. This ain't the way to behave. Let's get you home.' He took Kit's arm.

Kit shook him off. 'Nah, not before I say what I came to say.'

'You've said enough,' snapped Vittore.

'Not by a long shot,' said Kit, shaking his head.

He was still grinning, swaying, and Ruby thought that he wouldn't even remember this tomorrow, he was so pissed. But Vittore would.

Kit, you fool.

Daisy had told her Kit was drinking. She hadn't yet seen him drunk, but today he was far gone, almost insensible. *Is this my fault?* she wondered in anguish.

She knew that Kit had a lot to bear. He'd lost a woman he truly loved, and Michael, all in the space of a few months. It was enough to bring the strongest man down. And her efforts to reconnect with him, with this precious son she had lost at birth and then refound, were still being met with suspicion and sometimes with downright fury.

'I just wanted to tell you all how pleased I am that Tito's dead,' said Kit.

'Oh God . . .' said Ruby, putting a hand to her mouth. 'Bella, I'm sorry . . .'

'Don't apologize for me,' roared Kit, coming closer to his mother.

It was then that Vittore stepped forward, swift as a viper. Suddenly, shockingly, he grabbed Kit's head.

Ruby let out a yell.

Rob shouted: 'Hey!' and moved to intervene.

'Get off me, you wop son of a bitch,' snarled Kit.

But Vittore didn't headbutt Kit: he just held him. Then he flicked a thumb against his own front teeth and ran a fingernail down his own cheek. He released Kit, who staggered back, shocked out of his stupor, the grin gone from his face. Vittore said something under his breath, his words harsh, his gaze deadly.

'That's enough,' said Rob, and grabbed Kit's arm.

Kit took a fumbling swing at Rob, but stumbled sideways. Effortlessly Rob dodged the blow, pushed Kit's arm behind his back and pulled him away, toward Ruby's car.

Ruby stood there, aware of Vittore's coldly contained rage, of Bella's distress.

'I'm sorry,' she repeated. 'He's drinking a lot. I know it's no excuse, but . . .' her voice trailed away.

There *was* no excuse. This had been terrible, an insult. She was still shaking from the suddenness with which Vittore had caught hold of Kit.

'Come, Mama,' said Vittore, and took Bella's arm and put her in the limousine.

'Wait—' started Ruby, following.

Vittore turned a snakelike gaze on her. '*Go away*,' he hissed.

Ruby's shoulders slumped. Moving among the staring crowds, she made her way to her own car. Rob was already behind the wheel, and Kit was laid out, eyes closed, in the back. She got in beside him, looked at him with disgust. This was her son, but at this moment she was *ashamed* of him.

'Back to yours?' asked Rob, his eyes meeting hers in the rear-view mirror.

Ruby nodded. Right now, she couldn't trust herself to speak. Kit had ruined everything. And she couldn't help thinking again of Bella's words.

Blood will flow.

She only hoped it wouldn't be Kit's. But after this? She very much feared that it would.

'Rob? Did you hear what Vittore said?' she asked him.

Rob shook his head.

'*Rob?*' she insisted.

Rob heaved a heavy sigh. 'It's an empty threat, Ruby.'

'What did he say?'

'He said, "You and yours," said Rob uneasily. Actually, what Rob had *really* heard Vittore say was: 'I'm going to rip the *heart* out of your family, out of each and every one of you.'

He wasn't about to tell Ruby *that*.

Instead, he shrugged. 'Big talk. That's all.'

Ruby looked at him. She thought he was lying, but she wasn't going to pursue it.

'Get us home,' she said.

16

'You bloody fool,' said Ruby, thrusting a cup of freshly ground black coffee into her son's hands.

Kit lay sprawled on her sofa at the Marlow house. He straightened, took the coffee, stared at it, then swallowed a mouthful. Lifted the cup in salute to his mother, who stood over him looking disapproving.

'Thank you, Mother dear,' he said.

'And you can *stop* that right away,' snapped Ruby. 'D'you think that was clever, turning up and making a show of yourself?'

Kit put the drink down on the side table. Looked up at her, then at Rob, who was standing over by the window, arms folded, watching. At least *Daisy* wasn't here giving him an ear-bashing too. She was out somewhere, either pretending she was loving the store work to arse-lick her way into Ruby's good books, or with Jody and the twins.

'Wanted to say my farewells,' said Kit. He was feeling steadier now, but faintly sick – and his head was starting to throb again.

'You should have stopped away.'

'Well, I didn't.'

'I talked to Bella Danieri today. She told me something important.'

'*Did* she now.'

'Can you not take that tone with me please?' said Ruby. 'Yes. She did.'

'So what's this nugget of pure gold she passed on to you then?'

'Jesus, mate . . .' said Rob, shaking his head.

Ruby crouched down so that she was on the same level as Kit. 'She told me none of her sons was responsible for Michael's death.'

Kit sat there a moment, staring at Ruby's face.

Then he started to laugh. He laughed so hard she thought he was about to shit himself.

'Yes. Hysterically funny,' said Ruby.

Kit wiped at his eyes; he was literally *crying* with laughter. Neither Rob nor Ruby looked even faintly amused.

'Look,' said Kit when he could get his breath, 'whether it was Tito who put the gun to Michael's head, or Vittore or that little shit Fabio, it's all the same to me. The order came from Tito. I *know* it did.'

'You don't know any such thing. You hated him because he'd hurt you in the past—'

'Hurt me? He fucking *crucified* me. He deserved everything he got.'

'But he didn't kill Michael.'

Kit shrugged, sipped more of the coffee. 'Fabio then. He's like a hyena, that one, giggling and shuffling and twitching around, always ready to pull some fucker apart once the big boys have taken their share. Michael was shot from behind. Isn't that Fabio's style?'

'At least you admit it's not Tito's.'

Kit gave a sour smile. 'I'm not admitting anything. What about Vittore?'

'What about him?'

'He'd do it.'

Ruby let out an exasperated breath. 'Kit – *none* of them

did it. Bella swore that was true. She said Tito came to her, but she said no. And neither he nor Fabio nor Vittore would disregard her wishes – not about Michael. He was married to her niece, he was *kin*. She wouldn't allow it. She made that very clear.'

'Michael should have struck first,' said Kit, now gazing mournfully at the floor. 'He should have let me sort it. I *told* him, let me do it. But he wouldn't.'

Ruby was silent, feeling Kit's anguish for the loss of his boss, the one man who had been like a father to him. His *real* father, Cornelius Bray, had discarded him; he'd grown up bounced around children's homes, feckless and footloose, back in the days when she hadn't known where he was or even if he was still alive. She had desperately tried to trace him, but it was Michael he had stumbled into, and Michael who had saved him from the gutter, raised him up. The loss of him was killing Kit, she could see that.

'It's too late for all that,' she said gently. 'Too late for regrets. But maybe not too late to let it all go. To admit to yourself that you were wrong, that the Danieri family weren't responsible.'

Kit gazed at her. 'I'm not admitting a damned thing,' he said.

Rob let out a heavy sigh.

'And *you* can shut up,' Kit told him.

'Oh, pardon me for giving a shit,' said Rob.

'*Look*,' said Ruby, shooting a glance between them. 'This has to stop. If we're lucky – and I'm sure Bella will be talking to him right now – Vittore will calm down. For God's sake, Kit, the last thing anyone wants is all-out war. Admit you were wrong. That you made a mistake. Let's do as Bella says and stop this, just drop it.'

But Kit was shaking his head.

'No! I have to know who did it,' he said. 'If what you say is true—'

'Kit! It is.'

'OK. I don't believe it, but let's say for the sake of argument that you're right. If it wasn't one of *them*, then who the fuck was it?'

'I don't know,' said Ruby, thinking of Michael, *her* Michael, thinking of his steel-grey eyes and the feel of his hair beneath her fingers, of his strong, handsome face, his laugh, his way of always finding the answers. Well, he couldn't find this one. He was gone. 'I loved him too, Kit. I really did. But maybe we'll *never* know.'

Kit was shaking his head. 'No. That don't cut it. I *have* to know. If the Danieris didn't pull the trigger, *someone* did. Someone who's still out there, who thinks they're home free.'

'Kit, mate . . .' said Rob.

Kit flashed him a look full of fury. 'Don't "mate" me. If it wasn't the Danieri mob, then it was someone else. And I *have* to know *who*.'

17

What surprised Daisy most about working at the store was the stark difference between the shop floors – all pristine clean and laden with everything so beautifully and temptingly arrayed, designed to prompt impulse purchases – and the warren of dark passageways and bare cloakrooms and business-like offices the staff occupied.

'Morning,' she greeted everyone she passed, wanting to be one of the girls, accepted, part of the pack. She put on her burgundy coverall with *Darkes* picked out in gold thread on the left breast pocket, checked her golden-blonde hair was tucked up neatly in its French pleat.

'Oh good *mawning*,' said Tessa Barclay in an affectedly 'posh' voice, nudging her friend Julie as they stood beside the big row of lockers where the staff put all their belongings during shop hours.

Daisy hurried from the locker room, their laughter ringing in her ears.

Just two weeks in, and she was learning the ropes at least. She checked the shelves she was responsible for and then went to the stockroom, gathering up what she needed. Then she went back, put the stock out on display and did a return trip, edged past Tessa and Julie who did their best to stand in her way while she puffed past them, arms laden with stock items. Ignoring them, she cleaned up, tidied everything.

She kept thinking about her little boys, her twins, and she ached for them, missed them so much. But she'd wanted this. And now she'd got it. Truth was, though, she *hated* it.

'I suppose these early *mawnings* are a bit of a strain on your ladyship, are they?' asked Tessa, flicking a look at Julie, who smirked.

Daisy felt her mouth go dry. They were still doing this. Mocking her whenever they got the chance, whispering to everyone else on the shop floor that she was Ruby Darke's daughter and only in here to spy on everyone and to *pretend* that she was working like any other ordinary person. They ignored her in the canteen, moving away from where she was sitting. Of course she could join Mum for lunch, but that would endorse everything they already thought about her: that she was Mummy's little rich girl, unable to take the heat. That nepotism was alive and well, right here at Darkes.

'Not really,' she said, keeping her eyes on the neat lines of the stock she was putting out on display. 'I'm up early with the twins anyway.'

'Oh! Surely not! Don't the *nanny* do all that for you?' asked Tessa.

'No,' said Daisy. 'She doesn't. I like to help her get them up and dressed, give them breakfast.'

'Then nanny takes over and you come and ponce around in Mummy's store,' said Tessa.

Daisy straightened and looked her tormentor in the eye. 'I work here. The same as you do.'

'Oh, she *works heah*,' said Julie in that horrible mockery of Daisy's voice, and Tessa giggled. 'Gawd alive.'

Daisy gritted her teeth. 'Look . . .' she started. She wanted to *hit* Tessa. And then Julie. This couple of utter bitches had set out to make her life a misery, and why? Because her mother owned the store? How was that in any way fair?

Doris, her section leader, came over. 'We're short-staffed on the tills, Daisy, will you cover? Store's open in ten.'

Relieved, Daisy nodded. Aware of Tessa and Julie sniggering behind her, she went across to the tills, feeling herself shaking with temper.

This is a waste of time, she thought in a sudden moment of clarity. *I'm not like Mum. I hate store work. I can't do this.*

But she'd wanted this, she reminded herself. Being a stay-at-home mother wasn't for her. Trouble was, she didn't know what *was* for her. The thought of her babies, little Matthew and Luke, kept her sane even if their father – her ex-husband Simon – drove her crazy with his stupid accusations and demands. And then there was Rob . . .

Her heart leapt when she thought of Rob, her mother's minder and chauffeur. Daisy had been exchanging looks with him for months, she knew he was interested. Now she had only to give him the slightest encouragement. And she couldn't wait. Marriage to Simon had been miserable, but she felt she could be happy with Rob. Their relationship was no relationship at all, not yet. It was at that tingling, exciting pre-courtship stage, when the other person is just a tantalizing mystery, when anything seems possible and the world – whatever its difficulties – seems like a fantastic place to be.

She took up her position on the till and fixed a smile on her face, teeth gritted, as the doors of Darkes opened and the customers streamed in.

18

'Hi! Rob!'

Daisy got back home shortly after six, and there was Rob out on the front drive, washing down the Mercedes in the fading half-light with his shirt sleeves rolled up. She thought he looked sexy as hell. His toffee-blond hair was flopping into his eyes. Her heart did a roll, just seeing him there. He glanced up, didn't smile.

'Oh. Hiya, Daise.'

'Busy?'

'Yeah.'

He carried on soaping the car. Daisy watched him working, imagining those strong, strong hands on her body. He was so *reliable*, Rob. You felt like you could count on him for anything. She'd had a pig of a day, but seeing him was the perfect salve to her wounded feelings. Her co-workers hated her. She was the boss's daughter, slumming it – that was how they saw her. They were determined not to give her a chance. But at least Rob didn't have any of those stupid preconceptions.

'How's it going at the store?' he asked, seeing that she was still standing there, watching him.

'Fine. Great!' she lied.

'Good,' said Rob.

'Rob . . .' Daisy stepped closer, and snagged her instep

on the hose, twisting her ankle and lurching sideways. Rob reached out, caught her arm, steadied her.

'Careful,' he said.

'Ow,' said Daisy. That *hurt*. God, why wasn't she any good at all this femme fatale business, like chic Auntie Vi? But no. She lumbered around the place, tripping over hoses and making a fool of herself.

'All right?' he asked, still holding her arm while she hopped on one leg.

'Yeah. Fine,' said Daisy, wincing.

'Sure?' Now he was smiling. Laughing at her. She was *sick* of being laughed at.

'Fine,' said Daisy, yanking her arm free and straightening herself up with all the dignity she could muster. 'See you,' she said, and limped off indoors.

Rob watched her go, and sighed. He knew where she was going with this, and – OK – he *had* wanted to go there too, quite badly. He thought she was the sexiest woman he'd seen in a long while, and he wanted to fuck her bandy. But he'd had time to think it through, and now he reckoned it would be a stupid move. She was too bloody *posh*, for a start. And too bossy. Plus, she had a shedload of baggage. She'd done that rich-girl-goes-crazy thing in her younger years, driven everyone nuts. Was she over all that shit yet? Who knew?

On top of that she had babies. Twins, for God's sake. Double the trouble. Plus there was that crazy little fat fucker of an ex-husband – not that he could give a shit about Simon Collins, but still, it was an unwanted complication. And she was the boss's sister, and Kit was almost off his head at the moment, there was trouble building up there with him and the Danieri mob. It was all a little too close for comfort. If he got together with Daisy and then they fell out, how would that sit with Kit, and with their mother Ruby?

Rob got back to polishing the car.

No. Best to steer well clear of the complications. Find a nice single girl down the pub, no kids, no hassle, no crazy lunatic exes or unwanted connections, and let off steam with her instead.

It was all Daisy could do to stay awake, but she forced herself to get up out of the cosy armchair in the twins' room and make her way downstairs to join her mother. The previous evening she'd been so exhausted she'd gone to bed as soon as she finished bathing the twins with Jody and tucked them in for the night. She didn't want to make a habit of being in bed by seven thirty.

She sat down on the sofa beside Ruby, kicked off her shoes and gingerly rubbed at her ankle. It was still sore, but she wasn't limping any more. No permanent damage. Not enough to cry off work tomorrow, which was a pity. *Fucking* store work.

'You OK?' asked Ruby.

Daisy looked up at her mother, wondering whether to come clean, but the strain on Ruby's face stopped her in her tracks. 'I'm fine, but what about you? You look as if you're worried sick.'

Ruby sighed. 'I can't stop thinking about what happened at the funeral yesterday . . .' She told Daisy about Kit showing up, and Bella's words to her.

'God, that sounds serious,' said Daisy. It certainly put all *her* petty concerns into perspective.

'It's that all right. But if Bella can rein in Vittore and Fabio, Kit might yet get away with it.'

'Do you think she can?'

'Let's hope.'

19

Kit woke up alone and in pain. No luscious blonde Alison today, kicking off because he called her by someone else's name. Now, he couldn't remember whose name he'd called her by. *Same meat, different gravy.* It didn't matter, anyway.

The pain was a familiar morning companion. His head felt like someone had taken it off his shoulders and kicked it all around a football field, then booted it right out of the ground for an encore.

The drink.

He knew he had to stop that. He'd come home from his mother's late yesterday afternoon after the funeral – *was that wise, taunting the Danieris as they buried Tito?* – and then he'd got drunk again. Roaring, shit-faced drunk. He must have fallen across the bed fully dressed, and now he was awake, and he felt like death warmed over and served up as freshly minted.

He opened his eyes and it was light, it was morning, and oh God he didn't want another day, another *fucking* day without Michael, without Gilda. He pushed himself up into a sitting position and his brain started banging away inside his skull.

'Shit,' he groaned. There was a three-quarter-empty bottle of Bell's on the bedside table. He reached for it.

Hair of the dog, right? Make it all better. Maybe a prairie oyster later, settle my stomach, feels like it's doing backflips in there, what the hell . . . ?

Her face rose up in front of him, sea-green eyes laughing into his, the faint fairy jangle of gold that had followed her everywhere like her perfume, which was sweet strawberries and hay meadows. Not that he'd ever *smelled* a hay meadow, but if he had he just knew it would smell the same as her skin.

Gilda.

He'd truly loved her, and now she was gone.

He screwed up his eyes, wrenched out the cork, put the bottle to his lips and drank. Then he set it aside, tossed the cork fuck knew where, and lay back, eyes closed, feeling the whisky burn a hot tingling track all the way down to his toes.

Now he could see another face. Granite-jawed, set with a strong mouth and dark grey eyes that matched the thick thatch of hair. Those eyes were looking at him with disapproval.

Michael? Boss . . .

Kit felt his eyes fill with tears that spilled over. It was the drink. He was turning into a pitiful, booze-soaked alkie, maudlin and seeing faces of dead loved ones and blubbing like a fucking *baby*. Michael was looking disgusted with him. Well, he was disgusted with *himself*. He knew it was getting to be a major problem, the way he felt the pain and then automatically reached for the bottle to take it away.

He was scared of the pain. *Physical* pain he could handle. He was a gladiator, right? That was how he saw himself: tough as you like, nothing touched him. Rip his arm off, he'd come at you with the other one. But *this* – this soul-eating sense of loss, of something precious that was never, ever going to be replaced – this was too much.

So maybe he was, in fact, a fucking *coward*.

And what use was he, falling-down, rat-arsed drunk? He had . . .

Oh shit he had something important to do. What the hell was it?

Yeah, he had to . . . find out who murdered Michael, who *really* did it, because Tito and his brothers didn't. Was that true, though? *Could* it be?

Oh, and incidentally, just a minor detail, Kit, but didn't you kill Tito because you believed he did Michael?

'Fuck,' he muttered.

He hauled himself back into a sitting position. Looked again at the bottle and felt an uncomfortable stab of self-loathing. He was like a sodding baby with that bottle, a baby on its mother's teat. *Gimme comfort, take the pain away, don't let me think, don't let me feel, it hurts.*

He had no regrets about taking out Tito: Tito had been a bastard through and through, and he was now frying in hell, Kit was convinced of that. But what Ruby told him tormented him. That there could be someone still out there, laughing in secret because they'd done it, got away with it, they'd taken Michael Ward's life and never been made to pay the price.

Kit swung his legs over the edge of the bed. Everything in the room spun. Bile surged into his throat.

Somehow, he kept it down. Managed to stand up, too.

Up and at 'em, soldier! he told himself, and then he looked at the whisky bottle again, and he could *taste* it, it was good and it was as cosily enfolding as a warm blanket on a cold night, the booze, the blessed booze.

He picked up the bottle. No cork – where was the cork? Ah, no matter.

Raised it to his lips. *Smelled* it, rich alcohol, so soothing, taking the pain away.

But . . . he paused.

Maybe he had to *feel* that pain to be able to do this, find whoever had robbed Michael of his life. Maybe. He took a couple of steps over to the bathroom door, opened it, with the whisky bottle still in his hand. Then he went over to the sink, fully intending to pour all the remaining golden happy-juice down the plughole.

Instead, he left the bottle in the sink – *careful now, don't be a cunt and spill it!* – and looked at himself in the mirror. Café au lait skin looking a little grey, a little *bleached*, black hair, a handsome, well-sculpted face and blue, blue eyes with big dark shadows underneath them. His face. The face of Kit Miller. Only not. The stranger in the mirror was a nameless, unwanted boy, and 'Kit Miller' was actually a construct of some long-ago care worker in a children's home. His *mother* was Ruby Darke. His *father* was Cornelius Bray, who had also fathered Daisy – and neither of his parents had ever wanted him. He'd been cast aside, left to rot.

'So who the hell *are* you, pal?' he asked his reflection.

And his reflection answered: 'Michael's right hand. His number one man.'

Except, he wasn't *that* any more. Because Michael was gone. Now, everything that had been Michael's was Kit's – the restaurants, the boozers, the clubs, the wedge from the streets, the fortune Michael made on the Albert Docks development. Kit hadn't totted it all up, but he guessed he was now a sodding millionaire, and that was funny, because once upon a time money was the one thing he'd wanted. He'd been destitute as a child, not a pot to piss in, reliant on charity in children's homes. Now, he had it all. And he didn't want it.

What he wanted was a home life, a *real* life, a family maybe.

Gilda . . .

He wanted her back. And he wanted Michael back too.
Ah, impossible dreams.

He looked at the bottle.

My little friend.

He picked it up, took a swig.

Hold it down to a dull roar, right?

There was still some left in the bottle. He placed it carefully back in the sink, went towards the shower. He'd clean up, and then there was that nice liquid treat waiting there, a little something in reserve, right?

Right.

And then . . . maybe he'd try and start to think. Or maybe . . . maybe he'd decide not to face any of it. Maybe he'd take a razor blade, skip the shower, have a nice deep hot bath instead, you didn't feel it in a bath. Maybe that would be a plan: finish the drinking, finish with the whole stinking sorry mess that his life was these days, just open his wrists and lie there until it was over.

He thought of Vittore Danieri – those hate-filled eyes beneath that widow's peak of receding dark hair, the guy looked like fucking *Dracula* or something – Vittore hissing at him '*I'll rip the heart out of you . . .*'

Vittore had marked him, like Cain. Vittore had made a promise, a solemn oath that one day, one day soon, he was going to hurt him, maybe hurt Daisy or Ruby too. But maybe, Kit thought with a grim little smile, maybe he'd jump the gun, how about that? Take himself out of this whole shitty scene before Vittore took the matter out of his hands and did it for him.

He looked at the bath for long, long moments.

Then he leaned in and started the shower running.

OK, maybe not today. Maybe tomorrow.

20

'Please, Vittore, don't,' said Maria.

Ah, that was music to his ears. People begging, pleading, he loved it. What Vittore Danieri liked best about being the boss was seeing the abject fear in people's – even his wife's – eyes when he talked to them. He *loved* that. Relished it. He'd waited a damned long time for it, too, and would have had to wait a damned sight longer, if Tito hadn't come to such an unfortunate end.

In Vittore's eyes, Tito hadn't been right for the boss's job anyway. Like their father Astorre, Tito had been too easily distracted by bedding dirty *puttas* both male and female, and forging dubious connections to MPs and to the nobility, neither of which held any interest for Vittore.

What Vittore loved above all else was control, *power.*

As the middle son, he'd felt the lack of it for most of his life. Tito had been their father's chosen one, his first born. Astorre Danieri had doted on his eldest boy: Tito could do no wrong in his eyes. Fabio was the one who *hadn't* been the girl Mama craved.

No need to mention Bianca, the longed-for girl Bella so wanted. Girls didn't even figure in Vittore's mindset, beyond their obvious talents for keeping house and popping out babies – and Bianca didn't seem prepared to settle down and do *that*. She wanted to fiddle in the business instead, and of course Tito had yielded to pressure from Mama and given her the Southampton place to try.

For years Vittore had occupied the middle ground, the dead zone of the sibling forever doomed to go unnoticed by the father he always tried so hard to impress. Oh, his mother adored him. He was her favourite. He knew people saw him as dull, blockish, but Mama cooed over him, couldn't bear the thought of him marrying, desperate to keep him all for herself.

'Those dirty girls, you don't want to mix with them, my angel, my little Vittore,' Bella told him as a child, a teenager, a young man, all the while the music of Italy, of their home-land, playing in the background as Mama wore the old vinyl out.

'*Torna a Surriento*', that was a favourite of hers. And '*O Sole Mio*'.

'They carry on like *puttas*, like whores these days! This "permissive society", I spit on it. You could catch anything from them. Diseases. Your cock could drop off.'

Mama was right, no doubt about it. He'd had no interest in women, until Maria came along, black-haired, doe-eyed, a body like a fallen angel. For the first time in his life Vittore had felt the strong sexual pull of a woman. Maria had seemed so pure and innocent, and they had dated.

'She's a nice enough girl,' said Bella after the first couple of dates.

At this point, Vittore had been allowed to kiss Maria, deep and long.

'Still seeing Maria?' Mama asked after the fifth date, the sixth. Not looking too happy about it, not really.

Around about this time, Maria had let him undo her bra, gaze at her amazingly full naked breasts and touch her large dark nipples. It drove him crazy, touching them, feeling how soft her breasts were.

'I heard she's a *putta*,' came his mother's warning after the tenth date. 'You want to be careful. I won't always be here to protect you, Vito. You know my health's not good.'

Putta or not, he wanted this. When Maria let him lift her skirt and stare at the dark bush between her legs, oh God, he wanted all there was of this.

'How come you're still seeing that girl?' raged Bella after the twentieth date, when it was obvious that Vittore and Maria were 'going steady'. 'Are you trying to break your mother's heart? Didn't I tell you what these women are like?'

There were hysterical tears from Bella at news of the engagement, and then a flat refusal to attend the wedding.

'I may not live that long,' sniffed Bella, clutching at her chest when they named the date. 'I have this condition, as you know. My heart.'

I have a condition too, thought Vittore. *It's a pain in the arse, and you know what? It's you, Mama.*

He knew there was fuck-all wrong with his mother's heart. Her nose had been put out of joint by her favourite son finally growing a pair, that was all. He wanted a normal life, a family. And whether his mother liked it or not, he was going to have it.

Not that it had all been plain sailing. His mother's drip-drip-drip of acidic words seemed to have penetrated deep into the core of him. *Girls are dirty*, he heard in his head. *You want to catch something off them, syphilis maybe? Your penis will rot with sores – you want that, Vittore?*

Despite all that he wanted to bed Maria on their wedding night. Though he knew he was a bit undersized, on his own he could achieve a decent hard-on and jerk himself off to his complete satisfaction. But when they climbed into bed together, he couldn't do a thing. She was so pretty, big-breasted, small-waisted, with opulent full buttocks. Jesus, he wanted to fuck her so badly! But his cock was limp.

'It doesn't matter,' said Maria. 'We have all the time we need, don't worry.'

Maria couldn't believe she'd finally got Vittore up the aisle. Bella had pulled all sorts of tricks to prevent it, but here they were at last – married.

Vittore's little problem persisted for six, seven, eight months – by which time he was so desperate to have her that he felt he was going out of his mind. Then came the erections – full, amazing erections – but the mere sight of her naked body was enough to make him fire off too soon, before he could get in the bed with her.

Finally, a year into the marriage, consummation was achieved. He got drunk, fell into bed one night and there she was, his wife, and the drink relaxed him enough – not too much – to allow him to roll onto Maria – who was still a virgin – and shove his cock hard into her. It was over in three seconds.

Thereafter, that was the way it always seemed to be. And by that time, he suspected that Maria really didn't care any more.

But miracles did happen. His love life might have been blighted, but other things were going good. Tito's debauched reign had been swept away. The sign over the door of the club had been changed from Tito's to Vito's. Petty drug dealers who had circulated in the club selling their wares were ousted, and now Vittore's own doormen did discreet deals instead. The sex palace Tito had run above the club, pimping highly paid prostitutes to his upmarket friends, Vittore had quickly, with a shudder of distaste, swept away.

At long last he was in charge. But he'd come home to find that Maria hadn't even cleaned the place up. Was it too much to expect that she should keep their rooms clean and tidy, the way Mama would? Maybe Mama was right: all girls were dirty slovens.

'You think I want to live in a place like this, in a *tip*?' he shouted.

This was supposed to be where she would bear and raise his children; the place should be pristine, the way he liked it. That was all he wanted in life – a wife who did as she was told, as any good wife should. But today he'd come home to find the clumsy bitch had dropped a pot plant and now there was dirt all over the living-room carpet, the carpet *he'd* paid for, sweated for, and there was orange juice spilled on it by the fireplace and not mopped up, for God's sake, and the mantelpiece was caked in dust. Mama always kept an *immaculate* home.

Vittore was still seething over Kit Miller showing up at the funeral. He had promised the bastard that retribution was on its way, but when he had taken Mama home, she had told him, yet again:

'You won't touch him, Vittore. I told you, and you swore to behave yourself. This ends here, you understand?'

Actually he *didn't* understand. Actually he thought she was crazy and he was sick of hearing her *opinions* about what didn't concern her. Who was the boss now, after all? She was just an old woman, her time was done. He loved her but at the same time he hated her for what she had done to him, ruining him as a man. And was she crazy? That bastard Miller had insulted them, having the audacity to show up at Tito's funeral and crow about his death. There *had* to be revenge for that.

And what if the low rumble of rumours and suspicion should prove to be true? What if it wasn't one of Tito's other enemies but Miller himself who snatched Tito's life away? Wouldn't they be justified in taking action then? But no. His hands were tied by an old woman's apron strings, and he resented it, *hated* it.

He was sick of listening to Mama.

Why should he pay attention to what an old woman had to say about anything? Tito might have done. And Fabio might, too. But *he*, Vittore, was the boss.

Now all he wanted was to release this pent-up resentment, and here was Maria, who didn't seem to have a clue how to keep a house decent and tidy, and *whumph*, he slapped Maria, knocked her down, and suddenly he was aroused, he got down on the dirty floor with her and slapped her again, then pulled her pants down and unzipped himself, wild with lust now, he knew his cock wasn't very big but now to him it looked huge, impressive. He pushed her legs open and thrust it into her, pushed once, twice, three times, and then came.

'Dirty *whore*,' he groaned. 'Dirty fucking *whore!*'

Maria lay there sobbing as Vittore pulled out of her, zipped his trousers, scrambled to his feet.

'*Basta!* Get this place cleaned up, for God's sake,' he yelled above her crying, and went off into the bathroom to clean up.

He slammed the door shut after him, still furious, and kicked the white-painted wooden bath panel. It rattled, and one end flopped out of position.

'*Madonna!*' Vittore cursed loudly, and stooped down to see what was happening, had the screw come loose?

But there was no screw there, just the hole where it should be. He looked around on the floor: nothing. He pushed the panel back into place, but it swung out again at the tap end, leaving a gap six inches wide this time. Vittore's eyes caught a glint of something in the gap –

maybe plastic or silver. He reached in, and pulled out a foil packet of pills. Looked at it, and realized.

That *bitch*.

Maria lay there stunned, wondering why the man she had once thought she loved could only achieve an erection when he beat her, shouted out his hate for her, called her a dirty whore. She sat up slowly, her face burning, her thighs trembling from the force he'd used on her.

I hate him, she thought. *I hate him and I hate* her, *that old bitch. We will never be free of her.*

It galled her that Vittore hadn't had the guts to break away from Mama Bella after they'd married. Maria had envisaged a home of her own, but what had she got? A few rooms inside Mama's own home, so Bella could keep control of her favourite boy – and of his wife. Bella bullied her mercilessly; nothing Maria ever did was good enough. All it took was a few 'spasms' of Bella's supposedly frail heart (which to Maria's knowledge had never been proven to be frail) and Vittore caved in, agreeing that he and his new wife would stay under the family roof.

Numbly she sat up, crawled aching and sore to her feet.

She wished – so much – that they had buried *Vittore* today, not Tito.

Oh yeah – and that fucking old bitch Bella. She wished they'd put her in the ground too. That day couldn't come soon enough.

21

'The man's untouchable,' said Gilberto.

'You think?' asked Astorre.

'For sure.'

Despite the trauma of his father's death, Astorre was doing well in his business life. He had sussed out Corvetto's security arrangements and seen how good they were, how thorough. But he would wait. He was of the opinion that everyone was vulnerable, everyone had a weak spot; it was just a matter of finding Corvetto's, and he had all the time in the world to do that. Revenge truly was a dish best served cold.

Astorre's home life was troubled. After successfully delivering Tito, who was a strong boy, Bella had a succession of miscarriages and one painful, awful stillbirth – a daughter! – that broke her heart clean in two. Finally, after an eight-year wait, there came another son, a living son, Vittore, and Bella couldn't believe it; she doted on this unexpected child, lavished all her love on him. Even her husband felt pushed aside by this new, tiny interloper and when their love life resumed after a year or so Astorre still felt unwelcome in his own bed. So he took a mistress, and seldom attended to his marital duties with Bella.

More miscarriages followed Vittore's birth; but after a twelve-

year gap at last the news was good. Bella was pregnant again, and this time it would be the girl she longed for.

'Look how the baby carries all the way round, not just a little bump at the front,' she said gleefully to anyone who would listen, when she was huge and in the seventh month of her pregnancy. 'It's a girl. A little bambina, at last.'

When she went into labour, there was a ferociously long struggle to bring her daughter into the world. Exhausted, wrung out with the agony and blood loss, Bella gave one final desperate push and then looked down as the child spiralled out of her body. Her triumph turned to ashes in her mouth as she saw squirming there not the girl she had wanted so much but a puny little boy. Her heartbreak at being denied a daughter yet again was compounded by the doctors warning her and Astorre that this should be her last child.

'But I want a little girl to complete my family,' she cried when they broke the news.

'It's not safe,' said the doctor, and she was forced to accept that.

But it grieved her, the lack of a daughter. She had Tito. And she had Vittore, her favourite, her own little love. Now she had baby Fabio too, but he was a disappointment, always pushed away. She craved a girl. Longed for one. Without a daughter, her family would never be complete.

22

Someone was knocking at the front door. No, they were *hammering* on it, in perfect counterpoint to the steady throbbing of Kit's head.

'You'd better open this door,' said a voice. 'Or else I'm going to get Rob to kick it off its hinges.'

Kit closed his eyes again. Now where was he . . . ? He looked around him with sore eyes. He was in his own living room. He was dressed. He had . . . oh yeah. He'd got out of the shower, got himself all ready to roll, and then he'd come downstairs, sat down on his huge brown leather sofa – and fallen asleep. And there was the bottle, right there beside him, his ever-useful and strictly non-judgemental companion.

He reached for it.

Empty.

. *Fuck*.

'Kit! Open this bloody door! I know you're in there!'

Kit groaned and lurched to his feet. Staggered. Thought that he was going to fall straight back down, arse over tit. But no: slowly, the room stopped revolving. He tottered out to the hall, over to the door, and opened it.

Daisy was standing there, Rob at her shoulder. She looked flushed, angry, anxious.

'Oh, it's you,' said Kit, turning away from the door and going back into the living room. He went to the sofa and flopped down upon it.

Daisy came and stood in front of him. Her eyes took in the state of him, the empty whisky bottle by his side.

'Just *look* at you,' she said in disgust.

Kit got his eyes open again. Stared up at her. 'Shouldn't you be stacking a shelf somewhere?'

'Oh, shut up. Ruby was worried about you, she asked me to come, see you were OK.'

'And you brought Rob, too. All right, mate?' Kit raised an unsteady hand.

Rob said nothing.

'As you can see, I'm perfectly bloody fine,' said Kit. 'So the pair of you can fuck off.'

'We're not going anywhere. Make some coffee, Rob,' said Daisy, sitting down on the sofa and tossing the empty bottle aside.

'Yeah, hurry up and do the business, Robbo old son,' Kit shouted after Rob as he went out to the kitchen. 'Do as the boss lady says.'

Daisy's flush deepened. 'Don't be horrible to Rob,' she snapped. 'He'd take a bullet for you – don't you *dare* make fun of him.'

'Ah.' Kit laid his aching head on the sofa and closed his eyes with a smile. 'You got a crush on him, aintcha? I can tell, Daise.'

Daisy surged to her feet. 'Will you shut up?' she yelled. 'Don't you realize the *trouble* you're in?'

Kit opened his bleary eyes and squinted up at his twin sister – not that they looked alike, apart from the blue eyes. Hers were clear and bright; his, from a brief glance in the bathroom mirror earlier today, looked like two orange-red piss-holes in the snow.

Oh, he knew he was in trouble. He knew that Vittore Danieri was going to be looking to carve a good-sized chunk of meat out of his arse for turning up at the funeral. But somehow he couldn't get himself to care.

Rob was out in the kitchen, filling the kettle and putting it on to boil, then opening cupboards, rattling cups. All Kit wanted was to close his eyes again, forget it all.

I seek oblivion, he thought with sudden clarity. *I seek death.*

But there was no eternal peace here, only Daisy pacing back and forth. After a bit Rob came in with a mug of black coffee in his bear-like paw and placed it on the coffee table, not looking his boss in the eye.

Daisy was still stalking about the room, shooting filthy looks at Kit. 'Ruby told me what you did. Turning up at the funeral. How the hell could you do something so stupid?'

'Stupidity comes naturally to me. Didn't you know?'

'Oh, do shut up.'

'*Oh, do shut up,*' said Kit, mimicking her.

Daisy blushed bright red. Her eyes turned frosty. He'd hit a nerve. '*Don't* mock me,' she ordered, moving in on him. For a moment she looked mad enough to slap the crap out of him.

'Have some coffee,' advised Rob, standing over his boss with arms folded.

'*Fuck* your coffee,' said Kit. 'And fuck you too.'

Rob shook his head. He looked more sad than angry.

'Mate, you got to stop this,' he said, 'or one day Vittore's going to be on you and you'll be too pissed to even realize you're dead.'

'Fuck off.'

'You're such an idiot,' said Daisy. 'Ruby told me what Vittore did when you—'

'And did she tell you that none of the Danieri brothers were responsible for Michael's death?' asked Kit. He reached for the coffee, took a sip. Sour. Horrible. He put it back down.

'She did,' said Daisy. 'Yes.'

'And I'm supposed to believe that?'

'What reason do you have to disbelieve it?' asked Daisy, starting her pacing again. 'Apparently the Danieri boys hold their mother in very high esteem. Something you might find hard to understand, I imagine.'

Kit stiffened. 'Hey, don't start on *me*. Start on her over in Marlow, the great Ruby Darke. *I'm* not the one who abandoned their kid.'

'I'm not getting into all that again,' sighed Daisy. They'd argued about this on more than one occasion, her saying that Ruby had no choice, her family had turned on her when they found out she was pregnant out of wedlock and there was no way she could raise two babies all by herself, not in those days. To which Kit always said *bullshit*.

'Good,' said Kit. 'Because I don't fucking well want to hear it, not from you, not from anyone. Got that?'

Daisy and Rob looked at each other.

'Mate . . .' started Rob, turning despairing eyes on Kit.

'Kit,' said Daisy. 'You've insulted Vittore's family by doing what you did.'

Kit shrugged and squinted up at her. His sister, his twin. OK, she might have got the glamorous end of it growing up – the pony clubs, the coming-out balls, all that hoity-toity shit, but she was no fool; you didn't have to draw *her* any pictures. He had another slug of the coffee. It was still the pits.

Daisy sat down beside Kit. 'I loved Michael,' she said quietly.

'We all did,' said Rob.

Kit looked at Daisy's face. Then at Rob's.

'So who's going to say it?' asked Kit.

'What?' asked Daisy.

'What?' asked Rob.

'The bleeding obvious. If those Eyeties didn't do it, who did?'

'We all want to know the answer to that question,' said Daisy. It tormented her, the thought of Michael dying alone in an alley, shot through the head – and she had seen the fallout, the heart-rending grief Ruby had suffered when she lost him. She wanted to find out who did this. Not for revenge. For her own peace of mind. 'Don't you want to know? Kit?'

'Of course I fucking well do,' he said. Took another swig, finished the coffee. His head still hurt. He *still* wished he could just sleep, die, anything rather than have to face what he knew he must, this thing that would hound him to the grave if he didn't hunt it down and wring the truth out of it. It hurt him, *destroyed* him, that someone had killed Michael, rubbed out his life. And the thing that made it worse? It had happened on *his* watch.

'So who the hell did it? If they didn't?' he said aloud, and clutched at his head.

'We don't know. But for sure we *have* to find out,' said Rob.

Rob knew how badly Michael's passing had hurt Kit. It was as if he'd been locked into a downward spiral ever since, added to which he now had Vittore out for his blood. The way things were going, Kit wouldn't live long enough to track down Michael's killer. Kit and Rob had almost grown up together working for Michael. He didn't want to lose him.

I'll watch his back, he promised himself. *What more can I do?*

'Where do we start?' asked Kit. 'We don't have a fucking clue, do we?'

'He had enemies,' shrugged Rob.

'We *all* got those.'

'We have to start thinking,' said Daisy firmly. 'And *stop* drinking.'

23

Fabio was waiting, spying out the land, taking it nice and easy. He had his stake money together, his *own* money, nothing from the family coffers, nothing that Vittore with his smug superior smirk dealt out to him from petty cash like he was doing him some sort of fucking favour.

He hated Vittore, always had. Tito had been OK, had a bit of life in him, but Vittore was like a wet tea towel over a chip-pan fire: he seemed to extinguish life wherever he went. Yet despite that, Vittore was Mama's little darling. Not her youngest son, no. He'd been ousted by Bianca, the daughter Mama had always wanted – only she wasn't a *real* daughter, just a bought-in one, a ready-made thing – like shop cake.

Feeling the anger rise inside him, Fabio reminded himself that none of that mattered any more. He was his own man. Let Vittore worry about the family, the honour of the Danieris and that shit Kit Miller. Fabio didn't care. He had other concerns.

As he came downstairs into the hall, he could hear Mama in the kitchen making breakfast. From her sitting room drifted the sounds he'd grown up with, the sounds of old Italy, someone singing '*Bésame Mucho*'. Poor old Mama, clinging on to old ways and old days. Bella's speech was still heavily accented, but her sons had quickly smoothed out their vowels and now sounded pretty much English.

As he reached the bottom stair, pulling on his jacket, he paused to admire his reflection in the mirror there and was gratified to see that the caramel-coloured flecks of wool in his Donegal tweed jacket exactly matched the lustrous brown of his eyes. Then he saw Maria, wearing a pink silk house robe, come out of the hall door that led into the set of rooms she and Vittore shared. Poor cow, didn't even have a home of her own. What kind of a man went on living under his mama's roof after he tied the knot? Yeah, Mama had gone all hysterical when Vittore took Maria for a bride; there'd been tears, heart murmurs, all that crap – but a real man wouldn't have caved in and thrown her a sop by promising to go on living here with her.

'Hey, Maria,' he greeted her, wishing she hadn't come out at this precise moment. He had lots to do today, and he always found his brother's wife incredibly dull. He liked vibrant, chatty women, and that wasn't Maria at all. She was pretty and she had a dynamite body, all hot curves and that great fall of black hair, but she had no conversation whatsoever.

Then he saw her face, the bruise on her cheek, the eye-socket above it turning black. Maria clutched her robe closed at the neck, shrinking back against the door she'd just come through.

'Wow! What happened to you?' he asked, half-smiling.

'Nothing,' she said, her gaze averted.

'It don't look like nothing.'

'I fell over, it was stupid of me. I hit my face on the fire-place.'

'Ah. Well, be more careful. You want to put something on that, take down the swelling,' said Fabio cheerfully, thinking that robe revealed more than it concealed, and he was right: she had a *great* body.

'Maria!' It was Mama, appearing in the kitchen doorway, her voice like the crack of a whip.

Vittore saw Maria literally *shrink* back.

'Isn't it time you got dressed? And what happened to your face?' asked Bella.

'She fell over,' said Fabio, since Maria appeared to have been struck dumb.

'That was careless.' Bella made a shooing motion. 'Go on, Maria, get dressed, I need a hand in here . . .'

As Bella bustled off into the kitchen, Fabio's eyes met Maria's. He thought she looked like a whipped dog. But she wasn't his concern.

'I'll catch you later,' he called over his shoulder as he headed out the front door.

'Where's Fabby?' asked Bella, reappearing in the kitchen doorway a moment later.

'He went out,' said Maria.

'That boy!' tutted Bella, before turning impatiently to her daughter-in-law. 'What are you doing, still standing there? Get some clothes on, hurry up.'

Maria retreated to her own small section of the house, closed the door and leaned against it. If only she'd married Fabio instead of Vittore – she wouldn't be living in this place, that much was certain.

24

Naples, 1946

After baby Fabio's arrival, the old safe Italy had been blasted into smithereens. The beginning of the end had come last year, when Mussolini, Il Duce, had been captured by the communists, the fucking partisans. Il Duce had been tried, killed and then his corpse strung up in Milan, with his mistress and colleagues hanging at his side.

The war was over now, but the devastation remained. Poverty stalked the streets, a poverty so extreme that even the fish in the aquarium, rare expensive species that had been kept safe for years, were hauled out and eaten. Orphans and scugnizzi – the children who lived in the gutters of Napoli – hustled into restaurants and were thrown hunks of bread if they were lucky, maybe a dollop of the soft cheese they made on Vesuvius, the one with lamb's intestines added.

Astorre's family had come through the war relatively unscathed. He had managed to avoid being drafted into the army, and he'd kept Tito, who was now a strapping twenty-one-year-old, out of it, too, though it had taken all his remaining influence and that of any contacts still breathing to achieve this. But with the partisans in control his position was dangerously vulnerable, even though he'd had the sense to withdraw from the deposed Fascist Party.

At any moment Astorre expected a heavy knock at the door, to be marched outside and shot, then deposited in a shallow grave. His only defence was to move his family out of their home in town to a hovel in the country, scraping a living off the soil as best he could, skulking around the port looking for work or contraband, keeping his profile and that of his family as low as possible. Fear was their constant companion.

What made it so much harder to bear was the fact that Corvetto, who called himself a communist, All for one and one for all, brother! *– and what shit that was – had grown more powerful than ever. The bastard lived like a* barone *in his sprawling fenced-off estate with its olive groves and lemon trees, with guards on the gate and dogs roaming free. The fat turd dined on the best food and wine, nothing but the finest for him. And whenever he left his compound he was surrounded by body-guards. But he was still just a man. He could still be killed.*

Time and again Astorre went to the compound, hiding in the shrubbery as he watched Corvetto's place, the comings and goings. And as he watched, he remembered that day when the volcano had poured out its lava, poisoning the atmosphere, and he'd run through the ash-covered streets with Gilberto, the pair of them choking and breathless, falling into the police station to see his father's torn, ruined, blood-covered body.

Twenty long, hard years Astorre had been waiting for his revenge. Now he was afraid he might have waited too long. Corvetto was a hugely influential figure among the partisans, and if he was hit there would be hell to pay. Astorre thought of this, late into the night when Bella was asleep and he lay sleepless, staring at the ceiling in their hovel, sweating in the heat.

If – when – he hit Corvetto, he would have to take his family and run. Not just out of Napoli, but out of the country itself.

That thought broke his heart.

But he would do it.

It would be worth it, that sacrifice, to have his revenge for the death of his dear Papa. He was camorristi, after all, and to one of that ancient brotherhood, revenge was everything.

And by God, he swore he would have it.

25

Bianca often felt like a mushroom – kept in the dark and fed horseshit. From the word go, to her brothers she had always been the little one, the useless girl, the outsider who'd come in from the cold. She was deemed to have no part in the dark and dangerous world her family inhabited. Bianca knew all this. She also knew that this was the reason why, when she had started to kick against her enforced exclusion, the men of the family had gone into conference and decided that OK, they would throw her a little something to shut her up.

And so she was put in charge of a washed-up drinking club behind the old city walls in Southampton.

Near enough for Vittore to keep an eye on me, she thought. *But far enough outside London to be sure I don't try to get involved in any of the big stuff.*

She knew she was being palmed off, kept quiet. But she *also* knew that if she made a success of Dante's, her brothers might – just might – start to look at her in a different light. So that was what she was determined to do.

If life gives you lemons, you make lemonade, right?
Right.

So here she was, cast into the outer darkness but about to make a kick-arse success out of something the brothers were sure she was going to fail at.

She wasn't going to fail.

No way.

It hurt that even Tito, Tito whom she had so adored, treated her dismissively, as if she was a liability, not a thinking, fully functioning human being who, given a chance, could be a useful member of the family. She knew she wasn't a team player; she was, in fact, a natural boss – a leader, not a follower. And there were already enough bosses in the family. The Danieri boys, being bossed around by a mere female? Unthinkable. Unless her name was Mama Bella.

Having such a powerful mama figure in their lives didn't seem to have done the boys much good. Bianca thought of Tito, who had never married. And mean, bossy Vittore with his meek little wife Maria, who was so obviously scared to death of him – and of Mama too. And Fabio, whose cruel butterfly mentality was of the fuck 'em and forget 'em variety. None of the brothers had what she would call *easy* relationships with women.

Bianca thought of her own romantic past. A few boyfriends, nothing serious. Of course, she had never introduced any of them to her family. God forbid. Any male coming within fifty yards of her would get a hell of a grilling from the brothers, and run a mile. Not that there were any prospects at the moment. She was too busy with the business, there was no time for relationships.

Maybe she was better on her own. Into her mind drifted the image of the man who had stared at her while she'd been stuck in London traffic en route to Tito's funeral. The fiercely intelligent blue eyes, so startling, so full of pain and so strikingly *odd* in that dark-skinned face. The sensual mouth, the noble face, the close-cropped black hair . . .

Shit, what was wrong with her?

She was standing here pie-eyed, daydreaming about a man she had seen once, in a car, and would never see again.

Get a grip, girl, she told herself. And turned her attention back to the paperwork on her desk.

26

Kit was standing in the flat above Sheila's restaurant. *His* restaurant, now that Michael was gone; he'd inherited it along with all the other restaurants, clubs, shops, stalls, properties and a thriving loan business. He hadn't set foot in Sheila's, or the little office at the back where Michael had worked, controlled his legitimate and his criminal empire, not since they'd found Michael shot dead in that alley. He'd . . .

let things slide.

Yeah. That was it. He'd let things slip away because nothing really seemed to matter any more. He'd left it to Rob and the other boys to pick up the slack, and he shouldn't have. If Michael was here, he'd kick his arse, hard. But Michael was gone. So here Kit was, feeling hung-over, his head banging away like a brass band. He was looking around, and wondering what the fuck he was looking *for*.

You know what you're looking for. You're looking for answers.

Yeah, that was it. Answers to who killed Michael Ward.

Kit stared around the flat. It was big and tastefully furnished, decked out in neutrals – beiges and pale antiqued pinks and fine powder blues. He saw a feminine hand at work here – probably Ruby's. He glanced at Rob, who was standing there inside the open door to the flat. From downstairs, faintly, came the sounds of pots and pans clanging in the kitchens. Savoury aromas were floating up the stairs, making Kit feel nauseous. He could hear silverware being laid out front-of-house, the waiting staff talking, laughing, polishing glasses.

Everything was as normal.

Only it wasn't; it would never be normal again.

Kit went through the little sitting area and into the bedroom. He opened the wardrobe door: empty. He heaved a sigh. Ruby would have done this: cleared out all Michael's clothes, his Savile Row suits and his costly handmade shoes.

He closed the wardrobe door, went to the dressing table. Same again, empty. Then he looked in the bedside tables. Nothing.

Rob had followed him through. He was standing in the bedroom doorway, arms folded, watching.

'You can go if you want,' said Kit. 'Fuck-all to see here, anyway. Don't Ruby need you?'

'I've put Reg on that,' said Rob.

Kit looked at Rob. Reg was a big white-haired ex-boxer who had pulled out of the breaking game after some hernia trouble. Chauffeuring Ruby would be a doddle for him.

'Yeah? You didn't ask me about that,' said Kit.

'You weren't in a fit state to ask.'

'So you went ahead and did it.'

Rob shrugged again. *You need me more right now than Ruby does*, he thought, but didn't say it. Kit was notorious for being Mr Self-sufficiency. The slightest hint that he was showing weakness and he'd kick off like a madman.

Kit let out a heavy sigh and sat down on the bed. He felt weak.

Too much drink.

His head ached and he was tired and he wanted . . .

You want the bottle, right? You want to forget all this reality shit and hide away with your old pal Jack Daniels.

He shook his head, tried to concentrate.

'Did Michael ever keep . . . I dunno . . . maybe a diary? Anything like that?' he asked.

Rob looked at him. 'You kidding? Write stuff down for one of the straight filth to pick up on?'

Kit was aware that he'd said something stupid, made himself look a cunt. He took a sharp breath. *Come on.*

'What about his personal effects? His wallet, cufflinks, comb, that sort of shit?'

'Ruby cleared out this flat, so I guess she's got them.'

'She still got her key then?'

'Must have.'

Kit surveyed the room. This was too much, he couldn't do this. He closed his eyes, rubbed a weary hand over them and wished for a drink. At any moment he expected Michael to walk in the door, but that wasn't going to happen. He had started to *feel*, that was where it had all gone wrong. In the kids' homes, he had grown a hard shell of indifference over his heart. It was the only way; when you care for nothing and no one, not a damned thing in the world can hurt you.

But then he'd fallen for Gilda, and he'd grown close to Michael. Between the two of them they'd smashed Kit's shell wide open, laid bare his innermost soul, opened it wide to anguish, to loss, to grief. He was tormented by memories of Gilda's laugh, the feel of her skin against his. And Michael's sudden warm grin, the pressure of his hand on Kit's shoulder.

'You done good, son,' he would say, and Kit would feel like he'd won gold in the Olympics, the feeling was that bloody good.

He was never going to have that feeling again. It killed him to think it, but there was no getting away from the truth.

'What about the filth?' he asked Rob. 'We got quite a few in there on the take, right? What are they saying about what happened to Michael?'

'I've spoken to them. Word is it's been sidelined.'

Now Kit was paying attention. 'Sidelined?'

'Shunted into a dark place at the back of a filing cabinet,' said Rob. 'You think the Old Bill give a shit about Michael's death? Think again.'

'But there must be something,' said Kit. 'Crime scene forensics. *Something*.'

'There is, for sure.'

'Then I want it.'

'I'll see what I can do.'

'Don't *see*. Fucking well do it, OK?'

Rob's face stiffened. 'Fine. It's done. Look—'

'*What?*' Kit snapped, coming irritably to his feet. To his shame, he staggered slightly. And then felt a twat, because he knew Rob could see his unsteadiness and was about to mention it.

'Mate, you're not up to any of this. Not right now.'

Consumed with fury, Kit hurled himself across the room and grabbed the front of Rob's shirt and rammed him against the door.

'You *what?*' he shouted in Rob's face.

'Mate—' said Rob.

'I ain't your mate. I'm your *boss*. You wouldn't speak to Michael Ward like that, you don't speak to *me* like that either.'

'Truth hurts, yeah?' asked Rob, panting a little because Kit was pressing on his windpipe. But he didn't raise a hand to defend himself. Not even when Kit's face twisted with rage and he raised a fist.

'Go on then,' gasped Rob. 'If it makes you feel any better, *do it*. But you know I'm right. You're a fucking *mess*.'

Kit stood there frozen for long moments. Then he let Rob go, literally flung him to one side. They were both gasping, like fighters after a bout. Kit felt sick that he had nearly punched his best mate's lights out. He knew Rob wouldn't have fought back. Rob was better than that. He was so loyal that he would have let Kit kick all kinds of crap out of him without raising a finger to defend himself.

And what does that make me? wondered Kit. Right now he couldn't even look Rob in the eye.

When Rob spoke, his voice was low: 'Listen. Take a couple of days away, yeah? Sort yourself out. I'll see what I can do here, look into it, and then you can come back and we'll figure this out properly. But first, take some time. You need it. You know you do. You're no fucking good like this. You're embarrassing yourself.'

Rob was right. Kit hated it, but he *knew* Rob was right.

'You'd better go,' he said.

'Yeah. But think about what I've said, OK?'

And then Rob was gone, closing the door softly behind him.

Shit, I was going to deck him. I really was. Rob, of all people.

In the stillness of the flat, Kit looked around him. Michael wasn't here any more.

If I was, I'd knock your stupid block off came into Kit's brain, and he was able to raise a painful smile.

Yeah, that was the truth. Michael would hate to see him like this. His eyes went over to the drinks trolley, still loaded with whisky, wine, gin – everything you needed to get thoroughly, hopelessly smashed. Ruby'd missed a trick there.

He turned away from it, sickened with himself. Quietly, he left the flat, locked it behind him, and went downstairs. Rob was right. He needed a break. Then maybe he'd start to think more clearly.

27

Kit went back to his house, threw a few things into an overnight bag. Then he came downstairs and thought again about a drink.

You tosser, don't you dare, came Michael's voice, loud and clear in Kit's head, so clearly that Kit actually looked around, certain he'd see Michael standing there. But he wasn't. Of course not.

Kit put his bag down and went over to the drinks on the sideboard. He gathered up the bottles and strode into the hall cloakroom with them clutched to his chest. Put them in the sink. Looked at them. Thought of how close he'd come to punching Rob in the head.

How long before he turned that stupid drunken anger of his on Daisy, or Ruby? If he did *that*, he'd never be able to live with himself. He didn't beat on women: never had, never would. But his temper when he was in the drink was so unstable, it was like sweating gelignite.

Carefully, deliberately, he unscrewed the cap of each bottle and let the contents run away down the drain. The smell of the alcohol came to him, warm as a caress, rising to swirl around him.

No. You're done with that, right?

With all the bottles emptied, he picked up his overnight bag, switched off the lights and went out, locking the door behind him. He made his way down the front steps, to where the Bentley was parked. In the yellowish gloom of the street lights, he could see something had happened to the car. Cautiously he moved closer.

All down the driver's side, someone had taken a key or a knife and gouged a long line in the paintwork. He looked down. The tyres had been slashed. He walked around the car. The other side was the same – the paintwork savaged, the tyres in ribbons.

Kit's heart was thudding hard in his chest, he could feel the steady beat of a headache restarting over his right eye.

Just a little taster, right, Vittore? he thought.

He wasn't going anywhere in the Bentley tonight. He would phone Rob later, get him to sort it. He walked further along the road to the junction, expecting to be jumped at any moment, wondering would he be sorry or relieved if that should happen? But it didn't.

Not this time.

He saw a black cab coming, its golden light aglow. He flagged it down, and got in.

28

Three weeks into learning how the store worked from the ground up, and Daisy was still stacking shelves and serving customers and smiling very sweetly while her co-workers abused her.

'And how *is* her ladyship this mawning?' asked Tessa as Daisy loaded up with stock in the stores, counting packs.

Shit.

Daisy didn't answer. She just kept loading the products into her hand basket.

'Ooh, she's not talking to us,' said Julie, mouth turning down in mock offence. 'Thinks she's *above* us, I suppose.'

She was so sick of these horrible cows.

'Well, she is. The heir-apparent to this whole shebang, that's what her ladyship is. *Far* too good to *parse* the time of day with the likes of us.'

Daisy stopped loading her basket and turned to them.

'A dog in the street's too good for that,' she said.

Tessa's mouth dropped open. '*What* did you say?'

'You heard,' said Daisy, and swept past her tormentors.

Or at least she started to. One of them – she thought later that it must have been Julie – stuck out a foot, and Daisy went sprawling to the concrete floor. The basket handles came off her arm, spraying the contents over the floor. One of the packs burst open, and purple bubble bath splashed out in a glutinous arc, spattering the nearby pallets.

Searing pain lanced through Daisy's knee and her elbow. Wincing, she lay there, winded. Then she looked up. Tessa and Julie were smirking down at her. At that instant, something snapped in Daisy's head. She lunged to her feet, hardly feeling the pain. She ran at them, grabbed them both by the hair, slammed their heads back against the partition wall. Saw two pairs of eyes open wide with shock in the instant before she took a firmer grip and banged their heads together in fury.

Both girls squawked then, and Tessa started yelling that she couldn't do this.

'No? Bloody well *watch* me,' hissed Daisy.

'What's going on?' asked someone nearby.

Daisy, panting, turned her head. Doris Blanchard was standing right beside her.

Suddenly Daisy became aware that her arm was sore, her knee was throbbing. *Everything* hurt. But the hot rage that had flooded through her had blanked it all out. Slowly, she came to. Saw the fright on the faces of her two tormentors. Julie was crying. Tessa was saying she'd *get* Daisy for this.

She let them go. Doris was staring at her.

'We'd better clear up this mess . . .' said Doris, looking around her and then back at Daisy, like she'd never seen her before.

'These two can do that. *Can't* you, girls?' said Daisy.

'Don't want anyone slipping on this, do we?' asked Doris nervously. 'Come on, Daisy, you can give us a hand . . .'

'Actually, I can't,' said Daisy. She pulled off the Darkes uniform and threw it on the floor. Then she went straight up to Ruby's office to tell her that she was done with working here – but Ruby had already gone home.

Daisy piled gratefully into her Mini and headed back to Ruby's place in Marlow. She saw Ruby's Mercedes on the drive, saw the hose there and the moisture on the driveway. Rob was washing the car. She got out of the Mini, locked it, and went over to where Rob was, behind the Merc's bonnet.

'Hi . . .' she started to say, then Reg straightened up, thirty years older than Rob, white-haired and pug-nosed and sporting a matching set of cauliflower ears from his days punching it out in the boxing ring.

'Oh!' she said in surprise.

'Sorry, were you expecting Rob?' he asked. 'He's helping Kit out, he had some jobs for him. I've taken over driving Ruby.'

'Oh,' said Daisy, her guts creased with disappointment. She'd had the day from hell, she was going to have to break it to Ruby that she was quitting the store, and now no Rob.

'Will he be doing that for long?' she asked.

Reg shrugged. 'Who knows.'

'Oh. OK,' said Daisy, feeling her heart sink all the way to her aching feet.

Then her eyes fell on the other car parked up on the drive, a red BMW. Of course. Simon was bringing Jody the nanny and the twins back from their day with him. Daisy and Simon had argued about this – every conversation with Simon ended in an argument – but as usual he had won. Daisy thought the twins far too young to be removed from the familiarity of home. But of course, Simon disputed that.

'They're *my* kids,' he'd raged. 'And for God's sake the

nanny will be with them. *One fucking day.* Is that too much to ask, you bitch?'

'Oh yeah,' said Reg, his eyes following hers. 'Your husband's here.'

'Ex-husband,' said Daisy, and trudged on indoors.

29

At first Maria had asked Tito to intervene, but Tito had been indifferent to her pleas.

'Come between a man and his wife?' he had scoffed at her. 'No. Absolutely not.'

A man and his wife. That phraseology told Maria everything she wanted to know about Tito's attitude; that it wasn't a mile away from Vittore's own. Tito was dead now but it was clear what his opinion of women had been. The man was important: *the wife* was not. The wife was an appendage, to be treated as the man chose within the sanctity of marriage, within the privacy of *his* own four walls.

The beatings were the worst thing. The pain and indignity. And he seemed to *need* to hurt her; only then could be become aroused enough to mount her. She knew how much Vittore wanted a family, kids – to prove himself a man, presumably – but she had got the Pill from her doctor and she'd been careful to take them, and even more careful to keep them hidden away in the little place behind the bath panel. But he'd found them, destroyed them. And he'd said he would *kill* her if he found any more, that it was a sin against the Catholic faith, against *nature*. Then he beat her again – more carefully this time, avoiding her face – to make her understand the error of her ways.

The last thing she wanted was a child of *his*.

Impotent anger boiled inside her. She started to spend his money feverishly, on things that didn't matter, things she bought, unwrapped and then discarded, because it was a way of hurting him, of having some small revenge.

And then she thought that there could be bigger, better vengeance against her hated husband. Not divorce, of course. They were Catholic: there could never be divorce. But there were other ways.

So Maria went to Fabio. She knew the family all discounted Fab, thought him the weak, vain baby, not bright enough to run the family, and they all thanked God for Vittore, who was dull but sensible.

Maria's lip curled in instinctive dislike every time she so much as *thought* about her husband. She loathed everything about him: his square body, his dull, menacing brown eyes. The truth was, she'd never loved him. She married him because she needed a meal ticket, a way to escape her own miserable family background. Even back then, the very thought of him touching her made her want to puke. Not that he did *that* very often. He was hung like a worm and seemed to have little appetite for sex, except after he'd given her a beating – and she tried as best she could not to give him an excuse to do that.

She had to bide her time, waiting until she was certain Vittore was busy about town and would not be home until late, and Bella was in her own part of the house watching TV – Bella never stirred in the evenings, thank God. Only then did she ask Fabio if they could have a talk.

'A *talk*?' said Fabio, astonished to be approached by Maria. She had always been the quiet dutiful little wife, always in Vittore's shadow. At family gatherings, she barely uttered a word. And now she wanted to *talk*?

Fabio had a lot of stuff going down. He didn't have time for chats with Maria, he couldn't see any advantage in it.

'I'm busy . . .' he started.

'I know you are. Of course you are. I just need to speak to you, please, Fabio, on a family matter.'

Family matter? He was puzzled. But she *was* family, and he was flattered. No one ever sought his opinion about anything.

'Meet me tomorrow, in the park,' he said.

What would Vittore say if he knew she had been in contact with his younger brother about a *family* matter? He'd be seething mad about it, Fabio knew. And that appealed to him, the fact that he was going to lend a sympathetic ear to Maria over something she didn't want to discuss with know-all Mama's favourite Vittore.

So he walked over to the park next day, and there she was – though he almost didn't recognize her at first. Around the house, his sister-in-law was always close-mouthed, eyes permanently downcast. He barely noticed her; she was more part of the furniture than part of the family.

But today she looked different.

She'd done her hair, brushed it until it shone in the watery spring sunlight. She was wearing a little make-up and a form-fitting purple dress instead of the black shapeless garments she usually covered her body with.

'Thank you for coming,' she said to him.

Fabio had to admit that Maria was a nice-looking girl, although obviously cowed from her marriage to Vittore. He wondered about that, how it was with the two of them. Despite Mama's objections to the union, the marriage seemed to have stuck. There were no children, true, but she seemed to be a devoted wife.

But now, this. A secret meeting! He was intrigued.

'Hi, Maria,' he said, and sat down with her on a bench. 'What's all this about then?'

Maria stared at his face. Then, unsmiling, she indicated her own. 'It's about this, Fab.'

Fab peered at her cheek. Beneath the film of make-up, it looked faintly blue.

'What? That bruise there? You fell against the fireplace, you said.'

'I know. I lied.'

Fabio frowned. 'How did it happen, then?'

Maria gulped down a breath. 'Vito hit me. He hits me all the time.'

'He *what*?' This was the first Fabio had heard about it.

She nodded. 'It's true.'

Fabio was silent.

'I asked Tito to have a word with him. He wouldn't.'

Fabio shrugged. 'Maybe you should tell Mama. She has more say with Vittore than anyone.'

'Mama Bella hates me. She always has. Do you think I don't know that?' Maria sniffed. 'I think you're a bigger man than your brother, Fabio. I think *you* could speak to Vittore for me, warn him off.'

Fabio looked at her. He was flattered that she was confiding in him, but this wasn't his business. If he dared speak to Vittore about it, Vittore would be livid. He had no intention of provoking his brother, knowing what he was like when he flew into one of his rages. Still, she had come to him; of course she had. He was getting to be a big man now, a businessman in his own right, and clearly she respected him enough to entrust him with this.

'I'll see what I can do,' he said. He'd do nothing.

'You will?' Maria smiled. She was really quite pretty, he thought.

She reached out, put a small hand on his thigh. 'You're so nice,' she said, smiling into his eyes.

Things were *really* looking up.

30

Naples, 1947

Astorre's opportunity had come at last. Patience had triumphed. The baker Lattarullo was heard in his shop moaning about how when he took fresh bread into Corvetto's compound every day, Corvetto always insisted on coming down to the kitchens and prodding the produce, asking, Is it stale? Are you bringing me yesterday's bread, not fresh like I ordered?

'The man's a pig,' said Lattarullo to anyone who would listen. 'He insults me.'

Bella, who'd been in the shop buying what little bread she could afford, went home and reported this to Astorre.

Astorre knew that Lattarullo was a decent, hard-working man. He was also the widowed father of a beautiful daughter, whom he adored.

It pained Astorre to do it. But he knew he had to, to avenge his dead father Franco's soul. Here Tito played his part, spiriting the girl Luisa away to an isolated place, a little falling-down hut near the family's home, and kept her there.

Meanwhile, Astorre called upon the baker Lattarullo and told him that unless he performed a certain task on Astorre's behalf, his daughter would be killed.

The man started gabbling away, begging for his daughter's safe return.

'That is guaranteed,' said Astorre, making calming motions with his hands. The poor bastard was doomed, he just didn't know it yet. 'All will be well, I promise you. But first you have to do something for me.'

Lattarullo passed a desperate night in his bakery, Astorre standing at his side. The baker worked, kneading the dough, flour misting the air. All the time he prayed for his child to be returned to him unharmed.

'She'll be fine,' said Astorre. 'So long as you do this for me.'

In the morning, as usual, Lattarullo drove out to the Corvetto compound in his truck, the covered section at the back piled high with bread for all the estate workers. The guards let him in, holding the snarling dogs tight on their leashes.

'Go on up,' said one, grinning and grabbing a loaf out from under the cover, pulling it apart, eating. Then he paused. 'Hold on,' he said, and he went around the back of the truck and poked hard at the covers. Then again and again, each poke more vicious than the last.

Lattarullo's heart was in his mouth.

'You'll damage the goods,' he warned, his voice trembling, sweat pouring down his brow as the day's heat intensified.

The guard drew back with a grin. 'Go on. Up you go.'

Lattarullo drove up to the house, parked in his usual spot outside the kitchen door. He switched off the engine with a shaking hand, took his basket and threw back the cover at the rear of the truck. He piled bread into the basket, his eyes furtive as they moved left and right. Another guard holding a rifle lingered by the door, watching him.

'All right, my friend? Hot day, uh?' he asked.

'Yes,' said Lattarullo unsteadily.

He took the basket filled with bread into the kitchen. There was the cook, smiling a welcome, her fat black lapdog at her feet as usual. The dog got up at Lattarullo's entrance and hobbled bow-legged toward him.

And here came Corvetto, bustling in from the hall, slapping the baker on the shoulder, taking up a loaf from the basket. Lattarullo felt so terrified now, so overwhelmed at what was required of him, that he thought he might faint.

'These are fresh today, huh?' Corvetto asked, his gaze teasing and offensive to a craftsman such as Lattarullo. Of course the bread was fresh. It was the finest in Napoli.

'Yes, fresh,' said Lattarullo. His mind was full of Luisa, his beautiful girl; he was doing this for her.

Corvetto tore a hunk from the loaf and popped it into his grinning mouth. He chewed thoughtfully. Then he coughed. The cook poured water from the carafe and pushed it towards him, on the kitchen table. Corvetto coughed again, swigged some of the water.

'Are you—' started the cook, but she didn't finish the sentence.

Lattarullo drew the knife out of his pocket. He'd honed it last night, for just this purpose.

My lovely Luisa, he thought. After he did this, he would be dead, but she would be safe at least. He had Astorre's word on that.

With a desperate shriek, he drove the knife in an upstroke into Corvetto's fat neck. Lattarullo had strong hands from his work in the bakery, and he used that strength now to pull the blade across. Blood spurted out in an arterial jet from the rapidly opening wound and Corvetto fell back, his mouth gaping wide, the remnants of Lattarullo's bread falling out of it. Blood poured from his mouth and drenched his clothes. Lattarullo was spattered in blood, so was the cook and her dog, the walls, the table, the ceiling.

The cook screamed. The dog started barking, a high panicky sound. Corvetto fell to the floor, gasping uselessly, his windpipe sliced in two, his eyes wide open in terror. He could see his own *life ebbing away as the blood pulsed out of his throat. His hands pawed at the wound, as if he could stop the flow; he couldn't. The cook said afterwards that you could see in his eyes that he knew it.*

The guard ran in from outside the kitchen door, alerted by the woman's screams and the dog's wild barking. He saw Lattarullo standing there with the bloodied knife in his hand.

Luisa, thought Lattarullo.

The guard raised the rifle, and shot him in the head. The baker fell dead across Corvetto's body.

Soon, Corvetto let out one last wheezing groan. He was dead too. Finally, Astorre's revenge was complete.

31

Simon was in the small sitting room at the front of the Victorian villa, and the look on Ruby's face when Daisy entered told her that Ruby wasn't sorry for the interruption at all.

'We have the Dubai contract now, so we're rammed right up to next year,' Simon was telling Daisy's mother in his usual bragging tones. 'Oh – Daisy,' he said, getting to his feet. He came over and kissed his ex-wife's cheek.

She *hated* him kissing her cheek. She wished he would just vanish from the planet, but he was the twins' father.

He was still an attractive man, actually rather sexy – short, squat, powerfully built, with his thick russet-red hair and sharp hazel eyes. But his too-quick temper was betrayed by his high facial colour.

The Red Dwarf, people called him, and it suited him: he could kick off in spectacular style. A late order, a missed dinner, a mistake on an invoice, a misheard conversation. Anything would do it.

'How are you, sweetheart?' he asked.

I'm not your damned sweetheart, thought Daisy, teeth gritted.

'Fine,' she said.

Ruby shot her a sympathetic look. Ruby knew exactly how Daisy felt about her ex.

'I was telling your mother about the new contract,' he said.

'Yes, I heard. Well done for that. Has Jody taken the twins upstairs, Mum?' asked Daisy, wanting an excuse to get away from him.

When Ruby nodded, Daisy said: 'Good, I'll go on up.'

Jody was getting the twins into the bath, and for a while the misery of Daisy's day was forgotten amid the splashes and laughs as the babies were bathed, fed and then put to bed. When she heard Simon's BMW being driven away, Daisy headed downstairs. Ruby was closing the front door. She smiled at Daisy and linked her arm through her daughter's as they went back into the sitting room.

'It's always so quiet the minute he's gone,' sighed Ruby. 'He seems to suck the air out of a room, doesn't he? What an exhausting man. Drink, Daisy?' she offered. Ruby always had a sherry after work: she'd earned it, after all.

Into Daisy's mind came a vision of Kit, spark-out drunk on the sofa. She'd never been an angel: her youth had been full of reckless rebellion, so much so that she'd scared herself. Only when she'd been reunited as an adult with her mother had she found any peace.

'No thanks,' she said.

'How's Kit?' asked Ruby.

'He's going to take a break,' she said. 'I think he needs it.'

'Good for him,' said Ruby. She was hurt that Kit hadn't phoned to let her know what he was doing, but at least a break would get him clear of Vittore, and that was a good thing. She stood up. 'Come on, I'm starving. Let's sort out dinner.'

'Mum?' said Daisy.

'Hm?'

Oh what the hell. Best to just come out with it.

'I've quit the store.'

Simon drove to his home deep in the pitch-dark Berkshire countryside, his mood lifting as he turned the BMW into the drive. He loved his house. It was big, white, impressive. Daisy had hated it, called it The Mausoleum, said it was miles from anywhere and cold as the Arctic tundra. No matter. Daisy was the past, anyway. Of course he would like to meet someone new, someone who could be a *proper* mother to his twins, not like her. Some lovely docile woman who adored being at home, who would be there waiting for him at the end of the day with the house all warm and welcoming, a hot meal cooked, ready to listen to his woes; that was his dream.

As he pulled up outside the garage block he gave a sharp sigh, seeing the house in total darkness. No warm, accommodating woman waiting for him. He'd heat something up himself, or maybe not bother, just grab a whisky and a sandwich. In the headlights he could see that the damned gardener had left one of the garage doors open again; he had *told* the bloody man about that on more than one occasion; there were thieves even out here, and some valuable stuff was stored in the garage. Why didn't the fool listen?

Simon switched off the engine and all was suddenly blackness and silence but for the ticking of the engine as it started to cool. He got out, locked the car, stalked over to the open garage door, muttering in annoyance.

'Hey,' said a voice to his left.

He literally jumped. The shock of hearing someone in this place, in this dense dark country silence, was immense. He whirled around, his heart in his mouth. Saw a shadowy shape moving.

'Who the hell are you?' Simon demanded.

Then the strip light that hung from the beams inside the garage flickered on. He saw two men inside, big burly men in black coats. One of them, older and taller than the other, had a long puckered purple knife scar running the length of his left cheek. It was hideous. The scarred one was pushing an old chair into the centre of the concrete floor. The other one . . .

Simon felt his bowels contract as he saw what the other one was doing.

He turned to run.

The man who had spoken on his left moved in, grabbed him; another one came from the right. He started to resist, but to his shock one of them drew a gun and held it to his head.

'Shut up,' he said, and Simon instantly stopped struggling.

They nudged him towards the garage, towards the scarred one with the chair – and the other one with the rope that he had thrown over one of the beams after tying it into a noose.

32

Daisy woke to the sound of knocking. Her first thought was *Matthew and Luke*. With a mother's instant alertness, she sprang up in bed and reached for the bedside light, turned it on. Blinking, she checked the alarm clock. Seven thirty in the morning. Outside, it was still dark and raining steadily. She couldn't hear a sound from the nursery.

An owl hooted in the woods. Nothing else could be heard.

Had she dreamed it?

Then it came again. Knocking. Someone was at the front door. Her heartbeat picking up, she grabbed her robe and put it on, shuffled her feet into slippers and went out onto the landing to find her mother at the top of the stairs, flicking on the light. Ruby's face was anxious.

'Should I call Reg?' asked Daisy. Maybe Reg, who was staying in the flat over the garage that was usually occupied by Rob, hadn't heard a car pull up. But Daisy peered down into the gloom of the hallway and could see flashing lights, *blue* lights. 'I think it's the police,' she said, and hurried down there, switching on lights as she went, Ruby following close at her heels.

Daisy was unlocking the door when Ruby stayed her hand. Ruby was thinking of Vittore, threatening Kit. *You and yours*, he'd hissed. She didn't think Rob had relayed the full version to her, but she knew enough to be wary. What if these *weren't* real policemen?

'Who's there?' she called out.

'Police, can you open the door please?'

Ruby hesitated. Where the hell was Reg when you needed him? She wished Rob was here instead. Rob would have been on the spot the instant anyone showed up. Then she heard other voices outside: Reg was out there. Better late than never. There was another knock at the door.

'Open up, Miss Darke, police are here,' said Reg's foghorn voice.

Ruby glanced at Daisy, who looked as alarmed as she felt. Nothing good could ever come of a police visit at this early hour, they both knew that. She unlocked the door and opened it.

Reg was standing there in pyjamas and dressing gown, his white hair standing on end, with two uniformed police, one male, one female. Their patrol car was on the drive, lights still flashing, a radio blasting out intermittent, unde-cipherable words.

'You're Miss Darke?' asked the woman. Ruby didn't think she looked big enough or old enough to be a girl guide, let alone a police officer.

'Yes, I'm Miss Darke,' she said, swallowing hard.

'Is there a Mrs Collins here? A Mrs Daisy Collins?'

'I'm Mrs Collins – or I was,' said Daisy. 'What's this about?'

'Can we come in, please?'

Ruby led the way into the sitting room, followed by Daisy, Reg and the two officers. They all sat down.

'There's been an incident,' said the male police officer.

Kit, thought Ruby in sudden terror. She knew how low he'd been the past few months. 'Oh God,' she said.

'Do you know a person who lives at . . .' he got out his

notebook and reeled off the address of the white house in Berkshire, where Daisy had spent her brief and unhappy marriage with Simon.

Daisy stared open-mouthed at him. She felt the colour drain from her face. Felt her head start to hum. She looked at Ruby. 'That's Simon's house. My husband's,' she said, forgetting about calling him her ex.

The female officer cleared her throat. 'Your name and this address were in a notebook we found on him. I'm sorry,' she said gently. 'I'm afraid your husband is dead.'

33

Kit checked into a hotel overlooking Brighton seafront, then unpacked the essentials, opened the minibar, looked inside, closed it. He phoned Rob and told him about the Bentley.

'Shit,' said Rob.

'Yeah,' said Kit, looking out of his window and the rolling grey white-flecked breakers roaring in, driven by a fierce wind. Time off in sunny England, he thought. Should have taken himself off to the Costas.

'I'll see to it,' said Rob. 'You think it was Vittore?'

'Don't you?'

'Mm.'

'Watch your back.'

'You watch yours, Kit.'

'I'll phone again in a couple of days, OK?'

'Yeah. Or you want me to phone you?'

'No, I'll be moving around.'

Kit had another look at the contents of the minibar after he put the phone down. Then he picked up his jacket and went out into the rain to play tourist. He'd never been to Brighton before. Who knew? Maybe he'd enjoy it.

He joined a bunch of people trailing a guide around the Pavilion, and heard all about George IV and his mistress.

Then he got a bite to eat and wandered the Lanes, browsing the antique shops. Maybe he should take Daisy something, and Ruby . . . nah. Why should he bother with her? He thought that it might be nice to have a normal relationship with your mother, a real close mother-and-son bond, but they didn't have it and he wasn't about to fool himself that they ever would.

Far too much water had flowed under *that* particular bridge.

Because it had been Michael's dying wish, he'd promised her this Christmas past that he'd make an effort to forgive and forget, but fuck it to hell, it was *too hard*. The truth was, he despised his mother. Wanted *nothing* to do with her. Could *never* forgive her for abandoning him as a baby.

After he'd bought a present for Daisy – a silver necklace with a titanium butterfly pendant that flickered with rainbows like oil on water – he made his way back to his hotel room. Again he gravitated towards the minibar, taking a long look at the contents before closing the door on it and going out for the evening.

He took in a club, listened to the music – Barry White, Queen and Sweet, all booming out in time to the flashing strobes – and he picked up a girl. He'd done this many times in London; he was good-looking and could turn on the charm when needed, it was easy. As always, he adhered to the bachelor's code all his boys followed, and gave a false name. For tonight, he was Tony Mobley. Him and the girl ended up back in his hotel room having frantic, impersonal sex. Frantic or not, Kit was careful to use a Durex. Raised as an unwanted and fatherless child himself, there was no way on God's earth he was going to inflict that fate on some other poor bastard.

By the time he checked out two days later, he'd looked

inside the minibar eight times – he'd counted – but so far he hadn't touched a drop.

From Brighton he caught the train into Chichester, and there he finally started to relax a bit, to lose that feeling of being under a cloud, being watched, being *pursued*.

On top of that, his head was clearer. So was his tongue when he looked at it in the morning after long, peaceful nights of sleep lulled by the sound of waves on a shoreline. He ate well, drank tea or water, took walks along the beach, and began to feel almost human again.

I needed this, he thought. *I didn't know it, but I did. Rob called it right.*

He stopped off in Portsmouth for a night, took in the *Victory,* Nelson's flagship, then moved on to Southampton to stay in the Skyways hotel. This would be his last night of freedom: tomorrow he would return to the Smoke, stop behaving like an arsehole, take charge again.

No more drinking himself into a stupor.

No. What good did it do, after all? When you sobered up, the problems were still there. And you felt like shit into the bargain.

No more of that.

So what he was going to do on this, his last evening, was take in one of the clubs. The girl on reception at the hotel told him there was a new one that was pretty good, just around the corner. He'd have a half pint of shandy, that was his limit – and thank Christ none of the boys were here to see him doing that, sipping watered-down beer like a cunt – maybe chat up a bird or two, then back to bed and out of Southampton Central tomorrow morning, home to London.

34

The club Kit went to was all tricked out in black and blood-red, big gold signs screaming UNDER NEW MANAGEMENT! outside the entrance, doormen ushering people inside, the bass beat of the music so loud that it shook the strobe-lit dance floor where go-go dancers gyrated in devil horns in large gold cages suspended from a coal-black ceiling. Fake flame machines blew licking fronds of what looked like fire up the walls.

The place was packed. Kit fought his way to the bar, ordered the pitiful half a shandy that was going to last him all night. He turned with people jostling him out of the way, and some joker jogged his arm. He decanted his drink over the front of a girl of almost birdlike delicacy, with striking white-blonde hair. She was wearing a white lace minidress that revealed perfect legs.

'What the fuck are you *doing*?' she burst out, swiping at the front of her dress.

'Sorry,' said Kit, and then he did a double-take. Looked again. And thought, *Shit, it's her.*

She was staring right back at him.

They both said it at the same time: 'Don't I know you?'

'I'm Bianca,' she told him half an hour later, after she'd gone upstairs to change out of the soiled minidress and returned. They were sitting in one of the little alcoves, her with a gin and tonic in front of her on the low black-lacquered table, Kit with a fresh shandy.

'Tony,' said Kit, remembering the bachelor drill. If you're going to shag her, you don't give your own name. What if there are comebacks? You'd be a fool to give out your real name. And he fully intended to shag her if he could. He was *desperate* to do that. 'I'm Tony Mobley.'

'Hi, Tony,' she said, and smiled and held out a hand.

'Hi yourself, Bianca,' he said, and clasped her slender white hand in his larger, darker one.

Oh yes, he wanted to get her into bed as soon as he possibly could. He couldn't stop staring at her. The mini-dress had been replaced by another, also white: this one was soft sheeny satin, briefly cut without sleeves and with a big scooped neck and a high hemline. It clung to every curve. There was a teardrop pearl on a silver chain nestling in the shadowy hollow between her breasts. He wanted to rip the dress open and see her. He wanted, right now, to take her somewhere quiet, push her dress up out of the way and fuck her brains out, he was *consumed* by lust like he had never known before.

'I saw you,' he said. 'In a car, in London. In my head I called you the Bride. Because your hair's almost white, and you're so pale . . .' *Jesus, am I sounding like a cunt or what?*

'I saw you too,' said Bianca, thinking: *You're the most beautiful man I've ever seen in my life.* But she couldn't say that. She was embarrassed to. She felt like someone had snatched her breath away, hollowed out her stomach and left an echoing void there. She'd seen him just once, on that terrible day, the day of Tito's funeral, and she'd thought she would never see him again. Now here he was, talking to her, and she felt she'd lost all her usual panache. She was cool: everyone said so. That frosty virgin queen image was something she was always careful to promote. But now, almost shivering with excitement, she was struggling to maintain even an iota of it.

'What were you doing in London?' she asked.

Watch yourself, thought Kit. All right, he wanted her. Badly. More than he had ever wanted a woman before, including Gilda. This was no slow burn. This was immediate and powerful, something he had never experienced before, something entirely new to him – and fucking scary, actually. But he wasn't about to blow his cover. 'Business, that's all. I go there sometimes.'

'What line of business are you in?'

'Oh, restaurants, security . . . all sorts, really.'

'A bit of an entrepreneur,' said Bianca.

'That's right.' Kit looked around. 'And you run this place. Is that what you were doing in London? You have other clubs there?'

Bianca shook her head. 'I only run this one. I was up there for family stuff.' Her smile faded.

Kit remembered she'd been wearing a black veil, travelling in a long black limo. *Sad* family stuff, he thought. Then the beat of the music slowed, the lights dipped: now Gladys Knight was crooning.

'I love this song,' said Bianca as 'Help Me Make It Through the Night' filled the club with smoky, soulful tones.

'Want to dance?' asked Kit. He wanted to hold her. Couldn't understand it, marvelled at it, but that was a fact: he couldn't wait to *touch* this woman, body to body.

She looked into his eyes. 'Yeah. Why not?'

And then they were on the dance floor with all the other smooching couples, shuffling around, her arms around his neck, his hands on the back of her waist, pulling her in tight against his body. His nose was nuzzling in at the sweet, fragrant base of her throat, and he was thinking *This is heaven*.

He pulled her in closer, closer.

And then he realized he had an erection, and it was pressing against her. *Shit*, he thought. He eased himself back from her, and Bianca lifted her head from his shoulder and looked directly into his eyes.

'Let's go upstairs,' she said.

35

By Wednesday morning Simon's father, Sir Bradley Collins, had formally identified his son's body. Simon's mother had been so hysterical the doctor had prescribed a strong dose of tranquilisers, and Daisy couldn't do it, she was too shocked, too distraught.

Why she should be in floods of tears over Simon's death was beyond her. She had never really loved him, any more than he loved her. Theirs had been a marriage of convenience; Simon had wanted to marry into the Bray line and reap all the rewards that ties to the late Lord Cornelius Bray would net him. For Daisy, marriage to Simon had been an escape from her own wild and turbulent youth, a safe harbour after stormy seas. But aside from producing two beautiful baby boys, the marriage had been a disaster. Daisy's free spirit meant she could never be the dutiful wife that Simon desired, and he had punished her for it.

Divorced and glad of it, Daisy was amazed at the anguish she was going through now. Whatever else he might have been, Simon was the twins' father. Now her boys had been denied the chance to know their father, and her tears were as much for them as for her ex-husband. Never in her wildest dreams would she have believed that he was capable of suicide. But according to the police, he had gone home after his visit to Marlow, composed a brief note to his parents saying he was sorry to end it this way, and then he had hanged himself from a beam in the garage. The cleaner, passing the open garage door on her way up to the house the next morning, had seen him hanging there and called the police.

Her initial reaction when the police broke the news had been, *No, this must be a mistake, he* can't *be dead.* But then Sir Bradley called in at Ruby's on his way home from the hospital morgue; one look at his grief-stricken face, suddenly aged and riven with sorrow, told Daisy that there was no mistake. Simon was dead.

'My poor boy,' said Sir Bradley, his eyes bleak with pain. 'If only he'd talked to me, if only he'd told me he was in such despair . . .'

Ruby sat him down, gave him a brandy, while Daisy stood looking at him in stunned disbelief.

'I don't understand,' she said. 'He was here that evening, telling Ruby about the new contract and how well he was doing. He'd just spent a day with the babies. He was *happy*.'

'He certainly *seemed* fine,' sighed Ruby. 'But obviously he wasn't.'

'For God's sake, what does it matter?' Sir Bradley burst out. 'He's dead!'

'When will they release the . . . when can we arrange the funeral?' asked Ruby.

'Soon,' he said, and started to cry, great gut-wrenching sobs of loss.

Ruby took his hand in hers and squeezed it tight. Bleakly she looked up at Daisy.

'I wish Kit was here,' said Daisy helplessly, though even as she said it she was wondering what comfort Kit could provide in his present condition. He used to be so tough, almost invulnerable, but since Michael's death he was a shadow of his former self, intent on drowning his sorrows in booze. Still, he was her brother, and she wanted him here, to help her get through this.

'So do I,' said Ruby, putting a comforting arm around Sir Bradley's shoulders. He looked a broken man. 'So do I.'

To Ruby, it seemed as if everyone around her was coming apart: Kit taking to drink, Simon killing himself, and Daisy . . . Right now, Daisy was the most worrying of the lot.

She waited until Sir Bradley had composed himself and was ready to leave, walked with him to his car to make sure he was OK, then returned to the sitting room. Daisy was pacing up and down, arms wrapped around her body as if for warmth.

Ruby went to her, gently led her to the couch, then sat down beside her. She'd been putting off having this conversation, but it couldn't wait any longer.

'I keep thinking over and over that this is a nightmare, that I'll wake up,' said Daisy, shaking her head. 'Simon, killing himself? I can't take it in.'

'Sometimes people can't admit to anyone else that they've got problems. You're a bit like that yourself.'

Daisy looked at her mother. 'What do you mean?'

'Doris Blanchard told me what happened at the store. About Tessa and Julie . . .'

Daisy had given no explanation as to why she wanted to leave the store, and the shattering news of Simon's death had prevented Ruby from raising the matter with her daughter, but yesterday she'd had to spend a few hours at Darkes dealing with some matters that couldn't keep and she'd taken the opportunity to speak to Daisy's section leader. She was shocked when Doris Blanchard told her that Daisy had assaulted two members of staff.

'She did *what*?' Ruby had asked Doris in disbelief.

'I saw it, Miss Darke. I'm sorry, I don't doubt there was provocation – Tessa and Julie can be a right pair of madams – but they're talking about pressing charges . . .'

'Send them up, will you?'

Doris had done so.

Tessa and Julie, no longer so full of cocky swagger, had come into Ruby's office and told her that Daisy had laid into them over nothing, a bit of teasing, that was all.

'Teasing?' asked Ruby.

'Just a bit. Nothing serious.'

'What sort of teasing?' asked Ruby, watching them with cold eyes.

Tessa swallowed hard. 'Nothing, really . . .'

'Nothing? Are you sure about that?'

'It's her voice. Her accent,' blurted out Julie.

Tessa shot her a *shut up* look.

'What about it?' asked Ruby, but she could see it now. Daisy sounded 'posh', and she was the boss's daughter. These two had decided to make her suffer for it. 'Look – do you think that was a kind thing to do?' she said, fixing them with an icy stare. 'Mock someone over the way they speak? Do you?'

'No,' said Julie meekly.

'No,' echoed Tessa.

'I ought to sack you both on the spot.' Ruby was furious; she hated the thought of Daisy being victimized in this way.

'Oh, don't. Please. We're really sorry,' said Tessa.

Ruby stared at them for a long, frosty moment.

'Get back to work,' she snapped, and they scuttled out of the office.

'Why didn't you tell me they were picking on you?' said Ruby now, arm around her daughter's shoulders. 'Am I really that unapproachable?'

'No. It's just that I wanted to manage it on my own, that was all. And in the end I didn't. I lost my temper.'

Ruby was silent for a beat. 'You could come back, work in another department, if you wanted to.'

'I don't know.' She'd been so relieved when she quit, and until Simon's death had blighted everything she'd been relishing the prospect of spending time with the twins. But now her mind was in such turmoil, trying to come to terms with his suicide, that she couldn't concentrate on much else.

Resolving to drop the subject for now, Ruby sighed and glanced out onto the drive where Reg was patiently polishing the Merc. 'Reg does his best, but I miss Rob about the place. Don't you?'

Daisy could only nod. Oh yes, she missed Rob. *So* much. But with Kit away, Rob was busy filling in for him, keeping the business running smoothly. Rob had more important things to worry about than two bereaved women.

'Rob's Mr Sensible,' said Daisy bracingly. 'He'll look after everything until Kit gets back. He can rely on Rob.'

Still, she wished both Kit and Rob were here. The world seemed a safer more secure place when those two were about. Even if Kit was reeling around drunk, or being rotten or neglectful to Ruby – and he often was – she wanted him *here*.

'Rob said Kit would only be gone a few days, but it's nearly a week now,' Daisy fretted.

'He'll be back,' Ruby insisted. But she felt a tiny shiver of unease as she said it, Vittore Danieri's words reverberating in her mind: *You and yours*.

36

Bianca was moving ahead of Kit up the stairs as if she couldn't quite believe what she was doing, her legs feeling shaky beneath her, her mind focused totally on what was to come. How often did she do crazy things like this, take a complete stranger up to her flat with the full intention of going to bed with him?

Never, that was how often.

She was wary of men. With good reason. They always tried to screw her over in business, she was used to that. And her brothers Vittore and Fabio – resentful, she knew, of this little *principessa* who had suddenly been brought into their exclusively masculine conclave – had made her painfully familiar with jokey male put-downs of the female species from an early age. Not Tito, though. He alone had been kind to her.

What she absolutely *never* did was act impulsively. She didn't know this man. All she knew was that she had seen him once, fleetingly, and thought *Oh my God, will you look at him?* Now by some miracle he was here, and she couldn't let this moment pass by. She was moving as if in a dream, her mouth dry with apprehension, her body weak. She had never, not once in her life, felt this way before.

Kit was kissing her before she even had the door open, his tongue exploring her mouth, his teeth nipping at her lips. They all but fell through the door, Kit slamming it shut behind them. Blindly, Bianca reached out and shot the bolt. Gasping, panting, they kissed and clawed at each other like adversaries, Kit struggling with the zip on her dress and then giving up, *fuck* the dress, and instead he did what he had been dreaming of all evening since that moment when he'd accidentally thrown his drink down her front; he pushed the damned dress up, out of the way, saw the lacy panties there, white, of *course* they were white, and he ripped them off her, paused, saw the swansdown powder-puff of white-blonde curls. It was the most erotic thing he'd ever seen.

'Jesus, Bianca,' he groaned, turning, pushing her back against the closed door.

She was pulling at his belt, unzipping him with trembling fingers. He helped her, tugging his pants out of the way, letting his cock spring free. Bianca touched him, and he felt he was almost on the point of losing control. He shoved her hand away, lifted her, spread her legs, felt her wetness with the tip of his cock and, groaning, he thrust up and in, *deep* in, and she cried out, locking her legs around his waist, while he drove himself furiously into her.

'Oh God, yes, *yes*,' she moaned, half-crying, and that was it, that was enough.

Kit came, the exquisite sensation of orgasm shaking his entire body. Bianca wrapped her arms tight around his neck, muffling her scream of delight against his throat.

Oh Jesus what was that? Kit wondered, coming back down to earth. His breathing slowed, steadied.

No Durex. I bloody forgot to use a Durex. What the hell . . . ?

He didn't care. Maybe she was on the Pill, anyway. He felt euphoric. Nothing on earth had ever felt as good as this. Still lodged inside her, he carried her over to the bed and sank down on it with her wrapped tight in his arms. Slowly he kicked off his shoes and socks, slid off his trousers and pants, moved away from her to get rid of his shirt, tie and jacket.

Naked, his hands now steady enough to do it, he unzipped her dress and Bianca knelt up and wriggled out of it.

'No, let me,' he said, when she reached back to unclasp her white lacy bra.

Her hands fell and Kit reached behind her, undid the bra, pulling it off and down her arms.

'Christ,' he murmured, staring at her. She was so beautiful – full-breasted but with tiny nipples of the softest shell-pink. He cupped one breast in his hand, feeling the weight and coolness of it, and the contrast between his dark skin and hers, so white, was starkly erotic. She moaned at his touch and he felt her nipple harden.

He felt *himself* harden too, so quickly. Kit pushed her back, opened her legs and entered her again. This was heaven on earth. Which was kind of funny, when you considered where they were, in a club called Dante's, all painted red and black like an inferno – like hell.

But this wasn't hell. This was bliss. He felt he'd die of it, just before he came again, emptying himself into her carelessly, without thought, without a single solitary qualm.

37

Fabio's break into big-time drug dealing came when a Jamaican business acquaintance approached him and said he'd been stitched up.

'In what way?' asked Fabio, all ears. This boy was a big dealer in the Camden Lock area, well respected; Fab couldn't imagine anyone trying to go toe-to-toe with him. Cross him and he'd be at you with a ruddy great machete, splice your head wide open and use it for a cup to drink out of.

'Guy stole a kilo of coke off me.'

'That's bad,' said Fabio. 'Disrespectful.'

'It is. And I want it back.'

'So why you coming to me?'

'He's one of your lot.' Meaning an Italian immigrant, like Fab and his family, someone who lived in the Italian quarter around Clerkenwell Road or Farringdon or Rosebery Avenue.

'What's his name?'

The Jamaican told him the man's name. Fab knew the family; most of the people from the old country knew each other; Italians were warm, generous people, community-orientated. Seeing a chance to do himself a favour and make a profit, Fab took some of his boys round to the house where the man's mother lived. Politely, Fabio announced himself and said that he had come to see Georgio.

The woman made an exasperated gesture, a puffing-out of the cheeks. 'He's in there,' she waved them through, calling after them: 'Not that you'll get any sense out of him.'

Mama was right. Georgio had been busy snorting what should have been the Jamaican's profits. He was out of it on the sofa, the TV bellowing out canned laughter while four idiots in *Doctor on the Go* played at being medics. Fabio thought that this cunt was going to need a doctor for real, very soon. He turned it off. Georgio's eyes flickered open. Fabio looked at the boy in disgust. Fabio prided himself on keeping fit, on maintaining his perfect physique, but this wreck was pot-bellied, wearing a mouldy old tracksuit, his hair uncombed, a two-day stubble on his unwashed chin.

'I was . . . watching that . . .' said Georgio, looking around in bemusement at the men staring down at him.

Fabio got straight to the point.

'You've thieved off an acquaintance of mine. I'm not happy. What, you sniffed all the stash up your stupid nose?'

'No, I—'

Two of the boys lifted him off the sofa. He let out a squawk as they jammed him up against the wall, rattling the brass crucifix hanging there. It fell off the wall and hit the carpet with a thud.

'Don't!' he shouted. 'I still got most of it.'

'Where is it?' asked Fab.

Georgio indicated the sideboard. Fabio threw open the door and sure enough, there it was, all packaged up. Fabio grabbed it and weighed it in his hand. Georgio hadn't done it too much damage. He thought there was maybe still around thirty-seven ounces left.

Mama, alerted by her baby's shout, was now standing in the open doorway into the hall, a hand to her mouth, her eyes wide with fear. Fabio glanced at her, nodded to his boys. They dropped Georgio, and he sat down hard on the floor beside the crucifix and started crying.

'I'm taking this now and be grateful I don't have them rip a chunk out of your arse too,' Fabio told him. Then he slipped the stash into a bag he'd brought along for the purpose, nodded respectfully to Mama, and led the way outside.

Back at home, he called his Jamaican friend and told him he had the drugs in his possession.

'That's great. There'll be a reward for you, of course.'

'Too right there will,' said Fabio. 'I'm keeping half the stash in payment for its collection.'

There was stunned silence from the other end.

'You *what*?' yelled the Jamaican. 'Man, don't you mess with me. I was going to give you ten thou for fetching it back.'

'That's not good enough. I take half. That's the deal.'

Fabio had already worked out that a full kilo of the stuff was worth a thousand per ounce. The maths was simple: he had thirty-seven thousand pounds' worth of goods in his hands.

'Look, be grateful. You get half your stuff back instead of none,' said Fab.

'You thieving *spic*!' said the Jamaican.

'Hey! It's business, my *melanzana* pal. No offence. And you came to me, remember – I didn't *ask* for the job. Going there to get it, handling the goods – I took all sorts of risks for you.'

The Jamaican was quieter now.

'A quarter,' he offered.

'No. I'm keeping half. My boys will bring your share back to you today.'

Fabio put the phone down, feeling the adrenaline buzzing

through him. There was a big grin on his face. He could shift the stuff easily in the Danieri clubs. Everything was coming together for him at last. He went home, got washed up, then went and met Maria in the secret place they'd agreed. So much for Mama's 'good old days'! These new ones were pretty fucking good, too.

38

Naples, 1947

The satisfaction of Astorre's final revenge on Corvetto was short-lived. When word filtered back to Astorre that the deed was done, he contacted Tito, his eldest son, who was holding Luisa in safety until Lattarullo did as Astorre commanded.

'You can free the girl now. God knows she's got a world of pain coming to her, the loss of her father.' Astorre gave an extravagant shrug. 'But what could I do? Twenty years I've waited to make Corvetto pay for what he did. At last he's in hell where he . . .'

Instead of celebrating with his father, Tito was acting strangely, not meeting his father's eyes.

Astorre stiffened as he looked at his son's face. 'What is it?' *he asked.*

'The girl . . .' *said Tito. He spread his palms.*

'What about the girl?' *Now he was looking more closely at Tito he could see scratch-marks on his boy's face.* 'What is this?'

'I thought I'd have a little fun with her, that's all. Fuck her, maybe.'

Astorre stared at him. 'You kiss your mother with that mouth?' *he snapped.*

'The little bitch fought, scratched me – look, you see the marks?' *Tito indicated his face.*

'You weren't supposed to have fun with her,' said Astorre. 'You were to keep her safe until her father killed Corvetto, that was all.'

'Papa, what can I say? I'm human and the girl was pretty.'

Astorre's mouth dropped open. 'Was?'

Tito shrugged. 'She fought me,' he said. 'There was no need for that. And it was hot, I forgot about covering my face. Foolish of me, but there it is: she'd know we were behind this. The girl was dead anyway, Papa . . .' Tito's voice trailed away and he made a twisting motion with his hands.

Astorre thought that there had been every need for the girl to resist; Luisa Lattarullo was a decent girl, a virgin no doubt. And Tito had clearly raped then strangled her. Or maybe he had choked her to death while he was taking his pleasure, who knew? It was entirely probable that Tito had left his face uncovered quite deliberately, simply for the thrill of combining sex with a kill. Astorre himself was no angel, but sometimes Tito chilled him to the core. This wasn't the first time he'd heard about his son being dangerously rough with women. But this time . . . this time Tito had gone the full way toward depravity. Astorre felt sick. He made war on men, yes: but women? Never.

'You disposed of the body?' he asked his son.

'Of course, Papa. It won't be found.'

Astorre had to think this over. The girl and her unfortunate father apart, he knew that Corvetto had many friends, and they knew, they all knew, that Astorre had sworn vengeance on the man. From a camorristi, such a threat was never an idle one.

And now Lattarullo's family would be anxious to discover why their formerly placid kinsman had sliced Corvetto's throat from ear to ear — and what had become of his only daughter, who would soon be reported as missing.

Someone was going to link it all to him, he knew it. And when that happened, the Danieris were finished; they'd be hanged, every last one of them, in the local square, Bella included. The

Carabinieri would turn a blind eye as a lynch mob beat their door down, dragged them out one by one, and killed them.

He had known this would be a possibility, this outcome. His hometown was no longer as he remembered it; the place had been ravaged by war, wrecked by it, with desperate beggars in the streets and out in the countryside. There was no such thing as safety in Naples these days. So Tito's rash input had made Astorre's decision easier. The whole family – Astorre and Bella, twenty-two-year-old Tito, fourteen-year-old Vittore and Fabio, Bella's despised boy-child – would have to flee.

39

'I have to go back soon,' said Kit sleepily, lying in Bianca's bed with her – both of them naked and clinging to each other.

He kissed her silky white-blonde hair. He didn't want to move from this bed in a century, that was the truth. After losing Gilda, then Michael, he had felt cursed: but here tonight in Bianca's arms, he felt *blessed*. This was so peaceful, so *right*, a time outside of reality. But he could feel that reality starting to press upon him. Soon, very soon, he would have to go back, pick up the reins again.

Find out who did that to Michael.

Yes, he had to do that.

'Up to London,' said Bianca, her eyes closed.

'Mm.'

'No! Stay here,' she said, a frown forming between her brows.

'And do what?'

'Dunno. Be my willing sex slave. Anything. Don't care.'

'Honey, I *am* your willing sex slave.'

He'd never known anything like this, as *intense* as this. They'd spent the past couple of days mooching around town, then they'd fallen into bed at night to feast on each other like wild animals. He had never felt so tired, or relaxed, or completely happy as this before. And he felt like an arsehole too, because he still hadn't told her his real name; some slight remnant of his usual caution refused to let him enlighten her in that respect. To her, he was still Tony.

And he hadn't checked she was on the Pill. He'd broken his own rule, hadn't used a condom with her once. Crazy. He thought about it and found that he could shove it to the back of his mind in a compartment marked *don't care*. He knew very little about her and she knew nothing about him, but what the hell? If she got pregnant, he'd marry her. He wouldn't hesitate, not even for a moment.

'If you go, you won't come back,' she said, and her eyes opened and gazed sadly into his.

'Yeah, I will.' *I couldn't keep away.*

'Will you give me your number?' she asked, kissing his shoulder, inhaling the scent of his skin.

'Nah, I'll phone you. And I'll be back as soon as I can, OK?'

Bianca heaved a sigh. 'OK.'

Kit turned to her. 'Don't be sad,' he said, nuzzling his nose into her throat. 'This is only the beginning, you silly mare.'

'Talk's cheap,' said Bianca, wrapping her arms and legs around him, holding him to her.

'There are things I have to do,' said Kit, feeling the excitement building again. He just couldn't get enough of her. 'Important things. But *listen*. Nothing comes between you and me. You got that? So shut up for fuck's sake, and kiss me,' he murmured against her mouth.

Bianca smiled, and obeyed. She didn't want this magical time to end. She had a fear of abandonment, of being left. She'd often wondered where that fear had come from, because it didn't make sense. She was a strong, self-sufficient woman. Whenever she probed her memory, trying to account for the fear, the same hazy images came to her: a blonde woman, smiling; a strong, tanned arm furred with blond hairs, holding her. Some sort of foreign language. *Lefse*, she thought. Was that even a word? What did it mean? And *aquavit*.

Now she looked at Kit and felt that old deep-buried fear all over again. Would she lose him, like she'd lost her darling Tito? She was so afraid that he would turn out to be just another man, taking his pleasures and moving on. And she wasn't even on the Pill.

Bianca dismissed the fear, kissed him, gave herself up to the emotion of the moment all over again, and refused to think about the future, because this was so good it couldn't be real, it couldn't last. She knew it.

40

Almost a week after Simon's death, Daisy bought a bouquet of flowers. Then she drove to the white house in Berkshire where for a while she had shared married life with Simon. She didn't want to go up to the house, she couldn't *bear* to see the garage where *it* had happened, so she parked up the Mini at the bottom of the drive and got out.

For days she'd been wanting to come here and pay her respects but it had taken her until now to gather up the courage. The lane was very quiet. She could hear a robin singing high up in the huge bare willow beside the gate. With a heavy heart she walked over to the verge. The wind gusted, and she pulled her mac more securely around her as there came a spattering of cold rain. Shivering, she took the bouquet and laid it on the ground beside the gate.

The robin stopped singing. Suddenly, there was only silence. Was Simon here, watching her?

'I never meant to be such a rotten failure as a wife,' she murmured. 'And I think I almost loved you, once.'

No answer came.

Of course not. Simon wasn't here, he was dead and gone. He'd *killed* himself. She hated the thought that he'd been so miserable, that he'd had no one he felt he could turn to. She swiped angrily at the tears on her face. God, she was so fucking hormonal; half the time she didn't even know

159

what she was crying *about*. At least today she did. She was crying for Simon, for their sons, for all the hopes and dreams that now would never be.

She could hear a car coming along the lane from the direction of the town, the same way she'd just come, and it sounded as if it was travelling quite fast. Daisy stepped onto the verge so that it could easily pass by.

The car that approached was long and dark with tinted windows. And instead of passing, the driver pulled in on the verge about ten paces from where Daisy was standing. She felt a prickle of unease, but told herself this must be someone who'd known Simon and was coming to pay their respects, just as she was. She braced herself to make polite conversation, to receive commiserations. She didn't want to, but one had to be polite.

The car's powerful engine fell silent. Then all four doors opened, and four bulky men got out, dressed in heavy black coats. Daisy's heartbeat picked up speed. These weren't mourners, they didn't carry any flowers. They looked like thugs, like the men she often saw hanging around Kit, and around Michael when he was alive. She knew what Kit was into, the life he led. In the past, she'd experienced frightening things in his company. Yes, she knew what he was, what Michael had been too, and what Rob was, and it did alarm her – but, at the same time, it fascinated her too, and excited her more than she cared to admit.

Slowly, the men walked towards her. The driver hung back, as did the man who'd been in the front passenger seat, though he was close enough for her to see that his face was hideously scarred. The two men who'd got out of the back of the car kept walking until they were standing right in front of her. They were both dark-haired, but one of them was square, blockish, with a sinister vulpine look, while the other was thinner, taller, younger with film-star good looks, marred by vicious intent in his eyes and the cruel smile on his face.

What is this? she wondered in a paroxysm of fear. *What do they want?*

She was out in the middle of nowhere, utterly alone. The Mini was twenty yards away. If she ran, right now, would they try to stop her? But Daisy didn't think she was capable of running. She felt frozen with terror.

The handsome mean-eyed one moved in closer. Daisy took a stumbling step backward, her breathing unsteady. Then the other one, the bulky one who seemed to be in charge, spoke.

'Daisy Darke, right?' He gave a smile that chilled her to the bone. 'Formerly Daisy Bray, *then* Daisy Collins, and after the divorce you changed your name, didn't you? To Darke. Same as your birth mother, Ruby Darke.'

'Who the hell are you?' asked Daisy shakily. She had never felt so vulnerable. *Oh my God the twins,* she thought. *If anything happens to me, they'll have nothing left. No parents at all.*

'He's Vittore Danieri,' said the younger one, who was standing too close, unnervingly close, to her. 'And I'm Fabio, his brother. Such a pity about your ex-husband,' he said, smirking.

Daisy felt her mouth go dry as dust. 'How do you know about what happened to Simon?'

This amused all four of them greatly.

'How do we know about what happened to Simon Collins?' Fabio asked his brother with a grin.

'You mean the Simon Collins who was the brother-in-law of Kit Miller?' asked Vittore.

'*That's* the one,' said Fabio, striking his head as if it had just come to him in a flash. His eyes grinned into Daisy's as he came in even closer to her.

Daisy shrank back. They were going to hurt her, she was sure of that now. She was powerless to stop this. These were Tito's brothers, and they wanted revenge.

'Simon Collins was father to Miller's nephews, too,' said Vittore, looking straight into Daisy fear-stricken eyes.

'Such a shame, what happened. Hung himself, didn't he?' said Fabio.

He leaned in till Daisy could smell his breath, could feel the heat and the hatred radiating off him like poison gas. She glanced behind her: she was on the outside edge of the verge, there was nowhere left to go but the ditch. She could run up the drive, but there would be no one in the house to help her. Simon had lived here alone after they split up.

They were going to attack her. She knew it. They'd followed her out from the town to this place, where Simon had killed himself.

But had he?

For days it had been tormenting her, the sheer weirdness of Simon's death, given his fiery aggressive nature, his business successes, his clear and very genuine delight in his twin sons. She'd been struggling to believe that he could have taken his own life. And now . . . these men. These horrible people. They *knew* how he'd died.

Because he didn't hang himself: they murdered him. They must have forced him to write that suicide note . . . how? Threatened his parents? Threatened to harm the twins? Yes. Then he would do whatever they told him to. And then . . . they killed him, and made it look as if he'd killed himself.

Daisy swallowed hard. She knew she daren't let on how terrified she was. You didn't show fear when you dealt with wild dogs; you faced them down.

The robin started singing again, high up in the tree. Was that the last sound, the last beautiful thing she would ever know, that haunting birdsong? She hardly dared breathe. She was afraid she was about to faint, drenched as she was in cold sweat and sick with fear. The four men were silent, watching her. She felt they could smell her terror, like pheromones drifting in the gusty spring air.

Then Vittore spoke: 'This time, you can go,' he said.

'But maybe not next time,' said Fabio with a grin. And he leaned in closer, closer.

Daisy shrank into herself. But he wasn't reaching for her. Instead, he was bending, snatching up the bright bouquet of flowers, the one she had laid there for Simon. With a final triumphant sneer, he whacked the bouquet against the trunk of the tree, scattering the blooms, shredding them, killing them. Daisy flinched. Then he tossed the remnants of the bouquet onto the verge. Gave her a twisted smile. And turned away.

Vittore touched his fingers to his brow in an ironic salute. The four men left her standing there, and got into their car. One of Vittore's heavies started the engine, then the car shot forward, missing her by inches. Soon it was gone, roaring away into the distance.

The minute it was out of sight, Daisy fell to her knees on the mud-churned verge, clutching her hands to her face, amazed that she was still in one piece. Breathless with fright, she crouched like that for long minutes until the fear started to grip her again, the fear that they might come back, change their minds, do dreadful things to her.

Like they did to Simon.

Simon's death hadn't been an accident: Vittore had wiped Simon out, and in so doing he had deprived Matt and Luke of their father.

Somehow she managed to drag herself to her feet and stagger back to the Mini. She had to get home, to where she was safe.

But would she be safe? Could she be safe anywhere *now?*

They must have followed her out here. They'd been watching and waiting their chance with Simon, and they'd got it. And now they were watching her.

She started the engine and drove, very carefully, trembling like a leaf in a high wind, back to Ruby's place.

41

'Where the *fuck* did you get to?' demanded Rob, hurrying across the minute Kit showed up at Sheila's restaurant, said hi to the head barman and ordered a pineapple Britvic.

It wasn't the welcome Kit had been expecting. He blinked in surprise. Rob looked agitated, and that was a surprise too. Rob was solid, usually. The barman set down the juice in front of Kit.

'There you go, boss,' he said.

'Get you something?' Kit asked Rob, watching him curiously.

Rob shook his head and the barman moved off to polish glasses.

'I told you,' said Kit. 'I've been down on the coast, taking the air.'

'For a couple of days, wasn't that the deal? Not a fucking *week*.'

'Things came up.' He thought of Bianca. 'Important things.' He wasn't ready to tell Rob about her, not yet. Rob had a stick up his arse, best let him get *that* out of the way first. 'You get the car fixed up?'

'What?' Rob stared at him.

'What's wrong with you? The cunting *car*. I asked you to fix it.'

'Right, yeah, that.' Rob swiped a hand through his hair as if the car was the *last* thing on his mind. 'Yeah, it's done. It's over at the yard, locked up tight. Didn't want to risk parking it out on the street again and having to do the same damned job a second time.'

'Good.' Kit sipped his juice, still staring at Rob. 'Anything else I should know about? You tapped up our boys in the Bill, got some stuff about Michael?'

'Yeah, I did that. I'll talk that through with you later, OK?'

'Sure.'

Kit glanced around the restaurant. It was packed: Saturday night. The tills were ringing. All was right with the world. Except he wasn't where he wanted to be. Soonest, he was going to get Bianca up here with him. She could get a manager in at Dante's, and then they could be together properly. He was completely smitten. He was half-smiling, wanting to ask Rob, *You ever been in love, mate?* But he didn't want to make himself look like a soft-centred cunt. He had his image to protect.

'So, everything else running smooth?' he asked.

And then Rob told him about Simon, and how Daisy had been approached on the road, scared half out of her wits.

Kit's smile died on his face. He grew very still.

'You got Reg out at the Marlow house, right?' he said at last.

'Reg and two more of the boys. Taking no chances. Daise and Ruby have been climbing the walls.'

'Let's get over there then,' sighed Kit.

'My God, where have you *been*?' asked Daisy frantically when Reg ushered Kit into the sitting room. She and Ruby had been sitting huddled by the fire. They were wearing black, both of them. Ruby, it suited. Daisy, without her usual sunny array of bright colours, looked dreadful.

Kit was beginning to feel bad. There he'd been, having a sexual marathon with Bianca, happy as a pig in shit, and all *this* had been kicking off.

'I'm home now,' he said, and Daisy rushed forward and hugged him, hard.

Kit pushed her back a step. Her eyes were brimming with tears.

'You OK, Daise? They didn't touch you?' he asked, thinking that if any of the Danieri bastards had laid a hand on his sister then they'd be sorry.

Daisy shook her head. 'No, I'm fine. I was so *scared*, that's all. The instant I got back here, I called Rob, told him what happened, and he came straight over. Kit,' Daisy's voice trembled, 'we've had to send Jody and the twins away. Rob said it would be safest. I didn't *want* to do it. I can't believe it's even necessary. But—'

'Rob's right,' said Kit.

'They're stashed in one of our safe houses,' said Rob.

Daisy didn't know what was happening to her normally secure, orderly world. Suddenly it seemed to have tilted, spilling her over into chaos. A new year and a new job in Mum's store, she'd thought: well, she'd blown *that*. Then Simon, dying. Hideous, the shock of it. And almost worse, horrifically painful, she was being parted from her babies. She felt like she was going mad. She literally *hurt* when she thought about them. She was coming to realize what it truly meant, to be Kit Miller's kin.

'Could I at least phone through, check they're OK?' she pleaded.

Kit shook his head. 'Better not, Daise. It's too bloody easy to put a tap on a line, and who's to say there isn't one on this house phone? Safest to keep your distance. For you, *and* for them.'

He glanced at Rob, who gave him a bleak look in return. 'Poor Daisy was fucking traumatized,' he said. 'They must have been watching her all along. Maybe Ruby too, and this house. And who's to say they'll stop at scaring them, next time?'

Only then did Kit look beyond Daisy to where Ruby sat. His mother. Michael Ward had loved her, and he remembered the letter Michael had left for him, to be opened in the event of his death: *Don't be an arsehole. Give your mother a chance.*

'You all right?' he asked her roughly. To his annoyance, he found that he actually cared. He didn't want her frightened, or hurt.

Ruby nodded. She was made of tough stuff, he knew that. Well, she must be hard as fucking nails – after all, she'd abandoned him, her own kid, when he was even younger than Daisy's twins.

'It was suicide, right? Rob filled me in,' said Kit, going over to his mother and sitting down beside her. He didn't reach out, touch her hand, kiss her or anything.

'What we're thinking now is it wasn't suicide at all,' said Ruby, her face taut with suppressed anger. 'It could just as easily have happened when the twins and Jody were at the house with him. Do you think the Danieris would care?'

'You haven't told anyone about this . . . ?'

'No. We were waiting for you to come back. We've been going out of our minds here, and Rob didn't have a number to reach you on . . .'

'I know.' He felt like shit about that. There he'd been, happily getting his end away, and Daise and Rob and Ruby had been suffering a shedload of grief.

'They did it,' said Daisy, pacing around, her colour high with agitation. 'Kit, they *killed* him.'

'They said that?' asked Kit. 'They rigged it to look like suicide?'

'They made it obvious. And the implication was that they could just as easily kill me, too. I thought they were going to. I really did. God, Kit, it's been absolute murder. I'm a wreck, I haven't slept,' sobbed Daisy. 'He was the boys' *father.*'

Kit was struggling to take all this in. That his brother-in-law had got himself wasted was a big shock. Granted, Simon Collins was a prick, but the poor bastard hadn't deserved to die. And Daisy . . . the thought of the Danieri boys cornering her, throwing such a scare into her made him livid.

'Maybe it's time I had a chat with Vittore,' he said.

Ruby's eyes opened wide at that. 'No! Kit, don't go near him. *Promise* me you won't. This is exactly what Bella was afraid of, that things would escalate. If you go and see him, it can only make matters worse.'

Kit didn't agree, but he didn't say so. Daisy could have been badly hurt. And her kids could have been killed, and their nanny, along with their father. All because of *him*. Tension gripped him as he thought of what *could* have happened, while he was elsewhere having a bloody good time.

'Look,' he said finally. 'What we're going to do is this: Reg and the boys will stay here with you, OK?'

'Won't Rob stay too?' asked Ruby.

Kit looked at Ruby, at Daisy. He knew Daisy had a soft spot for Rob. He didn't think Rob felt the same, and that was sort of a relief. As Daisy's brother, he felt protective of her, and he wasn't entirely sure yet how he would feel if something should develop between his number one man and his own sister.

'No,' he said finally. 'I need him. Ruby . . .' He couldn't bring himself to call her 'Mum' . . .'There's something I've been meaning to ask you. Do you know where Michael was going, what he had planned to do, on the day he died?'

He didn't expect her to say yes, but she did.

'He was planning to call in on Joe,' said Ruby, wishing so much that he'd hug her, kiss her cheek, show *some* sort of feeling for her and not just for Daisy. But he wouldn't. She knew that.

Kit frowned. 'Your *brother* Joe?'

Ruby nodded.

'He didn't say what for?'

'No. He didn't.'

42

'Yes! Yes! Yes!' screamed Maria.

'Hey, hold it *down*, will ya?' said Fabio, laughing and thrusting and trying to get a hand over her mouth all at the same time.

Oh, this was better than any scenario he could have dreamed up, and he had dreamed up a *lot*. Over the years, the images he cooked up in his own head had been his only comfort. He *knew* Mama'd never wanted him. Time and again he'd heard her say how sure she was that he had been a girl, carrying all the way round, not at the front. He was sick to *death* of hearing her say that.

'But instead there he was, this scrawny little thing with a big dick,' Bella would say, shaking her head as if the bottom had dropped out of her world when Fabio popped out of her cooze. 'A *boy*, not a girl.'

Time and again. He was so *sick* of being the disappointment, the non-girl. Embarrassingly, Mama had dressed him as a girl at first. Vittore and Tito had never failed to see the funny side of that, fucking *bastards*. He'd been done up in pink booties and a hat, even the *nursery* was pink, painted in readiness for the expected female.

'Oh God, oh, Fabio . . .' moaned Maria loudly, thrashing around on the bed beneath him.

Jesus, he should have known she'd be a screamer.

Couldn't the noisy mare pipe down? They were in a cheap hotel way off the beaten track, but he didn't want to disturb the other guests, he didn't want to call any sort of attention to them. That would be stupid. And he wasn't stupid, no matter what the rest of the family might have to say about it.

When Mama'd sent him to school, she hadn't cut his hair, so it hung down past his shoulders like a girl's. Oh, how Vittore and Tito – and all his classmates – laughed. In desperation he himself had hacked the long strands off with a knife he stole out of art class. A wallop from Mama for doing that, but at least she seemed to get the message. He was *not* a girl. Thereafter, she kept his hair short.

Then who should arrive on the scene but Bianca. Before *her*, he'd been the stand-in, the stunt double, his mother – Jesus, she was demented – using him as a sort of dummy, a replacement for what he *should* have been at birth. Once Bianca came, things got worse. Instead of this *weird* attention, he got no attention at all. He was sent out to play, forgotten; what small place he had was taken up. There was no more room in the boat, and he was tossed out, shoved into the water to take his chances or drown.

He hated Bianca, but knew she had to be tolerated. The odd punch or two he managed to land on the little *principessa* was reported straight back to Mama, and Astorre had taken his belt to his youngest son at her insistence. Fabio hated Vittore, because Mama adored him so much. And he hated Tito too, swaggering about the place, impressing everyone with his bulky good looks and his largesse.

He hated them all.

But now he was having his revenge. He and his boys were shifting the Jamaican's gear around the family clubs, around Vito's, Fellows and Goldie's, but they were not giving Vittore so much as a taste. Not a *hint*. Fabio was making his own wedge right under Vittore's nose, but discreetly, carefully.

And this! Oh, this was the best thing of all.

He looked down at her, naked, sweaty, dishevelled. Maria was *quite* a handful. And it was pretty obvious that Vittore had not only been knocking her around but also letting her down in the bedroom department. Which was a crying shame. In Fabio's opinion, a woman like this needed a good seeing-to on a regular basis. And he was just the man to do it.

'Ah!' yelled Maria as she came, her excitement pushing him over the edge too. They locked together in an ecstatic clinch, then Fabio drew back and flopped onto the disarranged, cheap and rather scratchy sheets of the bed.

Gasping in a breath, he looked around the room and lit a cigarette. It was a pest-hole, this hotel. The wallpaper was peeling, there was a brown damp stain on the ceiling over by the window. The sheets were clean, though not the fine thousand-thread Egyptian cotton he was used to. But at least the place was off the Danieri patch and rented rooms by the hour. What more could he want?

To rub Vittore's nose in this, he thought, glancing back at Maria, who was now snuggling up against him with puppyish zeal.

But he couldn't. Vittore would kill him if he knew. So this revenge had to be a private one, gloated over in secret.

'Do you love me, Fabio?' she was asking him now.

'Yeah. I do,' he lied. Well, he loved the fact that he was screwing Vittore's wife. He loved *that*, for sure.

'And you'll talk to Vittore, like you promised?' she asked, kissing his shoulder.

'Of course,' he lied again.

43

'Well, say it,' said Kit.

'What?' asked Rob.

'That it's my fault, what happened to Simon,' said Kit.

It was late on Sunday night and Kit and Rob were in the little office behind the restaurant. Kit slumped down in the chair behind the desk that Michael Ward had once occupied. He could still smell the faint aroma of expensive cigars and Dunhill cigarettes in here: the ceiling was stained brown from all the years of nicotine. It was like Michael's ghost was in attendance, too.

Rob pulled up a chair and sat there and looked at his mate, his boss. He said nothing.

Kit went on: 'I turned up drunk at Tito's funeral. I provoked Vittore. And now we're in the shit because of it.'

Rob cleared his throat. 'Look, you were a mess. You were in mourning for Michael. Shit, I thought you were *never* going to pull out of it. And maybe you haven't, even now. These things take time.'

Kit eyed Rob speculatively.

'I behaved like a complete arsehole,' he said, shaking his head. 'God's sakes, *you* didn't go to fucking pieces.'

'Yeah, but I got a big family. Sisters, brothers, a mum – and a dad. He's an awkward, cantankerous old son of a bitch, but he's been there for me all my life. It'll break my heart when he goes. You never had any of that, did you? *Michael* was like a dad to you. The two of you were that close. And when you lost him – and especially losing him that way . . . well, it's understandable you'd go to pieces. Anybody would.'

Kit heaved a sigh. He wanted to go over to Vittore's place and torch it. Fulminating rage swept through him as he thought of Daisy, that they'd had the *front* to try to scare her that way. He leaned on the desk, pushed his hands through his hair, looked steadily at Rob.

'So what did you get from our boys down the cop shop?' he asked.

Rob placed a buff-coloured folder on the desk. Kit reached for it, but Rob kept his hand on it, holding it closed.

'There's things in there you really don't want to see. Morgue shots. Stuff like that,' he warned.

Kit looked Rob dead in the eye. He could see Rob's anxiety for him, he knew Rob was afraid that the contents of the folder would send him tumbling down the slippery slope again, hitting the bottle, that he wasn't up to seeing just what had been done to Michael.

'Yeah, I do.' *I need to,* he thought. *I need to know everything.*

Rob released the folder, and Kit pulled it towards him.

'They saying anything that could help?' asked Kit.

'Nothing except it's been shoved to one side. Other stuff's more important.' Rob leaned back in his chair, put his hands behind his head, and stared up at the dirty ceiling. 'Ruby reckoned Michael was having talks with her brother, didn't she? Joe Darke phoned her that night, when Michael didn't show up at his place.'

'Which is . . . ?'

'Over Chigwell way. You're his nephew, don't you know

this stuff? He's got a big fancy house out there, couple of acres with it.'

'Ruby go out there much?' asked Kit. He didn't know Joe at all.

Rob shook his head. 'They're not close. His old lady Betsy hates Ruby, although I heard they were mates once upon a time.'

'Wonder what they fell out over?'

'No idea. But that's all we've got right now. Michael went to Tito's club one day, and the day after that he *should* have gone to Joe's. But he never made it.'

Kit looked at the folder. 'Let's go on home and get some kip,' he said, picking it up and getting to his feet. 'First thing tomorrow, you and me are going to pay Ruby's brother a visit.'

After Rob dropped him off at his house, Kit took the folder into the kitchen and started spreading the contents across the table. He drew out the morgue reports and the photographs of the corpse. He caught his breath as the horrific black-and-white shots swam into view. Forced himself to look at the images of Michael, shot in the back of the head, his skull half-disintegrated. His right eye was gone, his fucking *soul* was gone, no life there whatsoever, all of it snatched from him by some bastard with a bloody great gun.

Kit surged to his feet. He ran to the sink and vomited. *Ah Jesus!*

He heaved until he felt like he was bringing his entire stomach up. Finally, panting, he washed out the sink, swooshed water around his mouth, snatched up a towel and dried himself. Then he tossed the towel aside and sat down at the table and looked again.

Michael, dead. No longer handsome, suave; no longer flashing that devil-may-care grin.

This isn't Michael, he told himself. *This is a shell, empty of life.*

Kit breathed deeply, and felt his heart racing in his chest, felt that sudden biting *urge* to go to the drinks cabinet, get something, glug it down.

But he'd chucked all the booze away, hadn't he?

Off-licence . . .

No. He could do this. He *had* to do this, and he couldn't do it if he was sodden with drink.

He pulled the folder towards him. Ballistics reports. A big-calibre gun firing soft-nosed bullets of lead that spread on impact, did maximum damage. They were called dumdums and during the drive home, Rob, who had a keen interest in munitions, had told him that the name came from the Dum Dum Arsenal near Calcutta in India, where the first expanding bullets were developed back in the 1890s by Captain Bertie-Clay of the British Army. Kit had sensed that the history lesson was Rob's way of trying to deal with the whole thing objectively, to try to focus on details instead of giving into the red mist that would take hold if you stopped thinking about the history of the bullet and thought about what it had been used for. The fact remained, whoever fired it hadn't wanted to take any chances. They had wanted to be sure that Michael Ward was dead.

But who did that finger on the trigger belong to?

44

Bianca sat and looked at the phone as if her will alone could make it ring.

It didn't.

Why hasn't he phoned me?

A little threadworm of fear uncurled in her stomach and a tiny voice in her brain whispered,

Because he's like all the others, he didn't mean any of it. Because, you fool, you were just a convenient lay and he said he loved you to get your legs open.

'Staring at it ain't going to make it ring,' said Cora, coming into the stockroom and tutting as she saw Bianca standing there.

Bianca instantly started making like normal. Like she didn't want to kill him or kiss him – she didn't know which. 'Don't know what you're on about.'

Cora gave a smile and a sigh of impatience. 'Yes you do. You're waiting for that Tony fella to call you, and so far he hasn't. Give the man a chance. And incidentally, we're getting low on the bitter lemon.'

'Put it on the list for the wholesalers.'

'Will do,' said Cora, and snatched up a box of ready-salted crisps. Then she paused. 'Don't you have a number to reach him on?'

Bianca gave her a sour look. 'No.'

'Oh.'

'What does that mean?' snapped Bianca. But she *knew* what it meant, she didn't need Cora or anyone else to draw her pictures. He hadn't given her a number to reach him on because he'd had a fine old time with her and that was it: end of the road.

'No offence. It seems odd that he didn't give you a number, that's all,' shrugged Cora.

'Well, he didn't.'

'You didn't ask?'

'Yes, I did. He said not to bother, he'd call me.'

'Right. What was his name again?'

'Tony. Tony Mobley.'

Cora hefted the box higher and gave a cheering smile to her boss.

'He'll call,' she reassured her. 'You wait and see.'

Then Bianca was alone in the stockroom again. Wearily, she sank down on a stool and thought *I have been such a fucking idiot.*

She had thought it was love, real love: something different, something special. It lanced her like a dagger, through and through, to think she'd been so callously duped.

Her eyes went again to the phone.

Ring, she thought. *Come on. For me!*

But he didn't call, not that day, or the next, or the one after that.

It was true, then. Mama was right. You couldn't trust *any* man.

They were *all* bastards.

45

Naples, 1947

Astorre still had old contacts in the port where he had once run contraband, and through these contacts he arranged passage for him and his family on a cargo vessel bound for England. The crossing was awful, through the Bay of Biscay all of them were sick, but soon they were in the English Channel and then they were sailing up the peaceful slate-grey Thames towards London's docks.

As the family stepped down onto dry land, swaying and feeling wrung out, dispossessed, the rain fell and the cold seeped into their bones. Three years earlier, Bella's sister and her husband and daughter Serafina had made this same trip – and her sister's husband had died not long after, having developed pneumonia. Bella could see why, breathing this damp dreadful air.

'Madre de Dios,' muttered Bella, looking fearfully around her as she held baby Fabio to her breast.

'It will be fine,' said Astorre.

It didn't take the Danieris long to realize that England, like their homeland, had suffered during this hideous war. Bomb sites were everywhere in the capital; children roamed the streets, begged, slept in gutters. Astorre had a little money, barely enough to get them board and lodgings in a stinking rat-hole of a tenement building.

Once installed in the place, Astorre took Tito out with him onto the streets to look around, to familiarize himself with London. The chill here was unbelievable, the damp and the fog seemed to permeate their very bones after the dry radiant Neapolitan sun. But they were tough and they were desperate.

Soon they sussed out that there was a pocket of Italian immigrants living in Clerkenwell – so many that it was called 'Little Italy' by the English. That was where Astorre wanted to be, among his own kind. Already, he missed the old country, but he knew that he would never go back. There were others who possessed the same deadly patience he had displayed; no matter how many years passed, it would never be safe for him or his family back in Napoli.

What he needed right now was more cash.

And that, at least, was a problem it would be easy to solve.

Astorre and Tito spied out and targeted a few clubs in London – 'up West', as the Londoners called the more salubrious part of their city. These particular clubs were owned by one man, a self-made heavy plant millionaire called Fred Cheeseman. Cheeseman's doormen were old lions, losing their teeth, unable to stand against bulky Astorre and his thuggish cub.

'All right. You can take over security on my doors,' Cheeseman told the Danieris. 'But I still run the bar and the business.'

Trying to talk tough, like he actually had a choice in the matter. As he spoke, Tito was standing at his father's shoulder, slapping a cosh rhythmically into the palm of his hand; big bulging-eyed Astorre was blocking out the light. Cheeseman, a short bald man, was terrified.

Cheeseman doled them out a contract, and hoped that would be the end of it – the fool. Within six months he'd caved in to extreme pressure and handed the clubs over. Astorre had even been so good as to pay him – a knock-down price, of course, a small salve to his wounded pride – and Cheeseman departed with his kneecaps intact.

'You got to take what you want in this life,' Astorre told his boys. And he did.

Soon they had money enough for their own home in London's 'Little Italy'. They became established and well respected in the area, running the clubs as fronts to launder the money they acquired by other means. The family worshipped together every Sunday – Mama Bella insisted – at St Peter's church, and they attended all the big Catholic festivals; particularly, Bella loved to see the Procession della Madonna del Carmine *passing through the packed streets in the summer. Still, she missed Napoli, and the old Italian songs filled the house as she remembered the old country with a nostalgic tear. But this was home now; it had to be. All that was missing, for Bella, was the daughter she longed for.*

Tito was growing into a robust man now. Vittore, his mother's little pet, was growing up fast too and showing signs of becoming a good businessman. Even Fabio, who had been a sickly sulky child – not exactly neglected but certainly not what Mama Bella wanted – was gaining strength as the Danieris surged forward, became established in their new environment.

But Bella still craved a daughter. Her sister had a girl – Serafina, who would later change her name to Sheila – but she had only sons. It broke her heart. Discreet enquiries by Astorre revealed that, as new immigrants, the Danieris would not be deemed suitable adoptive parents, and anyway they were in their forties now. They were simply too old.

'I want a girl,' sobbed Bella, clutching her chest when Astorre passed on the bad news.

He hated to see her pain; he still loved her, in his way.

So he decided. Bella wants a girl? She must have one.

46

Jay didn't want to tell Vittore what he knew. He was familiar with the Danieri taste for shooting the messenger. But he had worked for the family – particularly for Vittore – for a lot of years, and if the crap really started flying and it was discovered he'd said nothing, then he'd be even *deeper* in the shit. So he had to speak up.

They were in the room over the club that had been Tito's favourite – under Tito's reign this room had been opulent, all chandeliers, deeply padded couches, gold leaf and tarts on tap, playfully inviting you to suck chocolate buttons off their nipples. Now it was called Vito's and Vittore held sway. Things were plainer, less flamboyant, reflecting Vittore's own sober nature. The whole tone of the club had changed since Tito had got himself rubbed out. Everything was more low-key. All greys and browns. Fucking *dull*, really. Whatever Tito's faults – and they'd been many – at least he'd had a certain exuberant charm. Vittore had none. With Vittore, everything was business, everything was *cost*.

'So what's the problem, Jay?' Vittore asked him, sitting down on one of the functional stone-coloured marl Habitat sofas and indicating that his employee should sit too.

Jay sat down. He was a tall man for an Italian, fortyish, his face deeply scarred purple down the left cheek by a knife attack back in his twenties. He was a good worker.

Diligent. Dedicated to the family that had kept him in sharp suits and cannelloni for a long time.

'It's Fab,' said Jay.

'What about him?'

'He's been doing some moonlighting, working on his own.'

'So?' This wasn't news. Vittore had always been aware that Fab had deals cooking outside the normal run of things. The normal run of things was the clubs, through which the family washed clean all the money that came in from other sources, *criminal* sources. It made him uneasy, but that was Fabio. He was crazy. You just had to accept that.

'Bank jobs, drug stuff, you know,' said Jay. 'Other things too. More serious things.'

'Such as?'

Jay looked uncomfortable.

'Go on,' Vittore prompted.

'A guy I know had a shipment of coke snatched. He's a straight man, sound. He asked Fab and his boys to get the cargo back for him.'

'And did they?' Vittore was frowning, wondering where all this was leading. Fabio should never have acted on any of this without first discussing it with him, gaining his permission – and where was his fucking cut of the proceeds? The boss *always* took a cut, and he was boss now, had the cheeky little cunt forgotten that?

'They did, but Fabio stiffed him, boss. Took him for sixty per cent of the value of the entire load. Guy says he's seriously out of pocket. He was going to pay them, pay them well, but he's saying around town Fabio screwed him over royally.'

Vittore was silent, thinking. This was bad. If word of this spread and they got a reputation among the other firms for sharp practice, tempers would flare.

'Maybe you could talk to him,' suggested Jay. 'I think he may be offloading the stuff around the clubs.'

'Yeah. Maybe I will,' said Vittore. 'Meanwhile, keep an eye on him, will you? And report back to me.'

Vittore was thinking that his brother was a pain in the arse. He had enough on his plate already, what with Miller to sort out. He'd started on that, only a little thing, but every little thing felt good. He wouldn't take just one big bite out of that cake, he would nibble at it, savour it.

I'll tear the heart out of each and every one of you, he thought. And he would. He'd do it. Slowly. Inch by inch.

47

Joe Darke's place was a big square executive-type house set in two acres of prime Chigwell real-estate. It had high walls and electronic gates, and an intercom to vet visitors.

'You can come on up,' said a high-pitched female voice when Rob climbed out of the car and pressed the button and said that Kit Miller was here to speak to Mr Joe Darke. There was a soft click, and the gates swung inwards.

Rob got back behind the driver's seat, gave Kit a look and then drove on up the winding driveway flanked by purple rhododendrons. He stopped outside the front porch, which was porticoed, with faux Corinthian columns.

'Some place,' said Kit. 'You met him before?'

'No. I thought maybe you had.'

Kit shook his head. This was his uncle they'd come to visit, but Kit didn't know him at all. He'd had another uncle once: Joe and Ruby's eldest brother, Charlie; but Charlie was gone. He had cousins too. Joe and his wife Betsy had two kids, Nadine and Billy, about ten and eight years old. Ruby had told him Joe wasn't in good health these days; apart from that, he knew nothing about these people. He didn't particularly want to, either, but he was puzzled by the fact that Michael had been planning to visit Joe the night he died.

He had thought Michael kept him informed of his every

move. As his right-hand man – just as Rob was now his – he expected to be put in the picture about any meetings or appointments, for the sake of security. But Michael hadn't kept him informed. If he *had*, he might not be lying in the cold earth right now.

Rob rang the doorbell. A big-dog sort of bark started up in the hall, mingling with that same high-pitched female voice berating it.

'Shut up, Prince. *Shut up*,' the voice yelled, and then the door was opened and there was Betsy Darke, clinging on to the rhinestone-encrusted collar of a black-and-tan German shepherd who seemed intent on yanking her arm clean out of its socket; clearly, Prince wanted to eat whoever was standing on the step.

Both men thought that Betsy looked in pretty good shape, considering she was in her early fifties. Her blonde hair was cut in a bob and expertly streaked with strands of white, gold and subtle ivory, which flattered her mahogany tan. She was wearing a pink velour tracksuit and spangled trainers. Her hands, French-manicured to within an inch of their life, bristled with silver rings on every finger and both thumbs. There was the merest suggestion of crow's feet around her pretty, avaricious blue eyes. She was a good-looking woman, but you could see from the first glance that she was a man-eating tart; her smile was too white, too big, her eyes too flirtatious.

'Mrs Darke?' asked Kit.

'Oh, don't you be so formal,' said Betsy with a coquet-tish smile, fluttering her eyelashes at the pair of them like she wasn't old enough to be *both* their mothers. 'You're Kit, Ruby's boy? My God. Aren't you the handsome one! We meet at last.' Then her tone became one of iron command: 'Prince, *basket*.'

Prince stopped lunging toward Rob and Kit, turned meek as a kitten and loped off across the hall.

'You got him well trained,' said Rob.

Yeah, and I hear you got your husband pretty well whipped too, thought Kit as they moved into the hall. *Bet you had that poor bastard doctored a long time ago.* He knew Ruby had no affection for Betsy, and he could see why: they were as unalike as it was possible for two women to be. Much as he despised her, he had to admit that Ruby had a quiet dignity about her; but Betsy was like her home – flashy and eager for attention.

'Joe's in the conservatory,' said Betsy, leading the way, and they followed her jiggling arse across the cavernous hall and past where Prince lay, tongue lolling after all the excitement, in his basket.

They stepped out into the conservatory, which looked out through lush interior greenery onto even greener fields, with ponies grazing in a paddock, and a line of oaks some distance away; *ah, the proceeds of all those dodgy deals clearly paid dividends.*

Kit was shocked to see an elderly looking man, drawn and yellow-white in skin colour, wearing a dressing gown and pyjamas, with an oxygen mask over his face. Tubes led down to a red metal canister. Ruby had told him that Joe's health wasn't good, but he hadn't expected *this.* His uncle was not yet sixty years old, yet he looked a hundred. The hands resting in his lap were like a mummy's claws, the fingers on his right hand stained yellow from nicotine.

'Joe, your visitors are here.' Betsy gave them a look of sparkling, almost girlish enticement.

If she don't try to touch up one or both of us before we're out of here, I'm a bloody Dutchman, thought Kit.

Then Betsy turned a different look altogether on her husband. Impatient, irritable.

Joe Darke opened his eyes, pulled the oxygen mask away from his face. His voice was hoarse, his breathing laboured.

'Kit Miller, uh? The boy who copped the whole effing gold mine.' He smiled, revealing nicotine-stained teeth.

'We're sorry to trouble you when you're ill,' said Kit.

Betsy's mouth twisted. 'It's emphysema, the doctors say. The bloody cigarettes – he never could leave the damned things alone. Been smoking since he was ten years old. It won't get better.'

'I'm sorry to hear that,' said Kit, seeing the flash of hurt in the sick man's eyes at this cold summary of the situation.

'You boys want some tea? Coffee?' asked Betsy, and the flirtatious manner was back again – the smile, the eyes, she was really working it.

'Yeah. Coffee, thanks,' said Kit, to get rid of her for five minutes.

'Same for me,' said Rob.

Betsy departed, with a provocative wiggle.

'Sit down, sit down,' said Joe, making shaky motions with one hand.

Kit and Rob sat. It was hot in the conservatory, moisture beading on the glass. A purple bougainvillea was coming into flower in one corner, a huge grapevine was sending tangling fronds out over the roof in the other. There was a lemon tree, sporting a couple of tiny green fruit. It was like a fucking jungle, foliage pressing in on all sides. You half-expected to see a puma or monkeys loitering among the shrubbery, not a sick and frail man with skin the colour of old parchment.

'What did you mean by that?' asked Kit. 'The gold mine thing?'

'Well, it's the truth, ain't it?' Joe took a long, wheezing

pull at the mask, then laid it down on his lap. 'You *did* get the gold mine. You got it *all*.'

It was true that Michael had left everything he owned to Kit. But to have him back again . . . ah God, he would happily hand it over, lose the whole lot. How the hell could money compensate for the loss of Michael?

'What if I did?' asked Kit, wondering where this was leading.

Joe shrugged. 'Just saying,' he said.

'Michael was planning to pay you a visit the day after he died,' Rob chipped in.

'He was. Yes. And he never arrived. So I phoned the restaurant, and then I heard the news. Sad, sad news.' Joe coughed, lifted the mask and inhaled oxygen again.

'You know what he was coming to see you about?' asked Kit. 'Only, I was his number one. And I wasn't aware that he planned to come out here, I wasn't aware that you did *any* sort of business together. I believe your only connection is your sister and my mother, Ruby, who was sort of Michael's old lady.'

'That, young man, is correct,' said Joe. 'I asked Michael to come out, because I had some information for him that I didn't want to tell him over the phone.'

Kit frowned. 'What was this information?'

Joe inhaled another hit from the bottle. 'I'd had word from his son.'

Rob and Kit looked at each other. His *what*?

Joe was nodding his head.

'You heard me right. Michael and his wife Sheila had a son: Gabriel.'

48

Betsy was back, bearing a tray with two steaming mugs of coffee and a plate of biscuits. She beamed at Kit and Rob, then gave a look of blank dislike to her husband.

'There!' she said, placing the coffees on a low table in front of them. 'Help yourself to the biscuits. Can I get you anything else . . . ?'

'Bets,' said Joe.

'Yes?' She turned to him and there was that chameleon thing again, the fake charm dropping away to reveal the ugly heartfelt contempt.

'Fuck off, for Christ's sake,' said Joe, and took another deep drag on his oxygen.

Betsy went red in the face.

'We got things to discuss,' said Joe. 'So go in the kitchen and look at your fuckin' brochures, will you? Work out how you're going to spend the next few thousand I've sweated blood over, yeah?'

Betsy turned on her heel, lips clenched. Rob stood up, quickly touched her arm.

'You got a loo I can use, Mrs Darke?'

'Sure,' she said, and they went off into the main body of the house.

'This is some place,' they heard Rob say, and Betsy chattering in reply.

Joe turned his attention to Kit.

'She's cost me a fortune ever since the day I married her.' He inhaled deeply from the mask, the moisture from his struggling breath misting the transparent plastic. 'Now she's having the kitchen refitted because she don't like the colour of the units. She's had the fucking fishpond moved four times. Every six months, regular as clockwork, we got decorators indoors doing something or other. It's a pain in the fuckin' arse.'

'Joe . . . you said Michael had a son,' said Kit.

Joe was nodding.

'What's the deal here then, Joe?' Kit asked his uncle.

His *uncle*.

He'd never even met the man before. But this was his kin.

Some kin. Everyone said his late uncle Charlie was the one who'd cast him into a succession of care homes. He had only to think about it and he was back there. The bleak monotony of those places, the Christmases pasting together home-made garlands to hang around the stark hallways, the mealtimes when boiled cabbage was forced down his reluctant throat, the meagre accommodation, the cold, the rarely washed bedclothes, nights spent top-and-tailing because there weren't enough beds to go round – a kid at one end of the bed, a kid at the other, someone's cheesy feet stuck right under your nose all night. A fucking nightmare.

Charlie had been responsible for that. But surely Joe had known, too?

'Gabe and me go back a long way,' said Joe. His voice was growing hoarser, as if conversation exhausted him. 'He was one of my boys, back in the day. He fell out with his mum and dad as a teenager, dunno why. Michael washed his hands of him. Being a bad lad was all he knew, so he came to my lads and said did I have something for him? As it happens, I did. But Gabe, poor Gabe . . .' Joe heaved a sigh. 'Gabe's trouble, see, is money burns a hole in his pocket the minute he's got it. I think he's into drugs, probably got hooked on that crap inside. That can happen. He thinks the world owes him a living. It don't.'

Kit was silent, taking it in as Rob rejoined them and sat down. Whatever this Gabe had done as a teenager, it must have been pretty damned bad to make his parents disown him.

'He came out of the Scrubs about a week before Michael died,' said Joe.

'What was he in for?' asked Rob, who'd overheard the last bit of this.

'GBH.'

Kit gave his uncle a wry smile. 'Got a bit of a temper, has he? And he phoned you.' Had he phoned Michael too? Tried to make contact again, to repair the fractured relationship with his father? Michael hadn't said a thing about any of this.

'He wanted to know if I'd take him back on.'

'And you said . . . ?' Kit prompted. He wasn't sure how he felt about all this; displaced, angry, disappointed. Michael hadn't confided in him, and he *should* have.

Joe let out a loud *hmph* of disgust. 'I said sod off out of it. I made it clear he'd done working for me. The boys didn't like him, he was a jittery little fucker, off his head half the time. You know what I think? I think something *happened* to Gabe, something bad way back in his past. Anyway, I didn't want him around. I was glad to be rid of him. He wasn't happy about it, but fuck him.'

'You got an address for him?' asked Rob.

Joe shook his head, raised one quivering hand to his brow. He looked tired, thought Rob. Tired to death.

'I didn't ask for one. The boy's trouble. And he's money-hungry, he can never get enough of the stuff. You know the sort, they're always scammin' some poor bastard and thinking up stupid schemes, always grubbing around in the dirt for cash – but they never seem to have a pot to piss in?' Joe's eyes wandered to the open door into the house. Betsy's radio was loudly playing Showaddywaddy's 'Three Steps to Heaven' in the kitchen she was about to have remodelled, at Joe's expense. 'So I'm glad you called. I wanted to warn you he's out. That's the reason I asked Michael to come over, to tell him.'

'And Michael never made it.'

'No. He never did.'

Rob took a swig of coffee. He wondered how Kit felt about this. Kit had been Michael's blue-eyed boy for a long time; but Gabe was his actual *son*. Gabe was Michael's blood.

Joe managed a weak smile. 'And there you are, as I said – sitting on top of the gold mine.'

Kit gave Joe a level stare. He had worked diligently for Michael for years to earn the right to be his number one. And Michael's monetary decisions had been his alone; there had been no coercion on Kit's part.

'What are you saying?' he asked Joe.

'I'm saying Gabe's a greedy little tick and he's going to want it. All of it. The restaurants, the clubs, the flats, the dosh – everything. He'll want it *all*.'

Kit took a sip of the coffee, then said: 'It was Michael's wish that I should carry on where he left off. He knew I could do it. He *trusted* me to do it.'

He thought then of his dangerous flirtation with the booze. He'd been dry for a couple of weeks now, and one of the reasons he'd managed that was because he'd been sure that Michael would be disgusted with such weakness.

'What would this Gabe character do with it all?' he asked Joe.

Joe let out a guffaw of grating laughter which faded into a painful cough. 'He'd piss the whole lot up against the fuckin' wall,' he said, eyes watering. 'Spend it on alcohol, cigarettes and loose women. And the rest he'd just bloody squander.'

Kit had to smile. Poor bastard. He was up shit creek, but he still had a sense of humour.

'You really got no address for him? Not even a number?'

Joe shook his head.

'You think he's going to come calling over Michael's money?' asked Kit.

'Gabe?' Joe gave a dry smile and took another pull at the oxygen. 'Oh yeah. He'll come.'

49

1953

Tito wasn't going to rush this. He was like a cheetah, stalking fleet-footed gazelle; he had to be sure of his choice before he broke cover. He took his work seriously. Papa Astorre had spoken to Mama Bella and now Astorre told him what she wanted.

'A little blonde girl,' said Astorre. 'Not a baby. Maybe two, three years old? Young enough to forget, not old enough to remember the details.'

'People are going to talk,' warned Tito. 'Suddenly you have a child? A girl who doesn't even look like one of us?'

'We'll cook up a story. Something plausible. Besides, no one around us would talk. They wouldn't dare.' Astorre made a slicing motion, one finger against his cheek. 'Do it some distance away,' he said.

'The parents . . . ?' asked Tito, thinking of blonde women.

Astorre shrugged. He would leave that to Tito. Snatch the girl without a fight if he could, but if not . . .

'That's your affair,' he said. 'Just see to it, uh?'

Tito promised that he would.

Tito took his cousin Gabriel along for the ride, knowing that if Michael Ward heard what his nineteen-year-old son was up to he would be furious and disgusted. Gabe was forever hanging around the Danieri boys, and it was obvious he hero-worshipped Tito, who was now a full-grown camorristi of twenty-eight. It amused Tito, seeing the way Gabe tried to emulate him, making out he was tough and cool and didn't give a shit for anything.

Gabe was very impressed with the fact that Tito ran the clubs for the family, and that he had his own flat over the club that bore his name. There were women there, lots of women, Tito had his pick of them. Generously, he let Gabe have his pick, too, and that made Gabe worship him all the more.

'We're going on a little road trip,' Tito said, and Gabe was flattered that he'd been asked to go along, to help out.

Gabe was flattered if Tito so much as talked to him, and Tito knew it.

For a while, Gabe found the trip almost enjoyable. He'd thought that Tito would be doing a job or two on the way, maybe stitching someone up, doing a few deals, but no: this seemed to be purely pleasure, purely a break in the country. That puzzled Gabe, but he didn't object. He was with Tito, and he loved that.

He knew his dad didn't like Tito, even though they were related by marriage, but Gabe got a kick out of defying his father, going against his express wish that he steer well clear of Tito and the other Danieri boys.

They set off – not in Tito's usual flashy Jag, but in an old Jeep, the sort left here by American GIs during the war. Tito had packed a tent, it was a real road trip, a total adventure. They stopped off at B&Bs in the country. Tito shaved off his beard and wore shabby, casual clothes, which wasn't like him. They gave false names wherever they stayed.

Yeah, it was fun and Tito was a charming companion. He could be scary, Gabe knew that, but right now he was being treated as Tito's equal, as a friend, even, and he liked that. They went up through the Lake District, and then up further, to the Scottish Borders. All the while Gabe had a sense that Tito was searching for something, waiting for something to catch his eye.

They came back down, to the north Yorkshire moors, found a campsite and pitched their tent. It was fun, yes, but now Gabe was getting tired of it. All they did was drive, and stop off in pubs, and look around the campsites where they stayed for a night or two, then move on. He wanted to go back to London.

'Patience,' said Tito, when Gabe asked if they were going home soon.

After they'd pitched their tent on this latest site, they went to the shop at the centre of camp to buy provisions. There was a pretty young blonde woman toting a basket around the narrow aisles, holding a little silver-white-blonde girl by the hand, cooing to her in some foreign language.

'You see?' said Tito in triumph, grinning broadly at Gabe. 'Patience pays off.'

50

Kit and Rob drove from Joe's place back to Ruby's in Marlow.

'We thought all we had to worry about was Vittore and Fabio,' said Rob with a frustrated exhalation of breath. 'Now we got this Gabe character crawling out of the fucking woodwork.'

'We'll deal with him, if he shows his face,' said Kit. He didn't like the way all this was stacking up. Simon dying the way he did, and Daisy getting intimidated, and that business with Vittore at Tito's funeral – shit he'd been so *stupid* that day – and now there was Gabe to add to the mix. Michael's one and only legitimate son – and heir. Except he hadn't inherited a bean.

Kit was pleased to see one of his boys on Ruby's gate, and to note that the instant they pulled in and approached the house, Reg and another handy-looking lad were there to find out what was going on. When they saw it was Kit and Rob, they waved and withdrew.

'What you ought to get here,' said Rob when Ruby let them in, 'is a ruddy big dog. Your brother's got one over at his gaff, great monster of a thing, looks like it wants to tear your throat out.'

'I don't like dogs,' said Ruby, leading the way into the sitting room.

'Where's Daise?' asked Kit. Ruby had told him Daisy no longer worked at the store.

'Upstairs. All this has really upset her.'

'We're not stopping,' said Kit. 'I just wanted to ask you about Michael's personal effects. You know, like his wallet, his comb – things he'd carry around in his pocket. Do you still have them?'

Ruby grimaced. 'Yes, I do. I haven't been able to look at them, not since . . .' Her voice trailed away. 'I'll get them for you,' she said, and quickly left the room.

'What d'you want that stuff for?' asked Rob.

'Dunno. Maybe there's something in there that will tell us what Michael was doing. I just want to see, that's all.'

'You going to tell Ruby about the Gabe Ward thing?'

'Dunno about that, either,' said Kit. The whole way home he'd been going back and forth over everything that Joe had told them. Was it just a coincidence that one week after Gabe got out of jail, Michael was shot dead?

Had Michael – and he was just kicking the idea around, turning it over, looking at it from all angles – had Michael told Gabe about his plans to leave everything to Kit? Had they argued? Had Gabe, fresh from doing bird for GBH, and according to Uncle Joe, unstable, lost it and killed his own father?

Could it have been Gabe who did the deed?

This was disturbing. He had no idea where this Gabe was, or what he intended to do next. And even more disturbing was the discovery that there were parts of Michael's life he knew nothing about, that Michael had kept from him.

And the Bentley, scratched to hell and the tyres all slashed. He'd been thinking Vittore. But was he wrong? Was that Gabe at work?

Ruby returned carrying a smallish plastic see-through bag as if it was radioactive. She handed it to Kit.

'You can keep it,' she said. 'I don't want it. It just reminds me . . .'

 . . . of all I've lost.

The words hung unspoken in the air between them.

Kit could see Michael's wallet in there. His heart clenched on a churning wave of fresh grief as he saw the Dunhill lighter and gold cigarette case, so much a part of the boss that it was like he was here in the room. Matchbooks. A South African Krugerrand set into a big, heavily ridged gold ring. A Rolex watch. A wallet. A comb.

'You don't want to keep the watch?' he asked, swallowing hard past a lump in his throat. He reached into the bag, pulled out the Krugerrand ring. 'How about this? Look, it's engraved.'

Ruby looked at it. *I'm Still in Love with You* was etched in tiny Italic script on the inside of the band.

'Michael never wore rings,' she said, then she shrugged. 'Probably his wife Sheila gave it to him years ago and he carried it around with him for sentimental reasons. No, I don't want it. Keep the Rolex. He would have loved you to have that, I'm sure. That and his record collection; I'm glad you kept that. It'll remind you of him.' Ruby looked keenly at Kit's face. 'How was Joe?'

'Pretty bad. Too much smoking. You ought to go see him.'

'I don't think Betsy would make me very welcome.'

'What's the story there? Why'd you fall out with her?'

'Betsy don't get on with women. She only likes men. Preferably *young* ones.'

Kit had seen this with his own eyes; Ruby wasn't giving him any bullshit.

'Right,' he said, then hesitated. 'We'd better get back.'

'Call anytime,' she said, hope and eagerness plain in her voice. It hurt Rob to hear it. He liked Ruby, and he wished Kit would stop treating her so coldly.

'Thanks,' said Kit, and left the room with Rob in tow.

Ruby sat there and stared at the closed door for long moments.

Kit still hates me, she thought.

She felt tears start in her eyes. She gulped, blinked, *refused* to cry. Instead, she stood up, breathed deeply. She'd go out. Do something. Anything. Take her mind off the fact that her son, whom she loved to distraction, still, despite all her efforts, despised her.

In the car while Rob drove, Kit examined the items in the bag. There were a couple of fifties and some loose change in the black leather wallet. A comb, still with strands of Michael's thick iron-grey hair attached to it. He touched the strands, thought about Michael combing his hair for the last time, not knowing . . .

Shut up with that.

He put the comb aside, picked up the ring. It was heavy, the mount a solid lump of gold, a costly item with the springbok bounding on the gold coin. He turned it over, looked at the hallmark, reading the inscription again.

I'm Still in Love with You.

'Ruby's right,' he said to Rob. 'I never saw Michael wear this or any other ring. Did you?'

Rob shook his head.

'But he was carrying it around with him. Why was he doing that?'

Rob shrugged. 'So what? I got all sorts of shit in my pockets, haven't you?'

Kit let out a sharp sigh. It worried him that Michael had had secrets from him, but of course it was only natural that he would. After all, Kit *wasn't* his blood, he wasn't his son. And Rob was right. The inscription on the ring, even the ring itself, probably meant fuck-all.

'I want you to phone around when we get back, see if you can find any addresses or contact numbers for this Gabe.'

'Will do.'

If there were any answers to be had, Kit wasn't seeing them. And he wondered if he ever would. He leaned back, closed his eyes. Thought of those carefree days with Bianca . . .

He'd phone her, as soon as he got home. He needed to hear her voice.

51

Bianca was worn out with staring at the fucking phone. Days had gone by and it felt like that was all she'd done: stared at it, willed it to ring. Well, it had. Suppliers, workers, Mama Bella, everyone had phoned in. But not the only one she wanted to hear from. Not *him*.

Her weekend bag was packed and her coat was on, ready to go and visit Bella, she hadn't been up to the Smoke since Tito's funeral – ah, God what a day *that* had been – and still here she was, thinking *Ring, come on, dammit!* While the girls looked on, shaking their heads as if thinking, *Christ, Bianca Danieri's been screwed over – didn't see that one coming.*

'Well, I'm off,' she said to the assembled troops. 'Cora's in charge, OK.'

'Have a good one,' said the barman.

'We'll be fine here,' said Cora.

She knew they would. Sensible people, well trained: she'd surrounded herself with a good team. Tanya, the single weak link in an otherwise strong chain, she'd sacked and replaced with someone better.

'Well – bye then.' Bianca went out and threw her bag in the car, a beaten-up old cream Morgan. She already had the soft leather top down. It was a golden day, beautiful, spring in all its glory; a person should be happy, in love, ebullient, on a day like this.

She was in love. But it was a tragic sort of love, a one-way street, because he *hadn't phoned*.

Bianca started the engine, listened to its deep throaty roar. She loved to drive, to feel the wind whipping through her hair. She slipped on her shades and heaved a sharp sigh. She knew what Cora and Claire and the rest were thinking. She'd been done over. Used, then dumped. And they were right. She was furious with herself, and even more furious with him. Tony Mobley. The bastard.

'Fuck it,' she muttered, and slipped into first, and shot off towards London.

She was better than this. She was camorristi. Tito had drummed into her the ways of the Camorra, how to be proud, how to be vengeful. She remembered everything he had taught her so well.

Behind her, in Dante's, the phone started ringing.

'Is Bianca there?' asked Kit, slumped on his sofa, wanting to hear her, speak to her. He'd put one of Michael's LPs on the stereo, he had a bundle of them, a lot of Henry Mancini and some good Everly Brothers stuff, some Elvis, Roy Orbison, Billy Fury. Billy was currently singing 'Jealousy' to a hard tango beat.

Jesus he'd missed Bianca so much – but with all the shit going down since he'd got back, he hadn't had a moment to get in touch.

'Nope. Who's calling?' asked a stern female voice.

'K— um . . . Tony,' said Kit.

'Tony Mobley?'

'Yeah. Can I speak to her? Who is that?'

'It's Cora. She's not here.'

'Where is she then?' He felt his stomach drop away, he was that disappointed. And the business with the fake name, what a fucking embarrassment that was turning out to be.

Old habits die hard.

Yeah, he'd become used to the usual deceptions most bachelors practised to keep themselves out of the firing line. But with Bianca . . . the minute the lie had come out of his mouth, he had wanted to snatch it back. It felt wrong, distasteful.

'I can't tell you that.'

'Come on. You can.'

'No can do.'

'Give me a clue, yeah?'

'No. She'd kill me if she knew I'd given out her whereabouts to a total stranger.'

'I'm not a stranger. I'm . . .' *oh shit* '. . . Tony. So you know about me? Did we meet when I came in the club recently?'

'We did meet. Briefly. When Bianca's not here, I manage the place.'

'I remember you. Tall redhead, right?'

'Yeah. OK. Right.'

'So you know I'm not a stranger. Tell me where she is.'

'No,' said Cora.

Cora placed the phone carefully on its cradle.

'Who was that?' asked Claire, passing by with the barman lugging a crate of mixers behind her.

'Nobody,' said Cora, and went back out into the bar. All men were wasters, especially the gorgeous ones. Maybe Bianca just needed to learn that lesson the hard way.

52

'Got some more news,' said Jay in Vittore's ear.

He had just joined his boss at the busy bar in the Danieri club called Goldie's. It was late evening and the place was full of customers. 'Waterloo', Abba's big hit from last year's Eurovision, was banging out of the speakers at a colossal volume. People were bopping on the strobe-lit dance floor in flares and cheesecloth tie-dye tops, and waitresses in gold miniskirts, gold boots and gold nipple tassels were shimmying around among the punters, carrying trays of drinks to tables and corner banquettes.

Vittore had been watching these girls with disdain. As he had tidied up Tito's – now transformed as Vito's – so he intended to clean up this place too. These girls were dirty whores, flaunting themselves. They disgusted him and they would have to go.

'Let's discuss this upstairs,' said Vittore, and led the way up to the office.

Jay followed and closed the door behind him, deadening the noise. Vittore sat down behind the desk. Jay sat, too.

'So?' asked Vittore, looking at his henchman's ugly face, at the long scar running down his left cheek, disfiguring the mouth on that side. Jay wasn't pretty, but he was loyal and straight.

'You asked me to keep an eye on Fabio,' said Jay.

'Yeah?' Vittore spread his hands. *So?*

'It's bad, Vittore.'

Vittore stared at Jay. This man had worked for him for a lot of years. He trusted him.

'Tell me,' said Vittore, and Jay did.

For days Bianca mooched around at Mama Bella's, feeling miserable, rejected, ready to slit her throat. Then finally she thought, fuck him. He was just a man, just another fucking man, and she was tougher than this. She still had her life, her job, her family, and there were plenty of other men in the world. The last bit she told herself, over and over, but she didn't believe it.

Tony Mobley had *become* her world.

But not any more. He'd dumped her; that much was completely clear. So she had to get back on the horse, get back in the saddle, carry on.

'I'm going out,' she told Mama Bella, and she did, touching base with old friends and getting legless at Global Village, going on a reckless round of high-end shopping for designer gear that she threw in the wardrobe, didn't even bother to take the labels off, then off to Goldie's with her mates for a night of dancing – until dawn and a raging hangover stopped the fun.

'This is no way to behave,' Mama Bella scolded her next morning, as she lay groaning in her bed. 'What's the matter with you?'

'Leave me alone,' said Bianca, pulling the covers over her head. She thought of Tony, the rotten bastard, and the mixture of self-pity and hideous headache made her dissolve into tears. Whoever said love hurt? They were right. It did.

53

'Hi,' said the man, stepping out of the shadows.

Daisy was coming out of the back of Ruby's flagship store near Marble Arch and she nearly jumped out of her skin. Ruby had asked her to come over and collect a couple of files from Joan, and she'd happily obliged. Anything to keep busy, to stop mulling it all over, thinking of how much she missed the twins, how she felt literally sick and empty and *ached* to hold them. It had been nearly a fortnight since Simon's death, she still had his funeral to get through. And her nerves hadn't stopped jangling since that horrible experience on the road with the Danieri bastards.

On top of everything else, she was devastated at the distance Rob had suddenly placed between them. He practically ignored her now. Obviously he'd made some sort of decision, and their almost-romance was clearly off. That broke her heart. She adored him. Loved him. This wasn't just a crush, this was *serious*.

She was thinking of all this and coming out of the back of the store when suddenly there was this scruffy, sour-smelling man standing in front of her.

'Oh!' she said, startled.

He was smiling. The light wasn't too good out here, but she could see he was somewhere in his thirties and very skinny, almost gaunt. *Junkie*, she thought. He had puckish features with heavy-lidded eyes under arched brows. But there were big dark shadows all around his eye sockets. His grey-flecked hair was cut very short, there was a deep cleft in his chin and his mouth was thin.

As Daisy flinched away, he held up his hands in a *Hey! I'm harmless!* gesture, smiling at the same time.

'Whoa!' The smile widened to a grin. 'It's OK. I'm not a hooligan.'

People were flooding past them, coming out of the store to head home.

'Oh hello, Daisy. 'Night,' said Doris Blanchard, walking past in a group of chattering girls. Among them Daisy saw her tormentors, Tessa and Julie. They gave her hate-filled looks. She gave them back a look of blank uninterest. Fuck them.

'Good night, Doris,' said Daisy, then her eyes returned to the man standing in front of her. 'You startled me.'

'Sorry. My fault. Are you Daisy Darke?'

'How . . . ?'

He gave a smile. Daisy thought it had a flaky, mad edge to it. 'That woman just called you Daisy and it's an unusual name. Actually, I'm looking for *Ruby* Darke.'

'She's not in today.'

Daisy had done what she came for and now all she wanted was to hurry home. She felt jittery and exposed and miserable. It broke her heart that she couldn't go to the safe house to see the twins; Kit said it was too risky, that she might be spotted and that would place her babies in danger. But she had been allowed to speak to Jody very briefly from a phone box, only to be told that Matthew had been irritable for the past few days, feverish, coming down with a cold or something. And Luke would catch it. They did everything in tandem. And here she was, their mother, unable to see them, feed them, touch them, comfort them in any way. She hated all this, and was furious at the Danieri mob for causing this excruciating separation.

They're going to forget I'm their mother, she thought frantically. *They're going to start calling Jody 'Mum', their first words to her will be 'Mama'!*

'Gabe,' said the man blocking her path. He stuck out a hand. 'I'm Gabriel Ward. But everyone calls me Gabe.'

Daisy stared at him blankly. She was worried, distracted, and she most certainly didn't know or even *want* to know any Gabriel Ward.

Despite her misgivings, she shook his hand. It felt sweaty and unpleasant. He definitely had the look of a cokehead or a heroin addict. She wondered at the wisdom of abandoning the safety of Ruby's house and coming here today; maybe she should have got Reg to drive her. But she had been trying to overcome her own fears, to prove she could do it; and now look.

Everyone was leaving the store, the crowds of shop workers were thinning out, the place where they were standing, behind the big loading bays, was almost empty of life.

'Look, I have to go . . .' she said uneasily.

'Sure! Of course,' he said, and stepped aside. 'Only, I don't have an address for her, and I wanted to talk to her. She and my dad were close, I believe.'

Ward? thought Daisy.

She stopped, studied his face. 'You're not *related* to Michael? Michael Ward?'

He gave that mocking half-grin again. There was something about his eyes that she really didn't like. 'He was my dad.'

Daisy stared at him, thunderstruck. 'I didn't know Michael had any children.'

'I've been away for a while. Working.'

'Well, I'm sure Ruby would want to meet you,' she said politely. Actually she didn't think Ruby would like to meet this twitchy, wild-eyed person at all.

'So if you could give me her address . . .'

'I can't do that.'

'What?' He gave her a look of blinding innocence. 'Why not?'

'I just can't, that's all. Sorry.'

'But surely she wouldn't *mind*,' he said. 'I'm Michael's boy.'

'I told you: I can't.'

Gabe moved in closer. His smile had slipped. He let out a laugh, but it sounded harsh, forced. 'Oh, come on. This is silly.'

'No . . .' Daisy felt a shiver of alarm. She glanced down at her bag. 'Oh . . . oh for God's sake, I've left some files in the store. I'm sorry, I really have to go.'

Daisy hurried back inside, her heart beating hard. She half-expected him to follow her, to see through the thin-ness of her excuse to get away. The security guard was in his office and she went to the glass panel and leaned in close. Her eyes kept flicking toward the rear exit. At any moment, she expected Gabe to come in.

Henry looked up. He was portly and avuncular, and he smiled when he saw Daisy standing there.

'Help you, Miss Darke?' he asked, coming over.

'If anyone comes in asking for me, I've gone out the side entrance, OK?' said Daisy quickly.

'Sure. You all right?' he asked.

'Fine. Just got some things Mum wants me to do up in the office. Don't need any interruptions.'

'OK.' He was looking at her dubiously.

Daisy went back along the labyrinthine, echoing corridors and up to Ruby's den on the top floor, passing through

Joan's empty office. The store was almost deserted now, and suddenly she didn't like the feeling at all. She opened the inner door with her spare key, locked it behind her, and then went over to the desk, picked up the phone, and dialled.

He was there within half an hour, tapping at the locked office door.

'Daise? You in there?'

Daisy unlocked the door. Rob was standing in the hallway.

'What happened? You look like you've seen a ghost.'

Daisy composed herself. She was Lord Bray's daughter, she was the fabulous Ruby Darke's daughter, she absolutely *was not* going to fall to pieces. But she was getting so tired of feeling under threat all the time. The Danieri mob outside Simon's house – she'd nearly *died* of fright that day. And now this junkie stopping her at the back of the store, at first smiling, charming, then turning suddenly hostile.

'Do you know a Gabriel Ward?' she managed to get out.

Rob's attention sharpened. 'Kit's Uncle Joe was telling us about him. He's Michael's son. Got out of the big house not long ago.'

'Big house?' echoed Daisy.

'Prison, Daise.'

Not working then. 'He was here earlier. Waiting for me outside.'

Rob stared at her. 'Did he speak to you? What did he want?'

'He wanted Ruby's address. And when I wouldn't give it, he sort of . . . well, got aggressive in a pushy, smiley, spooky way. I think he may have been on something. You know, drugs. He looked spaced out.' Daisy took a breath. 'What was he in prison for?'

'Grievous.'

'What?'

'GBH. Grievous Bodily Harm.'

'Oh God.'

'Christ, Daise.'

'I came straight back inside and phoned you.'

'You did right.' Rob was frowning. 'Fuck's sake, Daise, will you please stop pissing around and stay where you're safest? We've got ourselves a situation here, you know that. You should have got Reg to drive you, you shouldn't have come in on your own.'

'Don't talk to me like that,' snapped Daisy, irritated because she knew he was right, she'd been stupid to do it.

'I'll talk to you any way I fucking-well like,' said Rob. 'Kit's the guvnor and he says I have to keep you safe. So whether you like that or not, I'll do that.' He took a breath. 'There was nobody hanging about the back entrance when I got here.'

'Good.' Daisy eyed him sulkily, stung by that rebuke. 'I didn't know Michael had a son.'

'Neither did any of us, until Kit and me went to talk to Joe. Joe thinks this Gabriel is spitting blood over Kit getting the firm. And it sounds like Joe's right. That's fucking annoying, him trying to come in sideways, starting with you and Ruby. Come on, Daise. Let's get you home.'

54

'Boss?' Scar-faced Jay put his head around the door of the office over Vito's. Downstairs, the club was humming and someone was hammering out a bouncy song that was pounding the floorboards beneath Jay's feet.

'What?' asked Vittore, who had been sitting behind his desk puffing on a thin cheroot and sipping a glass of wine from his own cellar, a very fine Chablis; he had a good palate and he appreciated things like that.

He'd been thinking about his brother and his wife and all that family shit, and trying not to. To distract himself, he had opened the bottle and then the post – just bills as usual. Then he'd tossed the letter-opener aside and begun leafing through the day's paper; inflation was riding high at 21 per cent, the Russians had put two more cosmonauts into space to link up with the Salyut 4 space station and Sinatra had successfully sued the BBC over some programme that had linked him to the Mafia.

'You are never gonna *believe* who's downstairs in the club asking for a meet.'

Vittore sat up. 'Who?' he asked, stubbing out the cheroot in a red Murano glass ashtray, a gaudy remnant of Tito's reign.

Jay told him.

'You're right,' said Vittore, standing up. 'I *don't* believe it.'

What Kit was thinking was this: he would talk with Vittore, work out some sort of deal with the bastard if he could, have a proper sit-down. It grated on him, the thought of doing this; the Danieris were scum. But this whole thing was getting out of control. Simon's death, and then Daisy being so badly scared . . . he didn't want that. If Vittore had a problem, it was with *him* – not his family.

So he'd come over to Vito's with Rob for backup, and he'd ignored his own misgivings.

The last time he'd been in this place, inside this building . . . he thought about it, then tried to shove it back out of his mind.

The last time . . .

Gilda, lying dead

Tito's men, holding him down

And, ah shit, the pain, the God-awful pain

But that was then and this was now. *This* time, there was Rob to mind his back, and this time Tito was six feet under and he was dealing with Vittore, so maybe this could come out right. He'd caused all this crap, now it was down to him to sort it out.

'There he is,' said Rob, leaning in to Kit's ear. 'And this is a *bad* idea – did I already say that?'

Rob had said it at least a dozen times, but Kit wasn't listening. The place was packed and the noise of the sound system was awesome. People danced, drank, crowded at the blue-lit bar. Beyond the bar was a roped-off stairway, and it was down these stairs that Vittore was now coming, with the tall knife-scarred man behind him. Vittore's eyes were casting around in the dim lights and the flashing strobes.

He saw Kit. For a moment Vittore paused there; then he gestured for Kit to come over.

Once they were all upstairs in Vittore's office and Jay had checked that neither of them was carrying, Jay shut the door and leaned against it. Rob stood off to one side. Vittore sat down behind his desk, and Kit took a seat opposite.

'What you come here for?' asked Vittore, eyeing Kit coldly.

'To talk,' said Kit.

'So talk.'

'I don't like what's happening,' said Kit.

Vittore glanced up at Jay, back at Kit. 'And what *is* happening?' he asked.

'My ex-brother-in-law died,' said Kit. Gloria Gaynor was vibrating the floorboards under their feet with 'Never Can Say Goodbye'.

'That's very sad, I'm sorry,' said Vittore.

'Killed himself, that's the story,' said Kit.

'Tragic,' shrugged Vittore.

'But see, I think it's just that: a story. He was a stroppy little cunt, but one thing you could say in that fucker's favour, he was always *up*. Never down. He had a good business, a family, everything to live for.'

'Shit happens,' said Vittore, nodding sympathetically.

'Don't it though. There was even a suicide note – nice touch.'

'Nice in what way?' asked Vittore.

'Nice in the way that it made the picture complete. Man commits suicide, leaves note saying he can't go on.' Kit was eyeing Vittore without blinking. 'Thing is, this was a little tit who could go on for England. *This* cunt would go on when everyone else had fallen by the wayside and gone down the pub for a beer. Giving up, giving in? Not an option for this fucker.'

Vittore sat back in his chair. 'Surely you're not suggesting there was something *suspicious* about this man's death?' he asked.

'I'm not suggesting anything. I'm stating a fact. Simon Collins wouldn't kill himself. Now on to Daisy, and you showing up with your boys when she goes to her ex-husband's place to pay her respects, trying to frighten her – I'm really upset about this, Mr Danieri, *very* upset.'

'Oh, you are?' said Vittore.

Kit nodded. 'I am. OK, so I may have stepped on your toes a little—'

'A little?' Vittore was smiling. 'No. A *lot*. You offended me deeply, Mr Miller, turning up at my brother's funeral like you did.'

'I realize that. But we're both reasonable men, *business* men. Let's cool this down a bit, eh?'

'Cool it down? When you behave as you do, when the rumours on the street are so strong about who was behind my beloved brother's death? Have you *heard* those rumours, Mr Miller?'

Kit shook his head. 'Tito had plenty of enemies.'

'Yeah. He did. You were one of them, you made *that* obvious. So now I'm wondering, were you the one who took Tito from us, his family?'

'Tito's gone,' said Kit. 'My ex-brother-in-law is gone. These are sad times for *both* our families. But if that's your view, then maybe we can say that we're even. That enough's enough.'

This time it was Vittore's turn to shake his head. 'No, Mr Miller.'

Kit stared at him. 'No?'

'Let's wrap this up, shall we?' Vittore stood up and leaned

both hands, palms down, on the desk's tooled leather surface. His eyes gleamed with fury and the thin veneer of civility dropped away like a discarded mask. 'You shitting me, coming here? You think I give a fuck about anything you and your tribe are going through? *My* family concerns me. *Mine.* And you've insulted them and maybe worse, who knows? What I *do* know is that you're a dead man walking.'

Kit stood up too. He leaned in on the other side of the desk. Smiled thinly.

'I'm trying to be the bigger man here,' he said.

'You? You fucking *schifoso*!' yelled Vittore suddenly. *'Get the fuck out of my club!'*

'Yeah. I will,' said Kit, and snatched up the letter-opener and thumped it down, skewering Vittore's hand to the desk.

55

'Leave the bottle,' Bianca told the barman over the heavy thrum of the music in Vito's. Her friend Shula, who she'd known since school, was there with her at the bar for another night of fun, drink and dance. She was going to enjoy herself tonight if it bloody well killed her.

The barman poured champagne into two flutes, and left the bottle just like Bianca said. Shula was looking around, spying out the eye candy. Bianca couldn't bring herself to bother. She grabbed the flute and drank down the bubbly, then poured another.

'Steady with that,' shouted Shula, leaning forward to make herself heard. 'We got all night.'

Oh, and why didn't that prospect fill her with excitement like it used to? Now the thought of an all-nighter was utterly bloody tedious and pointless.

Stop it, you miserable bitch, Bianca told herself sternly. *Enjoy yourself.*

She was determined to do that. She *would* do that.

'Jesus, what happened to *him*?' asked Shula, pointing out Donato further down the bar.

Bianca looked. All the boys called him Pizza Face now, and word was that Fabio had given him both a bad limp and a face-full of cigarette burns when he'd been stupid enough to bring him bad news. Nevertheless, gang loyalty ran deep. Donato was still here, still serving the family.

'Dunno,' she said, uninterested.

'Dance?' suggested Shula.

'Not yet,' said Bianca, and caught the exasperation in Shula's eyes. She knew she was being a pain in the arse, but somehow she couldn't seem to stop. She downed the second glass of champagne. It didn't cheer her up, though. She poured another and brought it to her lips.

Then she froze.

There was a commotion on the stairs near the far end of the bar. Men were coming down, practically wrestling each other down the stairs – a big chunky blond bloke and Jay, her brother's right-hand man, shouting and screaming, and . . .

'Hey! Watch it!' said Shula as Bianca's hand twitched in shock, spilling champagne over Shula's lap.

It was Tony Mobley. Jay had managed to grab him halfway down the stairs and they were yelling at each other. The blond one ran up a couple of steps and punched Jay in the head. Jay fell, and then Tony and the blond came on down and walked through the surging unconcerned crowds to the front of the club.

Bianca jumped to her feet. 'Tony!' she shouted.

He walked on; didn't hear her.

'Fuck's sake . . .' Bianca was hurrying after the two men now, going out to the front of the club, looking at the doormen. Damn it, he was *gone*.

'Well, *that* was bloody clever,' said Rob as he and Kit hurried back to the car. 'Talk, you said. Cool things down, you said.'

'Shut up,' said Kit. All right, he'd lost it. He *knew* he'd lost it, he didn't need that pointing out to him. But there was something about that ugly, self-satisfied smirk on Vittore's face that had made him want to wipe it off.

Well, he'd done that.

Not very bloody clever at all. Rob was right.

Instead of rejoining Shula at the bar, Bianca made her way up to the office. Inside she found a scene of chaos: Vittore was behind the desk, his face ashen, clutching a bloody handkerchief to his left hand. He was cursing in Italian. Pizza-faced Donato had come up to see what was occurring, and Jay was standing over Vittore, saying they'd better get him to the hospital, get that cleaned up.

'What's going on?' she asked. 'What happened to your hand?'

'Fucker Miller put the paper knife through it,' said Vittore, grimacing with pain.

Bianca's mouth was working but no sound was coming out. She looked at the newspaper on the desk, the paper knife, the smear of blood there. Then she thought, *Tony was up here.*

'I saw two men go through the bar. Jay came down the stairs with them. I think I know one of them, Tony Mobley . . .'

'You're mistaken,' said Vittore through clenched teeth. He staggered to his feet, cradling his injured hand. 'Kit Miller was here with one of his crew.'

Bianca frowned. This was bad news. Tony could be one of Kit Miller's mob. This was terrible news.

'That big blond guy, that's Kit Miller?' she asked.

Jay was staring at her. 'No. Miller's the dark one.' He shifted his attention back to his boss. 'Come on, let's get you sorted out,' he said.

They pushed past Bianca. She stood there in the office after they'd gone, frozen and filled with horror and not wanting to believe it as the truth hit her like a runaway truck.

Miller's the dark one.

But she'd seen *Tony Mobley*. She hadn't been mistaken. That was him.

Only it wasn't him. He must have lied to her, given her a false name. Because he was Kit Miller. Her family's arch enemy.

He was the one who had turned up at Tito's funeral, after she'd gone home, and laughed at her beloved brother's death. A lot of people were saying he was the one who killed Tito in the first place.

Bianca felt the strength go out of her legs. She slumped forward, supporting herself against the desk. The world was spinning and her head hummed with the shock of it. She couldn't begin to believe it, but . . . if Tony *was* Kit Miller, had he targeted her deliberately? Had this all been part of his feud with her family, that he would screw the sister, maybe laugh about it among his friends, tell them he had *fucked* Bianca Danieri, fed her all sorts of bullshit, given her a false name, fooled her completely?

Because if Tony *was* Kit Miller, that's what he'd done.

Bianca's stomach turned over at the thought.

He'd done the very worst thing he could – made her fall in love with him. Made her believe his poisonous lies.

It was a nightmare, but it was true.

The man she had fallen in love with was Kit Miller.

Tony Mobley didn't even *exist*.

56

Lady Albermarle kept a house in Palace Court, Kensington, a big red-bricked monolith with huge bay windows and airy endless rooms, and she stayed there whenever she came up to town, which was often. When Ruby called in to see her old friend, Vi's elderly husband Anthony was in Oxfordshire tending the ancestral family acreage, as usual.

'Darling!' Vi greeted Ruby, air-kissing her on both cheeks.

'Hello, Vi,' said Ruby, struck by the fact that in all the years she'd known her, Violet had somehow managed to remain unchanged.

There was something eternally attractive about Vi, something so effortlessly chic that Ruby thought it was no wonder Vi's younger sister Betsy had resented her just about forever. But then Vi had always been the cleverer of the two. While she had deliberately wooed and then married old money, her younger sister had married less well, opting for Ruby's brother Joe. While Vi rubbed shoulders with aristocrats and celebrities, poor Betsy seemed forever doomed to chase after respectability and status like an amateur collector snatching uselessly after rare butterflies.

'You look wonderful,' said Ruby truthfully.

Vi did. She still, at fifty-eight years old, sported the same dark red bob she had worn all her life; she was slim, tall, the same striking forthright girl she had been in the days when she stomped the boards and posed naked at the Windmill Theatre with Ruby, way back in her youth. Her green eyes were vibrant, her lips were painted carmine red, and she moved around in flowing drifts of Missoni fabric and wafts of her signature scent, Devon Violets.

'Come in, sweetheart, it's so lovely to see you,' said Vi, ushering her into the drawing room and seating her upon a Louis Quinze chair before taking the seat opposite.

'Would you like tea?'

'No, nothing for me.' Ruby looked at Vi. This was her best, her oldest friend. They had grown up together, coming through the war, forging very separate paths in life. Ruby had transformed a small corner shop into a nationwide chain of department stores; Vi had snagged a viscount.

'How's Daisy? And those adorable twins? Is Daisy still looking to follow in her mother's footsteps?'

Ruby gave a rueful smile. 'She tried working at the store, but truly, I think she hated it.'

'I'm surprised *you're* not at work though, beavering away as always. You live for that business.'

Ruby smiled painfully. If Michael's death had taught her anything, it was that life is short. She needed cheering up, snapping out her low mood, and Vi – lovely Vi – was the one to do it. 'I just wanted to see you. So here I am, on a workday – and what's more I don't care.'

'Is everything OK?' Vi's brow wrinkled in concern.

Before Ruby could answer there was a quiet knock at the door. It opened slightly and a young man with bright blond hair and a stunningly attractive face put his head around it. He saw Ruby there and smiled: 'Sorry to interrupt, darling,' he said to Vi. 'What time did you say for dinner tonight?'

'Nine, sweetheart,' said Vi. 'You know I never eat before nine.'

The young man nodded and closed the door.

There was a moment's silence, in which the two women smiled at each other.

'He's very good looking,' said Ruby. 'And *very* young.'

'Isn't he.' Vi gave a satisfied smile. 'Now, what was I saying . . . ?'

'You were asking if everything was OK.' Ruby's face clouded. 'And it's not, I'm afraid. There was something . . . something awful . . .'

'What's happened? Has someone been hurt?'

Ruby nodded. 'Simon – Daisy's ex-husband. Oh, Vi, it's horrible. He committed suicide. Hung himself.'

'Oh God, how awful.' Vi looked aghast. 'Rubes, I'm so sorry.'

'It's the funeral on Friday. I'm dreading it, I really am. The worst of it is, Kit says Simon's death wasn't suicide at all, it was some sort of reprisal.'

'Reprisal for what?' asked Vi.

Ruby waved her hand tiredly. She had probably already said too much. 'Let's just say things have been pretty tough since Michael died.'

'And Kit? Are you and he getting on any better?'

Ruby's eyes were brimming with tears. She shook her head.

'Not good,' she said, and it all poured out then: that Kit had been drinking heavily, losing it; that he believed the Danieri family had been behind Michael Ward's death, even though Bella Danieri swore this wasn't true.

'What, she *genuinely* doesn't think her boys were respon-sible for Michael being shot? But, Rubes, it must be them,' said Vi with an incredulous little laugh. 'Of *course* it was them.'

'She says not. And I believe her. Kit is determined to find out who did it. He loved Michael so much, it nearly broke him when he died.'

'I was so sorry about Michael,' said Vi. 'I thought you were settled, you and him.'

'What about you, Vi? Are *you* settled?' Ruby indicated the door the delicious young man had appeared at.

'What, with dear old Anthony? Yes, I suppose so. Although I do have my diversions, as you know.'

Ruby knew. A procession of very young handsome 'walkers' attended Vi whenever she was in town. Ruby had met them. They were all beautiful, polished and charming; lovely diversions indeed.

'And you? There's no one else yet?' asked Vi, her eyes resting on Ruby's face.

'No. Of course not. Only . . .' Ruby hesitated.

'Only what?'

Ruby frowned. 'Someone's been in touch with me, a couple of times. He sent me flowers, asked me to call him, asked if he could call on me . . .'

Vi's eyes lit up with interest. 'Really? Who is he? Have you seen him?'

'We've both seen him. He was at Michael's funeral.'

'Is he part of that world then? Michael's world?'

Ruby looked at Vi. She knew exactly what Vi meant. Did this man, like Michael, inhabit that shady grey area that hovered between respectable business and the dodgy deals done on the London streets?

'Yes, I suppose he is.'

'What's his name? What does he look like? You say we both saw him?'

'He looks like . . .' Ruby paused, searching for the words . . .'He looks like a thug.'

'Oh, come on, Rubes, I need more than that. Is he handsome?' Vi was nearly hopping on her seat with excitement now.

Ruby thought about what she had so far seen of Thomas

Knox. She *had* noticed him at the funeral, watching her with hard blue eyes. The straight dark-blond hair, the firm mouth, the air of a lion walking through a jungle, knowing he was king of the beasts. He had nodded to her, she had nodded back. They hadn't exchanged a word. And then had come the flowers, the notes, the letter . . .

'I suppose he is handsome, yes,' she said cautiously. 'In a brutish sort of way.'

'Why don't I remember him? I don't usually miss a pretty face.'

Ruby shrugged. 'He isn't so much *pretty.* More . . . rugged.'

'So what are you planning to do? Will you take him up on his offer and call him?'

Ruby thought of Michael, how desperately she missed him. Thomas Knox was clearly a perilous man to mix with, essentially lawless and without scruple, the sort of person who would always live by his own rules and to hell with whatever society might say.

'I think he's dangerous,' she said.

'Maybe that's what you need: someone exciting.'

This drew a nervous laugh from Ruby. She reckoned she had more than enough excitement in her life for the time being.

'Do you think you'll get in touch with him?' asked Vi.

Ruby thought it over. Well, did she? Since Michael's death she had felt a bleak, aching loneliness that was close to complete despair. She would wake in the night, thinking *I will never love again. That's it for me. He's gone. There's nothing left.*

'No,' she said, finally.

But when she got home later that same day, she found that Knox had sent her another letter, assuring her of his best wishes and asking once again if they could meet.

57

1953

Tito was taking a keen interest in the foreign family. They were Swedish, Finnish, something like that. Gabe didn't give a shit. Gabe and Tito stood near the woman when she was at the checkout with her little girl; her English was faltering, barely enough to conduct the exchange of money for goods. But she smiled a lot, and kept up a steady stream of conversation with the little girl, saying 'Agneta' often.

That was the little girl's name, then: Agneta.

The child looked up at Gabe and Tito, and smiled shyly. Tito smiled back. Gabe didn't bother. He'd never felt less like smiling. He was sick and tired of all this wandering about the countryside, he hated it now. All he wanted was to go home. He thought of leaving Tito to it, but he couldn't do that; Tito would take offence, and Gabe had realized that you didn't ever, ever, want to offend Tito if you valued your life. Besides, he had no money for trains. However this situation developed, he was stuck with it.

They returned to their tent, but Tito's eyes were on the blonde woman and little Agneta as they walked to the far side of the site and a beige camper van parked there; a tall young man with white-blonde hair greeted them, took the shopping from the woman, swept little Agneta up into his arms. They could hear her tinkling laughter from where they stood.

Gabe was confused now as well as bored. Tito's entire attention seemed to be focused on the family, and this puzzled him. For two days Tito did little but squat at the mouth of their tent and watch the comings and goings of the two attractive adults and their daughter. Then, when the family folded the awning on their camper van and loaded their belongings, Tito hurriedly began packing, telling Gabe to get a move on, they were leaving.

'What is it with those two? How come you're watching them?' asked Gabe as he loaded up the Jeep.

Tito didn't deign to give him an answer.

Now Gabe was starting to feel apprehensive. He didn't know what Tito was playing at, but he didn't like the feel of this, not at all.

They followed the little family at a discreet distance as they left the camp site. The man – Lars, they had heard the woman call him on several occasions – drove fast, and Tito sped along to keep up. Eventually Lars pulled into the car park of a pub that offered bed and breakfast. Tito drove on past, parked the Jeep up at the side of the road.

'Come on,' he said, and hopped out.

Gabe followed him reluctantly into the pub, and they ordered beer and sandwiches. The couple were nowhere in sight. Tito beckoned Gabe to follow him, then they wandered over to the table where the visitor's book was laid out for B&B patrons.

Lars-Birger Blomdahl was written there, and today's date. The family were upstairs, being shown to their room.

Tito returned to the bar, apparently satisfied. Gabe trailed him to a table in the bar and soon their sandwiches came. Gabe found he couldn't eat. He felt apprehension gnawing at his guts. Something horrible was going on here. Something frightening.

58

Even as Ruby sat down for drinks in the American Bar at the Savoy with Thomas Knox, she was thinking *I shouldn't be here*. When she had talked to Vi, she had been sure that she wasn't going to get involved. Then had come the second letter. Uncertain, she had slept on her decision, and what she now thought was this: Knox could perhaps be useful to her and more specifically he could be useful to Kit. According to Rob, Knox's hard men and Kit's had always shown respect for each other, the two firms working side-by-side without any trouble. And if she could get Knox further onside then that could only be a good thing.

She could see that Kit was really up against it, struggling to come to terms with Michael's death and running the business, let alone facing the Danieri threat. And now there was this Gabe character to contend with, fresh out of prison and with a history of violence. Even if Kit could cope with him, she had been appalled to learn that Gabe had waylaid Daisy.

'Does he think he has a claim on Michael's estate?' she'd asked Kit when he filled in the blanks for her, telling her about his visit to Joe's.

Kit told her what Joe had said, trying to calm her fears by adding that he was going to track the guy down and sort him out.

But that would only mean more trouble, at a time when they had troubles enough. Ruby hated all this. Running the business, her stores – that she could cope with; that was sanity. But for as long as she could remember, there had also been that other element in her life, edging around her like a black fog, seeping into her peace of mind. The shady London underworld had always been there – first with her brothers, Charlie and Joe, then with Michael, and now with Kit. That world frightened her; she had never sought it but she seemed unable to escape it. The most she could hope for was to hold it at bay.

She almost wished she hadn't agreed to meet Knox. From a distance, what she had planned seemed manageable; but now, seeing him close-up, talking to him, she doubted her own ability to control this situation.

'What?' he asked, catching her staring at him.

'Nothing.' Ruby quickly looked away, sipped her wine. The bar was busy, the low background hum of conversation and clinking glasses soothing her jangling nerves. She was struck by the beauty of the place; she had never visited before and she was captivated by its Art Deco splendour, by its gold walls, floral gold-and-black seating and low black lacquered tables.

'Ruby.'

Ruby turned her eyes back to his.

'Relax, will you? I don't bite.'

She thought he probably *would* bite, if the occasion called for it. His vivid blue eyes were very fierce in a tanned face that was not much given to smiling. Despite his neat appearance, his cleverly tailored grey suit, the crisp white shirt and striped tie, despite the brushed straight blond hair and the sweet whiff of expensive sandalwood aftershave, she felt an aura of brutal power seeping out of Thomas Knox's pores, like mist coming off a mountain.

'You like it here?' he asked her.

'It's beautiful.'

'Some very famous people have used this for a watering hole. Monet. Katherine Hepburn. Sinatra . . .'

'Really.'

'Yeah, really. You know, I knew Michael – Mike – ever since school. I was gutted over what happened to him,' he said, his eyes holding hers.

Ruby swallowed hard. 'So was I.'

'It must have been a shock for you.'

'It was.'

'But life goes on.'

Ruby looked up at him challengingly. 'Does it?'

'Yeah, Ruby. It does.'

'Even if you don't want it to?' she asked.

He almost smiled. 'Even then.'

Ruby sat back and sipped her wine.

'How's your boy coping?'

'Kit?' *Now I should lie,* thought Ruby. *Now I should tell him that everything's fine, that Kit's coping magnificently.* 'Not well,' she said instead.

'Oh? How's that?' He eyed her curiously.

'He drank a lot after Michael's death,' she admitted.

'I heard he'd upset the Danieri boys. That's not a good idea.'

'A misunderstanding,' said Ruby.

He was staring at her, gauging her reactions. 'I heard he could have done the hit on Tito. That the two of them fell out over a woman.'

Ruby's face was blank. 'I didn't hear that.'

'You didn't? That's odd. Everyone else did.'

'He's very vulnerable at the moment,' said Ruby, choosing her words carefully.

'You can say that again.'

'You and Michael were closely associated, I hear,' said Ruby, her eyes holding his. 'I'm hoping you will continue that association, that level of cooperation, with Kit.'

Thomas sat back and there was that smile again, very brief. 'So that's it. You're rallying the troops. In case he hits trouble.'

Ruby nodded. 'He's going to hit trouble. I can see that. The more people he has behind him, the better.'

'He's a sound man, they tell me. And I know Mike valued him very highly. You must be proud.'

'Do you have children, Mr Knox?'

He shook his head.

'Then you've no idea what it's like. The fear for them – it never leaves you.'

He was silent for a moment. Then he said: 'All right. I'll keep an eye out for your boy.'

Ruby heaved a sigh of pure relief. 'Thank you,' she said.

'But what do I get out of this deal?' he asked.

'What?'

'You get my boys and me helping out if we can, that's fine.'

'Could you find Gabe Ward?' said Ruby suddenly.

'That toerag son of Mike's? I heard he was in stir.'

'He's out. And it looks like he's gunning for Kit. Kit's been trying to trace him to an address, but so far no luck.' Ruby took a breath. 'He stopped my daughter when she was leaving the store the other night. It frightened her badly. I'm not happy about that.'

'I'll see what I can do,' said Thomas. 'But, Ruby, a deal's a two-way thing.'

'What deal did you have in mind?' she asked.

The fierce eyes bored into hers. 'You and me.'

Ruby stared back at him, unblinking. 'You don't even

know me,' she said, feeling her mouth turn dry, feeling her heart start to pound hard and fast.

'I've been watching you for a long, long time,' he said in reply.

That was disconcerting. He'd been watching her – where? When she was with Michael? Watching her, *coveting* her, like she was a Ming vase or something? She'd seen the way he'd stared at her at the funeral. She had felt his eyes on her that day, several times. The remembrance made her uncomfortable.

'I'm not for sale, Mr Knox,' she said.

'Who said anything about that? We're doing a deal here.'

This was what she'd been afraid of. Dip a toe into the waters these sharks inhabited, and pretty soon you were up to your neck and wondering how the hell *that* happened. She'd brushed up against all this before. Did she really want to do it again?

'I'm afraid the sort of deal you have in mind is totally out of the question,' she said coldly.

He sat back in his chair, studying her.

'And if I find Gabe?' he asked.

Ruby swallowed hard. 'Then I'll be very grateful,' she said.

'*How* grateful?'

Damn, what am I getting myself into here? she wondered. She was going to have to handle this very, very carefully. She had underestimated the ruthlessness of Thomas Knox, but if she handled the situation the way she handled any other business negotiation, then perhaps she could come through unscathed. And she was doing this for Kit, she reminded herself. It was worth stepping onto the edge, taking a risk, to do that – even if he didn't appreciate it, even if he went on hating her. Even if that never changed, she still wanted to help him. He was her son.

Ruby drained her drink and stood up. She looked down at Knox.

'Why don't you find him first?' she said. '*Then* we'll talk about gratitude.'

'I've seen him,' said Ruby.

'Who?' said Vi at the other end of the phone. She wasn't at her London place, but back at the ancestral pile in Oxfordshire. Aged Anthony, her husband, spent most of his time there; he had no interest in city life, whereas Vi was a good-time girl right down to her expensive Italian shoes.

'*Him*. Thomas Knox.'

'Oh! Tell me more,' prompted Vi.

Ruby had not long returned from her meeting with Knox. Unable to settle, she'd given up any idea of going to bed and instead phoned Vi. Now, what to say?

'He's . . . scary,' she said finally.

'Who is that?' demanded a querulous male voice – Anthony's, she thought – in the background.

'It's Ruby. You remember?' said Vi.

'Oh.'

'Memory like a sieve, poor old darling,' said Vi into the phone. 'Probably hasn't a clue who you are. But never mind that, tell me more about this Knox person.'

'He's got this aura about him,' said Ruby.

'Like what?'

Ruby remembered those hard blue eyes staring into hers. 'Like . . . power, I suppose.'

'And he wants to get closer to you. How *thrilling*.' Vi sighed. 'Lucky girl.'

'But I'm not sure I want to get closer to him,' said Ruby. 'On the other hand, he's saying that he'll look out for Kit, so . . . maybe I should play him along a little.'

'That sounds risky. Kit's all right, isn't he?'

'I wish I knew the answer to that. He's into such dangerous things these days, plus he's obsessed with finding out who killed Michael. I'm frightened he might churn up something beyond his control.'

'He ought to just let it go.'

'I've told him.'

'What difference would knowing make? Michael will still be dead.'

'I've told him that, too.' *But he'd never, ever listen to me.*

'He'll drive himself crazy with this,' said Vi.

'Hm.'

'So – are you planning to see this fabulous man again?' asked Vi.

'I don't know,' said Ruby. 'I want to help Kit . . .'

'But it might cost you,' finished Vi.

'And how is life in Oxfordshire?' asked Ruby, desperate to change the subject.

'Too dull for words. Anthony took me out on the boat. We went fishing on the lake yesterday, he was trying to catch carp and I was catching a cold. I now know more about boilies than I ever wished to.'

'Boilies?'

'Ground bait, darling. Apparently the carp love them. I thought I might *expire* with boredom.'

After Ruby said goodnight to Vi and put the phone down, she sat there wondering what she was getting herself into. To keep Kit protected, she might have to go against her better judgement and see Thomas Knox again. To keep Kit protected, she'd do it. For that, she'd do *anything*.

59

Bianca had been doing some research. She felt calm, *dead* calm, now that she had absorbed the awful shock of what Kit Miller had done to her. How he must have laughed at her! She was only surprised that he hadn't yet grabbed the opportunity to mock Vittore with it, the fact that he'd deceived and screwed the fearsome Vittore Danieri's sister.

After the first realization of how she had been duped, a cold sanity had descended on her and she looked into Kit Miller – aka Tony Mobley – with a ruthless eye. She knew where his haunts were, soon she knew where he lived, where he drank, what he did with his time. She studied him as if he were an insect under a microscope. And when she finally turned up at Sheila's restaurant one lunchtime and he was standing at the bar, her expression of surprise and dismay was a work of art.

'Oh!' she said, as if amazed to see him. He wasn't the only one who could lie convincingly.

'Jesus – Bianca!' said Kit. He was struck anew by how beautiful she was, he was so damned pleased to see her and amazed that she'd come in here. 'Hi,' he said, and moved in for a kiss.

Bianca stopped him with a hand on his chest. 'You didn't call,' she said.

'Yes I did. You'd left for London, Cora said. She wouldn't give me your number.'

He was looking around now, and Bianca could almost read his mind. Someone might come up and call him Kit. He took her arm.

'Let's go outside, I want to talk to you.'

Bianca let him lead her out onto the pavement.

Kit couldn't stop staring at her. She looked fucking *beautiful*.

'I want to talk to you, too,' said Bianca. 'I saw you in Vito's the other night.'

'You what? I didn't see you. What were you doing there?'

'My family owns that club. And Fellows, and Goldie's too.'

He'd been so delighted to see her, and it would all be OK, he would explain the deception over the name, it was nothing, he would apologize . . . but now what was she saying? Kit felt a chill sink from his brain into his gut. It settled there, spreading out cold tentacles. She was saying . . .

'I'm Bianca Danieri.'

Kit could feel his mouth opening, but for several seconds no sound came out. Then he managed to speak. 'Wait, I . . .'

'I'm Bianca Danieri,' she repeated, her turquoise eyes ice-cold as they looked into his. 'And you . . . you're not Tony Mobley. You're Kit Miller.'

Shit, shit, shit, thought Kit.

'But you're . . . fuck it, you're not Italian.' His throat suddenly felt parched, raw. This couldn't be happening, this was a disaster. She was a Danieri. And she knew he'd lied to her, she knew who he was, what he was.

'I was adopted,' said Bianca. 'I've got three older brothers . . .' She hesitated, and tears sprang into her eyes.

'No, two. Vittore and Fabio. We lost Tito.' Her eyes held Kit's. 'Someone killed him.'

There were people pushing past them on the pavement. Kit drew Bianca to one side, and she flinched when he touched her.

'We have to talk about this,' he said.

'What? About the fact that you cheated me, lied to me, and that you might be the one who took my brother from me?'

'I can explain.'

'No you can't.'

'I can.' Kit pulled her into his arms. She resisted for a moment, then let him kiss her.

What Kit knew he should do now was leave Bianca the *fuck* alone, not pursue this, not rub the salt even deeper into the wounds. The decent thing at this stage would be to walk away.

But he couldn't walk away from Bianca. Danieri or not, he wanted her.

'Look, my car's over there. Come home with me. Let's talk, properly.'

Bianca thought that she couldn't hate herself more than she hated herself right now. She had the willpower of a louse. Before they were even in the door of Kit's house they were kissing, touching, crawling all over each other, stripping each other's clothes off in their haste to be skin to skin again, no barriers between them. *This* was what she remembered best about him, making love with him, and she wanted it; she wanted to block out the truth, forget it, and for a while she let herself do that, enjoyed the lie, lived it.

As for Kit, he had never felt anything like this before in his entire life; not with Gilda, not with *anyone*. It was beyond cruel that the fates had played this joke on him; that she was Tito's kin, his family.

Later, when they lay together on his bed, he said:

'Let's take off somewhere. Like Bermuda – they got pink sand there, can you believe that? Pink sand and tiger sharks, I heard. How about it?'

Somewhere all this won't follow us, somewhere I can make you forget.

Kit propped himself up on one arm and stared down at her. Jesus, she was beautiful with her silver-blonde hair and her white skin. He loved looking at her. 'I don't mean a holiday. I mean, permanent.'

'What?' She looked at his face. He was serious. And was *she* serious, doing this again? Falling into bed with him, knowing what he was, how he'd lied? 'I can't do that. Mama's still in mourning. I have to stay.'

'Come on. Let's do it.'

'I can't, don't ask me.' She was staring at him, smoothing her hands over his hard muscular chest. Thinking that she hated him, she *should* hate him, and she should feel ashamed, but . . . 'My family . . .'

'They mean a lot to you,' he said.

'I lost Tito. I can't lose them all.'

Kit was quiet for a moment. 'You loved him very much, didn't you, your eldest brother?'

'Very much,' she said. '*So* much.'

'He made a fuss of you, his little sis?'

'He was the only one who did.' Bianca sniffed and blinked back a tear. 'He used to take me shooting, you know. He said if I was going to be a true daughter of the Camorra, I would have to learn. There was a farmer who let us shoot on his fields, keep the rabbits down. Tito was a great shot, and he taught me too.'

'Go on.' This hurt, hearing about her and Tito, but despite himself he was fascinated.

'One day . . . I had a rabbit in my sights; I knew I could kill it, take it home for the pot. "Go on," he said. "Shoot." And I looked at this rabbit. Was it a boy rabbit, with a family waiting at home? Was it a *mother* rabbit, with babies in the burrow, and would those babies starve to death if I killed their mother?'

'So did you shoot it?'

She shook her head. 'I couldn't do it. I let off the shot so that Tito wouldn't realize I'd bottled it – but I pulled to the left and missed.'

Talking about Tito was like tearing at an open wound. Bianca swung her legs over the edge of the bed, started gathering her clothes.

'Hey . . .' said Kit.

'No, don't . . .' She was pulling on her blouse and when he reached for her she shrugged him aside. 'I shouldn't be here. I shouldn't be doing this. This is *wrong*.'

'No it's not. Let's have dinner.' He named a time and a date at a restaurant where neither his crew not Vittore's held sway. Neutral ground.

'I can't,' she said, pulling on her skirt, picking up tights, bra, pants, scuffing on shoes.

'I'll be there,' said Kit.

She didn't answer, just hurried from the bedroom.

Kit lay back, his heart sinking as he heard her go down the stairs. Then the front door slammed shut. He listened to the ticking of the clock beside his bed, the seconds passing, the minutes hurtling ever onward, the hours speeding swiftly by.

She'd loved Tito.

She loved him still.

He was going to lose her.

60

'You know what I heard?' asked Vittore of his younger brother Fabio when the two of them were alone upstairs in Fellows nightclub after closing.

Vittore was counting the night's takings, sorting the twenties and the tens into neat regular piles. His left hand was bandaged.

'No, what?' asked Fabio, relaxed after an evening's drinking. He yawned. He was shattered. Had to get home, get some sleep. Maria was turning out to be *very* demanding. 'What happened to that?' he asked, indicating Vittore's hand.

'That fuck Miller came in here for a meet and then stuck me with my own paper knife,' said Vittore grimly. 'But no matter about that, I'm going to *sort* that. I heard some fucker's been cutting in on the club drug business. And you know that whore bitch I'm married to?' asked Vittore, straightening a pile of pound notes. He flicked a glance up at his brother.

Fabio's face seemed to freeze. It was as if Vittore had read his mind; he'd been thinking of Maria, and now here was Vittore talking about her.

'You know what I heard? You won't believe it.' Vittore was flicking through the ones, counting them. Never missing a beat.

Bile lodged in Fabio's throat. 'Go on,' he said.

Jesus, did he sound as guilty as he felt?

'She's playing away with some bastard.'

Fabio tried to relax his facial muscles, but couldn't. He tried not to blink, not to break eye contact. Tried to look *innocent*. But Jesus – Vittore knew. Not just the drug stuff, but Maria too. He *knew*.

'You're joking,' he managed to get out.

'Hey! Does this face say joking?' asked Vittore.

'Well . . . do you know who . . . ?' He felt hot suddenly, clammy with sweat.

'No,' lied Vittore. He shot a chilling smile at his younger brother. 'But when I find him, you know what? I'm going to cut off his balls with a blunt carving knife. *After* I deal with her, of course.'

Fabio didn't go home that night. When he left Vittore, still counting out the takings, he went straight to a phone box and called Maria.

'H'lo?' She sounded half-asleep, like she was in bed already.

'He knows,' said Fabio.

There was a pause. '*What?*' she asked, suddenly wide awake, her voice full of panic.

'I said he knows. He spoke to me tonight about you, said you're playing away.'

'Does he know it's you?'

'I think he does. No, I'm fucking *sure* of it.' Fabio was still sweating despite the cool night air. This wasn't part of the deal. He had been having fun with Maria, screwing her, loving it, but Vittore finding out was his worst nightmare.

'Then we'll have to go away. Now. Tonight,' she said, her voice shaking.

'*What?*'

'You love me, I love you. We can go, right away. I'll pack . . .'

'Wait! Just a minute. Did I ever say I was going to run away with you? Ever? Once?'

Maria was silent for a long while. Then she said: 'You told me you loved me. You *said* that.'

Fabio let out a gusting breath. 'Shit, Maria, a man says a lot of things when he's in bed with a woman, that don't mean fuck-all.'

'What . . . ?' She sounded breathless with shock.

'Look, when he gets home you play innocent if he mentions it to you. You deny everything, and you *don't* mention my name to him, you hear me?'

'Fabio . . .' She was crying now, sobbing like a child.

'You hear me? You say one word to him, I'll cut your fucking throat myself!' shouted Fabio, and slammed the phone back onto the cradle.

61

Daisy had been dreading this, but here it was at last: the day of Simon's funeral. She stood in the church, Ruby at her side, and shivered. The wind gusted and moaned around the ancient Norman building set in gorgeous rolling Sussex countryside. The sun flitted teasingly from behind deep grey clouds. It was freezing the instant the sun vanished from the skies, then humid when the sun reappeared.

Daisy felt chilled to the bone as she sat beside Ruby near the front of the church, one row behind where Sir Bradley and Lady Collins sat, the pair of them nearly bent double with grief. They both seemed to have aged ten years overnight. Simon had been their only child; his loss must be awful for them.

It was awful for *her*, too. Simon's death and its ghastly aftermath had shaken her belief in everything. Where she was going in life, what she hoped to achieve. It all seemed like nonsense when life could be taken away so easily. She glanced back: there was Rob, sitting beside Kit. Their eyes met, and he nodded, then looked away.

Now they were carrying in the coffin, strewn with multi-coloured bouquets and the cream chrysanthemum wreath with DADDY on it that Daisy had ordered from Matthew and Luke, who were still tucked up in the safe house with Jody. There was a large congregation here to see Simon take his final journey – he'd been popular among work colleagues and friends. Lady Collins' narrow shoulders heaved as she wept. Her husband – who suddenly looked so frail himself – put an arm around her shoulders. Daisy didn't like her ex-in-laws – she never had – but standing here today, she pitied them, and wished there was a way she could ease their pain.

Ruby gave her arm a squeeze as the ceremony began. It was long, longer than Daisy would have expected, given that this was a Protestant ceremony and none of Simon's family had ever been keen churchgoers. As the choir sang 'Abide with Me' her eyes wandered around the packed pews, and she was surprised when they fell upon Vanessa Bray, the woman who had raised her from a baby until Ruby, her birth mother, had made herself known.

In her sixties now, Vanessa was stick-thin, her fine long bones showing off the plain black coat she wore to its best advantage. Daisy nudged Ruby, nodded over to where Vanessa stood on the other side of the aisle. She saw Ruby's eyes widen in surprise, but then of course Vanessa *would* come today. Daisy had still been living at Brayfield in Hampshire, under Vanessa and Cornelius Bray's roof, when she had agreed to marry Simon; he'd been Vanessa's son-in-law.

The ceremony dragged along, eulogy after eulogy being read by workmates, friends, and finally, heartbreakingly, by Sir Bradley himself, who broke down mid-sentence and couldn't go on.

'My son . . .' he said, in the midst of saying how good a worker Simon had been, and on those words he faltered and stopped, and wept, unable to continue. The vicar helped him back to his seat.

Then – at last – it was over.

'Thank God,' muttered Daisy when they were all able

to file outside into the biting wind. The pall-bearers were sliding the coffin back into the hearse to take its last journey, to the crematorium – Lady Collins had insisted they should have a proper church service first.

People were milling about, and in amongst the throng Ruby saw a group of men who looked familiar.

'Oh no,' she said, dry-mouthed.

'What is it?' asked Daisy.

Ruby indicated the men. The moment she saw them, the colour drained out of Daisy's face and she started to shake, reliving the terror she'd felt that day they approached her on the road outside Simon's house. There was no mistaking Vittore and Fabio Danieri, and as before they were flanked by two goons. She recognized the taller one with the big scar on his face.

Kit appeared by her side, his face thunderous. 'You see them?' he asked.

'We've seen them,' said Ruby, laying a hand on Kit's arm. 'Don't do anything stupid.'

'Well what the fuck are they doing here? Are they taking the piss?'

'That's exactly what they're doing,' snapped Ruby. 'Because you took the piss out of them at Tito's funeral. They're returning the compliment. *Don't* rise to it, for God's sake.'

Kit glared at the men, who stared back with clear hostility. The fucking cheek of them, but Ruby was right, this was tit-for-tat. Vittore touched a hand briefly to his brow in sardonic greeting. His other hand was bandaged, Kit saw with satisfaction.

Much as he wanted to march over there and smash Vittore's teeth down his throat, Kit knew he couldn't. The whole game had changed since he'd discovered Bianca's connection to these people. Now he was painfully aware that every strike against them would also be a strike against her. She loved her brothers. Of course she did. So his hands were tied.

Vittore and Fabio turned away as the hearse left, their two heavies following close at their heels.

'Thank God for that,' said Ruby with a shiver as the wind buffeted them. She was amazed Kit hadn't lost it and challenged them, but she was very glad he'd managed not to.

'Reg driving you two home?' asked Rob, his eyes avoiding Daisy's.

'Yes,' said Ruby.

Kit nodded, satisfied, and set off for his own car with Rob in tow. Ruby saw the hurt on Daisy's face but said nothing. She knew how Daisy felt about Rob, but if he didn't want that involvement, what could you do?

At that moment Vanessa emerged from the church, looking frail and very alone, and Daisy turned to Ruby.

'Would you mind . . . ?' she asked, indicating Vanessa.

'Of course not. Why would I? Go and have a word with her,' said Ruby. 'I'll wait in the car.'

The crowds of mourners were thinning out. Ruby went through the lychgate deep in thought. She felt sorry for Vanessa, who had raised Daisy and then lost her when she, Ruby, had come back into her daughter's life. If Daisy wanted to spend time with Vanessa, that was fine by her.

'Ruby?'

'Oh!' Startled from thought, she clutched a hand to her chest.

Thomas Knox was leaning against the old stone wall that surrounded the churchyard. When he saw her coming, he straightened up and approached her. Ruby looked anxiously ahead. Reg was waiting by the car, watching her, making sure she was safe. That reassured her. She *never* felt safe around Thomas Knox.

She hadn't thought she'd be seeing him again anytime soon after their meeting at the Savoy. But here he was. And he still disturbed her, with his expensive suits and his bold blue eyes. He really was very attractive, *startlingly* attractive, and just thinking that, just *feeling* it, made her uncomfortable, as if she was betraying Michael.

'Sorry, did I make you jump?' he asked.

'I didn't expect to see you here.'

He looked around at the departing mourners. 'Sad day, yeah? Your daughter's ex, I believe?'

'Yes. That's right.' He seemed to know every detail of her life. She hated that.

I've been watching you for a long, long time . . .

'I'm sorry to hear it,' he said.

'Thank you.'

Silence fell.

Ruby shifted anxiously. 'Um, was there something you wanted . . . ?'

He gazed into her eyes. Gave that tiny suggestion of a smile.

'I think we both know there's something I want, Ruby. But first things first. I've got you an address for Gabe Ward.'

'What?' Ruby was gobsmacked. Rob and Kit had been trying to locate Michael's son for days, with no success, yet Thomas Knox had managed it overnight.

'Yeah, here you go.' He slipped a piece of paper out of his pocket and handed it to her. Ruby took it.

'Now we need to talk about gratitude,' he said. 'Like you said we would, after I'd come up with that address.'

She hadn't *expected* him to find it. She hadn't anticipated this scenario at all. And now she was feeling panicky. 'Of course I'm grateful you've found it.'

'Remember the deal, Ruby. You and me. *That* was the deal.' She fumbled her bag open, put the paper inside, looking anywhere but at his face.

'I know,' she said.

'But . . . what? You didn't think I'd find the address, right? And if I *did*, you thought I'd be all gentlemanly about it, just let it go.'

That was exactly what she'd thought, or *hoped*, anyway. She ought to have known better. She was swimming among predators here, and she was just part of the food chain, about to be snapped up, swallowed whole.

'I never let go on a deal,' he said when she was silent. 'So – dinner tonight, I think. Don't you? My place. Then we'll discuss how grateful you are.'

'I don't . . .'

'I'll collect you at seven thirty.'

'Have you found *my* address too?' she asked, heart thumping. The flowers and the letters had gone to the store, not to her home.

'I've known your address for years.' And there it was again. That clear message: *I've been watching you for a long, long time.*

Had he been watching her, when she was with Michael, when she and Michael were lovers?

Yes. Of course he had.

'You're a very scary man, Mr Knox,' she said.

Again, that brief hint of a smile. 'As I said – I don't bite.'

I bet you do, she thought as he turned and walked away.

'Who's that?' asked Daisy, coming up to her mother. 'That man you were talking to?'

'Thomas Knox,' said Ruby, still feeling as if her heart was going to seize up. Her hands were trembling. She would hand Gabe Ward's address to Kit, tell him Knox had found it for her, and that he had the man's support too. She had achieved a lot.

But . . .

'He's rather gorgeous,' said Daisy consideringly, gazing after him. 'In a *heavy* sort of way. Don't you think?'

Ruby didn't comment. She thought Daisy had summed it up very well. 'Let's go home,' she said, and took Daisy's arm and steered her to the car, and the safety of Reg.

62

1953

It happened the following morning, and Gabe knew he would never forget it as long as he lived. It was a sunny day, breezy and bright. All wrong for what happened, Gabe always thought afterwards. The couple set out walking, wearing suitable clothes, with a pushchair in which sat the little girl in her pink jacket and white-frilled skirt. They chattered to her constantly, the strong young man and his pretty wife.

They walked, enjoying the morning sunshine, and Tito and Gabe followed quite a distance behind them.

'I don't understand this,' complained Gabe.

Tito was starting to frighten him. He couldn't figure out where this was going, but his guts were churning and he'd slept badly, scrunched up in the back of the Jeep alongside Tito. Tito slept deeply, snoring like a hog, and Gabe had spent long hours awake, staring into the blackness of the country night, wondering what would happen next. Dreading it, really. He wanted to run home, to get out of this situation any way he could.

'You'll grab the woman and the girl,' said Tito as they walked. 'I'll see to him.'

'Tito . . .' Gabe panted. He couldn't catch his breath. Suddenly, he was terrified. He wanted to shout out to the couple walking *ahead, tell them to run. But he couldn't. He was paralysed with fear.*

The road was very quiet, there was no noise, nothing except the wind whispering through the long grass on the verges. A hawk soared overhead, calling its weird desolate cry, and Gabe thought how terrifying that sound must be to the small, hunted creatures it stalked. There was no traffic. There was nothing. And now they were drawing closer to the couple and the child in the pushchair. Tito broke into a run, swinging some small thing out of his coat pocket. Gasping, his heart pounding crazily, Gabe followed.

63

After the funeral Kit and Rob went to the office behind Sheila's restaurant. Kit sat down behind the desk, the same desk where Michael had sat, opening the post and doling out work for the boys with Rob standing patiently at his side. Business as usual.

'Fats, you get over to Chiswick, chase up that dickhead Robbo, it's getting close to two thousand with the interest, I want that paid, OK? Either it's cash now or you take it out of his cheating arse,' said Kit.

Fats nodded. He was tall and skeleton-thin but strong as a whip. Everyone called him Fats; it was a standing joke. He ate like a horse, never gained a single pound.

'Who's on the milk round this week, Rob?' asked Kit. The milk round was collecting all the protection money that was paid into Kit's pocket from the shops, arcades, massage parlours, clubs and restaurants on his manor.

'Paulie,' said Rob, busy cleaning his fingernails with a flick knife.

'He's doing well with that. No problems?'

Rob shook his head. Paulie was built like a brick shit-house, no one ever gave him problems. Or if they did, they soon wished they hadn't bothered.

'Kit, the Bartons have asked me if you would show your face down there,' said Ashok. He was a handsome black-bearded Indian youngster, full of attitude and sharp as a tack. He reminded Kit of himself, at that age. Ashok's father and grandfather had served in the Indian army, and his own bearing was very upright, almost military.

'What's the problem?' asked Kit. The Barton family had run their restaurant for years, it was a decent establishment, and he was paid to keep trouble from their door.

'Some rough elements been showing up. Two big lads and their girls, taking the piss, making a nuisance of themselves, saying the food's shit and trying to get it for free. Fridays, Saturdays, they turn up. The Bartons will stand you a good meal, of course: whatever you want.'

'Sort out a date, OK?' Kit looked around at the assembled men. 'Anything else?'

They all shook their heads.

'All right,' said Kit. 'Off you go then.'

The boys departed. Rob shut the door after them, then took a seat across the desk from Kit, continuing with his manicure while Kit perused the post. There was the usual wad of bills, plus a large packet from the accountant's office, all the year's paperwork bundled up and returned. He tipped the stuff out on the desk and then had a sudden thought.

'Hey,' he said to Rob.

'Hm?' Rob paused, looked up from his nails.

'Phone bills, right? People Michael phoned on or near the date of his death. Might help us.'

Rob narrowed his eyes. 'You got 'em there?'

'I got *everything* here.' Everything legit, anyway. He sifted through the papers and there they were, quarterly bills for the office phone, all crossed through with Michael's looping hand, *Paid* and the cheque number and the date. The flat phone bills were here, too: but no calls had been made from that phone, except to Ruby's number.

Kit stuffed the rest of the papers back into the bag and

pored over the phone bills. Each call was itemized. He studied the dates. Michael had been killed in November last year. There was a list of numbers here, and the length of each call, and the charge made for it. He found the fortnight before the date of Michael's death, started looking through the numbers he'd dialled from this office.

'Take a look at these. You know any of them?'

Rob came round the desk and looked at the numbers. 'That's Joe Darke's, right there. He called Michael, that's what he said, and Michael phoned him back. There it is.'

Kit nodded. 'That's Ruby's work line. And her home line too.'

'That's Fats's place.'

'That's the line out to the flat over the garage at Ruby's house?'

'That's the one.' Rob knew the number well; for some time, he'd stayed in the flat Reg was currently occupying.

'That's the meat market, we deal with them all the time.'

'And the brewery.'

'And Billingsgate, for the fish.'

'That one?' Kit pointed.

'Dunno. Maybe it's in Michael's book.'

Kit pulled the address book out of the drawer. 'Leave me with this, I'll have a look through,' he said, and Rob left the room.

Kit searched the address book from front to back. Lots of phone numbers in there; but not this one. Probably it didn't matter, just some random thing. He picked up the phone and dialled a different number.

'Miss Darke's office,' said Joan, Ruby's PA.

'Joan, it's Kit, can I have a word with Ruby?'

'Hi, Kit, putting you through.'

There was a pause, then Ruby picked up, sounding anxious. 'Kit? Are you all right?'

'I'm fine. I have a phone number here, one that Michael called the day before his death. I was wondering if you knew whose it is.'

'Oh. Let me get a pen.' She was shuffling papers. 'Go on then.'

Kit gave her the number. Ruby was silent.

'You know it?' he asked.

'No. I don't. Look, let me check it out, I'll call you right back.'

'I'm at the office behind Sheila's,' he said and put the phone down. It might be nothing, nothing at all, but he wanted everything accounted for. He wanted to know what had been going on with Michael in the days before he died. And then, maybe, it would all start to make some sort of sense.

Minutes passed. The phone rang, and he snatched it up on the first ring.

'Ruby?'

'Yes, it's me. No, I don't have that number. But I forgot to tell you: I've got an address for Gabe Ward.'

Kit sat back in his chair. 'How the hell did you manage that?'

'Through an associate of Michael's – Thomas Knox.'

'I know him.'

'We've kept in touch.'

Kit was surprised. He thought Ruby was straight, right down the line. Granted, she'd got involved with Michael, but he didn't think for one minute that she bought into the life he'd been involved in. She'd loved the man, that much was obvious; but she'd chosen to ignore what he truly was.

'Give me the address then,' he said, and wrote it down as she reeled it off.

'Kit, take care,' she said.

He put the phone down.

Thought for a moment.

Then he dialled the mystery number and found himself talking to Lady Vanessa Bray, the widow of his own late father, Cornelius.

64

Ruby had been surprised by Thomas Knox's house. She had pictured him in smoky pool halls, dingy little offices, back alleys. She pictured him roughing people up, doing under-the-table deals. She hadn't pictured him living in a stately Georgian place in Hampstead, with comfortable, tasteful interior décor and a housekeeper who took care of the cooking, and took care of it very well, too.

They'd eaten dinner. A very nice dinner: tender lamb and croquette potatoes and fresh beans, followed by lemon tart, all washed down with a good red wine.

He was, clearly, a man of surprises.

But the entire time she was eating, Ruby was thinking about what Vi had once laughingly told her about men, when she was still young and naïve.

First they feed you, then they fuck you.

Which was true enough, Ruby had long since discovered. Now she found herself remembering Knox's words to her at Simon's funeral: *We'll discuss how grateful you are.*

She didn't doubt that he was going to exact some return for his trouble, and she wondered how she felt about that. The truth was – and she wasn't proud of this – he intrigued her. Not too many months since Michael's death, and here she was being wined and dined by another man. She didn't like the thought of it. But . . . he was hellishly attractive.

Too attractive. Those cold, cold blue eyes . . . she sensed that if she stared into them too long, she'd drown in them. Completely lose it. She was a full-grown woman, she was Ruby Darke the Ice Queen of Retail, she wasn't used to feeling this way, and it annoyed her.

Now they were sitting on a big buff-coloured sofa, the lights were dimmed, there was music playing. 'The Look of Love', Dusty Springfield. A classic. Yet the ambient lighting, the soft suggestive music, only added to her annoyance. She was annoyed at herself, at the way he was making her feel.

It's called desire, whispered a treacherous voice in her head. *You remember that, don't you?*

'You know what I think?' she said.

'No,' said Thomas Knox, loosening his tie, leaning back, staring at her. 'What do you think?'

She was no fool, and it was time he was made aware of that fact. 'I think you already had Gabe's address,' she said. 'That was much too fast.'

He shrugged. 'Maybe I did.'

'*Did* you?'

A hint of a smile. 'That would be telling, wouldn't it?'

'For God's sake,' said Ruby, shaking her head.

'What?'

'You're so . . . so . . .'

'So what?'

'Mysterious.'

He raised his eyebrows at her, took a sip of wine.

'There's nothing mysterious about me, Ruby. I fulfilled my part of the deal, that's all. And I think it's past time you fulfilled yours.'

Ruby's eyes narrowed. 'You had that address already. I know it.'

'You don't know. You're guessing.'

'And you're not telling.'

No. I'm not.' He drained his glass, put it aside. 'I did what I said I would do. I got you the address. Now it's your turn.'

Ruby stared at him. 'So what do you want from me?' she asked.

'Oh, come on. We *both* know the answer to that one.'

'Thomas . . .'

'That's nice.'

'What?'

'That's the first time you've said my name.'

'Hm. Well – Thomas – I have Gabe's address now. And I've passed it on to Kit. I've got what I wanted.'

'Not all of it, though.'

'Go on.'

'You also want me to give Kit my backing. Which I am fully prepared to do, of course. For a price.'

'Go on then. Name it.'

Dusty had given way to something else. Sounded like Henry Mancini, a sultry tinkling on the piano, a suggestion of a muted horn. Music intended for seduction.

Those hard blue eyes drilled into hers.

'Oh, I dunno. We'll start with the top, shall we? See how we go from there.'

Ruby stared at him. 'What?' She hadn't a clue what he meant.

'The top you're wearing.' Again that smile, there and then quickly gone. 'Take it off.'

'I'm not a whore, Mr Knox,' said Ruby coldly. 'If you want one, I suggest you look elsewhere.'

'So we're back to "Mr Knox" again,' he noted. 'You weren't so coy in the war though, were you? Posing nude at the Windmill. Bedding that lecherous bastard Cornelius

Bray. Having his illegitimate twins, I believe, who were liquorice allsorts, one half-black – Kit – and the other white – Daisy.'

Ruby's mouth opened in shock.

'Bray only wanted to own up to the white kid though, didn't he,' Thomas went on. 'So him and his childless missus Vanessa brought up Daisy, and poor old dark-skinned Kit was stuffed out of sight – by Charlie your brother, I believe – in a kids' home. Took you a long, long time to find Kit, didn't it? And he still hasn't forgiven you for letting him be taken.'

'Shut up,' said Ruby.

'Then Michael Ward helped you find your boy and you became his lover. You're not exactly a nervous virgin, are you? You're a woman of the world. Tough in business, I've been told. You must be, to have done so well with it. And you have this cool air about you. I like that, it's sort of challenging. Yet there's this hot sensuality in your eyes, and in the way you move. A woman like you, Ruby, needs a lover.'

Ruby stood up. She hated the fact that, despite all her best intentions, she could feel a hard pulse beating deep in the pit of her belly. He had aroused her, talking this way. 'Have you quite finished?' she asked.

'No. I haven't. You know what I'd like?'

'No. I don't.'

'I'd like to see you naked in my bed.'

Ruby gulped, tried to compose herself. She felt flushed suddenly, unstable. Today had been horrible, stressful; she told herself that she was just feeling the after-effects of that, and too much wine.

When she could trust herself to speak she said: 'If I "needed" a lover, Mr Knox – it wouldn't be you.' She snatched up her bag and went to the door.

'So . . .' his words drifted after her . . .'You *don't* want me keeping an eye out for Kit then?'

Ruby stopped. Looked back at him. 'You bastard.'

'Been called worse,' he shrugged.

65

1953

'Here, little bambina, look at this. Chocolate,' said Tito, dandling the three-year-old Agneta on his knee as Gabe drove.

Gabe didn't know how he was driving. He didn't know how he was managing to keep sane. What he had just seen . . .

No. He couldn't think about it. He couldn't.

And the little girl had been there, she'd seen it all. Gabe glanced at the girl. She wasn't crying any more. She seemed very calm – almost dazed, he thought – and her huge turquoise eyes were gazing up at Tito's smiling face. Her hands reached for the chocolate he was offering.

Jesus, look at that, thought Gabe, wondering if he was going to throw up again. He didn't think there was anything left in his stomach to bring up. Then he saw the small smear of blood on Agneta's jacket and felt his guts heave afresh. He stopped the Jeep, pulled in quickly to the side of the road, jumped out and vomited one more time.

Ah Jesus.

Ah God, he couldn't think about it, he couldn't . . .

His stomach heaved and he retched.

'Gabe's not well,' Tito was telling the little girl. 'Poor Gabe, hm? Is that nice, that chocolate?'

Gasping, wiping at his mouth, shivering with the aftermath

of the shock he'd suffered, the awful things that Tito had made him do, Gabe fell back into the driver's seat and looked again at the little girl Tito had snatched.

She'd sat there in silence in the pushchair while they'd done it, got the spades from the Jeep . . . but no. He couldn't think about it. All he could think was that Dad had been right; Tito *really* was *a monster.*

She was eating the chocolate and smiling up at Tito's face. Numb, Gabe thought of that thing he'd heard about baby birds . . . that imprinting thing. The first thing they saw, they attached to, they loved. He looked at the child's face, at the adoring way she was staring up at Tito.

Jesus, was he going to be sick again? Was he going to pass out?

He was shuddering, revolted. His eyes kept darting back, looking at that small bloodstain on the girl's pink jacket . . .

'Come on, bambina, eat up,' said Tito at the smiling child as Gabe drove south, towards London, towards home and sanity.

Ah God just get me there. Please get me there, thought Gabe.

66

'Holy *shit*,' said Rob, as Kit drove the Bentley up to the front entrance of Brayfield House next day.

Kit could understand Rob's astonishment; he remembered the effect the place had had on him, back in the day when he first met Daisy. Built of glowing rose-red brick with cream stone quoins at the corners, the Elizabethan manor was a pink jewel in the morning light, set amidst an expanse of lush green watercress beds and rolling sheep-dotted fields. It had two outer gables and a smaller central one, and a stunningly beautiful clock tower stood off to one side. And this humble abode had been home to the Bray family for four generations.

Kit steered the big car around the turning circle, at the centre of which was a huge circular stone and bronze non-working fountain, covered in algae and verdigris, depicting Neptune arising with rippling muscles and a fish's tail from a sea of starfish and leaping dolphins.

'So Daisy grew up here?' asked Rob as Kit turned off the engine.

'Yep,' said Kit.

'Oh *shit*.' Rob was transfixed.

The pieces were finally falling together: Daisy with her cut-glass accent and her impeccable manners, this place . . . He thanked God that he'd had the sense to pull back from her because, *look* at this. She'd grown up taking this for granted. What could he ever offer a girl like her? He'd been raised on a council estate, part of a big boisterous and not entirely honest family; it had taken him years of hard graft to work his way up to his present position: her mother's minder – a fucking bodyguard and a head breaker. He was *so far* beneath her on the social scale, he was the bottom dregs of society while she was plainly an out-and-out nob.

No, he'd pulled out of all that in the nick of time. What could it ever have brought either of them but trouble?

Kit wasn't noticing the house. Impressive as Brayfield was, his mind was on Michael, and what he could have been doing, phoning Vanessa Bray the day before his death.

When he'd called the number yesterday and she'd picked up, he'd been both surprised and bewildered. Michael and Vanessa surely had nothing in common, nothing to talk about. And when he'd questioned Vanessa about the call, she'd been evasive. His request to come and see her, talk about it, had been firmly rebuffed. But he'd persisted, and finally she'd agreed.

'I can't spare you much time,' she'd said, her accent reminding him of Daisy. The elite tones of the Home Counties, frosty from Vanessa, full of warmth from Daisy.

'That's all right,' he said.

'Ten o'clock tomorrow morning then.'

'I'll be there.'

She put the phone down.

Now here they were. They left the car and went up the front steps and pulled the bell. Way back in the house, the thing chimed and echoed.

Must be big as a fucking football pitch in there, thought Rob.

He half-expected some tailcoated flunkey to come to the door, saying, *I'll see if the mistress is at home to visitors.* Or, *The tradesman's entrance is at the back of the house.*

But no. There was a pause, and then Lady Bray herself opened the door. Small, weak-looking, with long greyhound features. Her hair was blonde, fading to grey, her deep-lidded eyes were a milky blue, and her lips were thin. She wore no make-up, and was dressed in old jeans and a work-man's shirt and black socks, no shoes. There was a hole in one, and her big toe was poking through, Kit noticed.

'Oh! It's you. Well . . . do come in,' she said, seeming flustered that Kit had kept the appointment.

Kit and Rob followed Vanessa down a cavernous hallway and into a room that seemed to burst with vivid sunlight. All done out in faded golds and duck-egg blue, it had big French doors that led out to a terrace and beyond that to a huge garden. The doors were wide open to admit the first faint suggestions of the coming summer. Bees hummed near the doors, and fresh country air wafted in.

'Do sit down,' said Vanessa, and Kit and Rob sat like a pair of bookends on one threadbare and no doubt horrif-ically expensive tapestry-covered sofa. Vanessa sat oppo-site, on a small Victorian nursing chair covered in thinning cream velvet. 'Well now,' she began briskly, 'as I told you on the phone, I know very little about any of this.'

Kit leaned forward, clasping his hands loosely between his knees, mirroring her posture.

'I have no idea why Michael phoned you, Lady Bray,' he said. 'It might help if you can tell us anything about the conversation you had with him.'

'Help what?' she asked. 'The man is dead.'

Kit drew a breath. 'Michael was *murdered*, Lady Bray. And we're trying to find out more about the events surrounding his murder.'

'Surely that's a matter for the authorities, for the police?' she said.

She was stonewalling him. Kit could feel it. Could feel his irritation rising in response, too.

'The police don't seem too interested,' said Rob.

Vanessa turned her head and stared at Rob as if surprised to see him there. 'And why is that?' she asked.

'Michael . . . had a reputation,' said Kit.

'Cornelius always said he was a crook. But then Cornelius liked crooks. He was fascinated by them.'

Rob shot a look at Kit. Coming from Cornelius Bray, who'd strong-armed and shagged his way through the establishment to get himself a seat in the Lords, that was pretty damned rich.

'And when crooks get themselves killed, I don't suppose anyone is too surprised,' said Vanessa.

'Even crooks have people who care for them,' said Kit.

'And did you?'

'What?'

'Did you "care" for Michael Ward?'

'Yes, I did. He was like a father to me. A *real* one.'

'Then I am sincerely sorry for your loss,' said Vanessa.

'Can you tell me what you spoke about?'

'You're looking for revenge,' said Vanessa.

'I want to find out who killed him.'

'And then what?'

'I don't know.'

Vanessa was silent, staring at Kit's face. 'You look very like your mother,' she said. 'You have that same *physical* look about you.'

She sneered the words. But Kit reminded himself that this was the woman whose husband had betrayed her, fathering both him and Daisy on the beauteous Ruby Darke.

Of course that must have hurt weak, barren, *useless* Vanessa. Of course she must be bitter.

'What did you talk about that day?' he asked. 'Please tell me.'

'He phoned to see how I was,' said Vanessa. 'I was quite impressed by that, actually. That he made the effort to enquire.'

'Because you'd lost your husband not too long before?'

'Because of that, yes. It was considerate of him, I thought.'

'And that's all?' asked Rob.

Vanessa turned her hands up. 'What other reason could there possibly be?'

'They're gone then,' said Ivan, Vanessa's gardener, coming to the French doors ten minutes later.

Vanessa smiled at him – small, whip-thin, red-bearded Ivan. He'd been with her for years and she was very fond of him. Fonder, truth be told, than she had ever been of big handsome blond Cornelius, her husband.

'Yes – they're gone.'

'And they believed what you said?'

'They seemed to.'

'Good.' He paused. 'So . . . do you think they'll come back?'

'No. Why should they?'

67

1953

Tito dropped Gabe off at his parents' house, where he still lived.

'You keep this quiet, yes?' said Tito, giving him one last icy glinting glance. 'This is never mentioned, capisce?'

Gabriel nodded. He went indoors, into his father's house, and his mother Sheila was out somewhere, he didn't know where but he was glad because he knew she would see something was wrong the instant she laid eyes on him.

The first thing he did was take a bath. Try to wash the whole horrible episode off. He scrubbed at his skin with a nail brush until it was a vivid, angry pink, scrubbing harder and harder, more and more desperately, but it was no good, still he could see it, could see Tito doing it, and the little girl at first silent – and wasn't there a word for that, wasn't it catatonic? *– and then smiling up at him so trustingly. Finally he sat there in the bath and just cried. He'd always thought of himself as tough, a bit of a handful, but Christ he was nothing compared to Tito. Tito was a fucking psycho.*

Bella would never forget the day when Tito put the little girl in her arms. She was sitting at the kitchen table and he walked in carrying the child, the most beautiful child she had ever seen.

Silver-white hair and huge turquoise eyes. Dressed in a little white frilly skirt, sandals and a pink jacket.

Seven-year-old Fabio, leaning against the table, stared curiously at the little girl.

'Fabby!' said Bella sharply. 'Go out and play now. Go on!'

Sulkily, Fabio did as he was told. The little girl let out a cry, held up her hands to Tito.

'No, bambina, this is your mama, your new mama,' he said, and she looked at Bella. Bella stared back at her, a tremulous smile on her face.

'She's so beautiful,' said Bella in wonder. 'Where did you . . . ?' Then Bella stopped herself. She had instigated this; she had wanted a daughter, and now she had one. A shiver of guilt, of apprehension, shuddered through her, but she squashed it. She was not about to question the good luck that had brought her such fortune.

'What are you going to call her?' asked Tito.

Bella looked at the girl, who was clutching with tiny perfect hands into the front of Bella's dress. 'She's so white. Pale, and all this white hair. So pretty. I'll call her the white one. I'll call her Bianca.'

Now Bella's eyes moved on. She was frowning at the small bloodstain on the pink jacket. She looked up at Tito.

'Ask no questions, Mama,' he said sternly. 'When you've got her some new clothes you burn that, all right? And you'll have to tell Fabby and Vittore that the adoption came through at last.'

'And other people? The neighbours? Our friends?'

Tito shrugged. 'Tell them the same. If anyone pries, I'll sort it. Not that they will.'

Bella nodded dazedly. No one questioned the Danieri family over their way of life or what happened in their household. You didn't ever look too closely at what they did. It would be dangerous.

'Beautiful little Bianca,' said Bella, stroking the child's pale hair.

Tito withdrew. He had to get rid of the Jeep. He'd done his part, and now Mama would be satisfied. The girl whimpered when he left the room, but Mama Bella soothed her.

68

'Well, what other reason could there be for Michael calling her ladyship?' Kit asked Rob when they were in the car and heading down the drive, Brayfield's massive bulk disappearing into the distance behind them.

'Don't tell me you reckon she was telling the truth?' Rob shook his head. 'Can you honestly see Michael arsing around making courtesy calls to some inbred aristo? He hated Cornelius Bray's guts for the way the bastard treated Ruby. And as for "her ladyship", that damned woman took Daisy off Ruby – d'you think for one moment Michael would have much to say to her?'

'Seriously? No.'

Rob was shaking his head as Kit turned into the lane, big froths of cream cow parsley crowding in on either side of them. There was a glimpse of the cress beds as the Bentley shot over the bridge and then they were heading into Brayfield village. Rob thought it was all too quaintly *country*, with its thatched cottages and its stream with ducks lazing on the grassy bank in the sunshine. It looked like something off a chocolate box.

'I can't believe Daisy grew up in that place,' said Rob.

Kit shot Rob a look. Rich people were 'nobs' to Rob, and he mocked them mercilessly, often putting on a cuttingly accurate imitation 'posh' accent. He never did it when he was around Daisy, Kit noticed, but Rob's council-estate upbringing and the staunch lower-class ethics of his parents had clearly left a mark.

Kit wondered whether he should say anything, and then thought what the hell. This was Rob, his oldest pal. And Daisy was his sister, his twin.

'Daisy likes you a lot,' he said.

'I know.'

'I think she thought you liked her too.'

Rob looked at Kit. 'I *do* like her.'

'So . . . ?'

'So what? It's not going anywhere, is it?' He gestured over his shoulder. 'Come on, mate, get real. Look at that fucking place. That's where she came from.'

'No,' said Kit. 'If you're going to be picky about it, she was born in the East End like me, she was illegitimate like me, and Ruby's dad – our granddad Ted – ran a corner shop. *That's* Daisy's real background.'

'Come on. She grew up in a stately home.'

'Daisy's a diamond.'

'I know that. But—'

'You don't think it can go anywhere, you and her,' finished Kit.

'How can it? Look, what am I? I break heads for a living, I used to mind Ruby. That's all I am, that's what I do. Have you any idea what it would be like, trying to introduce Daisy to my family? They'd laugh their heads off at her. *And* at me.'

'OK.'

'You know it's true.'

Kit didn't see that it mattered where Daisy had been brought up or how posh she spoke, but to Rob it was obviously a problem. Which, come to think of it, made Rob the snob – not Daisy, who happily mixed in with anyone. But he could see it was no good pushing Rob into a corner on this.

'I met a girl,' said Kit when the silence deepened as he drove them back towards London.

'Oh?' Rob looked at him with interest.

'Her name's Bianca. She dresses in white. She's got this platinum blonde hair and she's pale-skinned with these big blue eyes and a fantastic body.'

'Right . . .' Rob paused, waiting for Kit to go on. Kit didn't. '*And . . . ?*' Rob prompted him at last.

Kit knew he could tell Rob anything, anything at all, and Rob would listen, sympathize – and then do whatever was necessary to ensure his mate was protected from any comebacks. But *this* . . .

'I met her in Southampton. She runs a club there at the Back of the Walls – Dante's.'

'That's why you took so long coming back?'

'That's right.'

'You keeping in touch then?'

Kit flicked a glance at Rob. *Ah shit*, he thought.

'She was adopted,' he said.

'Right.'

'An Italian immigrant family adopted her after they came to England.'

'OK.'

Kit let out a sharp breath. 'Astorre and Bella Danieri adopted her.'

Rob was silent for long moments. Then he turned his head and stared at Kit. 'You *what*?'

'I had no idea, OK? You know how it is when you're screwing around, having fun? That's how it started. I thought it was a quick fuck and then goodbye. Jump on, smash the life out of it, sorted. I gave her a false name.'

'That's good.'

'Only, as soon as I'd done that, I realized there was something more going on.'

'No . . .' Rob was shaking his head again, and now he raised his shovel-like hands and clutched at his temples and shut his eyes and said: 'Tell me you're not doing this. Tell me you're not even *thinking* of doing this.'

Kit was silent.

'She'll find out who you are. As soon as she connects Kit Miller with *you*, what the fuck's she going to think then? Kit – *you killed Tito.* You killed her brother. This is a bloody disaster, mate.'

'I know that.'

'She don't know yet though? She don't know who you are?'

'She saw us in Vito's the other night. She knows I'm Kit Miller.'

'Jesus.' Rob half-turned in his seat and stared at Kit. 'Listen, you got to stop this. You got to step away from this girl, right now. Or I tell you, Vittore and Fabio will rip your guts out and serve them up fried if they find out that you and her . . . You haven't met up with her again since you've been back, have you? She been up here? You been jumping on her bones again?'

Kit nodded.

'*Shit. Shit. Shit.*' Rob thumped his head against the leather headrest three times. 'Kit, listen to me, for the love of God. This has got to *stop.*'

'I know,' said Kit.

'Good. I'm glad you know.'

Kit sighed. He knew Rob was right. But still . . . he was going to see Bianca tonight, and Rob wouldn't know a damned thing about it. He was sucking the last of the sweetness out of the situation before it all turned sour. Which it would; he knew that. The whole enterprise was doomed. There was no getting away from the fact.

'So. What we doing now?' asked Rob.

'Ruby got an address for this Gabe Ward character.'

'Where'd she get that?'

'An old associate of Michael's, she said.'

'Right.' Rob looked bemused. It wasn't like Ruby, hanging around dodgy types. She'd made an exception for Michael, but then Michael Ward had been an exceptional man. 'So . . . ?'

'I thought we'd pay the little tick a visit,' said Kit.

69

1953

'There's something the matter with Gabe,' Sheila told Michael
a week after Gabe's return.

Michael looked at her. 'What?'

'Your son, Gabe,' said Sheila with a sigh.

These Englishmen, they were so taciturn, so unfeeling. She
was Italian by birth, she'd come over to England before the war.
Her name had been Serafina then, but after her parents died
she had adopted the more English-sounding name, Sheila. And
she had met and married Michael, a well-to-do businessman,
and they had a son.

Sheila was warmer, more intuitive than Michael – she was
Italian, after all – and she loved her son Gabe with a passion.
Oh, Sheila knew he was troubled, she knew that he had been
getting on his father's nerves, pushing the boundaries as young
men liked to do, testing himself, challenging his father's rule.
All of which was perfectly natural. But none of it had gone
down well with Michael.

'What's he up to now?' asked Michael, putting the evening
paper aside. It was all fucking trouble anyway. After the excitement of the Coronation, it was business as usual: doom and
disasters and moans about the state of the economy. There were
earthquakes and tidal waves in the Greek islands, the Ruskies

were accelerating the arms race and the French were threat-
ening a general strike.

Sheila was looking awkward.

'What?' asked Michael, watching her face. 'What is it?'

'I wasn't supposed to tell you,' she said.

'Tell me what?'

'You know he went away for a couple of weeks with a
friend . . . ?'

'Jesus, what's he been up to now?' Michael was fed up with
this. His son was not a son to be proud of. He cheated, he lied,
he was into the most pathetic kinds of petty thievery and ran
around getting girls into trouble, and he ought to know better.
Michael had spent a lot of time over the past four or five years
bailing Gabe out of silly situations, and he was sick of it. The
boy was nineteen now, and Michael was wondering when the
fuck the little idiot was going to grow up.

'I shouldn't tell you . . .' said Sheila.

'Well, you've told me half of it already, you may as well tell
me the rest. What is it?'

Sheila's eyes came back to his face. 'He was with Tito,' she
said quickly, making rapid calm-down motions with her hands.
'Now don't get angry. Gabe's really upset. Whatever Tito was
up to, it wasn't good. It's knocked Gabe for six. But he won't
tell me about it.'

Michael felt his temper flare. He tossed the paper aside. 'For
fuck's sake! I told him to stay away from Tito. Tito's bad news,
I warned him.'

'Please don't lose your temper. The boy's badly shaken, and
he won't tell me what's happened. Perhaps you could talk to
him . . . ?'

I'd rather throttle the little bastard, thought Michael, *but*
he tried to cool down for Sheila's sake. His private opinion was
that Gabe was no good and never would be. But he'd never say
as much to his wife.

'I'll talk to him,' he said.

'And no shouting?'

Michael almost smiled at that. 'No shouting,' he promised.

But that was before he heard the ghastly details about Gabe's road trip with Tito.

70

Gabe Ward's bedsit was out in Bermondsey, not too far from the Rotherhithe Tunnel. It was one of a big skyscraper block of flats near the vast sprawl of the river. The lift was out of order and there was graffiti scrawled all up the piss-stinking stairs. Kit and Rob trudged up to the sixth floor, along the draughty rubbish-strewn walkway, ducking here and there under washing lines and stepping over half-dead pot plants.

'Fucking tip,' commented Rob as they arrived at Gabe's door.

'Yeah,' said Kit. Ward lived in a shit-hole. And it reminded Kit painfully of some of the God-awful dumps he'd stayed in as a child. *Not* happy memories.

Kit looked at the doorbell, which was hanging off, wires still attached. He knocked on the door. It was scratched at the bottom as if an animal had been trying to gain entry. It could have used a coat of paint. In fact the entire block could have been considerably improved if someone were to knock the damned thing down and start again, from scratch.

They could hear a TV going inside the flat. Then there was movement, near the door.

'Who is it?' It was a male voice, quavering with nerves.

'Council maintenance,' Kit replied. It sounded thin, on a Saturday, but what the hell.

The door opened, just a crack. A pair of wide blood-shot eyes in an unshaven face looked out at them. There was a chain on the door. Gabe took one look at Kit and Rob standing there and tried to shut the door again, but Rob was faster; he shouldered it, and the chain popped out of its moorings with a tired crunch.

Gabe fell back and now they could see he had a knife in his hand. Inside, the flat looked no better than the outside. There was a dirty old sofa, a carpet stained from years of use. The smell in here was rank, musty. There was a piece of brownish foil on the coffee table, and a spoon and the sickly scent of burning.

Druggie, thought Kit.

'Don't be silly. You're going to hurt yourself with that,' said Rob, grabbing the hand with the knife in it and smacking Gabe upside the jaw. Gabe went down hard. Rob took the knife off him and tucked it into his belt.

'Who the hell are you?' moaned Gabe, clutching his chin.

'Oh, I think you know the answer to that. And just in case you don't, listen up. I'm Kit Miller,' said Kit, dragging Gabe back to his feet and slamming him hard against the wall beside the TV. He stared into Gabe's eyes. 'You got something you want to say to me?'

'I . . . wha . . . ?' Gabe's mouth was seeping blood where Rob had cuffed him. He looked bewildered, terrified.

'Sorry would be a start. An apology for shoving your ugly mug in my sister's face and trying to get my mother's address off her. That wasn't nice.'

'Wait—'

'You got anything to say, you say it to *me*. I been hearing you're not happy with my situation. That's tough. Understandable but tough.'

'But—'

'Listen, cunt.' Kit shook Gabe. 'Did I ask you to speak?

No. So just listen. Your dad trusted me. We were close. He wanted me to benefit when he wasn't here any longer. That was *his* decision. I didn't force it. I couldn't. You and him, you fell out years ago. Now you come around here, wanting what I've worked for, *slaved* for, poking your *stupid* nose in where it's not wanted, frightening my sister, thinking you're going to be allowed to throw a scare into my mother – you cheeky little prick.'

Gabe was silent now, panting, blood trickling down and dripping onto the front of his shirt. He was shaking like a sick old man.

'You got something to say then?' asked Kit, while Rob stood by, watching.

'*Have* you?' Kit jammed his fist further into Gabe's throat.

'No. No!' Gabe wheezed out. 'Don't, you're . . .'

'Throttling you?' Kit suggested. 'Listen, you turd, come near my family again and I won't play at this like I'm doing now, you got me? I'll finish the fucking job – and you with it.'

Kit stared at Gabe. This had frightened Daisy? All he saw was a pathetic wreck, more to be pitied than anything else. He let Gabe go, and the man sank down onto the grubby floor and stayed there.

Kit pointed a finger at him. 'What do you know about Michael's death, you tosser?' he demanded.

'What . . . ?'

Kit yanked him back to his feet. '*What do you know?*' he yelled in Gabe's face.

'I don't know anything!'

'You got out of stir a week before he died, and you were pissed off because you knew he was leaving everything to me, not you. That the truth?'

'Yeah, but . . .'

'But *what?* Did you meet him in that alley, shoot him when he turned his back? Was that it?'

'You think *I* did that, killed my own father?' Gabe almost laughed.

'You wouldn't be the first.'

'No! Not me.'

'You didn't, uh?' Kit stared hard at Gabe's face. 'I don't trust a word that comes out of your mouth,' he said.

'It's the truth!'

'Don't give me that. You wouldn't know truth if it bit you up the arse,' said Kit, and nodded to Rob. Rob handed him the knife.

'No . . .' said Gabe, eyes crazy with terror.

When Kit raised the knife, Gabe shrieked. Someone next door started banging on the wall, yelling at them to keep it down. Kit stood there, looking at the mess of a man in front of him. Gabe was wearing tattered jeans and a sweat-stinking grey T-shirt; Kit could smell his fear, could see the needle-marks criss-crossing his scrawny arms like blue cheese.

Slowly, he lowered his hand; gave the knife back to Rob. Then he grabbed Gabe's head, brought those madly swivelling eyes to meet his own.

'Here's the deal, so listen carefully, OK?'

Gabe was shuddering and crying.

'*I said OK?*' yelled Kit.

Gabe nodded frantically.

'Good. Real hard nut, ain't you? Now this is it: I hear you been trying to get close to my family, or doing *anything* that I find even a little bit annoying, I am coming for you and I am not going to fuck around nicely like I've done this time. I am going to kill you. Do you understand me?'

Tears, snot and blood mingling on his face, Gabe nodded.

'Say you understand.'

'I understand,' he gulped.

'Not so brave when you're not trying to scare women, are you?' said Kit. He gestured to Rob. 'What I'll do, if I need to call on you again, is I'll let Rob work on you. And then I'll finish you off. You got that?'

'Yeah . . . I got it,' said Gabe.

'First and last warning,' said Kit, and let him go. Then he walked out of the flat with Rob following close behind.

71

Somehow, Ruby found herself thinking more and more about Thomas Knox. She kept asking herself, *Would he be that much of an advantage onside anyway?* But she knew he would. And she had to think of Kit.

Ah yes, but is that really your only concern here? Hmm?

Ruby always tried to be honest with herself. And she was being honest now when she acknowledged that she was very attracted, physically, to Knox. She might dislike his methods, she might mistrust him – and oh, she did, she really did – but there was no denying that, when he looked at her, something happened. Something that hadn't happened since Michael was gunned down.

So, when Thomas Knox came to the store, presented himself at Joan her gatekeeper's door and asked to speak to Miss Darke, she knew she was in for a bumpy ride. That this was going to happen, whether she actively encouraged it or not.

'There's a man out here,' said Joan, coming frowning into her office and pushing the door closed behind her. 'He says his name is Thomas Knox, and that you're expecting him. There's nothing in the diary. You want me to call security?'

Well, she *had* been expecting him, sooner or later. She had known from the start that whatever obstacle she put up between Knox and herself would be swiftly broken down. And right now, she wasn't sure whether that frightened or delighted her. A bit of both, maybe.

'No, that won't be necessary,' said Ruby. 'Show Mr Knox in, will you, Joan?'

And there it was, the instant he came in the room and fixed her with those eyes. That *feeling*. She had thought all feeling was past and done, when Michael died. But no: there it was. She was still alive, still a fully functioning woman, after all. And now she realized how miserable she had been, how low she had sunk since Michael's death. In the brief time she had been coming under the influence of Thomas Knox's powerful aura, that misery had abated.

'You're a hard woman to track down,' he said, taking a seat and looking around her office with interest. There were awards on the walls. Best British Retailer. Businesswoman of the Year. And there were pictures of her shaking hands with royalty and celebs.

'That isn't true,' said Ruby. 'You've been tracking me for some time, Mr Knox. I suspect you know where I am, what I'm doing, every moment of every day.'

'You calling me a liar?' It seemed to amuse him.

'Yes, I am.'

He put a hand to his chest. 'I'm wounded,' he said.

'No, you're not.'

'Yes, I am. Last time we met you called me a bastard and walked out on me.'

'You *are* a bastard.' They were flirting and she was finding it hard not to smile.

'I was just doing a bit of business.'

'And trying to combine it with rather a lot of pleasure, as I recall.'

'Businesswoman of the Year, uh?' His eyes met hers.

'This is where you feel safest, am I right? Here at work. In control of things. You know it's Saturday, Ruby? It's the weekend, and here you are – working.'

'The store's open on a Saturday,' said Ruby.

He eyed her for long moments. 'You know, I look at you, sitting there behind your desk, and I begin to see you more clearly.'

Ruby cocked her head to one side and returned his stare. 'All right, what do you see?' she asked, amused.

'I see . . .' He pursed his lips, his eyes never leaving hers . . . 'I see a woman who hides from the world because the world once hurt her. I see a woman who buries her sexual nature beneath all this work stuff.'

'Really.'

'Yeah, really. That's what I see. Now let me buy you lunch. There's a hotel in Covent Garden, chef there does the best poached salmon I've ever eaten.'

'I usually eat at my desk.'

'Christ, throw me a bone, will you? Come and eat with me.'

'No.'

'Go on.'

Ruby looked at her watch. 'I suppose I can spare an hour . . .'

'Terrific.' He stood up. 'Let's go.'

Three hours later, lunch was over and they had checked into a room in the same hotel. Ruby was feeling a little tipsy from several glasses of Merlot but mostly she felt drugged with lust. The moment they were inside the room, Thomas Knox pulled her into his arms and kissed her very thoroughly. Ruby responded, dragging her hands through his hair, inhaling his scent, her tongue touching his. When they fell apart, they were both panting.

Thomas leaned back against the door and folded his arms over his chest.

'You ready to play ball then?' he asked, his voice husky with desire.

Ruby shrugged, her eyes playing with his.

'Are *you* ready to do what you promised, give Kit your full support?' she asked.

'I already said so.'

'Say it again then.'

'All right. I will.'

'I ought to get back to work.'

'You're such a prick-tease. And the firm won't founder because you're not there for an afternoon, will it.'

'Joan will wonder where I am.'

'Joan will *know* where you are, because while you were getting your stuff together I told her you would be spending the afternoon with me and you probably wouldn't be back in.'

'That was presumptuous of you.'

A flicker of a smile. 'As you said, I'm a bastard. So come on. Let's do this deal. The top. And don't pretend you don't know what I'm saying, not this time.'

Ruby felt suddenly reckless. She took off her jacket. Then, her eyes holding his, she slowly unbuttoned the front of her crisp businesslike white cotton blouse, then the cuffs.

'*And . . . ?*' he encouraged, making winding-up motions with one hand.

Ruby slipped the blouse off her shoulders and let it drop to the floor. She was wearing a lacy white bra, her burgundy skirt that matched the jacket she had already tossed aside, black tights, white pants, high black court shoes.

'Nice,' said Thomas. 'Go on.'

Ruby unhooked the bra, slipped the straps off her shoulders, let that too fall to the floor. His eyes were on her nude full breasts, and she felt her nipples rise and harden in response. Suddenly she felt breathless, flushed, weak.

'Better,' he said. 'Don't stop there.'

Her fingers fumbling, feeling awkward, Ruby reached up under her pencil skirt and yanked down the tights. Stepping out of her high-heeled shoes, hotly aware of him watching every move she made, she tossed the tights aside.

'And the rest,' he said.

Ruby stretched a hand behind her, freed the button on the waistband of her skirt, unzipped it. The silky lining slithered down her legs, and she stepped out of it, feeling smaller, somehow more vulnerable without her day-to-day armour, her work uniform. Her eyes met his. He looked so much bigger than her now that she was out of her heels – so tough and threatening, so invincibly *male*.

'All of it,' he said.

Ruby took a gulping breath and hooked her thumbs into either side of the white lace briefs she wore – her own label, everything she wore was her own label, the suit, the blouse, the bra, everything, and what was she thinking about *that* for at a time like this?

She pulled the briefs down over her long tanned legs and kicked them off. Stood there naked, trying to get her breath, while he was still fully clothed. She felt so aroused, flooding with wetness, ready for him.

Thomas stepped forward, came right up close to her, looming over her. He reached out a hand, cupped one breast, rubbed his thumb almost thoughtfully over her rock-hard nipple.

'Oh God,' groaned Ruby.

'Good?' he murmured, bending to kiss her throat. His teeth nipped hard at her shoulder, and she gasped with shock.

'You said you didn't bite,' she managed to murmur.

'I lied. Get on the bed.'

As if in a dream Ruby turned, feeling him touch her buttocks, smoothing over them, delving, slipping deeper . . .

'Oh . . . oh Jesus . . .' she moaned as he caught her around the waist, nearly snatching her breath away. He held her there against him for long moments, her back pressing into the front of his body so that she could feel how hard he was. Then he let her go.

'Go on. Hurry.'

Ruby went to the bed and lay down. He would take his clothes off now, she *wanted* him to take off his clothes and be naked with her, but he didn't. He got on the bed with her, pushed her back, opening her legs.

'Please . . .' she murmured, and all sense of shame was gone, to be replaced by heat, desire, total readiness. *This* was what he had wanted, all those times he had watched her, and now she wanted it too, she was weak but she was also powerful, enticing him, drawing him into her. 'Thomas, oh, Thomas please . . .'

But he didn't take off his clothes. Still fully dressed, he knelt between her legs and unbuckled his belt, unzipped himself, and plunged into her.

'Oh, you bastard,' shouted Ruby.

Thomas only laughed.

What was supposed to be lunch turned into a long day. Late in the afternoon they went back to Thomas's house, and after eating fruit and cheese in the big barnlike kitchen Thomas gave her the complete grand tour, finishing up in the room that housed a huge swimming pool surrounded by fake Corinthian columns and blue-skied, green-ivied trompe l'oeil. The whole effect was of a fabulous sunlit Roman bath house.

Ruby gazed at it, and laughed. 'For God's sake! A little bit extravagant, wouldn't you say?'

'Extravagant?' Thomas looked at her. 'Nah, I enjoy a swim, it's heated and it came with the house. I thought of changing it, but then I thought, what the hell? I like the idea of living like a king.'

'I can imagine you would,' said Ruby, smiling uncertainly. She didn't *know* this man. And she had fallen shamelessly into bed with him. Somehow, he had seduced her completely. Taken down her guard, smashed it to smithereens. But she still thought he was scary. And unknown. And – oh God – *extremely* sexy.

He started loosening his tie, unbuttoning his shirt. 'Coming for a dip then?' he asked.

Ruby stared at him. 'I don't have a swimsuit.'

'Sweetheart,' he said with a roguish smile, 'you don't need one.'

72

At seven years old, Bianca was forced to face the fact that her family was different to those of many of her school friends. It was brought home to her quite horribly. Bella and Astorre got her a puppy from Battersea Dog's Home. He was a Labrador crossed with some other thing, God knew what, with a flat silky ginger coat and a wide grinning face.

Bianca christened the puppy Joey, and she loved him absolutely and completely, grooming him, feeding him, poor little unloved mite. He'd been just like her, in an orphanage just like Mama Bella had told her, scrawny and unwanted; but now look. He was home. He was safe.

It was true that at first Bianca had thought her adoptive family was the same as any other. They were Italian immigrants, and her father and brothers were out every weekday and most weekends doing business.

When they were in, they muttered around the kitchen table and she heard snatches of their conversations, about money going through the businesses, 'laundering', they called it, and she gathered that there were three stages to this process – placement, layering and finally integration. At seven years old, she didn't know what the words meant, but as she grew, she listened, and she learned.

Tito told her that Daddy Astorre was Camorra from the streets of Naples, but there'd been big trouble and they had to *flee or die. Now, there was peace. There was church on Sundays and at least an illusion of security.*

Then there came the incident, and Bianca discovered how thin the illusion was, how insubstantial. That was when she realized that this family's secrets were darker and their ways more dangerous. They had power on the streets; and that meant they also had enemies.

She called Joey in from the garden one day, and he didn't come. She searched for him everywhere, she opened the gate into the back yard, she looked upstairs in the house, downstairs too. He was gone.

Bianca was in tears. Then there was a commotion inside the house, in the hall. She ran through from the kitchen, smiling because this meant they'd found Joey, that he was all right. Her father was shouting, the boys were clustered around the open doorway, there was something . . .

Bianca ran forward and her mother caught her. Bella looked shocked, strained.

'No! No, darling, come back . . .'

Bianca was still surging forward. Tito grabbed her arm, held her, but she could see . . .

There was blood. Something there, on the front doorstep. It was . . .

Bianca felt a scream building in her throat, building and building . . .

It was Joey.

It was just Joey's head.

Someone had cut her puppy's head off, and placed it right there on the step.

Bianca never asked for another pet, not after that.

73

Kit, Rob and a couple of the boys turned up as promised at the Barton restaurant at eight o'clock sharp. Kit had decided to give it an hour, time for a snack or something, a small drink, then his duty would be discharged, everyone could see that the Barton family's protection was right there on the spot and that any little tossers causing trouble here had better think again.

The family were effusive in their gratitude.

'You want steak? Aberdeen Angus, the finest, the sweetest steaks in the world,' offered Mr Barton.

Rob and the boys had the steak, Kit settled for the prawn starter, he'd be eating later with Bianca – assuming she showed up. The restaurant was packed and everyone seemed to be enjoying their meals. Then a couple of tough-looking young lads started to loudly complain about the food, playing up to their tarty-looking girlfriends.

'This the best you can do?' one was saying, loud enough for everyone in the place to hear. 'I can get *slop* like this off my old mum, any day of the week.'

'I'm sorry, sir. Can I bring you something else from the kitchen?' the waiter asked, red-faced as the other diners fell quiet, listening.

'I wouldn't risk eating anything that came out of that rat-hole. I heard you put cat food in your pies, the health people found a load of empty tins in the bin round the back.'

'Please, sir, if you can just keep your voice down . . .'

Samuel Barton was hovering anxiously by the till now, and his wife was starting to come over. Kit gave her a small headshake, and she stopped walking.

This them? he mouthed to her.

She nodded.

Kit stood up; so did Rob. Together they walked over to where the lads and their girls were sitting.

'You want to keep it down a bit, pal?' asked Kit of the one with laughing dark eyes, who seemed to be the ring-leader.

The waiter stepped back.

'Who the fuck invited you to join the party?' sneered the dark-haired one.

Kit eyed him steadily. His smile slipped a notch.

'Yeah, fuck off, mate,' said the other one, and the girls giggled.

'You're disturbing the other diners,' said Rob.

'So?'

'So, you ought to stop.'

'Yeah? Make me,' said the bolder one, standing up.

Kit shot out a hand and grabbed a rough handful of Big Mouth's testicles, and Big Mouth let out a noise some-where between a bellow and a scream. Kit's other hand gripped the back of his jacket, and he marched him out the door.

Rob hauled Big Mouth's partner in crime to his feet and followed. The two girls jumped up and started shouting as they trailed after their two ejected escorts.

Outside, Kit threw Big Mouth onto the pavement. Rob dumped the other one down beside him.

'Watchoo doin'?' shrieked one of the girls.

'Yeah, what the hell?' demanded the other one.

Big Mouth was hugging his groin. He yelled as Kit dragged him back to his feet. Rob took hold of the other one, and they yanked them both around the corner, out of sight of the main street.

'You don't come near this place, ever again, understood?' Kit told Big Mouth.

'There's no need for this,' shouted the other lad, sounding scared. Suddenly, this wasn't such a big laugh any more.

'There's every need,' said Rob, and punched him in the head.

When Kit and the boys left at ten to nine, the Bartons waved away all offers of payment, gave them bottles of wine and almond cakes wrapped in napkins, and thanked them for their time and trouble.

'No trouble,' said Kit. 'You need any help, you call us, OK?'

The boys drifted off to their cars, Rob and Kit to the Bentley.

'You drive. Drop me off at Gino's,' said Kit.

74

Vittore said nothing to Maria about what he'd heard from Jay, about the club drugs stroke Fabio had tried to pull on him, or about her and Fabio meeting up in a backstreet hotel for sex. It had happened several times, Jay said, and it made Vittore sick to think that he could have been screwing his wife after Fabio had been there.

Not that he screwed her much, not any more. Like the whores in the club, he despised her. Now he knew that Mama had been right all along: these women were filth, not to be trusted. Look at the way she had been taking those contraceptive pills, and keeping him in ignorance. He should have known, then and there, that she was a dirty *putta*.

Well, he would see to Fabio later. But first, he would sort out Maria.

He waited for the dust to settle. Maria was treading very carefully around him, and he just bet that Fabio had told her that he was on to them. He also bet that Fabio had ditched her straight away. Fabio had good looks and a swaggering way about him, but he was no one's idea of a knight in shining armour. If it came down to his skin or a woman's, then the woman would catch it, every time.

Well, let the bitch sweat it out. Let her think that she might have got away with it.

'There's something I wanted to talk to you about,' he said to his wife after supper one evening. She'd cooked rigatoni pomodoro, it was good; she wasn't a bad cook. Not in Mama's class, of course. He'd got one of his favourite reds from the cellar to wash it down with.

Maria had cleaned away the dishes and returned to the dining room, where Vittore was still swigging back the wine.

He's drinking a lot, she thought with a little niggle of fear.

Ever since Fabio's phone call, she had been on tenterhooks. But perhaps . . . perhaps Fabio had been mistaken, because Vittore was acting normally, like everything was fine. And slowly, inch by inch, she had begun to relax. Tonight, she thought that he would want to make love. He might knock her around a bit first – this was Vittore, after all – but she was used to that. Then he would screw her, and fall into a disgusting drunken sleep, after which she could do what she usually did and go off to the spare bedroom to sleep in peace instead of having to listen to him snoring.

She'd wake tomorrow with a few bruises, but all would be well, all would be the same, with Mama hollering at her to help out in the kitchen, and Vittore being his usual cold self, and maybe . . . maybe Fabio hadn't meant what he'd said, maybe he'd just been scared that night. And so perhaps soon they could resume their love-making, and be a bit more careful, of course, a bit more cautious, so that Vittore would never suspect again . . .

Vittore had drained his glass and was now looking at the empty bottle of wine.

'Go down and get me another bottle of this,' he said to Maria.

Anything to keep you happy, you pig, she thought, and she went through to their small kitchen – nowhere near as grand as Mama's – and opened the cellar door. It was then that she heard movement behind her, and started to turn as she stood at the top of the cellar steps, her hand reaching for the light switch. Below her, darkness yawned like the mouth of hell. She *hated* the cellar, it gave her the creeps.

The crashing blow on the back of her head was so hard that it was a sheer sickening impact, she felt barely any pain at all. She teetered forward, her feet slipping from underneath her, and went hurtling end over end down the steps, crying out just once, very briefly; then she was silent.

The poker still in his hand, Vittore flicked the switch. Light flooded the cellar, showing the neat rows of bottles stored down there – and Maria, crumpled in a heap at the base of the steps. Vittore descended the stairs slowly. When he got to the bottom he bent over Maria. Her eyes were wide open but they didn't see him. Where he'd struck her, there was no blood; nothing at all. He reached down, felt her neck which was bent at an extreme angle. Not a pulse, no sign of life.

'*Basta!*' he cursed her, and just to make sure he hit her head once more, as hard as he could, with the poker, hearing the *crunch* as her skull split open.

Then, panting, he made his way back up the stairs, flicking off the light behind him, closing the cellar door. He went through to the lounge, put the poker down on the hearth; then he phoned Jay, and told him what he wanted done.

75

Gino's was a small Italian place not on Kit's manor and not on the Danieris' patch either. He took a table near the door so he could keep an eye out for Bianca in case she showed. He thought that maybe she wouldn't; that he'd blown all his chances with her, and maybe that wouldn't be a bad thing. But . . . he couldn't wait to see her again. Stupid, self-destructive though that might be, it was the truth.

When she came in through the door he felt that same dry-mouthed, heart-thumping excitement he'd felt the very first time he'd seen her. She was dressed in white, taking off her thin summer coat to reveal a crocheted white minidress. It had some sort of flesh-coloured lining, so that you could almost think she was naked underneath, but she wasn't.

He stood up and she turned, her eyes meeting his. Her expression was very serious, her face paler than ever. Carrying a small clutch bag, she came over to where he sat. Kit kissed her on the mouth. The waiter hurried to hold out her seat.

'Thank you,' she said, sitting down.

'You OK?' asked Kit. She looked washed out, as if she'd been crying.

'Bad day,' she said with a little twist of a smile.

'Well, let's have a good evening, take the sting out of it,' he said.

'Yeah,' she said, her eyes holding his. 'Let's.'

The waiter came, brought bread and water, took their drinks order, gave them menus.

'Actually, I don't think I'm very hungry,' said Bianca, perusing the appetizing treats on offer. She felt that if she ate a single morsel, she would throw it straight back up. Sitting across the table from him seemed surreal. She could still hardly believe it. This was not Tony. This was *him*. The evil creature who might have stolen Tito's life away. The one who had insulted their entire family. The one who had wounded Vittore.

'You sure you're OK?' Kit frowned at her. She looked sickly, as if she was coming down with something. Jesus, she could be pregnant for all he knew. Carrying his baby. The thought of it was so sweet and at the same time so painful, given that he knew such a thing could never be.

'I'm fine. As I said, bad day.'

'You want to talk about it?'

'No. I don't.'

'Might help.'

'Trust me. It won't.' She went back to studying the menu. 'I'll have the carbonara,' she said, putting it aside. She wouldn't eat it. She couldn't. She felt sick to her stomach just being here, just looking at him, just breathing the same air. She couldn't believe she'd been weak enough to sleep with him again, even when she *knew* who and what he was; she hated herself for it.

'Me too.' Kit put his menu on top of hers. The waiter came back, took their order. Kit was watching her. She didn't look him in the eye.

'Bianca? We have to discuss this.'

'I can't. Not right now,' she said, and sat there in stony

silence until their meals arrived. At which point she said: 'I can't eat this.'

Kit hadn't even picked up his knife and fork.

'Were you ever planning to tell me you're not Tony Mobley?' she asked. 'If I hadn't seen you at Vito's, would you ever have told me the truth?'

Kit felt his guts turn over as she spoke the words.

Ah shit, he thought. 'I didn't know you were part of that family.'

'My brothers think you could be the one who killed Tito.' Now her voice shook with stifled emotion. 'I *loved* Tito. When I was a girl, I could always turn to him. I adored him.'

'Jesus . . .'

A tear escaped, spilled over and ran down her cheek. She stared at him, eyes red-raw with pain. 'I loved him so much!'

'Bianca, wait—'

'No! I think you *knew* who I was, right from the start. And then – what? – I suppose you thought you'd have a game with me? Not content with wrecking my family, you thought you'd have even more revenge on us? You weren't finished there. You thought, *I know, I'll fuck the brains out of the sister too, I'll make her believe I love her and shag her senseless* – is that how it was?'

'No,' said Kit. 'It wasn't like that. I didn't know you were a Danieri. I *didn't.*'

'Then why the lie about your name? Come on. I would really like to understand.'

'Bianca! I had no idea who you were when I first met you. None at all. It was never about revenge, it was never about Tito – although I honestly believed that he killed Michael, the man who was like a father to me. It was *never* about that with you and me. I saw you and I wanted you.

Straight away. It was like a fucking thunderbolt or something. That's never happened to me before.'

'It's never happened to me, either. Before.' She grabbed a tissue out of her bag, mopped irritably at her face.

'I never meant to hurt you,' said Kit. 'You've got to believe that.'

'Why should I believe a word you say? You *lied* to me, didn't even tell me your real name.'

Kit was shaking his head. 'I made up a name because that's what men do when they're out shagging around, Bianca.'

'Oh, thanks for that,' she said, her mouth dropping open in outrage.

'Listen. When men want casual sex, they don't give their real names, they'd be a *cunt* to do that. And that's what I was doing, until I met you. And you know what? The minute I said that stupid name I wished I hadn't. I wanted to be honest with you, because – for fuck's sake! – it was something special with you. It meant a lot. Ever since then, it's been killing me. When you told me that you're Tito's and Vittore's and Fabio's sister, I knew you were going to hate me. I just hoped it wouldn't be so soon, that's all. That we'd have more time.'

'Well, time's up,' snapped Bianca, picking up her bag and jumping to her feet.

She ran towards the door, snatching her coat from the hook. Kit threw some money onto the table and rushed after her.

'Bianca, wait. Maybe we can work this out. Come on. We *have* to,' said Kit as she went out the door and started off along the windblown street.

Bianca kept walking.

'We don't have to do anything,' she flung back at him,

walking fast, head down, pulling on her coat, hurrying away from him.

The street was quiet, dark but for the pale yellowish wash from the sodium lights. Cabs passed by now and then, a couple of people were out walking their dogs. It was starting to rain. Kit caught her arm. She was shivering with cold or despair, he couldn't tell which.

'Look, we have to get over this. Somehow,' he said.

They were near a pub, and music was seeping out. The juke in there was playing 'Laughter in the Rain' by Neil Sedaka. He could hear it. It was horribly ironic.

'*Get over it?*' she echoed. In the dim light her eyes looked almost demented with fury. She was fumbling in her bag again, searching for a hankie. She lunged at him, and he saw hatred, real cold hatred, on her face. It staggered him, made him step back.

'You've *destroyed* me, you've *lied* to me, you've *betrayed* me,' she spat at him. 'You think we can get over any of that? You're *crazy*.'

And then he saw it. The glint of metal in her hand.

'Oh no. Honey, don't—' he said, half-turning away from her.

Bianca's hand was shaking as she pointed the gun at him. She hadn't been looking for a tissue, she'd been trying to find *that*.

'Don't do this,' he said, 'don't—'

He hadn't even finished what he was saying when Bianca let out a hopeless cry and shot him in the chest.

76

Kit discovered that being shot isn't like in the movies. In the movies, the hero takes a bullet and crawls on, defeats the baddie, gets the girl. In real life, he found it was a little different.

Those celluloid heroes don't scream and collapse with pain when a piece of metal is fired at high velocity into their flesh. Kit did. And they don't lie there helpless and trembling afterwards, either; Kit did. His body went instantly into shock; suddenly he was shaking and disorientated, his chest heaving. Every cell had flown into panic mode, screaming *What the hell was that? What's happened?*

He could see her standing over him, could see the smoking gun in her hand. Such a small gun, and it had floored him. Kit Miller, all-round tough bastard, lord of the manor. Flat out on the wet grubby pavement, unable to move a muscle.

'Bianca,' he tried to say, but he couldn't get his breath.

Her hand holding the gun was trembling, but she was aiming at him again, aiming at his head this time; she was really going to do it, she was going to kill him.

He closed his eyes, make it easier for her. He wanted to hold her, one last time, but that was out of the question. He knew he deserved this. He knew he had it coming.

This was how it was for Michael, he thought. And maybe Michael was up there somewhere, waiting for him right this minute – and this was such a God-awful mess that it wouldn't be too bad to just go now, would it?

'Bianca,' he tried again, but what came out of his mouth was one long bubbling groan.

One minute more, she'd pull the trigger, and that would be it. Eyes closed, his heart thundering, clammy sick sweat mingling with the hardening rain, he waited. Maybe the shot he'd already taken would be enough to do the job, anyway. Felt like enough. He could feel all his systems closing down, his strength ebbing away.

So this is what it's like to die.

He waited. He was standing on the edge of an abyss, at the bottom of which was death, and freedom. No more torment. No more trouble.

She would fire the gun again, any second.

He waited.

Finally, when it didn't come, he forced his eyes open. They felt tired, heavy. One last glimpse of her, maybe. That would be good.

But she wasn't there.

She was gone.

Wendy Metcalfe and her boyfriend Sammy Spears came out of the pub. They were off home, get a Chinese on the way, and now this was all a bit inconvenient because there was this drunk lying there waiting to trip someone up. A person could break their fucking neck over the inebriated bastard.

'Hey!' said Sammy, poking Kit with his shoe.

'Is he pissed?' asked Wendy, peering impatiently at the man on the pavement.

It was raining out here and rain flattened her hair, she hated getting her hair wet, it was nightmare hair, thin and fine, her dad's hair not her mum's, sod her luck, and she didn't have an umbrella because they'd said blue skies on the forecast and of course that was bollocks, as per usual. It was also pretty dark, only the light from the street lamps and the pub windows to illuminate anything, that and the swishing intermittent lighthouse sweep of passing car head-lights.

'Of course he's pissed,' said Sammy in disgust.

Wendy peered closer. 'There's blood on his shirt. Isn't that blood?'

Sammy had a look just to humour her. 'Shit! Looks like it. D'you reckon he's been in a fight, someone's knifed him?'

'Dunno.' There was a lot of blood. Wendy looked at the man's face; his eyes were closed. Maybe he was not drunk but dead, who knew? She withdrew quickly with a shudder. 'I'm going back in, phone 999,' she decided. At least then she wouldn't be standing here in the rain, getting her fucking hair ruined.

77

When Bianca got home in a state of hysteria, babbling that she'd done it, she'd killed him, Bella phoned her favourite, her Vittore, who showed up an hour later with Fabio in tow.

'She says she shot Kit Miller,' said Bella, as Bianca sat hunched over a glass of brandy at the kitchen table.

'Where's the gun?' asked Vittore.

Bella motioned to Bianca's bag, there on the table.

Fabio took up the bag, opened it. There was the gun, a .22, a dainty little thing but deadly at close range.

'I'll get rid of it,' said Fabio. 'And the bag's got to go too. Residue.'

Fabio left the room. Vittore and Bella sat down at the table and looked at Bianca.

'Was he dead?' asked Vittore.

'Yes, I think so,' said Bianca, and started to cry again. She'd hated him but she'd loved him too, and now he was gone. He'd deceived her, lied to her, probably snatched Tito away from her, but she *loved* him.

'How did any of this happen?' asked Vittore.

Bianca told him in halting sentences punctuated by crying fits, about Kit coming into Dante's, calling himself Tony Mobley. She couldn't tell Vittore all of it, of their affair, of how passionate and deep and fiery it had been, that it had been love, or at least she had thought so.

'Who saw you together tonight?' he asked, scratching at his bandaged hand. It was healing, and it itched like crazy.

'She's tired, let her—' started Bella.

'*Who?*' shouted Vittore.

Bianca flinched. 'People in the restaurant. Gino's. The waiter. I don't think anyone actually noticed us.'

Vittore looked at his adopted sister. Bianca never passed unnoticed anywhere; she was far too striking for that. But maybe they could scrape their way out of this.

'We were near a pub, there was a jukebox playing very loud. No one would have heard the . . . the shot. And there was no one about, it was raining.'

'That was lucky,' said Vittore. He was thinking fast. It would be even luckier if Miller was pronounced dead at the scene. If not, things could get a little untidy. The bastard might recover, might name Bianca as the shooter. That outcome had to be prevented at all costs. He'd get some of the boys out, check the hospitals.

'She's very upset,' said Bella, patting Bianca's hand.

'I should have cleared this up sooner myself,' said Vittore. 'Then Bianca would never have got involved with any of this. You see, Mama? Sometimes action is necessary.'

Bella nodded grimly. *This* was what she had been trying to avoid. A child of hers or of Ruby Darke's ending up on a slab. But despite all her best efforts, she'd been unable to prevent it.

'Have a bath, Bianca. Scrub your fingernails in case there's cordite on your hands. But first bag up all the clothes you were wearing tonight and give them to me – I'll burn them.' Vittore eyed his sister dispassionately. 'You did good. Tomorrow, you go back down to Southampton and you stay there. Don't worry about it. That bastard deserves to fry in hell.'

78

The ambulance came, blue lights flashing, siren wailing, the medics piling out into the rainy night: a crowd gathered, interested, as people always are, in death and disaster. They watched the medics check to see if Kit still had a pulse – which amazingly he did – then they checked his blood pressure.

The onlookers watched them give him oxygen as the police arrived, and Wendy stepped forward and told them she and Sammy had found him out here on the pavement. As the medics attached an IV line and fastened an oxygen mask over Kit's face, Wendy said that no, she didn't know the man, Sammy didn't either, they'd just come out of the pub and nearly fallen over him lying there on the pavement, that was all.

'Someone stab the poor bastard?' asked Sammy.

'It looks like a bullet wound so far as we can ascertain, sir,' said the policeman. Another one came up, had a look at Kit.

'Jesus!' he said.

'You know him?' asked his partner.

'Looks like Kit Miller – local businessman.' The officer knew Kit. He knew Kit's boys. He fucking well ought to, he was on their payroll.

The medics were wrapping the victim in blankets, lifting

313

him carefully onto a gurney, strapping him in, loading him into the back of the ambulance. There was blood on the spot where he'd lain, but now the rain started to wash the pavement clean. Soon, it would be as if he'd never been there at all.

'We'll need a statement,' said the first policeman to Wendy as the medics slammed the ambulance doors and the siren started up.

'Yeah, sure,' said Wendy, thinking that this was what it was like, scum on the streets these days. People getting themselves shot, for Christ's sake.

It was indeed Kit Miller who nearly got himself wasted that night. There was a driver's licence in his coat pocket and a handful of belongings – a wallet stuffed with more money than most of A&E had seen in a year, comb, a red card with Dante's emblazoned across it in gold, a handkerchief, not much else.

'An inch to the right and he'd be in G4,' said the surgeon as he fished around for the bullet that had smashed through Kit's chest wall before being deflected by one of his ribs, just missing his heart. It had embedded itself in his upper left arm, tearing an artery in the process. G4 was the morgue, down in the bowels of the building.

'Clamp,' he barked, and the nurse hurried forward, stemmed the bleeding. 'Ah, look. Here it is.' The surgeon held a tiny pellet of silver in his bloody gloved hand. 'Small calibre, you see? Any bigger and it would have killed him right then and there.'

'Blood pressure's falling,' said a nurse, and alarms sounded as Kit went into cardiac arrest.

PC Halligan, the second policeman to show up at the scene of the incident, put through a call to a number he knew very well; Rob answered. Within fifteen minutes, Rob had phoned Ruby, dressed, and was on his way to the hospital.

'Can you tell me how Kit Miller's doing?' asked Rob when he got to the hospital and stood at the receptionist's desk.

'Kit Miller?'

'He was brought in by ambulance. Gunshot wound. Maybe an hour ago?' Rob was saying these things, but he could scarcely believe they were coming out of his mouth. Kit had been shot in the chest. It looked bad. That was all Halligan told him on the phone, apart from the fact that he'd been found collapsed on the pavement outside a pub near to Gino's, where he'd asked Rob to drop him off earlier.

'Are you a relative?'

'His brother,' lied Rob.

He was asked to wait. Ten minutes of anxious pacing later, he was told: 'Your brother's in surgery. If you'd care to take a seat . . . ?'

Ruby and Daisy arrived half an hour later, having been driven from Marlow by Reg. Their faces were drained of colour and life, their eyes desperate. He got to his feet and Ruby flung herself into his arms, sobbing. He looked over her shoulder at Daisy.

'How is he?' she asked. 'Have you heard anything?'

He shook his head. 'They're operating now.'

'You said a gunshot wound?' Daisy's eyes filled with tears, but she blinked them back, swallowing hard. Trying to keep it together.

'He took a shot in the chest,' said Rob. 'It could be bad.'

Ruby stepped back, looked up at him. 'No! I can't lose him,' she cried.

Daisy reached out and hugged her mother. 'Kit's tough.

He'll pull through,' she said, managing to get some conviction into her voice.

'Course he will,' said Rob. 'Sit down, I'll fetch us some coffee.'

'You know the worst thing?' Ruby said to Daisy as the minutes drifted into hours in the dingy little waiting room. People had been coming and going the whole time they sat there, but it was quietening down now. This was the middle of the night, the time when people died if they were going to.

'No. What?' asked Daisy. Rob was sitting opposite the two women, arms folded, keeping watch.

'He still hadn't forgiven me for abandoning him when he was a baby. And now . . .' Ruby was shaking her head, more despairing tears slipping down her cheeks.

'Don't say it,' said Daisy, squeezing Ruby's hand. 'He's going to get better. And if he has any hang-ups about the past, he's going to get over them. It's all going to be fine.'

Platitudes. The sort of thing that everyone says to people sitting in hospital waiting rooms. Ruby knew Daisy's words for the comforting lies that they were. But she was grateful for them. Daisy cared. Daisy loved her. Kit, he'd not been able to . . . yet. She'd been hoping, over these last few months since Michael died, that it would all come right somehow. But the gap between them seemed too wide; unbridgeable.

And now she was thinking about Thomas Knox, who had promised her he would watch over Kit. And he had let *this* happen.

'Mrs . . . Miller?' asked a tall, thin, tired-looking man, suddenly appearing at the door in a green surgical gown, his mask pushed down around his neck. There was blood on the front of the gown. *Kit's blood*, thought Ruby. Oh, Jesus . . .

'I'm Kit Miller's mother,' she said, stumbling to her feet.

The man paused, looked at Daisy, at Rob.

'His brother and sister,' said Ruby. 'How is he?'

'I'm afraid his condition is critical,' said the surgeon. 'The bullet missed his heart, smashed a rib, did a fair bit of collateral damage . . .'

Ruby felt her legs dissolve like water. She sank back down into the chair.

'. . . but he's still with us. He's not out of danger. He's suffered a severe trauma and serious loss of blood. We're keeping him deeply sedated for the time being and we'll be monitoring him closely in ICU for the next twenty-four hours.'

'When can we see him?' asked Daisy, pale as milk.

'Not yet. Go home, get a few hours' sleep. Come back tomorrow; hopefully his condition will have improved by then. In the meantime, there's nothing you can do here. You'll be better off at home.'

Ruby and Daisy looked at Rob. 'I'll stay here in case I'm needed,' he said. 'Come on, let's go find Reg downstairs, get you two home.'

'I want to stay,' said Ruby.

'No. The doc's right, time to go.'

The surgeon departed, and Rob escorted Daisy and Ruby downstairs and out to the car park where Reg was waiting with the Merc. Having got them safely inside, Rob went back into the hospital, found a payphone and called Ashok. He told him what had happened, and to get himself to the hospital at eight a.m. to take over. Then he returned to the now deserted waiting room, took off his jacket and made it into a pillow, and laid himself out across four of the chairs to try to get some sleep.

79

Someone was knocking on the door of Thomas Knox's Hampstead home.

'What the fuck?' he asked of no one in particular. He sat up, switched on the bedside light. It was four in the morning, and someone was out there playing silly buggers. He slipped on his robe, and went over to the window. There was a black Mercedes parked up on the drive, he could just about make out a grey-haired bloke sitting at the wheel.

He made his way downstairs, flicking on lights as he went. Flung the front door open. Ruby shot inside like an Exocet, slamming the door shut behind her. Since leaving the hospital, she'd been fulminating with rage against Thomas Knox. He'd promised he was going to look out for Kit, and now Kit was in intensive care. So she'd dropped Daisy off, and then she'd got Reg to drive her over here, because she was so devastated, so furious, that she felt if she didn't get some of this rage out then she would explode.

Ruby strode straight past Thomas and into the sitting room. She flicked on the lights in there. He followed her, his eyes curious, as she stalked around the place like a caged panther.

'You *promised*,' she spat out at last, coming at him with eyes full of fury, poking him hard in the chest with one finger. 'You promised you were going to watch out for him.'

Thomas stared at her. 'What's happened?'

'You mean you don't know? You're supposed to know everything, aren't you? But you don't know my boy's laid up in hospital with a bullet wound in his chest!'

'When did all this go down?'

'Last night. He got shot.'

'Jesus! Who?'

'Who shot him? I have no idea. Nobody seems to know. But you didn't even know he'd *been* shot, and you should. You're supposed to be on the ball.'

'Ruby, I said I'd keep an eye on him and I'll stick to that, but I can't stop harm coming to him twenty-four hours of the day – how could I?'

Ruby rounded on him in fury. 'Are you serious? You *seduced* me and promised me . . .'

Now Thomas's eyes hardened. 'Hey! As I recall, you didn't seem too reluctant. You were panting for it like a fucking porn star.'

Ruby's eyes flared with rage. She slapped him, hard, across the face.

To her surprise, Thomas slapped her right back in return and pushed her until she hit the wall. More startled than hurt, she glared at him as he held her there, pinned, immobile.

'Oh, now this is the *real* Ruby Darke,' he hissed against her mouth. 'This is the East End alley cat, not the cool business lady. This is the genuine article.'

'Why was I so stupid as to get involved with you, to believe what you said?' she gasped out. It shamed her, mortified her, that she had been cavorting with Thomas Knox in expensive hotel rooms, swimming naked with him in his pool, while Kit had been going through some sort of awful crisis.

'While we're on the subject of stupid, what about Kit fucking the Danieri sister – how's *that* for stupid?'

Ruby grew still, staring at him. 'What are you talking about?' she whispered.

'I been hearing about it around town. I got people on the streets. They were starting to notice, Kit and Bianca Danieri. So if you're looking for someone with a good reason to shoot your boy, I'd look to Vittore or Fabio, since Kit was busy turking their baby *principessa*. If you think they were going to be happy when they found that out, you're off your head.'

'Bianca . . . ?' Ruby repeated numbly. 'I didn't know they had a sister.'

'She runs a club down south, I heard. Dante's.'

Ruby's eyes grew distant. Kit had been away on the south coast, and he'd been late coming back to London; she and Daisy had been frantic over Simon's death, they'd needed Kit to be there. Was this Bianca the reason he hadn't been? For God's sake, if that was true, how could he have been so foolish?

'There's much more to that girl than meets the eye,' said Thomas. 'More to that family, too. The story was that they adopted her, but Michael told me something different.'

'What do you mean?'

'Tito – did you know him?'

'Not much.'

'That's good, because he was a real bad bastard. Mike was tied to him in business and there was a family connection because of Sheila – but he hated the guy. And Mike's boy Gabe was like Tito's lapdog. Mike hated that, too. Told the boy to keep clear. But Gabe wouldn't. He hung around Tito, and saw more than he wanted to see. Came home one day, Mike told me, all shot to pieces. Gabe was never the same after that. And he confessed to Mike that he'd seen Tito snatch a little girl from her parents, and kill them. Bianca wasn't adopted like everyone thinks she was. She was taken.'

'Jesus,' said Ruby, and slumped against the wall. 'And this Bianca, she doesn't know?'

Thomas shook his head. 'She believes she was adopted. She idolized Tito. And she don't remember a thing about him offing her folks.'

Ruby was shaking her head at the ghastly picture he'd just painted. 'Poor girl,' she said.

'Yeah,' said Thomas.

Ruby closed her eyes, fighting back the tears. 'We could lose him,' she moaned. 'We could lose Kit. He could die.'

'Hey! You won't. He's tough as old boots, that one. Like his mum.'

'I love him, and you know what? He's never believed it.'

'You got time to work on that.'

Ruby let out a thin, sad laugh. 'I might not have. He's seriously hurt. He could die. Oh God, I'm sorry I hit you.'

They looked at each other. Then Thomas opened his arms and Ruby went into them, hugging him, feeling shattered from the horrors of this night and wondering where the hell they could all go from here.

'You want to stay here tonight?' he asked, kissing her forehead.

'I can't. I have to go home, in case the hospital phones.'

'He'll be all right.'

She didn't dare allow herself to believe that.

'Ruby?' he murmured against her brow.

'What?'

'There's something else. There are things I should have told you before, but didn't. I want to tell you now, but I'm worried you're so screwed up over Kit that it will be too much for you . . .'

'What is it?' asked Ruby, drawing her head away from his so she could look into his eyes.

'Nah. Let's leave it for now.'

'*No*. Whatever it is, tell me.'

Thomas stared into her eyes for a long time. Then he said: 'It's about Mike.'

'Michael? What about him?'

'Ruby – I'm sorry. I heard he was unfaithful to you.'

'*What?*'

'From dependable sources. He was seen with another woman. They were close, if you get me. That's all I know. More than that, I can't tell you.'

Ruby's eyes were anguished as they stared at his face. '*No*,' she said faintly.

'I'm sorry, Ruby. It's true.'

80

They were back at the hospital at two o'clock the following afternoon. Ashok was there, keeping watch, and when Rob arrived he headed off home with nothing of interest to report.

Rob, Daisy and Ruby went into intensive care to see Kit. He was out of it, fastened up to tubes and pumps and monitors, and his skin had a greyish tinge; he looked nothing like his usual robust self, and his chest was heavily band-aged, a drain attached to the left-hand side of it. Ruby started to cry the minute she saw him. Daisy hugged her. A dark-haired, bushy-browed nurse passed by, all kind smiles and compassion. 'Talk to him,' she said. 'He might hear you.'

Talk to him about what?

'When will we be able to speak to the doctors?' asked Ruby.

'They do their rounds at three thirty, they'll see you then,' said the nurse.

Rob patted Kit's hand, where the IV line ran in. 'All right, mate?' he said, having to swallow hard. It hurt him to see Kit like this. It hurt him that he hadn't been there to stop it.

Daisy wiped at her eyes and sat down beside Kit's bedside and spoke to him. 'You gave us all a terrible scare,' she said. 'We can't wait for you to get better. If only so we can shout at you to take care of yourself in future.'

Ruby could only stand there and watch. Her beautiful boy! Seeing him like this was agony. Daisy's bravery left her in awe, but then Daisy had been brought up to believe in the stiff upper lip, *noblesse oblige*; her class of woman – Vanessa's class – never crumbled.

When the doctors came, the surgeon who'd operated on Kit was among them. He said Kit was making progress, but that he wasn't out of the woods yet, and that the police would doubtless be in touch with the family to discuss the nature of Kit's injuries.

'It's not every day we get a gunshot victim in here,' he said.

After the doctors' rounds, Daisy and Ruby went home, but Rob stayed on. At ten o'clock that evening, one of the other boys would take over. Until then, he would do what he always tried so hard to do: watch Kit's back. This time, he wouldn't fail in his duty.

The following day, Ruby spoke to Daisy over breakfast. Neither of them had slept.

'This is a nightmare,' said Ruby, refusing food. She couldn't eat, the very thought of it made her guts heave. She could barely keep down a cup of coffee.

'He'll pull through,' insisted Daisy.

'Thomas Knox said he was going to look out for him,' said Ruby numbly. 'He promised.'

'Knox? The man outside the church?' Daisy was watching Ruby.

Ruby looked up at Daisy. 'We're . . . involved,' she said.

'Well, that's good, isn't it? I've been worried about you, since Michael died. That was awful for you.'

Ruby took a gulp of coffee. The strange and deeply

sexual nature of her relationship with Thomas was something she didn't feel able to discuss with anyone, especially
not her own daughter. With Michael, she had felt loved,
secure. With Thomas, it was so different: she was on tenterhooks. And now he had told her this thing, this terrible
thing.

'Thomas told me that Michael was unfaithful,' she blurted
out.

Daisy's mouth dropped open. 'He what?'

'He said there was another woman.'

Daisy was silent for a moment. 'Do you believe him?'

'Why would he lie?'

'To distance you from Michael? Maybe he's jealous of
how close you were.'

'I don't think so. I think he was telling the truth about
it.'

'But who's the woman?' Daisy was shocked by this reve-
lation.

'I don't know.'

'I can't believe it.'

'Neither could I,' said Ruby grimly. 'But the more I think
about it? The way Michael was behaving in the weeks before
his death? I'm starting to.'

Ruby's brain was in turmoil. She had spent a wretched
night again, wondering if at any moment the phone was
going to ring and it would be the hospital, saying *Your son
is dead, he passed peacefully away, we're so sorry.*

She had been afraid to sleep, afraid to even lie on the
bed, as if that might be inviting disaster. Now, hyped up
on coffee and dazed from lack of sleep, she sat there and
wondered what the hell was happening to her life.

Thomas
Michael
Kit

What Thomas had told her – that Michael had been unfaithful – devastated her. It had never occurred to her; in all the time they'd been together, not once had he given her cause to doubt him. And she had been utterly faithful to him. Had he lived, they would have married. Yet here was Thomas, telling her that Michael had betrayed her.

She had asked him to tell her who the woman was. 'Come on. You know everything, don't you?'

'Sweetheart, I don't know that.'

Maybe he was lying. If Michael could have lied to her, then so could Thomas. And that shocking thing he'd told her about the Danieri girl, Bianca, the one Kit seemed, according to Rob, to have become obsessed with . . .

She sank her head into her hands as she thought about Thomas. How easily he had reeled her in, how volatile and passionate their sudden affair was; how inappropriate. What was she thinking, getting involved with a cold-blooded crook like him? A man of secrets, a man who watched, who took note, who waited with the patience of a spider for Michael to come to grief, so that he could snatch her for himself.

And now Kit was lying in a hospital bed, teetering between life and death. She cast a fearful look at the phone. What if it rang, and they told her he was gone? She would never have the chance to make things right with him, never know the joy of having him love her as desperately as she loved him.

'I'll phone Joan,' said Daisy, watching her mother with concern. 'Tell her you won't be in to work for a while.'

Ruby nodded, wiping away the tears that were streaming down her face.

She couldn't think about work. Couldn't even form a sentence. All she could do was cry.

★

Kit was surrounded by icy windblown blackness. There was nobody there but him, and this faint but biting pain, chilling him, eating into him like frostbite. He could hear murmurings, far away. Could be from another world, it was so distant, so unconnected to anything that was happening with him. There was not a thought in his head, there was simply . . . nothing. So this was what it was like. This was death.

'Do you think he can hear me? Really?' Ruby asked the nurse. She was staring at Kit's face, so still in repose. Not the flicker of an eyelid. He looked dead to the world.

They let you in, mornings, in ICU. After all, the person laid up in here might not make it. It was a special consideration for the relatives, to be allowed in. The monitors beeped, pumps wheezed; this really was *intensive* care. It was a different nurse this time, a neat little pigtailed blonde. But she had the same smile. Patient. Kind.

'Try it. Talk to him.'

So Ruby gulped, cleared her throat. Felt foolish, didn't know where to begin. She started telling her son about living through the war, with a father who seemed to hate everything about her and with brothers, Charlie and Joe, who ducked and dived.

'Joe was the nicer of the two,' she told Kit.

She told him about the Windmill Theatre, and about Vi and about Cornelius Bray – the father Kit had never known, the father who had lavished whatever love he had upon Daisy, having washed his hands of his unacceptable and illegitimate dark-skinned son.

When she stopped talking, pouring her heart out to the man lying unconscious in the bed, the little blonde nurse was standing beside her, arms folded, listening. The nurse blinked; her eyes looked faintly red.

'I hope he can hear you,' she said.

Ruby nodded, and wiped at her eyes. She didn't think he could. 'Let's hope,' she said.

'Keep at it,' said the nurse.

Ruby did.

Daisy phoned Joan and told her to pass a memo round to all the heads of department that Ruby wouldn't be available for a while, probably the next fortnight, who knew? But they were to carry on as normal, and if there were any problems they couldn't manage, they were to inform Joan, and Joan would phone the Marlow house. Then Daisy would see what she could do to resolve them.

'You?' asked Joan, looking up from her notepad in surprise when Daisy said this.

'Yes, or I'll pass it on to Ruby if she's OK to take it. If not, it'll be down to me. Is that all right?'

'I'm sure it will be,' said Joan.

81

Bianca didn't know what to do with herself. She had gone back to work, back to Dante's, but her mind was all over the place.

I've killed him, she thought, over and over.

The man she loved, the one she had thought loved her, she had finished him, taken his life. If the police came and got her, hauled her away to a cell, she knew she deserved it, she would almost relish it. Instead, life went on. Life *dragged* on. And the everyday mechanics of living exhausted her.

She waited for the police to come, for that knock on the door in the middle of the night.

You did it. You're guilty. You ought to suffer.

And she *was* suffering. Every ghastly, endless day was a waking nightmare, during which she went through the motions of doing what she had done before she met him, the same endless drag of days, none of it having any meaning now that everything had changed. Nothing would ever be the same again.

'You OK?' Cora kept asking her.

'I'm fine.'

And then, even worse: 'Did you ever catch up with that Tony Mobley character?'

'No. No, I didn't.'

At night she lay sleepless in her bed, remembering the feel of his body against hers, the sweet sharp scent of him. She looked at the pills in the bathroom cabinet, thought about ending it. But then she thought of her mother. Bella'd had enough grief to last a lifetime, she couldn't inflict still more on her.

Vittore phoned, just once. 'You OK there?' he asked his sister.

'I'm fine,' she told him, same as she told everybody. She knew she should stop there, but the question nagged at her, the one she ought to ask, the one she *had* to ask, even though it would make him angry. 'Have you heard anything? Is he . . . ?'

Dead.

She braced herself for his answer.

Vittore was silent for long moments. 'He's in hospital, he's holding on, they say.'

Bianca slumped down onto her chair, pressing a hand to her mouth to stifle a sob. Her ears hummed, the world went momentarily black: he was *alive*.

'If he should pull through, this could get bad,' said Vittore.

'What?' He was alive. That was all she could think about. Tears flooded down her face like a waterfall. She was half-crying, half-laughing, thinking, *Oh, thank God it's true he's alive, he's alive!*

'They say he's out of it for now. But if he comes round, he'll name you, won't he?'

She wiped at her eyes, shuddering. He ought to name her. What she had done had been done in a moment of supreme madness, and if he were to recover, then she didn't care what happened to her any more, let her be punished, she didn't care about that.

'You got your passport up to date?' asked Vittore.

'What? Well . . . yes.'

'You may have to go.'

Bianca was shaking her head. She'd done an awful thing, a crazy thing, but the madness was past now, she could see things more clearly.

'I'm not going anywhere, Vittore,' she said.

'You'll do what you're fucking well told, *capisce*?' he snapped.

'No! Look. I . . . I made a mistake. I shouldn't have done it. I want to be with him. With Kit Miller. I can't help it.'

There was a moment's frozen silence.

Then Vittore hissed: 'Madonna! You think that's going to happen? You seriously think I'd let you? I'll kill you first!'

'Vittore . . .' Bianca felt her mouth go dry, her stomach lurch with fear. He meant it.

'No. No more! I'll keep my ear to the ground here. Stay in touch – don't make a move unless I tell you.'

Vittore was already making plans. He had someone singled out to take care of a simple clean-up job like this. Best take no chances. As for the crazy thing she'd just said, he was going to ignore it. She thought she could 'be' with Miller? No chance.

Bianca gulped. 'Look . . . Vittore—'

'Not another word,' he said, and slammed the phone down.

Slowly, shaking, Bianca placed the phone back in its cradle.

He was still alive.

Now she knew what she had to do. And fuck Vittore.

82

The murmuring voices were like someone having a whispered conversation in another room. Kit heard them all the time, drifting to him on a cold black wind. He couldn't make out what they were saying, but somehow it was a comfort, knowing that he wasn't completely alone here in the void.

'And then I had you, and Daisy,' said Ruby, sitting at Kit's bedside and holding on tight to his hand. 'I was an unmarried mother, and those were different times. I knew I couldn't give either of you what you would need to get on in life. Charlie was going on and on about how I'd shamed the family and I was a disgrace and I needn't expect any handouts from the family to help keep illegitimate kids. So Daisy went with Cornelius and his wife Vanessa, and you . . . Charlie told me you were going to a good home, with a nice married couple. It broke my heart, broke it clean in two, but I had to put you first, to forget about how *I* felt.'

A monitor was beeping; the dark-haired nurse with the bushy eyebrows hurried over.

Ruby stopped talking as the nurse examined a reading. Some figures were dropping. It meant nothing to her.

'Is everything all right?' she asked.

'Fine. His blood pressure's falling a little.' The nurse was pressing a buzzer beside the bed. 'Can you wait outside, just for a moment?'

The black wind had increased to such a force that his feet were no longer on the ground. It was carrying him now so that he floated, weightless, lifeless, and now he could see there was a tunnel, whirling and spinning, sucking him in. At the end of the tunnel he could see a tiny pinprick of light. The cold wind swept him onward, into the tunnel, whirling him into the distance, where the light awaited.

The consultant's eyes were brown and very kind, as he explained to Ruby four nightmarish hours later what had happened.

'Kit's pressure dropped and that told us there was sudden and significant bleeding. But, Mrs Miller . . .' Ruby had long since given up correcting them; at a time like this, what did it matter that she was Miss Darke? '. . . we've stopped that now, and he's resting comfortably.'

Ruby felt sick. This nice man was telling her that Kit had nearly died for a second time. She had never felt so helpless, so useless, as she did right now.

'Can I go back in? See him again?' she asked, dry-mouthed.

'Tomorrow. For today, let's just keep monitoring his signs, make sure he's back on an even keel.'

Ruby went home. Next day she returned to find Kit was lying there, looking exactly the same. The blonde nurse was on duty, beaming a smile as Ruby came in and took up her position by the bed.

'How's he doing?' she asked the nurse, Corinne.

'He's comfortable,' said Corinne. 'He's a real fighter.'

He's had to be, thought Ruby. No wonder he hated her. She should have been there, when he was growing up, looking out for him, but she had failed in the most basic of all mothering duties.

'Talk to him,' said Corinne.

So Ruby did, picking up the thread and telling him about what had happened after she had lost touch with him and with Daisy. How business had become her focus in life, because her children were missing.

'One corner shop,' she said. 'And I wanted to turn that into a chain . . .' She talked for nearly half an hour, telling him of her life without him, how difficult it had been and how lonely and yes, now she was a rich woman, she'd worked hard to become so, but she would give it all back, every penny, trade it all in a heartbeat, to have been able to spend that time with him.

Ruby looked at his lifeless face and squeezed his hand. The tears came again, hot and hard: Corinne, in passing, patted her heaving shoulder.

'Oh, Kit, please come back,' sobbed Ruby. 'Please, please don't leave me.'

For a while there were no voices, but now the tunnel was receding, that dim distant light had winked out, and he was back again in the inky-black wasteland, the ice-cold wind lashing at his skin, bringing with it the voices, the murmuring voices that he could almost hear clearly, sometimes. He made out words now and then: corner shop. Daisy. And this was a novelty – a whole sentence: please don't leave me.

Leave who?

Leave where?

83

Daisy and Rob arrived at the hospital that afternoon to find the usually calm Ashok looking tense and agitated.

'What's up?' Rob asked the minute he saw Ashok's face.

'I went down to the paper shop and when I came back there was some git up here asking about Kit,' said Ashok. 'He was right there, at the desk. He looked like a face and I heard him trying to pass himself off as a cousin of Kit's. I went up to him and said I didn't know Kit *had* any cousins, and he laughed it off and said OK he was a friend and wanted to see him, and was there anything wrong with *that*, but I tell you, the instant I called him on it he backed away and vamoosed.'

'One of Vittore's crew?' asked Rob.

Rob had been into Gino's where Kit had dined on Saturday night, asked the owner who he'd been with. A pale blonde young woman in a white dress and coat, he said, and she left in a hurry, Kit going after her.

Christ, that has to be Bianca Danieri, thought Rob.

Had her brothers done this then? Shot Kit?

'I'm certain of it,' said Ashok. 'He fucked right off. They're checking it out, Rob. They're worried Kit's going to come round and start talking.'

'They're trying to get to Kit?' asked Daisy, her voice high with anxiety. Her skin crawled at the thought.

Rob looked at Ashok. 'Double up,' he said. 'Cover any breaks, however short.'

Ashok nodded.

'Set up Fats and one of the other guys to come over. When they're here, tell them about this geezer, make sure they know Vittore's sniffing around. Then you go home, rest up. You done good.'

Rob and Daisy went into ICU; Ruby was still there.

'How's he doing?' asked Rob.

'He's holding on,' said Ruby. 'How's everything with you two?'

'Oh, fine.' Daisy sat down on the other side of Kit's bed, took his hand in hers. His hand felt hot and spongy; not lean and muscular, not like Kit's hand at all.

'I've been thinking . . .' said Daisy.

Ruby looked at her with weary, deeply shadowed eyes.

'. . . Rob and I ought to carry on with what Kit was doing. Trying to find out who was behind Michael's death.'

As Daisy said the words, Ruby thought of Thomas saying that Michael had been unfaithful to her. Unfaithful with who, though? He'd said he had no more information; it had just been word on the street. So was it even true? Or was Thomas, in his Machiavellian way, trying to destabilize her loyal attachment to Michael's memory, to have her transfer the whole of her affection to him?

'I can do that on my own, Daise,' said Rob.

'I can help,' said Daisy.

Rob made no attempt to conceal his amusement at this.

Daisy stood up, giving Rob a look of blazing contempt. 'I'm going to the loo,' she said, and swept past him.

'Don't treat her like a joke,' said Ruby.

'I'm not, I—'

'Shut your gob for a second and listen, will you? Let me tell you something you don't know about Daisy. You'll have heard all about her upbringing: the private girls' schools and so on. Oh, she had a fantastic education – if all you want in life is to make cakes and arrange flowers and play the grande dame at charitable functions. But she was never encouraged to achieve anything, and she left school with no exams behind her, and a typical upper-crust life mapped out in front of her: marriage to a wealthy man, two perfect children . . .'

'Well, she got the wealthy man,' said Rob, thinking of Simon, the twat. Dead now, poor bastard, and you had to show respect, but the fact was he'd been a bumptious little arsehole and nothing could alter that. 'And the two kids.'

'Don't be fooled, Rob. Daisy catches on fast, and she's a real force to be reckoned with.' Ruby hesitated. She thought of her daughter, who had – shockingly – shown she had a violent side, banging those two bullies' heads together. Maybe she had more in common with her twin brother than she wanted to think. 'She's going crazy with nothing to do except worry over Kit and being separated from the twins. So . . .'

There was an awkward silence.

'Ruby,' said Rob at last.

'Hm?'

'I'm sorry, but there's something you should know. Someone tried to get in here. Ashok thinks it was one of Vittore's lot.'

Ruby's eyes widened. 'Oh God.'

Rob's gaze shifted to Kit's still, unresponsive face. 'He's got to come out of it soon.'

'I hope,' said Ruby.

'The sooner we can get him moved to someplace more secure, the better.'

They fell silent as Daisy returned, tetchily yanking her

cardigan back onto her shoulder. She took up her position by Kit's bed.

Rob watched her. It was hard to believe that the voluptuous and oh-so-posh Daisy, whose clothes always seemed to be about to fall off her, who was always tripping over something like to break her bloody neck, could actually be clever. Mind you, she was Kit's twin; and sometimes when he looked in her eyes it was as if he saw Kit staring right back at him, and that was fucking spooky. He wasn't sure about this, especially when there was still this weird frisson of attraction between them. Daisy could prove a nuisance, an encumbrance. And there was a danger she might get far too close for comfort.

'Daise?' he said.

'Hm?' Daisy wouldn't look him in the eye, still hurt because he'd laughed off her offer of help.

Finally she glanced at him. Big China-blue eyes, kissable mouth, corn-gold hair tumbling in disarray like she'd just fallen out of bed, and oh God, all right, he really wanted her in bed, he had to admit that. He was going to have to be *very* careful here.

'Daise – here's what'll happen,' said Rob. 'You can help . . .'

'Great!'

'. . . but what I say goes, OK? You keep your mouth shut – or some fucker's going to eat you whole and spit out the bits. So I do the talking, right?'

Daisy nodded. 'Right,' she said.

'Long as that's understood . . .'

'Oh, it is. Absolutely.'

84

Before they left the hospital Rob made sure that Fats was in place and aware of what had happened on Ashok's watch.

'Nobody gets in to see him unless it's Ruby, me or Daise, got that?'

Ruby was still in there with Kit; she never seemed to leave his side.

From the hospital, Daisy and Rob went straight to Kit's house. Rob had a spare key, he let them in. Daisy pulled off her cardigan and dumped it on the leather couch, then said: 'So, how was Kit getting on with this? How far had he got?'

'Not far,' he said. He looked over at the side table, where Michael's little collection of belongings were still spread out, just as Kit had left them. 'We know Michael was due to go over to see Ruby's brother Joe on the night he was killed, but he never showed up. Joe wanted to tell Michael about Gabe having been released from Wandsworth a week before. Gabe was pissed off that Michael had left the whole of his fortune to Kit, not him.'

'That does seem hard,' said Daisy, walking over to the side table.

'Michael and his boy fell out when Gabe was a teenager. God knows what he got up to, but it can't have been good.

Michael was tolerant, up to a point. Push him beyond that? The shutters would come down, and you were out.'

'So these are the bits and pieces Michael was carrying with him at the time of his death?' asked Daisy, leaning over to peer at the little pile.

'Yep.'

'What's this ring? This Krugerrand?' Daisy picked it up, turned it over, looked at the inside. 'It's hallmarked. And there's an inscription: *I'm Still in Love with You.* Tiny script. Was he actually *wearing* the ring?'

'What difference does that make?'

'All the difference in the world.'

'I never saw him wear the thing when he was alive, that's for sure. Or any other ring, not even a wedding ring.'

'What else have we got?'

'Not much.' Rob joined her at the side table and stared at Michael's belongings. Not much to show, for a life. 'Michael spoke to Vanessa Bray on the phone the day he died.'

Daisy turned to Rob in surprise. 'Really? About what?'

'Kit and me went down to Brayfield to see her, ask her about it. She said that it had been a courtesy call, that Michael had been asking how she was, after losing your dad, Cornelius.'

Daisy was frowning. 'Why would Michael do that? He barely knew her. And I had the distinct impression he didn't like her very much.'

'Me too. It didn't ring true. I didn't like her much, either.'

'Vanessa's OK,' said Daisy.

'You would say that. You grew up there with her, didn't you? Down in upper-crust towers.'

Daisy's gaze turned icy. 'Vanessa's OK,' she repeated slowly. Then she chewed her lip. 'That Gabe . . . when he came to the store to find me, it gave me the creeps.'

'He likes tackling women.'

'Have you spoken to him? You and Kit?'

'We have.' Rob didn't elaborate on the precise nature of Kit's conversation with Gabe.

'Nothing?'

'Nothing at all.'

'Can I ask you something?'

'Go on,' said Rob.

'You dropped Kit off on Saturday, when he got shot. He was going to have dinner at Gino's. Do you know who he was meeting?'

'Not for sure, no.'

Daisy's eyes were resting on Rob's face. 'Do you have a suspicion?'

Rob heaved a sigh. 'Truth? Yeah, I do.'

'Who?'

'Bianca Danieri.'

'Were they . . . ?'

'They were.'

'But . . . you're kidding.' She shook her head in disbelief. 'No . . . Would she . . . ? He must have been out of his mind!'

Rob went and sat down on the couch. He leaned his head back, and addressed his next remarks to the ceiling. 'Kit told me he met her when he was down on the coast. He didn't have a clue who she was – and how would she know him? I don't think she'd ever set eyes on him up until that point. So there was Kit, keeping it light, or trying to, but it sounds like he fell pretty hard. Between you and me, I reckon Kit's a pushover where women are concerned. Easy meat. Because he never had his mother around when he was growing up, and he craved that: a woman to care for him. Also, he'd given Bianca a false name.'

'He what?' Daisy frowned, unable to make sense of this.

'Daise, it's what men do. When they're out on the pull, they give false names. Easier that way. No accidental pregnancies, no paternity suits, no brats to pay for.'

She stared at him, wide-eyed. 'Is that what you do?'

'I'm not proud of it.'

'And Kit did that?'

'He did. But he said that the minute he'd spun her the lie, he felt bad about it. Knew she could be something special. Anyway, I went to Gino's, and the owner's description of the woman with Kit matches the one Kit gave me of Bianca Danieri. So yeah, I think he met her the night he was shot.'

'But the Danieris hate Kit. They're convinced that he killed Tito, even if their mother's been trying to put the brakes on them doing anything about it.'

'I know that.'

'Yet here Kit was, having dinner with the Danieri sister – a woman he'd *lied* to, who had no idea about who he really was. Do you suppose her brothers used her as bait? That they staked Kit out that night and shot him?'

'Here's what I think,' said Rob. 'If Fabio Danieri wanted to kill you, he'd blow your arse straight to hell with a sawn-off shotgun. Showy, see? Big gun, big noise. *Look at me, here I am, I'm the man.* If Vittore wanted to ice someone, it would be sneaky: in the back with something mid-sized, unshowy but effective. But Kit was shot from the front with a .22 – a lady's gun. That's probably why he's still alive; because it was small bore.'

Daisy was staring at Rob's face. 'You're saying he met Bianca Danieri at Gino's that night. And you're saying . . . are you saying it was most likely *Bianca* who shot him? Could a woman do that, do you think? Shoot a man down in cold blood?'

'You don't know that family, Daise. They're dangerous. They're Camorra – that's like the Mafia, only nastier.'

'Do you think she did it because she found out he lied to her? Found out who he really was? That he was the man who shot her brother?'

'Must have done.'

'If Kit . . .' Daisy couldn't say it.

'If he dies? Then to hell with it, I'm pointing the finger. And if the filth don't get her, I will.'

The phone on the side table started ringing. Rob leaned over and snatched it up. 'Hello?'

'*There* you are,' said Fats. In the background as Fats spoke Rob could hear the general hubbub of a hospital corridor.

'What's up?'

'You better get over here quick,' said Fats.

'What's going on?' Rob glanced at Daisy, who was watching him anxiously.

'There's a girl here, feisty little blonde, kicking off like you wouldn't believe. Says she's the boss's girlfriend and she's got to see him.'

Rob's whole body stiffened. 'Check she's not carrying, make sure she's alone and then get her out of the building,' he said quickly.

'Got you,' said Fats and hung up.

'What is it?' asked Daisy as Rob put the phone down.

Rob looked at her.

'I think Bianca Danieri just pitched up at the hospital.'

'*What?*'

'Come on. Sounds like she's trying to finish the job. Let's get over there.'

85

'Get your fucking hands off me!' yelled Bianca as Fats hustled her out into the hospital grounds.

People turned and stared.

'She's OK,' he said to a couple who paused, their faces concerned. 'Just upset. We're visiting our nan.'

The couple went on their way. Fats pushed Bianca roughly down onto a bench.

'Now sit there and shut up,' he snarled.

'I want to see him, that's all. I *have* to see him,' said Bianca.

'Did you hear what I just said? *Shut the fuck up.*' Fats sat down beside her.

Bianca shut up. She sat there in silence until another couple approached the bench, a big young bruiser of a man and a tall golden-blonde girl. Fats stood up. The two newcomers stared down at Bianca.

'She's not carrying?' asked Rob.

'Nah,' said Fats. 'Not a thing.'

Bianca sprang to her feet. 'I don't want to *hurt* him, for God's sake! I just need to see him.'

It had been tormenting her, what she'd done to him, preying on her mind like an endlessly revolving nightmare. She'd shot Tony – *Kit* – in a fit of craziness and she hated herself for it. Now she knew he had survived, all she wanted was to see him, to be sure he was OK.

Daisy stepped forward and for a split second Rob thought she would flatten Bianca.

'You're not going anywhere near Kit,' she hissed in Bianca's face. 'You've done enough damage already.'

'I have to see him,' said Bianca through gritted teeth.

Daisy lunged forward. Rob grabbed her, held her back. 'Shut up, Daise,' he told her. 'Calm down.'

Daisy took a gulping breath, glaring at Bianca. After a moment, the tension went out of her and Rob let her go. She walked off a couple of paces and then came back, clutching her arms around her middle as if that was the only way she could prevent herself from grabbing hold of Bianca and choking the life out of her.

'We can use this,' said Daisy.

'What?' said Rob.

'This. She's walked straight into our hands. Vittore's trying to get to Kit, right? If we've got his sister, and you tell him so, he'll stop trying.'

Rob and Fats stared at each other.

'Could work,' said Fats.

Bianca was looking at the three of them, her eyes frantic. 'I don't want to hurt him, I swear.'

Daisy turned on her. 'You already have.'

'Look—'

'Shut up,' said Rob, and he grabbed Bianca's arm and led her away.

86

Fabio was feeling increasingly nervous. No, *terrified*. He sensed that something had happened, but he had no idea what. He didn't dare ask Vittore about it, so he asked Mama instead.

'I haven't seen Maria about the place recently,' he said, all casual. 'Is she OK?'

Bella gave a derisory *humph*. 'She's gone off to stay with her parents for a while, Vittore tells me. You'd think the woman's place would be at her husband's side, but oh no. Not her. She has to have a break, apparently.'

But discreet enquiries soon revealed that Maria was not at her parents' home. So where was she?

There had been a lot of activity in Maria's and Vittore's set of rooms the last few days. Passing through the hall, Fabio had seen that sneaky, ugly scar-faced fucker Jay going in and out, along with some of Vito's other boys. Soon, Vittore's wine collection, of which he had always been so proud, was stacked out in the hallway.

'Just a bit of decorating,' said Vittore, when Fabio stood there one day, eyeing the bottles.

He didn't question it. He was only grateful that Vittore hadn't tried to slit his throat yet. If Maria was gone, it was none of his business.

Then, more workmen showed up. Bricks were being taken

into Vittore's rooms, and a door came out. Then the plasterer showed up with his bucket and his pink powder.

Fabio passed Bella, who was out in the hall, sniffing.

'You smell anything out here?'

Fabio said he didn't, even though he thought he could, just a little.

'I'll get them to check the drains,' said Bella, and went back to her kitchen.

A few days later the painters and decorators arrived. And then one evening Fabio came home to find all the wine was gone from the hallway.

Fabio waited until Bella was out and Vittore was at work, until he was certain no one else was in the house. He took the spare key to Vittore's rooms from the hanging horseshoe in Bella's kitchen and, his heart beating furiously, he went into Vittore and Maria's section of the house and looked around.

All was pristine in the lounge and the bedroom. He didn't think to check the wardrobes because he felt panicky just being inside Vittore's territory. In the kitchen, everything looked much as it should. But he stood there, surveying the room, thinking *There's something's different about the place. What is it?*

And another thing. Lingering below the chemical tang of fresh paint, as he stood there in the kitchen he smelled something else, something that made him put a hand to his nose, pull a disgusted face.

'*Che puzzo!*' he burst out. *The smell.*

It was like chicken left in a rubbish bin for too long, like something decaying, something rotting.

He recoiled, feeling faintly sick, and hurried back out into the lounge, through there to the door, and he was afraid now, he was very afraid indeed, because he was thinking, *Vittore's going to come home and find me in here.*

And if that happened, he didn't know what would become of him.

Trembling, Fabio stepped out into the – mercifully empty – hall, turned the key and removed it, hurried over to Mama's kitchen and with a shaking hand hung the thing on the hook on the horseshoe. When that was done he leaned over the sink, poured water, gulped it down.

It was only then that he realized what was different in Vittore's kitchen.

The cellar door had been bricked up.

87

'Then I opened the Leicester store. By the mid-sixties I did a deal directly with the manufacturers. I went against the Wholesale Textile Association, cut out the middle men,' said Ruby, feeling as if she wanted to slump her head onto Kit's bed and sleep.

They'd told her that they were decreasing the level of Kit's tranquilizers now, but he looked just the same. He looked dead, but he was still breathing. So she sat there, talking and talking, saying anything that came into her head, her eyes gritty and red-raw, her voice fading sometimes to a hoarse whisper.

It didn't seem possible, not after all this time. But what was time? How much time had he spent here, in this strange black desert where his only companion was the howling, freezing wind that whipped at his flesh and bones, chilling him to the marrow? There were no stars above him, no cities around him, there was nothing. Just endless night and that strange whispering cacophony of voices that had now become one voice, saying his name, saying, Don't leave me, don't go. Slowly, oh so slowly, it couldn't be possible, could it? Was the black really starting to fade to grey? Or had he been looking at it for so long (and God alone knew how long) that his eyes were playing tricks on him?

★

Ruby's head was drooping. It was soporifically hot in intensive care, she was struggling to keep her eyes open. It was late, she'd been here for days, and now all she wanted was to sleep. She was exhausted from all this talking, from looking at Kit so hopefully, praying for a sign, however small, that he was coming back to her. She had run out of words, out of hope, out of strength. She was . . .

A hand grabbed her shoulder, shook it.

Ruby started awake from a half-doze, looking around, realizing that she had almost fallen asleep.

'What?' She dragged a hand through her hair, and gazed up at Corinne, the little blonde nurse.

'Look,' said Corinne, nodding to Kit.

Ruby looked. Nothing had changed. She felt crushing disappointment.

'Look at his eyes,' said Corinne.

Ruby looked. Kit's eyes were still closed, no change there. Except . . . well, something had changed. Just a little. Beneath the closed lids, Kit's eyes were flicking back and forth, like someone dreaming. This was different. She glanced at Corinne, then back at Kit. His eyes were closed, but yes, they *were* moving.

'Is he . . . ?' asked Ruby.

'He's beginning to come round,' said Corinne.

'Come round,' said a voice that floated past in the teeth of the gale. The greyness was lifting, and with it came a vague discomfort, but this was better than the blackness, the icy blast of the wind that numbed his flesh and clawed at his skin. This was better than the tunnel, too, even if there had been that enticing light at the end of it. He wasn't ready to go there, not yet. Or at least he didn't think so.

'Is he . . . ?' asked another voice.

Female voices.

They gave him no comfort, females. Deserted him, abandoned him, caused him pain.

Now he felt it, in his heart, in his chest.

Ruby

Bianca

Ah no, Gilda, he couldn't think about her. Too much pain.

Oh Jesus, it hurt.

'What's the matter with him, is he all right?' asked Ruby.

Kit was twisting in the bed now, as if fighting restraints; his eyes, beneath their closed lids, were flicking back and forth frantically, and his mouth was open in a silent scream.

'It's something he has to go through,' said Corinne reassuringly. 'This is a good sign. Wait outside now, if you would. We've things to do.'

What things?

Ruby stumbled to her feet.

'Outside,' said Corinne, and Ruby went, dazed and distressed, into the waiting room where Fats loitered, watching everyone with suspicious eyes. Ruby took refuge in the women's toilets, where she could be alone and cry her heart out in peace.

Fats was waiting for his replacement but the guy was late, silly bastard. Bladder bursting, he had to give in at last and respond to a call of nature. He strode off down the corridor, past the nurse's station, past the endless wards. He got to the men's toilets, hurriedly relieved himself, washed his hands. Then he made his way back as fast as he could.

There was a squat man with scarred, pockmarked red cheeks and black hair standing at the nurse's station, asking about his nephew Kit Miller. Fats knew that Kit had only two uncles, and one of them was long dead. The other was out at Chigwell, almost too old and infirm to walk, let alone make hospital visits. This bloke looked all wrong. He was too young. Too Latin. And he had a face like a pizza. He looked like someone had played join-the-dots on his face with a lit cigarette.

Tensing, Fats walked straight on past the man and dived into one of the sidewards. Instead of beds and bleeping monitors and hospital equipment it was full of decorators' gear, and the window was open wide to get rid of the smell of fresh paint. Fats stood there peering through the crack in the door, waiting.

Soon, the man came past, limping slightly. *So much the better.*

Fats stepped out quietly behind him, glanced around to check that he was unobserved, and kicked the man hard in the back of the knee. His weight took him down. Fats clamped a hand over his mouth to stifle a yell. Then he dragged him backward, off-balance, into the side ward and let the door swing closed behind them.

'Kit Miller might have an uncle, but you ain't it,' snarled Fats, running the man across the room to the window.

'*NO!*' the man tried to yell through the hand gagging his mouth, his legs scrabbling uselessly as Fats got him over the edge of the windowsill. For a moment he swung like a pendulum, then his weight and a hefty push took him over and out. A thin cry escaped him; then he was gone. When he hit the ground far below, he barely made a sound.

It was awful, a suicide like that. Not that it was the first time such a thing had happened within the hospital grounds, but still, it was shocking. Poor man jumping to his death, how low would you have to feel, to do that to yourself?

Corinne and a couple of the other ICU nurses heard about it within the hour.

'It's terrible. So sad,' said Corinne, on her coffee break.

'The good-looking one's coming round then,' said her colleague.

'Kit Miller? Yes, he's coming along fine.'

Corinne thought that Kit was good-looking, extremely so. But he had an air about him that disturbed her. And those burly men, hanging around in the waiting room, she didn't care for that. She'd asked Kit's brother, the big one with the sexy khaki-green eyes about it, and he had reassured her, though not entirely. He didn't look anything like Kit, for a start. But he'd told her Kit was an important businessman and these were his bodyguards. Still, it gave Corinne an uneasy feeling. And now Kit was coming round, the police would be here to question him. With gunshot vics, they always did.

88

Daisy and Rob dropped Bianca off at one of Kit's safe houses near Lambeth – not the one where Jody and the twins were being concealed, he told Daisy, so she mustn't start on about seeing them.

'I won't,' she snapped.

'Good.'

This enforced separation from her babies was torture, but Daisy understood that it was for the twins' safety and that had to be paramount. Again she thought of Simon, dying the way he did. No, Matthew and Luke were safer where they were, even if it *did* crucify her to be apart from them.

On the way to the safe house, they picked up two of Kit's most dependable men, to watch over Bianca.

'Do they know what happened? That it was her . . . ?' Daisy asked Rob when the two men were out of earshot.

'They know,' said Rob. 'All the boys know.'

'Tell them you don't want her hurt, or touched. That's very important. She's not to be let outside the door, or allowed to make phone calls. Tell them they're to keep her in perfect health, that you'll be very cross if they disobey you.'

'*Very cross?*'

'You know what I mean,' she said.

Rob was shaking his head at her. 'Are we sure about this?' he wondered.

'Perfectly sure. They're trying to get to Kit in case he talks to the police. But now we have Bianca – and you're going to tell them that. They'll back away.'

'You hope.'

'They will. She's our one and only bargaining chip now that Vittore's stepping up the pressure, but we have to look after her really well. It's vital.'

'And never mind what's she's done,' said Rob sourly.

'Precisely. *Forget* that,' said Daisy with a flash of steely determination in her eyes.

After dropping Bianca off, Daisy insisted that they call by Michael's flat. Rob parked outside Sheila's restaurant and led the way to the side door. He was about to put the key in the lock when he saw that it had been forced.

He paused, looked at Daisy. Held a finger to his lips.

He pushed the door gently, and it swung inward. Seeing no one there, he ran up the stairs, Daisy following close behind.

'Christ,' said Rob in a whisper when he found the flat door busted too. 'Stop here a minute, Daise,' he said quietly, and ducked swiftly inside, looking left and right at a scene of chaos.

He moved through the main lounge, into the kitchen; then into the bedroom and the bathroom. It seemed every drawer had been tipped onto the floor, every cupboard ransacked. The mattress had been slashed open, there was stuffing all over the place. The bathroom cabinets had been emptied, creams and vials and deodorants smashed on the tiled floor. The sofas in the lounge had been given the same treatment as the bed, the cushions thrown carelessly aside, the coverings ripped. Even the curtains had been pulled down from their tracks. In the kitchen, it looked as though a whirlwind had hit. There was food all over the floor, smashed eggs and spilled milk, and the refrigerator door was hanging open.

The place had been comprehensively turned over.

'Jesus,' said Daisy, standing thunderstruck in the open doorway. 'Do you think they've taken anything?'

Rob stood in the centre of the lounge, looking around him in wonder.

'How the fuck would I know? *Look* at this shit.'

Daisy moved inside, feeling a bit bolder now she knew some lunatic wasn't lurking in a corner somewhere. She looked around, at the sofas, the cushions, the . . .

'Why slash the sofas open?' she asked him.

'Hm? Oh. They did the mattress too.'

'Yes, but why?'

'I dunno, Daise,' said Rob irritably. 'It's been a bloody long week. And now this . . .'

'They must have been looking for something,' said Daisy.

'What?'

'Don't you think so? I wonder what's missing.'

'Daise – I *don't know*. I never did a fucking inventory of the place.'

Daisy surveyed the wreckage. 'What were they looking for?' she wondered aloud.

'Fuck knows. Maybe nothing. Maybe they just smashed up the place for the hell of it.'

Rob was tired, and he was thinking that possibly they'd done a stupid thing, taking Bianca. Vittore had been beyond fury when he'd phoned him and let him know the score. His best friend was laid up in a hospital bed hovering somewhere between life and death. He'd had *enough*. He walked to the door.

'Where are you going?' said Daisy.

'Home,' he said. 'I need to sleep.'

'No, I want to look in the office downstairs.'

'Oh, for fuck's—'

'What?'

'Daise, enough.'

'No! The office.'

'God, you're a stroppy cow, has anyone ever told you that?' said Rob, thinking that he'd have to get the locks repaired and the boys in, tidy the damned place up; it was just one bloody thing after another lately.

He followed Daisy downstairs and into the restaurant where the staff were getting ready for the evening's trade. Daisy and Rob wove their way through the bar, through the restaurant, and over to the office.

'Oh for fuck's sake,' said Rob.

Daisy peered past his shoulder. The door was slightly ajar. And the lock looked . . .

'It's been broken into,' she said.

'Oh, first prize! Give the lady a coconut,' said Rob, and pushed the door open. He flicked on the light. 'Damn, will you look at this? How the hell did this happen and no one see or hear?'

Daisy came in behind Rob and eased the door closed behind them. All the filing cabinets had been emptied and overturned. There were papers all over the place, the desk had been flipped onto its back, Michael's chair – *Kit's* chair – had been thrown aside, the seat slashed open, the stuffing pulled out.

Rob went over to the desk.

Daisy stared all around her.

'Somebody's *definitely* looking for something,' she said.

'Yeah, but what?'

'I wonder if they found it?'

'Daise . . .'

'Maybe they didn't.'

'Hm.'

'Maybe you and Kit have already taken it away. Perhaps what someone wants is the stuff that Michael was carrying around with him.'

On the way out, they stopped at the bar and questioned Terry, the head barman.

'You seen anyone hanging about the office?' asked Rob.

'No, why?'

'It's been broken into. Turned upside-down. The flat upstairs, too.'

'Get out of it! Really? Well, I was on last night and I didn't notice anything. Mind you, that lock's a pissy little thing, one good shove and it'd give. Keely!' He called over to a brunette who was busy polishing glasses. 'You see anyone hanging around the office yesterday or today? Someone's been in there.'

Keely shook her head: no.

'Bridge was on too,' said Terry. 'Bridge!' he called, and a blonde girl appeared from the back, eyebrows raised in enquiry. 'Bridge, you see anyone around the office last night or today? They're saying someone's been in there, and the flat upstairs.'

'No, I haven't. Sorry.' Bridget turned away, then she stopped and looked back at them. 'Wait on, I saw a bloke with a beard loitering near the side entrance yesterday evening. But he was that skinny, I wouldn't have thought he could break the lock. Didn't look like he had an ounce of strength in him.'

At that moment, Ashok appeared in the restaurant doorway. He saw Rob and came straight over.

'We had some trouble at the hospital,' he said. 'I didn't want to risk telling you over the phone, so I've been driving all over—'

'What's happened?'

'Another one tried to get to Kit.'

'What's this?' asked Daisy.

'It sorted?' asked Rob.

Ashok grinned. 'Bloke had a nasty accident, decided to end it all.'

89

When he took the call at the club, Vittore couldn't believe it. This was not a day for good news. 'Pizza-face' Donato had fallen to his death from a hospital window and then Miller's right-hand man had the brass neck to tell him that he should call his dogs off, because they had Bianca.

A bluff?

He phoned Dante's in Southampton and asked Cora, was Bianca there?

She wasn't. Days ago, she'd said she was going up to London, and no one at the club had seen or heard from her since.

First, he had to tell Mama. She wailed and screamed like a madwoman.

'What will they do to her?' she sobbed. 'My baby!'

'They'll do nothing, Mama,' said Vittore. 'She has to be kept safe, or else what do they have left?'

But Bella went on with her hysterical breast-beating.

Fabio came into the kitchen, alerted by all the noise. 'What's going on?'

Vittore filled him in.

'We can't allow this,' said Fabio, clenching his fists.

'It's done,' said Vittore, watching his younger brother with cynical eyes. Like *he* cared about Bianca. Not that

Vittore did either, not really, only insofar as her behaviour reflected upon him and the Danieri name. She was becoming a liability. He couldn't have her telling the world she was in love with that bastard Kit Miller. He couldn't have Miller scoring points over them. No way. And it wasn't as if Bianca was truly blood, he reminded himself.

'What do you mean? We stand by? Do nothing?'

'Yeah, we do nothing. For the time being. What else can we do? Now shut up and get out of my way.'

Fabio glared at his older brother. Who was he, telling *him* what to do? He had his own business now, he didn't have to answer to Vittore any more. He had even tupped the mama's boy's wife. And still Vittore thought he could tell him what to do?

Fuck him.

But then he remembered that bricked-up cellar door, and Maria, gone God knew where, and that smell. And suddenly the fear was back, crawling up his spine as he looked at Vittore.

He's going to get me, thought Fabio.

And then he had another thought.

Unless I get him first.

90

Someone was calling his name, right by his ear.

The voice was so close that it startled him. All the sounds before had been distant, ethereal, ghost-echoes of his own thoughts. But this was a definite, firm, *Kit*.

It was grey, light-grey now, and he could hear things beeping, monitors or something, and it was like being talked up from hypnosis or some such bollocks; he was coming up and he would wake when someone went *click* with their fingers.

Three . . .

Coming awake, coming back to the land of the living . . .

Two . . .

. . . stretching, feeling that he'd had enough of that other world with its blackness and its chilling winds . . .

One.

His eyes flickered open. Owwww. Bright in here. Lights all over the place, and someone leaning over him, a blonde pigtail tickling his collarbone, his heartbeat accelerating, what the fuck . . . ? A kind face, young, pretty and that blonde was straight out of a bottle . . .

'Kit?' she said, and smiled and put a soft warm hand to his face. 'Hello, Kit. You're fine, you're in hospital. Just rest there for now, everything's going to be OK.'

What happened? he wanted to say, but even as his brain

formed the words, it came back to him. Dinner with Bianca. Outside in the rain. The gun in her hand. The terrible ripping pain in his chest, and then nothing.

The nurse's face withdrew and he saw Ruby sitting there. She was holding his hand and she was crying and laughing at the same time.

'You're back,' she was saying. 'Thank God, you're back.'

'Yeah,' he said, but he made no sound. He felt so tired, like he'd run a mile.

The nurse's face floated into view. 'Rest now. You're doing so well,' she said.

He was exhausted. His eyes drooped, and closed again. No wasteland this time, though. This time there was only the warm familiar darkness of sleep.

91

Rob drove Daisy back to Kit's house and they let themselves in, relieved to find that the lock was intact and inside the place was, apparently, untouched.

'Well, thank fuck for that,' said Rob.

Daisy walked over to where Michael's belongings were still spread out on the side table. Rob joined her. They both stared at the bits and pieces there. The gold Dunhill lighter, the cigarette case, the comb, the Krugerrand set in the ridged heavy gold mount of the ring, three matchbooks, a Rolex, a wad of twenty-pound notes and some change in a plain black wallet.

'Is this all? I mean, were there any other items that Michael was carrying, that Kit would have kept for himself?' asked Daisy. Rob shook his head. 'Kit was so sure that Tito killed Michael,' she said.

'Bella Danieri says not. Not Tito, and not Fabio or Vittore either.'

'Motives, then. What motive would anyone else have for doing that?'

'Money and honey,' said Rob.

'Hm?'

'Money,' said Rob. 'That points straight to Gabriel Ward. He found out he wasn't getting a bean, and killed his dad in a rage.'

'It's possible.'

'Honey?'

'That's possible too.' Daisy thought of her mother. 'Rob . . . what do you know about Thomas Knox?'

'Tom Knox? He's a hard man, a real face. In charge of a firm. Like Michael was. Like Kit is now.'

'I think Ruby's been seeing him. He was outside the church after Simon's funeral, waiting to speak to her. The way he looks at her . . .'

'What?' asked Rob, when she hesitated.

'Just he seems . . . as if the normal rules don't apply to him.'

'Daise – they don't. I didn't know Ruby was involved with him.'

'I'm thinking aloud, that's all . . . Honey, you said. Michael dies and suddenly there's Thomas Knox, making moves on Ruby. Knox could have wanted Michael out of the way. To clear the path to her.'

'Possible.'

Daisy was frowning. 'Did Michael strike you as secretive?'

'In what way?'

'Oh . . . hiding things. You know.'

'No, I don't know. What sort of things?'

Daisy looked at Rob. 'I don't want this going any further,' she said. 'This is just between us.'

'What is?'

'Apparently Michael had another woman. A *secret* woman. Thomas Knox told Ruby about it.'

Rob looked astonished. 'I don't believe it.'

'Neither did I, but it's true.'

'Bullshit. Maybe he cooked up the secret woman to turn Ruby off Michael's memory?'

'Maybe.' Daisy picked up the Krugerrand ring and turned

it over in her hand. 'But I'm looking at this inscription: *I'm Still in Love with You*. Ruby didn't give this to him. Michael didn't wear rings, as a general rule. We don't think his wife gave it to him . . .'

'There's no way of knowing that.'

'Why would she give him a ring? She knew he wouldn't wear it. And why was it in his pocket, instead of in a drawer somewhere? Why was he carrying it around with him?'

'Jesus,' said Rob. 'I don't know.'

Daisy put the ring down. 'So what else is there?' she asked.

'Well . . .' Rob glanced around the flat. 'There's Michael's record collection, Kit kept that.'

Daisy knew that Kit was into modern stuff with a hard aggressive beat, but Michael's taste had been for the music of the fifties, the era he'd grown up in – Billy Fury, Bobby Darren, artists like that. The music of a bygone age.

Rob stood up and went over to the stereo, opened a door and lifted out a thick wodge of LPs. He took them over to the sofa.

'Well, here we are,' he sighed.

Daisy spread the covers out and took a look. 'That's Kit's,' said Rob, and tossed Queen's *Sheer Heart Attack* to one side. 'That too,' he said, shuffling past an old dog-eared copy of *Their Satanic Majesties Request* by the Stones. 'These are Michael's.' Now they were into Michael's era: some Tony Bennett and Vic Damone, a little Johnny Rae, a soupçon of the big O.

'Roy Orbison,' said Rob, and sighed again, heavily. 'That's one of the newer ones for Michael, but he liked the Big O. Always said that man could really sing.'

Daisy was looking at the cover. 'The title on the cover: *I'm Still in Love with You*,' she said. 'That's odd, isn't it? The same as the ring.'

Now she was pulling out the white inner sleeve. 'Oh, look at this!' she said, and her voice was full of excitement. 'Look, Rob.'

Rob looked. There was handwriting in the bottom right-hand corner. It read: *I'm still in love with you*. 'What about the writing?'

'I don't recognize it,' said Daisy, squinting hard at it. 'This album was released last year, but that's the same inscription as the one on the ring.'

'So if this is from that same person, the same woman, that's not his wife Sheila's handwriting. It can't be.'

'Maybe it's Ruby . . . ? I don't think so, though. Oh . . .'

Rob looked at her. 'Oh what?' he asked.

'I don't know,' she said vacantly.

'Do you know the writing? Daise?'

'No, but I just thought of something.'

'Well, go on then.'

'It's too stupid.'

'I said go on.'

'Michael phoning Vanessa to see how she was . . .'

Rob stared at Daisy's face. 'Oh, come on. You're kidding! Michael and her ladyship? Don't make me laugh.'

'She's a lonely rich widow,' said Daisy.

'Daise – the woman's as dried-up as a nun's twat,' said Rob.

'Rob!'

'Come on. It's the truth.'

Daisy was flushed with sudden temper. 'It might be, but I don't want to hear it! She was all I knew as a child, and she loved me. She did her best for me. So don't talk about her like that, OK?'

Rob shrugged. 'OK,' he said.

Daisy heaved a sigh. Michael and Vanessa as lovers?

Vanessa buying Michael rings and LPs, little love tokens? Surely not . . .

'No, Vanessa hates popular music. She's into Dvořák and Holst, a little Wagner,' said Daisy.

They both fell silent, staring at the sleeve of the LP.

'But someone wrote that,' said Rob. 'Looks like the same person who had the ring inscribed, too.'

'Yes,' said Daisy. 'I don't think it's Ruby's writing, though. And I don't think it's Vanessa's hand either. Too loopy.'

'Well, whose is it?'

'Don't know . . . But, Rob . . .'

'Hm?'

'I've had a thought about Bridge's skinny bloke with the beard.'

92

Bianca was being kept in comfort but she was still in a state of misery. She was lying on a bed in a strange house, thinking of Kit gravely ill in hospital. Her big fear was that her brothers would get to him, finish him off. She knew it wasn't beyond them to do that.

She hated him, but she loved him too. She was so torn over Kit Miller that she thought she might go mad.

He probably killed Tito.

Yes, that was true. But . . . she loved him.

He lied to you.

Also true. No denying it.

Are you mad?

Yes. Maybe she was.

There was a knock on the door. She heard the key turn in the lock and one of the men entered, the slim, cold-eyed one, bringing her dinner on a tray. She was a prisoner here, confined. Oh, she had a comfy bedroom, a television, a radio, her own bathroom to use. But she was a prisoner nonetheless. Which was really no more than she deserved, after the awful thing she'd done.

What if he dies? she wondered.

If he did . . . then she might as well be dead, too.

If he didn't, if he lived, then he could grass her up to the police, and it would all be over for her. Maybe these people – his people – would simply hand her over to the law, let them deal with her. Or maybe they would deal with her themselves.

Unsmiling, not speaking, the man put the tray down on a low table. She saw the food there. Fish and chips. The thought of eating anything made her guts heave.

She didn't thank the man.

She turned her back on him, faced the wall. Presently she heard him leave the room, heard the key turn in the lock once more.

93

Kit was out of intensive and into high care within a week.

'He's a strong one,' said Corinne to Ruby.

'Yes, he is,' said Ruby. She was so relieved that Kit was getting better, and she stayed with him as much as she could. Fully conscious now, growing stronger day by day, he moved his hand away when she tried to hold it.

'You don't have to stay here,' he said at one point.

'I want to,' said Ruby.

'Was that your voice I heard when I was out of it?' he asked.

Ruby was startled by the question. So he had heard her. 'I expect it was. I stayed here, I talked to you. The nurses said it would help.'

It had helped. Even though he might deny it to anyone who asked, Kit knew that Ruby's voice had comforted him in the bleak blackness of unconsciousness, had wormed its way through, like a single bright thread tethering him to the earth. But was she telling the truth? Would she really have taken the time, the trouble?

He looked at her. His mother. She looked shitty, not her usual elegant self; she looked like she'd been through the mill.

'You been to see Uncle Joe yet?' asked Kit, thinking of that dark place with its screaming winds, that tunnel he had glimpsed but not gone through. Pretty soon, he knew that Uncle Joe was going to make that same trip, and he wouldn't be coming back.

'No.' Ruby looked awkward. 'We fell out some years ago. Or at least, me and Betsy did. So Joe took her side – of course he did – and the whole thing got sort of lost and forgotten. We exchange cards at Christmas. And I keep them all, every one, which I suppose is stupid. That's about as far as it goes these days.'

'Fuck Betsy,' said Kit. 'Go and see him. Say goodbye, if nothing else.'

Rob and Daisy came in, all smiles because they could tell he was on the mend.

'Hiya, mate,' said Rob.

'Kit! You're looking better,' said Daisy, planting a kiss on her brother's cheek.

'I'm feeling it,' said Kit. 'Why don't you and Ruby slip outside while I have a chat to Rob.'

'Oh God. Man talk. Come on, Mum,' sighed Daisy.

'So how the fuck are you?' Rob asked Kit.

'Pretty much OK,' said Kit. They were still dosing him with morphine for residual pain, but the wound was healing and he could feel himself getting stronger, day by day.

'I understand you've been lumbered with Daisy,' said Kit.

'She's a good kid. And bright.' Rob went on to tell Kit about Bianca trying to bust her way into the ward, and Daisy's plan of holding her for insurance purposes. About the 'suicide', and about the other one who'd come in, claiming to be a relative. 'The Bill spoken to you yet?'

'Yeah, they have. And I didn't see anything, can't remember anything – you get the picture.' Kit was frowning. 'I don't want Bianca touched, you understand?'

'She won't be.'

'Make sure of it.'

'I will.'

'You looking after Daise?'

'Goes without saying. Listen, have you got somewhere in the office at the restaurant or in Michael's flat where you'd hide something worth a bob or two, something someone might want to find and take back?'

Kit looked at Rob. 'What you telling me?'

'Michael's flat was turned over. And the office behind the restaurant. It's OK, I've had it all tidied up. But somebody was searching for something. Maybe they found it, who knows? Would you have left anything about the place that was, I dunno, *sensitive*?'

'Nothing that I know of,' said Kit.

'Well, where would you hide something like that?' asked Rob. He'd spent days puzzling over this and had been back to the flat for a second look, but had drawn a blank. He'd been even more stumped when Daisy told him her theory about the identity of the bearded man seen loitering outside Sheila's. 'Where would Michael have put something like that?'

'There's a cubbyhole under the carpet beneath the desk,' said Kit, lowering his voice. 'A couple of the floorboards are loose, and Michael used to tuck anything really valuable in the back there. I don't use it. You could try that. Why? What are you thinking you'll find?'

Rob shrugged. 'Haven't got a fucking clue. But I'll take a look.'

Kit wondered what he would do without Rob. Good, solid, dependable Rob – you could always rely on him to pick up any slack. He hated being laid up like this. It sounded as though all sorts of shit was happening and here he was, unable to do a thing about it.

'You got Bianca safe?' he asked.

'Course.'

'Rob, I want her kept that way. No funny business.'

'After what she did to you?'

'She could have killed me. She didn't.'

'She gave it a bloody good go.'

'She pulled to the left. Missed the heart.'

'Didn't know you *had* one.'

'Then she was looking down at me, the gun pointing straight at my head. She could have pulled the trigger and finished me – she didn't.'

'Must be love,' scoffed Rob. 'Mate, she damned near killed you and here you are saying what a peach she is and not to harm a hair on her head. You mad?'

'You wouldn't know, you berk. You never been in love in your life. Oh, and incidentally . . .'

'Yeah, what?'

'I want to see her.'

'Fuck's sake!'

'There's something I wanted to talk to you about,' said Daisy when she and Ruby had bought their coffees and seated themselves at a table in the canteen.

'Oh? You want sugar in yours? No? OK. Go ahead.'

'Thomas Knox.'

'What about him?' Ruby sipped her drink.

'Are you . . . very involved with him?'

Up to the hilt, thought Ruby. Her mind kept running through everything Thomas had told her. That shocking thing about Bianca Danieri. And about Michael, and his son Gabe.

Aloud, she said: 'A bit. Why?'

'Rob and I were discussing who would have had a motive to kill Michael.'

'And . . . ?'

'I think that Thomas might have had a motive.'

'What?' Ruby was staring at Daisy's face.

'I know you won't want to hear this,' said Daisy.

'Hear what?'

Daisy took a breath. 'Mum, he's been pursuing you. He's made no secret of the fact that he wants to get close to you, am I right?'

Ruby flushed lightly, thinking of Thomas at the hotel, then swimming in his pool, and afterwards in his bed. She wasn't about to share any of that with Daisy.

'So?' she asked.

'Mum . . .' Daisy was being as delicate as she could. 'There was an obstacle to Thomas Knox's pursuit of you, wasn't there? You told me he'd been watching you for years – *coveting* you, was the phrase you used – and there was only one thing in his way. That thing was Michael, Mum. It was Michael.'

Ruby was silent, staring at her daughter's face. 'What are you saying?'

'Thomas Knox had a motive. He wanted to get to you. And he couldn't, not with Michael alive.'

'Jesus, what . . . I mean, really . . .'

'Think about it,' said Daisy.

Ruby fell silent again. At last she said: 'This is ridiculous.'

'Mum . . .'

'No! Seriously, Daisy, this is mad. Thomas and Michael knew each other from school, they grew up together . . .'

'And there you were, in mourning for Michael. And suddenly here's Thomas, ready with the tea and sympathy.'

Ruby was shaking her head. *Thomas?* She was in his thrall, she knew it. Her affair with him had been amazingly – shamefully – hot, lustful. Nothing like the relationship she'd had with Michael. And now Daisy was asking her to believe that the man she was involved with had *killed* Michael, simply to get her?

No. It couldn't be.

Could it?

Oh God in heaven. Perhaps it *could* be true. And worse – she had been so dazed with passion, so completely under his spell, that she hadn't even given such a foul possibility a thought until this moment.

Daisy was watching her mother's face closely. She hated having to do this. But if Knox had removed Michael because he was a barrier to Ruby, then Ruby needed to know, she had to be made aware. 'I'm sorry,' she said.

Ruby shook her head again, covered her mouth with her hand; suddenly her eyes were full of tears and she was blinking them back. She picked up the cup, drank, put it down again with a shaking hand.

'It's not your fault,' she said.

'I'm really sorry,' said Daisy. She couldn't think of anything else to say.

94

'He wants to see her,' said Rob when Daisy and Ruby joined him later.

Ruby looked aghast. She'd had enough shocks recently. First Daisy's thunderbolt about Thomas Knox, now this. 'What, this Bianca woman? Are you serious? She tried to kill him!'

'I'll bring her in tomorrow evening,' said Rob. 'Maybe it's best you stay away.'

Ruby stared at him. This was crazy.

'I don't want her anywhere near him,' she said forcefully.

'It's what he wants, Ruby.'

Daisy gave Ruby's arm a squeeze. 'We have to respect his wishes,' she said.

'But he must be bloody insane! She could try it again, finish him off this time. I can't agree to this,' said Ruby, tight-lipped.

'You don't have to. Kit wants it, and what Kit wants, he gets,' said Rob more firmly.

Ruby opened her mouth to speak, then shut it like a clamp when she saw the determination on Rob's face. She turned on her heel and stormed off.

★

'You know what?' Fats was holding court in the office with two other members of the Miller crew. 'That arsehole had so much blubber that he must have bounced three feet off the fucking ground when he hit.'

Everyone laughed; they stopped when Rob came in.

'What's this?' he asked.

'That Eyetie trying to sneak in on the boss at the hospital. Big boy. I always say a boy like that's easy to take down. His weight'll defeat him. Got him in the back of the knee and—'

'Fats,' said Rob. 'Shut the fuck up. You think it's funny – one of the Danieri crew throwing himself out of a hospital window when Kit's in a room a few doors down? You reckon the Old Bill's laughing? Do you have any idea the trouble I'll have to go to, to see that it's buried?'

Fats shrugged uneasily. He'd done his job, hadn't he? Stopped that wop bastard dead.

'Soon as Kit came round the police were in there, questioning him about the shooting. He handled it; we were home clear. All that could change if they find out the guy who took a high-dive from the window had a helping hand. You think Kit needs any more crap, you dumb fuck?'

The boys were silent. Rob turned away from them in disgust.

'I'm not happy with any of this,' he said, and stalked out of the room.

'No shit,' muttered Fats.

Next evening, Rob took a pale, silent Bianca to the hospital. Throughout her enforced stay at the Lambeth safe house, she had been biddable, subdued, and her demeanour didn't change even when they entered the maze of corridors and wound their way to the private room Kit now occupied.

Ashok was on guard.

'All OK?' Rob asked him.

'Fine,' he said, glaring at Bianca.

'Go on home,' said Rob, and Ashok departed.

Rob glanced at Bianca. 'You OK for this?'

She nodded: didn't speak.

'Sorry about this,' said Rob, 'but I need you to spread your arms.' And there in an empty waiting room he frisked her with cool expertise.

'Come on then,' he said when it was done.

Rob led the way into Kit's room. The moment they walked through the door, Kit's eyes fastened on Bianca and stayed there.

Bianca and Rob stopped at the foot of the bed.

'Rob, you can go,' said Kit, his eyes still fixed on her.

'I'd rather stay,' said Rob. The woman was a crazy Danieri, who knew what she was going to pull? She might grab a syringe, stick Kit with it. She was capable of anything.

Kit's eyes flicked to meet his. 'Go,' he said.

Rob sighed and started towards the door. He groaned when he saw Ruby appear there, about to come in and no doubt kick off. He'd told her to stay away. But she was looking past him, arrested by the scene at Kit's bedside.

Rob paused beside her in the doorway and looked back too.

'Come to finish the job off?' Kit asked Bianca.

Bianca bit her lip and shook her head as she approached him. Tears filled her eyes as she stared down at his face.

'I want to hate you,' she gulped out. 'But I can't.'

She moved closer and slowly reached out a trembling hand. Kit grasped her hand, twined his fingers into hers. Suddenly the tears overflowed and poured down Bianca's cheeks. The strength left her and she fell to her knees beside the bed.

'Oh God,' she managed to say. Over and over, she kissed

his hand, sobbing and murmuring that she was sorry, she was so, so sorry. Kit placed his other hand on her head, smoothing her silky white-blonde hair.

'It's all right,' he said to her. 'Really. It's all right. I'm sorry too.' *Sorry for Tito. Sorry I caused you pain. Sorry I lied to you.*

'I can't hate you,' sobbed Bianca. 'I can't do it.'

'I know.'

'You don't know. You *can't.*'

'You pulled to the left. Like the rabbit, right? You could have finished me, shot me straight through the heart, but you didn't. And when you were aiming at my head, you couldn't do it then, either.'

'Oh Jesus, I'm so . . . did it hurt?'

'Stung a bit,' he said.

Rob and Ruby stood in the doorway. They looked at each other. Then Rob took Ruby's arm. 'Let's give them a minute,' he said, and led her out to the waiting room.

'I don't understand any of this,' said Ruby.

'Join the fucking club,' said Rob.

95

Outside the hospital, Thomas Knox was waiting for Ruby.

He knew I was here because he watches me, all the time, she thought. Once it had made her shiver with lust, that thought. Now there was fear, too, and a cold hard stab of dread.

'You got Reg here with the car?' Rob asked her.

'Just over there.'

'Good. I'll catch up with you tomorrow then, OK?'

'Fine. Thanks.'

Rob went back inside.

Reg had the Merc parked up and he was standing, leaning against the bonnet, watching her.

'Hey,' said Thomas, coming forward and kissing her cheek.

He wanted Michael out of the way to get to you, said Daisy's voice in her head.

Ruby stiffened.

Thomas drew back, stared at her face. 'What's up?' he asked.

Ruby shook her head. 'Nothing, it's just . . .'

'Just what?' he prompted when she hesitated.

'It's just that I don't think I can do this any more. You and me. I can't.'

He was still staring at her, trying to fathom her reasoning.

'Something happened?' he asked. 'Is Kit all right?'

'He's fine.' *He's crazy and he's got that lunatic girl who nearly killed him at his bedside, but he's fine.*

'Then what? What's changed your mind all of a sudden?'

'Nothing. But I don't want to go on with this.'

Now his eyes were fierce. He grabbed her arm. 'Bullshit. Something's happened.'

Yeah, I've found out that you might have killed Michael just to have me, and you know what? That makes me feel sick, like I may as well have pulled the trigger and killed him myself.

Reg was coming toward them now, his face anxious.

'Nothing's happened. It's over. That's all.'

'Not until I say.'

'No! *I* say it's over,' said Ruby angrily. 'And it is.'

She pulled her arm free and barged past him, towards Reg.

'All right, Miss Darke?' he asked.

'Fine, Reg.' She glanced back, just once, and Thomas Knox was still standing there, watching her go. She turned away, and told Reg where she wanted to be taken next.

The last time Ruby had been to Joe's big house in Chigwell, she had been attending her eldest brother's funeral after Charlie died drunk in a hit-and-run. She remembered the day vividly; she hadn't wanted to come, but Charlie was her brother, blood was thicker than water and all that sentimental bullshit. And she recalled the way Betsy – who long, long ago had been her best friend – had lorded about the place while hosting the funeral tea, showing her grandly embellished palatial home and her swanky new pool house off to all the East End faces and their wives, letting them know how much better than them Joe was doing with his business dealings.

Poor bloody Joe, thought Ruby as Reg stopped at the gates and announced her arrival into the intercom. He could have done a lot better, a lot nicer, than Betsy, but there you go. Who knew what brought people together?

That train of thought led her back to Thomas Knox, and she pushed it aside. She'd done the right thing. Finished it. Kit was safe enough with his boys around him; she should never have got involved with Thomas, never asked him to find Gabe's address or anything else. The thought that he could have killed Michael tormented her.

Was it possible he'd been so determined to have her that he'd have stopped at nothing, even removing Michael from the scene?

She was afraid that *she* had caused Michael's death. It made her feel nauseous to consider it as a possibility, but there it was, right in front of her. Her own guilt.

A squawking voice emerged from the intercom, and Reg answered it. The gates started to open, and Reg got back in the Merc and drove up to the house along a deep dark avenue of shrubbery, the headlights forging a path. Reg parked the Merc in front of the house and Ruby peered out at it, lit by the porch light. To her eye, then as now, the place looked tacky, like it was trying too hard to be something it wasn't. There was a white van parked up on the drive, and the sound of hammering was coming loud and clear from inside the house. Someone was working late.

Reg waited in the car and she stepped up onto the porch and rang the bell. The door swung inward. Instantly the sound of hammering and drilling was louder. Betsy stood there in white high-heeled mules, a filmy turquoise beach cover-up that clearly showed a bikini beneath. She was holding onto a lunging German shepherd by its rhinestone-studded collar. The dog was wagging its tail madly.

'Jesus, it *is* you,' said Betsy. Seeing the direction of Ruby's gaze, she shrugged. 'Just got out of the pool. I like a swim in the evening.'

And there she was, Ruby's friend from when they were

kids, Ruby's best friend in those days – before she became attached to Betsy's older sister Vi when they worked together at the Windmill Theatre.

Straight out of the pool or not, Betsy was wearing a lot of make-up, an extremely deep tan and a very expensive tiger-striped blonde hairdo. Her eyes were pale blue and still fiercely acquisitive, her mouth open in a fake smile that revealed a set of startlingly white crowns. Ruby could feel Betsy's eyes moving up and down her body, assessing her shape and itemizing the value and the brand of every bit of clothing she wore.

No change here then, thought Ruby.

Life was one long bitching contest to Betsy, it always had been. Whatever anyone else had, Betsy wanted it – only bigger and better. It drove her crazy that her sister Vi had married into the aristocracy, outdoing her in the marriage stakes.

'Yeah, it's me. Thought I'd pop in.'

'What, after all this time?'

'Kit told me Joe's not well.'

Betsy's lip curled. 'He never fucking is, these days. I suppose you'd better come in. Prince, *basket*.'

The dog dived obediently for its basket at the side of the hall.

'Come on. He's in the conservatory, he lives in there, loves it,' Betsy threw back over her shoulder as she sashayed through the hall and into the big glass structure at the rear of the property. As they passed the kitchen, Betsy flashed her fake glittery smile that way. A scene of apparent devastation greeted Ruby; all the units had been ripped out and as she glanced in there, the integral oven was being lobbed out the door onto the terrace by two burly men.

'I'm having the kitchen refitted,' said Betsy with a triumphant smirk. 'Walnut units this time; nice and tasteful.'

Ruby didn't comment; she knew of old that Betsy had the decorators in every six months, that she was never satisfied with any improvement to her property for very long. Ruby thought of her own small Victorian villa, a far less opulent place than this, but infinitely more homely.

'Here's a visitor for you,' said Betsy, and Ruby entered the conservatory.

In amongst the scrambling bougainvillea, the grapevine and the datura with its big peachy trumpet flowers, sat Joe. It was hot in here, and the darkness outside seemed to press in against the glass.

God, he'd changed! Ruby couldn't believe that big, beefy Joe, once the scourge of the East End with brother Charlie at his side, had come to this. Now he looked thin, like the flesh was hanging off him. His features were gaunt, but his eyes were the same, a warm brown above the oxygen mask he had clamped to his face. But they had a frail and frightened expression in them that broke Ruby's heart.

'Joe?' she whispered, hardly believing it.

'Ruby!' he let out a rasping breath.

She was looking at the oxygen mask, the tubes, the bottle at the side of his chair.

'Hello, Joe.' Trying to hide her shock, Ruby came forward. Hesitantly she dropped a kiss onto his thin cheek, and pulled up a chair.

'Hello, girl. You all right then?' he asked, clasping her hand in one of his. It was icy cold and she nearly flinched away.

'I'm fine. Kit told me you're not well, so I've come to see you.'

Joe gave her an ironic look. 'Fuckin' bastard, innit? I'm dyin' on my feet here.'

'Emphysema,' chimed in Betsy. 'It's them bloody fags, rolling his own all those years. Too much fucking Old Holborn, that's what *this* is.'

'And all this noise going on,' complained Joe.

'They got to make a noise,' said Betsy. 'They're fitting a kitchen, for God's sake.'

'Yeah? Well go and make them some tea – lazy gits have only had ten cups so far today, may as well stand them another. Make us some too, while you're at it.'

Betsy flounced off to the kitchen. After a couple of seconds they heard her tinkling laughter mingling with men's voices and the crashing, crunching sounds of the kitchen being pulled inside out.

'She always was a bloody flirt,' said Joe. 'Sauntering about the fuckin' place with her arse hanging out and all those blokes in the sodding kitchen. Thinks I don't know, I suppose. Or don't give a shit if I do.'

'How you feeling, Joe?' asked Ruby.

'Fuckin' awful – how do I look?' Joe let the oxygen mask drop to his blanketed lap and gave a hoarse laugh. 'Does me good to see you though, Rubes. Keepin' all right?'

'Fine.'

'Glad one of us is. Not too long now, there I'll be – sitting on an effing cloud along with Charlie.'

'Don't say that.'

A fresh peal of laughter came floating through from the kitchen.

'Why not? It's the truth. And I'm not sorry. Had a goodish life, really. Only one real regret . . . and you know what that is?'

'No,' said Ruby. 'Go on, tell me.'

Joe cocked his head toward the kitchen. 'Aside from the fags? My one regret is that I wasted my time marrying that selfish cow.'

'Joe . . .' She didn't want to hear this. Ruby had always known that Joe could have done better for himself but she had hoped, up until this moment, that he was at least moderately happy in his marriage. It hurt her to see that he was not.

'Come on, Rubes, you know it's true. I was always second-best for Betsy, wasn't I? It was always Charlie for her. When he got sent down after the mail-van job, she settled for me.'

'Joe, come on . . .'

'What you mean, "come on"? I'm speaking the truth here. Drove me nuts for years, she did, saying why didn't I go and get my cut of the robbery – money-grubbing bitch. Currency changed, see, *times* changed. This is how she has her revenge on me, spendin' my fuckin' money non-stop.' Joe's watery eyes grew distant. 'Poor old Charlie, eh? He got done good and proper. It broke him you know, all that time in stir. He was never the same man after that. And then he steps out in the road drunk, and some fucker ploughs in, and that's him finished. Well, now *I'm* finished too.' Joe heaved a sigh. 'Could have got myself a nice warm woman, could have had my pick, they were all after me. Lord of the streets, I was. Not now, though. Too late.'

'How're the kids?' asked Ruby. It was an easier subject than Betsy and everything that had gone before. It was all old stuff, *dead* stuff, it didn't matter. While Ruby had been minding the shop, Charlie and Joe had taken to a career as criminals; she'd always known that there wouldn't be a happy ending to their saga.

'Nadine's getting the hump with everyone. Ten years old and already you can see she's her mother's daughter. Billy's a real live wire. It's bad for them, seeing me like this. Thank Christ they're at boarding school, takes them out of the way most of the time.'

'I'm sorry, Joe.'

'Good to see you though, girl. You're a tonic. Now where's that cow with the bloody tea . . . ?'

96

When Ruby got back to Marlow, there was a familiar car waiting on the drive. The Jag's headlights swept over it, showing Thomas Knox standing by the bonnet. Ruby felt her heartbeat pick up in panic, felt a wave of revulsion engulf her. He wasn't going to let this go.

'You want me to have a word with him, Miss Darke?' asked Reg, pulling up, switching off the engine.

Ruby thought that Thomas wouldn't stop this unless she gave him an explanation. She felt weary to the bone, but she had to sort this out, right now.

'No, that's OK, Reg.'

Ruby got out of the Merc and Reg drove it round to the garage which was some distance from the main house. She walked over to where Thomas lounged against his car.

'I want answers,' he said flatly, as she came and stood within two feet of him.

'I know. Come inside, it's cold out here.'

He followed her into the house, into the small sitting room at the front. Ruby kept her coat on. So did Thomas. She didn't offer him a seat. She stood several paces away from him and they confronted each other like strangers.

'I want answers too,' said Ruby.

'Oh? To what?'

'Did you do it?'

'Do what?'

Ruby hitched in a breath. 'Kill Michael. Was it you?'

'*What?*'

'You wanted to get to me. But you couldn't, could you? You knew I was with him, that nothing was going to come between us.' Suddenly her eyes were full of tears. 'So did you do it?'

Thomas looked at the floor. Then he glanced sharply at Ruby. 'You think I did?'

'I want you to tell me. Did you? Because if you did, this is *my* fault. Michael would be alive today if not for me.'

'You seriously think I'd do that?'

Ruby stared at him. Thought of all the things he'd said to her, how completely he'd seduced her.

'Because if you think that,' he snapped out, 'then you're right – we can't go on with this. Oh, and incidentally? I won't be looking out for your boy any more.'

Now Ruby felt fury building up in her. He'd duped her, deceived her, bedded her; and now she was thinking that Daisy was right about all this and he'd robbed her of Michael, who had truly loved her, then made her doubt that love by feeding her lies about another woman. There had been no one but her. She was sure of that. Thomas Knox had done his best to twist the truth, make her question everything she had ever believed in.

'I don't want a damned thing from you,' she told him furiously. 'And Kit will manage just fine without your help.'

'I dunno about that. He's treading a dangerous road, wouldn't you say? Getting mixed up with that crazy Danieri sister. Do you have any idea what he's up against? That family's Camorra, out of Naples – you don't mess with those people. Vittore's spitting blood over this. He's a proud man, he won't take any shit. If Kit wanted to, he could still name Bianca to the Bill as the one who shot him, and Vittore won't risk that happening. And the Danieris won't back down just because Kit's boys have got Bianca. They'll retaliate – maybe snatch Kit's sister,' he went on relentlessly. 'Before you know it, you could be getting her back in pieces, through the post – an ear, maybe, or a tongue – how about that for a thought? Maybe they'll snatch Daisy's kids and—'

'They're in a safe place,' said Ruby as his words struck home.

'Yeah? How safe?'

'Stop it! Shut up! I don't ever want to see you or speak to you again.'

Thomas's eyes were hard on her face. 'Sure about that?'

'Completely sure.'

'OK. But think about this: you got no proof I offed Mike. None at all. And everything I've just told you is true, so you'd better watch yourself. Oh, and what I told you before is true an' all: Michael *was* tied up with another woman.'

'Liar!' shouted Ruby.

'Nope. Not so.'

'Then give me a name. Give me *something*.'

'I don't have it. Besides, I thought you didn't want anything from me?'

'I don't.'

'Then, sweetheart – you're on your own,' he said, and left the room.

'You're a *liar*!' yelled Ruby after him.

He opened the front door, went outside and slammed it shut behind him. Presently Ruby heard his car start up, heard the motor being driven fast into the distance. She threw her bag onto the sofa in impotent rage. He was lying. There was no woman. Michael wouldn't do that to her. She knew it.

She had to believe that.

She *had* to.

97

It was getting late, the punters in Sheila's restaurant were thinning out, those remaining were drowsing and talking softly over coffee and brandies at the candlelit tables while a gifted young man sat in the corner, playing Spanish guitar.

Rob and Daisy headed straight through to the office, pushing the door closed behind them. The boys had been in, cleaned up the worst of the mess. Rob tucked a chair under the still-shattered lock to keep it that way. While Daisy watched, he went over to the desk, moved the chair aside, got down on his knees and lifted the rug to expose the floorboards.

He prised at a loose edge, and up it came: a foot-long insert in the boards. With that one out of the way, he pulled up another, then another. Now he was looking down into a little cubbyhole, which appeared to be empty.

He kept stuff tucked back there, out of the way, Kit had told Rob earlier.

Rob leaned down further. He stuck in his hand up to the elbow, and groped around.

'Anything?' asked Daisy, almost twitching with impatience.

Nothing.

A hard pang of disappointment hit Rob. He'd been so

sure that whatever the intruder had been looking for, it would be found here, in Michael's favourite hiding place.

'Fuck,' he muttered.

He took off his jacket, rolled up his shirt sleeves and got down further, pressing his whole body and his face into the floor. He inserted his arm again, right the way in, as far as it could go.

Nothing, nothing, fucking *nothing*.

His hand scrabbled around in there, he was blind, he didn't have a torch with him and anyway he could feel sod-all in there and this was a total waste of . . .

He stiffened. 'Something here,' he said to Daisy.

His fingers had brushed what felt like cardboard. He tried to grab it, failed. Pushed his face hard against the floor, gave himself a millimetre or two more to play with. Groped back in there, caught the edge of the thing: it was flat and again it slipped away. Grunting with effort, he grabbed the edge once more, and *aha!* He had it. This time, he kept a tight grip on the cardboard, eased it towards him, pulled it out, rolled over on the floor and took a look at what he'd found.

It was a stiff envelope, about fourteen inches by eleven, the sort pro photographers use to mail prints to clients. It was stuck down with brown tape. Rob sat up, slid his thumb-nail under the tape, prised it free. Daisy got down on her knees and peered at it in excitement.

'What is it?' she asked. 'Hurry up! Open it.'

Rob tipped it up. A small stack of ten-by-eight glossy black-and-white photographs fell out, into his hands. He put the envelope aside and they looked at what he'd netted.

Presently, he let out a low whistle.

Big surprise.

'Oh, good Lord,' said Daisy, mistress of understatement.

★

Next day Rob picked up a few toiletries and items of clothing from Kit's place, put them in a plastic carrier bag and went to the hospital. Kit was lying there, eyes closed. His skin had lost its deathly pallor. His left arm was tucked up in a sling, taking the weight off while it healed.

'Hey, Kit?' said Rob, sitting down at his bedside.

Kit's eyes opened.

'Hi,' he said.

Rob had been thinking it over. In ICU, the situation had been secure and he could keep a lid on things. In a private room, security became more difficult. Out on the streets that Kit ran, they had their own tame private doctors, even a fucking surgeon on the payroll, no questions asked.

'How you feeling?' asked Rob.

'OK.'

Kit felt about a million times better, now that he'd seen Bianca and reassured himself that she was all right. The filth had – of course – been in, asking him more questions. Who shot him? Did he see anyone? He hadn't, he said. Sorry, officer. They told him about a bloke who'd fallen or jumped to his death from a window just down the hall, Italian guy, no one seemed to know who he was or what he was doing in the hospital – had Kit heard anything about that? Kit said he hadn't. And the police had gone away again.

'You feel well enough to get the fuck out of here?' asked Rob.

Kit looked at his mate. 'They trying?'

'Twice.'

'The jumper?'

'Cops told you?'

'They did. Hey, Rob . . .'

'Hm?'

'I kept hearing a voice when I was out of it. Ruby said it was her.'

'Yeah, that's right.' Rob looked at his mate. 'She stayed here with you the whole time. We couldn't drag her away – and God knows we tried.'

Kit returned Rob's gaze. The Ice Queen of Retail, cold as fuck and putting business before her kids, had been here, talking to him, the entire time?

'She wouldn't leave you. All she did was stay by your bed, talking to you.'

Kit looked at him dubiously.

'It's true,' Rob assured him. Then his face darkened as he moved on to the subject that had been bothering him: 'Look, we've got Bianca stashed away. But these Danieri boys . . . I dunno. They're crazy. They might try again, whether we've got her for insurance or not. I don't want to take the chance . . .'

'So I guess we go,' said Kit.

Rob held up the carrier bag. 'Got your clothes in here.'

'OK, let's do it.'

98

Daisy slept late next morning. Ruby had departed for the store now that Kit was in the clear, and would then go on to the hospital to see him, but here *she* was, still in bed. Disconsolately she slipped on her robe and wandered up to the nursery. There was only silence; a few abandoned toys, the empty cots. She went downstairs and firmly resisted the impulse to phone Jody. Kit was right. The line might be tapped, and she could betray their whereabouts without meaning to.

She showered, dressed and then phoned Rob's flat number.

There was no answer.

Well, he was probably doing something for Kit. She knew better than to speculate as to what exactly that might entail. One thing she couldn't put to the back of her mind was the envelope Rob had discovered last night, and the shocking images they contained.

Neither could she shove away from her brain the fact that her brother seemed besotted by a madwoman who had damned near killed him. She had no idea where they were going to go from here with Bianca. She had no idea what mad scheme Kit was going to cook up next, and she dreaded going back to the hospital to hear about it.

She phoned the restaurant; was Rob there?

'Haven't seen him since yesterday,' said the bar manager.

She phoned Ruby's office.

'Rob? No, I haven't seen him since last night. Check with Reg.'

Daisy then phoned Reg's flat, all the while the tension and anxiety building in her until she felt just about ready to blow.

Reg picked up on the first ring. 'Yes?'

'Reg? It's Daisy. Do you know where Rob is today?'

'No idea,' said Reg. 'Have you tried . . .'

And so it went on. Daisy phoned pool halls, bars, restaurants, and no one had seen Rob.

Finally she gave up, put the phone down and wondered what the hell to do now.

What she was afraid of . . . no, she couldn't bear to even think it, it was too awful.

But try as she might she couldn't shake off the fear that Rob had decided to act alone on the contents of the brown cardboard envelope he'd unearthed last night.

If the man who had been searching for those photos was the same person who killed Michael Ward in that alley, then Rob could be walking into a very dangerous situation. The searcher would know Rob had seen the prints, would know the game was up, and he might decide that Rob needed getting out of the way, too.

Gripped with anxiety, Daisy gave up on the phone. Instead she tore down the stairs, ran out and got into her Mini, and drove like a bat out of hell.

She had made this journey a hundred thousand times, or so it felt. The whole route was so familiar to her that the car almost drove itself. Before long she was crossing over the bridge above the cress beds and turning into the driveway, barrelling the Mini full-pelt up the drive among the dripping rhododendrons until she reached the fountain of Neptune in front of the house.

Her fears escalated to fever pitch when she saw that Rob's car was there, on the drive.

'Oh no . . .' she gasped as she slammed on the hand-brake and turned off the engine.

She almost fell out of the car, and ran up the steps to Brayfield's front door and bashed her fist upon it. Nobody answered. Swearing, limp with fear, she hared off around the building to the back, heading for the French doors that led into Vanessa's blue-and-gold drawing room. They were standing open and she could hear raised voices coming from inside.

'I have not the faintest idea what you are talking about,' came Vanessa's voice, high with strain.

Daisy all but fell through the doors.

'Daisy!' Vanessa said in astonishment.

Rob was standing over Vanessa. And there was the card-board envelope. It was on a low table, and the prints were spread out on top of it. They were grainy, clearly taken with a long lens, but the content was unmistakable.

One showed Ivan and Vanessa, his hand on her shoulder in the garden; they were laughing together. Another showed them up against a tree, kissing. And another – most damning – showed Ivan, full-frontal naked, drawing back the curtains in what was clearly Vanessa's bedroom.

Jesus, it's like something out of a D.H. Lawrence novel, thought Daisy. *It's* Lady Chatterley's Lover.

The shock of seeing the prints again was just as strong as it had been last night when Rob first discovered them. Daisy had lived with Vanessa for years, she knew how highly strung she was, always generating her own anxieties – mostly about the state of her position in society. Respectability was everything to Vanessa. If these prints should ever be revealed

– if it should ever come to light that Lady Bray was having an affair with her gardener – then it would be truly disastrous for her. Her social circle would shun her, and she couldn't bear that.

And that's precisely why Ivan was tearing up Michael's flat and the office to find them, thought Daisy.

Now she could see what had been happening here. Michael had been blackmailing Vanessa with these prints, threatening to show them to the press. And she thought she knew why. For all that Vanessa and Cornelius Bray had put Ruby through, tearing her children away from her, tormenting her, Michael had decided that they should pay. Well, Cornelius was out of it; but there was still Vanessa.

As a motive for murder, getting rid of a blackmailer held a lot of weight.

Vanessa looked mortified. It was bad enough, this stranger turning up here again, after she'd thought they'd got rid of him and that ghastly thug Kit Miller. But now she saw Daisy looking at the prints, and drawing her own conclusions.

'It's not how it looks . . .' she said desperately.

'It looks like you're knocking off the gardener,' said Rob.

'Daisy, you have to believe—' said Vanessa.

'Believe what? That these photos aren't genuine? I can see they are.'

Vanessa's eyes dropped to her lap. 'This is very embarrassing,' she said.

'Michael was blackmailing you, wasn't he?' asked Daisy.

'That vile man!' burst out Vanessa. 'He came here and said that if I didn't pay up he'd show them to the press. So I agreed. I paid him. And then he said he was going to show them anyway, and—'

'And then what?' Rob demanded. 'Ivan killed him, right?'

Vanessa's milky blue eyes opened wide. 'No! How you can say that?'

'It's what I'd do, in his place,' said Rob. 'Remove the threat. Nice and clean. Always supposing Michael hadn't lodged a set of the prints elsewhere with instructions to open and publish if anything should happen to him.'

'Ivan was in the army, wasn't he? He knows all about guns,' said Daisy.

There was movement at the French windows and a male voice spoke.

'That may be true. But if I'd wanted to kill that bastard, I'd have done it with my own bare hands.'

Daisy and Rob turned as one, and saw that wiry, bearded Ivan had just stepped into the drawing room holding a twelve-bore shotgun.

99

'Oh God,' said Vanessa, putting a hand to her mouth. She surged to her feet, making entreating motions to Ivan. 'No, you mustn't . . .'

Rob pushed Daisy behind him and stared down the barrel of the gun. Ivan was much smaller than Rob, slight and sinewy, but he had eyes like a tiger and they glared with purpose.

'Get hold of the prints,' Ivan ordered Vanessa.

With trembling fingers, Vanessa did as she was told.

'That's no good,' said Daisy, having to swallow hard to get the words out. 'We have copies. *Several* copies,' she lied.

'What about the negatives?' asked Ivan.

'We don't have those. We can't find them.'

'But you found these.'

'Yeah, you missed them when you searched the office and the flat,' said Rob. 'But the negatives? No. Couldn't find them.'

'It was worth a try,' shrugged Ivan.

'Yeah, I'll give you that,' said Rob. 'Like offing Michael was worth a try too, I guess. End of blackmailer – end of blackmail.'

Ivan's lips twisted in a sneer. 'What, you think that was me? Sonny, if I'd truly intended to see the man gone, I'd have done it quietly, not with a gun.'

Daisy was staring at Ivan. She grabbed Rob's arm. 'Ivan was in the army,' she said.

'Special Air Services,' said Ivan.

'They're taught silent killing.'

'They're also taught guns,' said Rob. 'Dum-dum bullets. That says military to me.'

'I wouldn't have needed a gun to put that bastard's lights out,' said Ivan.

'But you're waving a gun around now,' said Rob.

'We're not interested in these prints,' Daisy said. 'I know Michael didn't need your money, he was just winding you up. Paying you back for what you put Ruby through. The only thing we're interested in is who killed him. That's all we want to know.'

'Ivan didn't do it,' snapped Vanessa. 'Of course he didn't. But I tell you – when that man died the way he did, we were just so pleased. So relieved the nightmare was over. Ivan decided he'd try to find the negatives, and any prints. Put the whole horrible incident safely away. But he couldn't find them.'

Daisy could feel herself shaking as she stared at Ivan holding the gun, pointing it straight at Rob's middle.

'Please put the gun down,' said Vanessa, her teeth chattering with fear as she glanced at Daisy's ashen face. 'There's really no need for that.'

Ivan stayed motionless for a moment. Then, slowly, he lowered the shotgun. He looked straight at Rob. 'I didn't kill Michael Ward,' he said, disgust obvious in his tone. 'But I wish I had. He deserved it.'

Daisy saw a muscle twitch in Rob's jaw. She knew he had idolized Michael.

Rob turned away from Ivan and looked at Vanessa.

'Keep the prints,' he said, and moved towards the French

windows followed by Daisy, both of them passing close by Ivan.

'What about the other copies?' snapped Ivan.

'That's our insurance,' said Rob, pausing on the threshold. 'Behave, and they stay out of the public eye. Don't, and the society pages will get an eyeful.'

Rob then stepped outside, grabbing Daisy's arm and walking her quickly round the side of the building.

'What the fuck are you doing, showing up here?' he asked her as he bundled her over to his car.

'I've got my—' she started.

'No leave the frigging Mini right there. There's no guarantee he won't come after us even now. Just get in the bloody car, you daft mare – and hurry up.'

Daisy got in Rob's car and he jumped in, started the engine and roared off full speed down the drive.

'Shit, that was scary!' said Daisy, clutching her chest. 'My car . . .'

'We'll pick it up when things have cooled down. You shouldn't have come. What the hell were you playing at?' Rob reached the end of the drive and steered the car quickly into the lane with a chirp of tyres.

'Me? How about you? You vanished without a word. I phoned round, trying to find you, and then it hit me. I knew you'd be down here on your own, playing the big man.'

'He could have shot us, Daisy. Both of us.'

'Jesus, don't you think I'm aware of that?' shrieked Daisy.

They tore through the village and out the other side, and onto the main road. Slowly, Daisy began to feel just a little safer.

'Daise, calm down.'

'Calm down? After everything that's been going on?'

She couldn't believe that they had just been standing in

Vanessa's drawing room with Ivan pointing a gun straight at Rob. What if she hadn't shown up? Would he have taken the opportunity to dispose of Rob? He could be dead right now. And knowing that, how awful it would be, how truly terrifying, brought it home to her all the more forcefully: she was in love with Rob.

And the worst thing was, it wasn't reciprocated.

100

Once they'd put a good distance between themselves and Brayfield, Rob pulled in at the side of the road and turned off the engine. He looked at Daisy.

'You great fool, he could have killed you!' she shouted, thumping his arm.

'Daise.'

'Oh, shut up. You had to play John Wayne, didn't you? Strutting down here on your own. Has it occurred to you what would have happened if I hadn't shown up? You could be in a hole somewhere! Do you seriously think he wouldn't have done it if I wasn't there as a witness? Vanessa wouldn't let him hurt me, so he couldn't hurt you. I've just absolutely fucking *saved* you, and all you can say is *calm down*!'

'Daise,' said Rob again.

'And you shouldn't have left the prints there. The police would have treated those as evidence, we could have given those photos to them and perhaps made a case.'

'The police don't give a shit about Michael's death, Daisy,' cut in Rob harshly. 'The case has been sidelined. We could hand photos of Lady Bray and her gardener swinging bollock-naked off the light fittings or boffing a bloody donkey, and they wouldn't give a toss. But when Ivan said he'd have used his bare hands? I think that was true.'

Daisy thought it was true too; Ivan was a real old-school

officer type, super-posh and tough as cowhide. She had always imagined him as the sort of man who would trek to the Pole with his toes blackening and dropping off through frostbite, and he wouldn't utter a word of complaint until he'd got there, achieved his goal.

'You know what? I honestly hate you,' snapped Daisy. She put her hands to her head and shook it, digging her fingers into her scalp. Then she threw her arms wide and sent him a desperate look. 'And who the hell gave Michael that LP, that ring? That's driving me *mad*.'

Christ, he thought, she looked so sexy with her hair all mussed up, her face flushed with temper and her chest heaving from the exertion of their run out of Brayfield. When she'd thrown her hands out like that, pneumatic things had happened in her chest area: a heavy delicious swaying movement that drew his eye. He had this terrible, fatal weakness for heavily stacked girls.

She was close, and she was available. Now he caught himself wondering how those fantastically alluring breasts of hers would feel under his hands if he were to lean over and slide them up under her bra. He could already imagine the feel of them, so heavy and cool and . . .

Whoa there, tiger, he thought suddenly.

What was he thinking? The blood rush of their narrow escape from that bearded twat Ivan had stirred him up, that was all, got his juices flowing. Big luscious bazookas or not, Daisy was rich, spoiled and spoke with a plum in her mouth. And she liked to be in charge. She wasn't for the likes of him.

'Am I wrong, or did that scrawny jumped-up little gnome actually call me "sonny" back there?' he wondered aloud.

'Yes. He did. But never mind that now, that's a blind alley.'

'What, you don't think it's possible he offed Michael?'

'No, I really don't. I believe Ivan was telling the absolute truth. Knowing Michael, he wanted revenge for the torment Vanessa had put Ruby through in the past, and he fished around until he found the perfect thing to sting Vanessa with. She cares for her reputation, for her standing in the community, above all else. And it's clear Ivan adores her and wanted to protect her reputation.'

'He's fucking her, if that's what you mean,' snorted Rob.

'Do you have to be so crude? The reason he was so intent on getting those photos back was to protect the name of the woman he loves. It's rather noble, if you ask me.'

'Jesus!'

'But I don't think for one minute that he'd shoot Michael in the back of the head. It seems a cowardly thing to do. I can't imagine an honourable old soldier like Ivan would ever stoop to that, can you?'

Rob slumped in his seat. Unless he was missing something obvious, she was right.

'So now we move on,' said Daisy, shaking her head. 'You know, I still can't believe that Michael was unfaithful to Ruby.'

Rob sent her a look. '*I* can't believe that Lady Bray would fuck her gardener, but she does.'

'I don't think it's quite like that,' said Daisy.

'Daise, it's *exactly* like that.'

'Look, Vanessa was always very fond of Ivan, they had much more in common than she ever had with my father. They got on well. And . . . I suppose this is the inevitable result.'

'I think you're fooling yourself with this LP-sleeve business, and the ring.'

'In what way?'

'It's another dead end. Penny to a pinch of shit it was

that little fucker Gabe killed Mike. Look to the nearest and dearest – isn't that what they always say?'

'Yes, but Gabe's never been near or dear to Michael. They parted company when he was in his teens.'

'And Gabe resented that,' said Rob. 'And it festered. Then he was banged up. Finally he gets out and he's on his uppers, low as you can get – and he finds out his dear old dad has cut him out of the money. Wham! He snaps.'

'God, I need some fresh air,' said Daisy, opening the car door and getting out onto the verge. Rob got out too, watching her, frowning. 'What about Thomas Knox?' Daisy turned to him. 'That man is fixated on Ruby.'

'So?' Rob shrugged. 'Ruby's a very attractive woman.'

'Yes, but Knox has had his eye on her for years. And what stood in the way of his *getting* her? Michael. That's all.'

Rob was silent for a minute. 'That LP sleeve – Ruby was close to Michael, maybe she'll recognize the writing.'

'Worth a try,' said Daisy.

'Sure is,' said Rob. 'Let's do it.'

They walked back to the car and it was then that Rob saw a lightweight motorbike zooming around the corner of the lane, closing in on them fast. The black-helmeted rider had his arm straight out, aiming something at Daisy.

Rob took two quick steps and grabbed Daisy in one swift movement. As the gunshots started to blast away the silence, he pushed her down onto the verge and threw his full weight on top of her.

He heard her give a thin shriek and for a moment all was chaos. He was scrabbling for his own weapon and thinking, *Slow, too fucking slow, he's going to stop and finish us.*

But the roar of the two-stroke engine was dying away.

Rob raised his head and saw bike and rider tearing off to their left, then vanishing from sight.

Silence returned. All he could hear now was Daisy's gasping breaths, all he could feel was her frantically racing heart against his rib cage.

'You all right?' he managed to get out.

He looked down and Daisy was staring up at him. She gulped twice: nodded.

'Sure? No damage?'

Daisy shook her head. 'You're heavy,' she pointed out.

Rob eased himself to his feet, slipped his gun back into its holster inside his jacket, and pulled her upright.

'You going to pass out?' he asked. He felt pretty shaken up himself. Daisy could be dead now if he hadn't happened to see that fucker coming.

Daisy took a huge breath. Shook her head again.

'He was trying to kill me,' she said. 'Wasn't he?'

You and yours, thought Rob. *I'll tear the heart out of every one of you.*

Despite the fact they had Bianca, Vittore was on the warpath. He'd sent his crew out to follow Kit's family, to find a chink in their armour and pierce it if they could. That bastard on the bike must have been watching them all day, just waiting his chance.

'Come on,' he said, bundling Daisy back into the car. 'Let's get you out of here.'

101

Kit was resting at home. When Ruby went to his house and let herself in with a spare key, he was sitting up in bed, staring pensively out of the window.

'Hi,' she said, feeling almost shy.

'Oh.' He looked round, saw it was her. 'It's you.'

'Yep, me again,' she said brightly, sitting down at his bedside. 'How you feeling?'

'All right.' Kit lay his head back against the pillow.

'You looked as though you were deep in thought,' said Ruby when the silence fell between them, same as it always did. And in that silence she thought, *He hates me, he will always hate me, because he thinks I abandoned him. This is the way it will always be between us.*

It broke her heart in a thousand pieces, to think that he would never come to terms with the past, that he would never forgive her.

'I was deep in thought,' said Kit, closing his eyes wearily. 'I was thinking what a royal fuck-up I've made of my life.'

'Meaning?'

His eyes opened. He turned his head and looked at her. 'Meaning I killed Tito for murdering Gilda and then Michael. I thought I was doing the right thing, the only thing I could do. But turns out Tito wasn't the one I was after. Whoever killed Michael is still out there, free as a bird.'

411

Ruby gulped, thinking of Thomas. God, she'd been so stupid, getting involved with him.

'He was Bianca's brother. And I killed him,' said Kit.

'Kit, she very nearly killed you.'

He shrugged, then winced.

'She didn't, though. She pulled to the left. Like the rabbit.'

'The what?'

'Tito took her rabbit shooting when she was young, but she couldn't do it. Thought of all the baby bunnies back at home: what if she killed their mother and they starved to death?' He gave a wry smile. 'That's what she did with me. She wanted to kill me, but she couldn't bring herself to do it. But you know what? Deep down, I don't think she'll ever forgive me for offing Tito. I really don't. How could she? So I've fucked it all up. Everything.'

Ruby was silent for a moment. Then she said: 'Once, I thought I'd done the same. Fucked my entire life up.'

'Yeah, when?' He gave her a cynical stare. 'Big successful business lady, that's you.'

'That might be me now, but back in the war it was all different. I fell in love with a rotten bastard and he knocked me up.'

Kit's eyes hardened. 'My dear late and unlamented old dad, eh? Cornelius Bray.'

'When I lost you, and Daisy . . . I felt as if I might as well be dead. That there was no future, no hope.'

'Yeah, yeah.' Kit looked unimpressed.

'But I survived it. I found Daisy, and then I found you too,' said Ruby.

Now Kit was staring at her. 'You still glad you did? Find me, I mean? Knowing what I am, that after you chucked me on the scrapheap . . .'

'I never did that. You were taken from me, I've told you.'

'After that, I got shoved around kids' homes and then

on the streets and then into being a bone-breaker for Michael. Yeah, I might have wedge in my pocket now. I might have property portfolios and shares in hotels and I might lunch at the Ivy along with the nobs and the celebs, but I'm still a bone-breaker – that's what you made me, those are my roots. Right down deep that's still what I am, even if I pay other people to do the dirty jobs now. I'm a heavy, knocking heads together, scaring the shit out of people to make a living.'

Ruby leaned forward and grabbed his hand. She was so sick of this. 'Kit, *I found you*,' she said fiercely. 'And I am glad, of *course* I'm glad. You're my son and I love you. Whether or not you ever love me, it doesn't matter. *I love you*. You're so like me, you even look like me. You're passionate, sensitive, impulsive, clever. You're not just a bone-breaker. You're not just a thug. Not you.'

Kit was watching his mother's face intently. 'What about Daise? Who's she take after, eh? Cornelius Bray?'

'She's got his looks,' shrugged Ruby, leaning back. 'And his intelligence. But you think you're scarred by what happened to you in your childhood? Well, Daisy is too. She may have had a privileged upbringing, but Cornelius was never there except to throw money at her, and for Vanessa I imagine it was like getting the wrong Christmas present. Vanessa wanted a quiet little girl. Daisy? She's not quiet. She's bright, robust and assertive. For Vanessa, I think Daisy came as a bit of a shock.'

'She's been pretty wild in the past,' said Kit, unable to suppress a slight smile.

'Those days are behind her. Having the twins settled her right down, there's no doubt about that. It's sheer hell for her, you know, being separated from them. Still, she's a work in progress.' Ruby squeezed Kit's hand. 'We all are, son.'

Kit's eyes grew cold and he snatched his hand away. 'Don't call me that.'

Ruby shrank back. 'Why not?' she asked. 'It's what you are.'

'Yeah. A fact you conveniently forgot for most of my lifetime.'

'I never forgot it. *Never.*' Ruby stared at his face, closed off with anger. 'I . . . I went to see your uncle Joe yesterday.'

'That wife of his! What a slapper. My God, I thought she was going eat Rob or me whole.' Then Kit sobered. 'It's good you went, anyway. He's pretty rough.'

'He's running out of time fast,' said Ruby sadly. Then she brightened. 'But you're not. You're on the mend.'

'Yeah, with my fucked-up life,' said Kit.

'Don't give up yet,' said Ruby. And then she told him what Thomas had told her about Bianca.

102

Reg drove Ruby home. There had been such sadness, such awful stress lately that she felt wrung-out, ready to crumble. She thought of the horror of nearly losing Kit; Joe, who was on his way out of this world; of Michael, who was gone, never to return; and Thomas Knox who had seduced her utterly, then ruined everything.

Exhausted, she leaned back against the soft leather upholstery and longed for sanity to be restored, to have nothing to concern her other than how many pairs of XL tights Darkes should stock and whether she ought to be changing her suppliers for skirting material, cutting herself a better deal.

She had been teetering on the edge of the criminal abyss for years, and she had always been careful not to get involved; but how could she not be? Kit was her blood, her precious boy. Whatever he did, whatever trouble he was in, she had to support him.

She thought of Daisy. Daisy who would never fit into shop work of any kind, whose upbringing worked against her just as much as Kit's did. Even now she was a mother, Daisy still seemed to be floating around, restless, looking for a direction in life. Ruby felt a stab of anxiety pierce her. Right now Daisy was out there somewhere with Rob, trying to find out who killed Michael. What if working with Rob, seeing that side of life, that dark, threatening, gutter side, drew her in, stimulated something in her?

Ruby sat up, told herself she was letting her imagination run riot. What she needed was a hot bath, a warm bed. The events of the last few weeks had left her shattered. She needed to rest, restore her strength. Then she could think about how to get them all back to some sort of normality. And . . .

Shouldn't there be two men on the gate?

Ruby felt a bolt of unease shoot from her feet to the top of her head. Her heartbeat quickened.

'Reg, stop,' she said, instantly alarmed.

Reg didn't answer. He kept on driving, right up to the house.

'Reg!' Ruby reached forward and tapped his shoulder. 'There was no one on the gate. Where are they?'

Reg glanced sideways; there was no question that he'd heard her. Then he looked stonily ahead.

He brought the Mercedes to a halt outside the front door. In the light from the porch, she could see a group of men standing there. Big men in black coats.

Oh no.

Ruby lunged across the seat and threw open the far door, getting ready to run. But someone got to it before she could, held it wide open. It was Fabio Danieri, and his smile was mocking.

Ruby looked at Reg. For a moment her eyes burned into his in the rear-view mirror, then he turned his face away. She saw a dull brick-red flush creep up from his neck to his cheeks. Reg had betrayed her. Of all people, *Reg*.

'Welcome home, Miss Darke,' said Fabio, leaning in with a manic little laugh. 'Sadly, you won't be stopping. In fact,

I don't know when you'll be coming home. Or should I say *if?*'

The other door opened, and Vittore Danieri got in and sat beside her. Ruby shrank back.

'Why don't you just drive,' Vittore told Reg. 'I'll direct you.' He turned his dark vulpine gaze on Ruby. 'Good evening, Miss Darke.'

Ruby said nothing. She was too terrified to say a word. Fabio piled in and both doors were quickly closed. Reg restarted the engine.

She could feel her pulse beating hard in her throat, almost choking off her air supply.

Jesus, they were taking her, they really were.

She thought of Kit, who still resented her, hated her for giving him up all those years ago. Her heart clenched as the bitter, hard pain of realization hit her full force. Kit would not pay to get her back. And if the Danieris wanted an exchange – her for Bianca – how would that work? Would he stand for it? She thought of Bianca by his bedside. Any fool could see that they were deeply in love. Would he really exchange his despised mother for the love of his life?

Answer: no.

Fabio leaned in and suddenly Ruby saw the knife in his hand, felt the horrifying prick of cold steel against her throat.

'Now, Ruby Darke, you choose. Where shall I cut you first?' he asked with a smile.

Over the frantic hammering of her pulse, Ruby could only hear Thomas's last angry words to her: that if this feud went on there could be bits of Daisy sent through the post to her. Bits of the twins. A finger – hadn't he said that? – a tongue . . .

But that wasn't how it was going to be, not at all.
It wouldn't be bits of Daisy or her kids.
It would be bits of *her*.

103

Rob and Daisy arrived at the Marlow house an hour later, and the first thing they noticed was that there were no guards on the gate. Rob stopped the car and climbed out. It was dark, and Daisy was feeling jumpy. Barely an hour ago, someone had tried to kill her. She sat looking tense as Rob scouted around. Then he came back to the car and got in behind the wheel.

'What's going on? Why aren't they there?' asked Daisy.

'Dunno,' he said. Inwardly he was thinking, *Gates wide open, nobody here. Fuck, what's going on?* He restarted the engine and drove on up to the house. They got out. The porch light was on, but the house was otherwise in darkness.

'Mum should be home by now,' said Daisy worriedly, opening the front door with her key and flipping on the hall lights. She started up the stairs.

'Whoa!' snapped Rob, grabbing her arm. 'Hold on, Daise. Let me check.'

He went upstairs on his own, while Daisy loitered, pacing nervously, in the hallway. When Rob came back down, his face was grim.

'Nobody up there,' he said.

They hurried into the kitchen, the sitting room, flicking on lights as they went.

'Mum!' called Daisy.

Nobody answered. The house was empty.

'She was visiting Kit at home today, right? She had no plans to go anywhere else afterwards – she didn't tell you anything?' asked Rob.

'No.'

'What the fuck . . . ?' muttered Rob. He went over to the phone. The answer machine's red light was blinking steadily. He pressed PLAY.

You have one new message. Press one to play your new message. Message reads . . .

'This is a message for Kit Miller,' said a low male voice. 'Message is, we have your mother. So you better stop fucking around and hand Bianca back, or this is going to get ugly, OK?'

The voice went on, naming a time and location when the exchange should take place – Ruby for Bianca.

Daisy was staring at Rob with horror writ large all over her face. 'My God,' she whispered.

And then they heard it – a low continuous thumping.

'What . . . ?' Daisy was almost too shocked to speak.

'It's coming from outside,' said Rob, and ran into the hall and back out through the front door. He paused on the step. Then he went and opened the boot of the car, took out a torch. 'Over there . . .' he said, and took off.

Daisy followed him and the thin beam of torchlight, stumbling in the dark, down beyond the lawn to the compost heaps and potting shed. The noise was coming from the shed. Rob pulled open the door, flashed the torch inside. There were two men lying on the floor, bound and gagged, amid the tools. The guards who should have been on the gate.

'Fuck,' said Rob.

He knelt down, freed the gag of one of the boys.

'Where's Reg?' he demanded.

'Well he ain't here,' said the man angrily. 'They jumped us, Rob. I'm so fucking sorry. We heard Ruby's car come in a while ago, maybe an hour, then it went out again straight away. Maybe Reg was driving, we don't know. Maybe Reg was *in* on it. We don't know that either. Fucking well get these ropes off us, will you?'

104

'I can't believe you have done this,' said Bella, beside herself.

'Hm?' asked Fabio distractedly.

They were all in the kitchen at the Danieri house – Fabio, his mother, a couple of the boys and a terrified-looking Ruby. Music was seeping from another room, an Italian tenor was singing '*Funiculi, funicula*'.

Bella couldn't believe what was happening. Her sons were a disgrace. They had sunk to the level of that monster Kit Miller, snatching women away from their homes. This would never have happened during the reign of her beloved Astorre. Her darling Bianca was a prisoner of that awful thug, and now they had this poor woman here, Miller's mother, who looked frightened out of her wits.

'When your brother hears of this . . .' she started, but the words died on her lips as Vittore came in, bringing with him a waft of chilly night air.

'As you can see, Mama, I know about it,' said Vittore, looking at her with cold eyes. 'In fact, I did it. I *ordered* it.'

'Then you must take her back to her home!' demanded Bella, coming to her feet. 'This family doesn't make war on women, surely? Shame on you, Vittore, for doing such a—'

Vittore's fist connected hard with her cheek, slamming Bella into her chair. She let out a shocked cry and then sat there, her eyes round with amazement and the beginnings of fear as she looked up at Vittore, her favourite son. He'd *struck* her.

'Shut your stupid mouth, Mama,' he ordered.

Fabio didn't even seem interested. He was pacing the room irritably.

'You *hit* me,' said Bella, staring at Vittore like he was a stranger.

'I should have done that years ago, you meddling cow.'

Bella's head snapped back at that, as if he'd dealt her another blow, harder than the first.

'Meddling in my *life*, fiddling around in my *marriage*, what the fuck gives you the right to do that?' demanded Vittore.

Fabio watched his older brother nervously. He was shocked and unsettled to see Vittore turning on Mama. *Something's changed,* he thought. *Yeah, he's done Maria for sure.*

Ruby sat silent, trying to be invisible. But all too soon Vittore's eyes turned to her.

'I've told them we have you,' he said softly, coming so close to her that she strained back against the chair. 'Now, let's see what they come back with. You think your boy Kit will give up Bianca, for you? I think he will.'

Ruby thanked God that Vittore didn't know her family situation. *If he knew, then he would realize this was a waste of time – and what might he do to me then?* she wondered. She didn't think for a minute that Kit would give up Bianca. Not for anything, and certainly not for her.

She knew she was doomed. Her shoulders slumped in defeat.

All she could do now was wait for the axe to fall.

105

Kit was up, dressed and walking, but it was perfectly clear to Rob and Daisy that he was far from fully recovered. He still looked grey around the gills, his arm was still bound up in a sling. A private nurse was coming in every day to tend his wound, and he was mending. But it was slow.

Now, they had to tell him this.

'They've got Ruby,' said Rob, not dressing it up.

'They *what*?'

'You heard. It was a snatch. Guys on the gate were tied up and put in the shed. Reg? I don't know. Maybe they've dumped him somewhere. Maybe he was in on it, who knows?'

'Shit.' Kit sat down.

'They want an exchange,' said Rob, standing over him.

'Right.'

Ruby for Bianca.

Only . . .

Kit thought about this. If they got Bianca back, what would they do? Spirit her away somewhere, far out of his reach? And if she insisted she wanted to be with him – and she would, he thought – what would Vittore do then? Wring her neck for dishonouring him, for going against the family code?

He thought of what Thomas had told Ruby, then Ruby

had told him about Bianca. His life seemed to be inextricably bound up with hers, and he couldn't let her go now. He just couldn't.

But they had Ruby. Vittore's words to him at Tito's funeral rang in his head: *I'll rip the heart out of you, out of every one of you.* Vittore had her. His mother. The very mother who had abandoned him, given him up.

Rob was staring down at him.

'What we gonna do?' he asked.

'We have to get her back,' said Daisy. 'We have to exchange them. Ruby for Bianca.'

Kit looked up at her. Then at Rob.

'Kit?' demanded Daisy, panic lacing her voice.

'What?' he asked.

'For God's sake! What are we going to do? We have to do something.'

Kit seemed about to speak. Then he sat back, said nothing.

Rob was watching him. He was afraid that Kit was going to say something like: *I've got Bianca. They can do whatever the hell they like with Ruby.* He exchanged an uneasy look with Daisy. He could see that she was thinking the same thing. He glanced back down at Kit. Years of anger and hurt there, all directed against Ruby. Was he really going to let it go now, come riding to Ruby's rescue when she needed him?

Rob didn't think so. And he could see that Daisy didn't, either.

106

Bianca was lying on the bed in the safe house, bored out of her brain, wondering when she would see him again.

He was probably the one who killed Tito.

She knew that. But she couldn't hate him. God knows, she had tried so hard to do it. Hate him as a true camorristi should hate. She'd shot him. Doing that had devastated her. Fearing him dead, she had thought she might as well be dead too.

No, she couldn't hate him.

Impossible.

When the key turned in the lock, she thought, *What's this? I've had supper.*

No one ever disturbed her except at mealtimes. It was part of her routine, her endlessly boring routine, that this was the case. So the only other living person she saw was the thin one with the cold eyes who came in to leave her a tray of food. He never spoke. He just put it down, and departed.

So what was this about? She tensed, turned away from the wall and sat up.

Kit was standing in the open doorway.

He didn't say anything. He just came in, closed the door behind him, leaned back against it.

Her heart beating hard, she stared at him, taking in every

detail. He looked stronger. He was dressed in jeans, a white shirt, a dark jacket draped over his shoulders. He seemed almost himself, but for the slight pallor of his skin and the sling still supporting the weight of his left arm.

Their eyes met and held.

'So I'm your prisoner,' she said.

'Yeah.' Kit walked forward, came to stand over her. 'Seems you are.'

Bianca stood up. He was very close.

For a moment she hesitated, then with a breathless moan she leaned in, snaking her arms around his neck, burying her fingers in his thick dark hair. His head dipped and he kissed her, long and deeply.

When the kiss ended, Bianca stayed there, her breath mingling with his. 'I love you so much,' she murmured. 'I shouldn't, but I do.'

'I know. Bianca . . .'

'Hm?'

'I have to talk to you. About Tito.'

'No . . .' She started to pull away. He held her fast.

'Honey, *yes*.'

'I can't!' She was shaking her head wildly. 'I don't want to hear it. I can't take it!'

'Look.' He grabbed her shoulders, shook her lightly. His eyes were intense as they bored into hers. 'Bianca, we have to somehow get past this, or it will wreck us. We have to talk.'

'But it's no good,' she said, almost sobbing. 'I can't . . .'

'Bianca. I'm sorry you lost your brother. *Really* sorry. But Tito did something awful to a woman I loved very much. He tortured her, killed her. I know you don't want to hear that about him, but he did.'

Bianca was staring at him; her skin, already pale, was now white as snow.

'And you see this? My hands? You asked me about them, remember?' Gingerly Kit held out hands, palms upward. The angry scar tissue right across them was horrible. 'Tito did this to me. The same night he killed that woman, he did this.'

Bianca was silent, staring at his hands.

Kit shook his head. 'I couldn't let it go, Bianca. How could I? The things he did to her . . . I won't tell you. It makes me want to puke just thinking about it. Tito . . . yeah, I know this is the last thing you want to hear, and I'm sorry. He was a sadist. A psycho. He was cruel right through to the bone, particularly with women. But Michael Ward – my old boss – he said that Tito was his wife's kin, that I mustn't do anything. So I didn't. I respected Michael's wishes. But once Michael was gone, I was free to act. And I did.'

Bianca was staring at him. All the colour had drained from her face and her eyes looked enormous. This was it, at last; now she knew for certain. All the rumours on the streets were true. Vittore and Fabio were right. He'd killed Tito.

'For fuck's sake, say something,' said Kit.

She swallowed convulsively. 'I loved him so much,' she said.

'I know.'

'And I love you,' she said, dragging a hand through her hair. 'God forgive me.'

'He's got fuck-all to forgive you for. You loved your brother, you didn't know that side of him. How could you? And Bianca – you and me, there's nothing wrong with that. Nothing that feels this right could possibly be wrong.'

Bianca put her head on his chest, slipped her arms around him, held him tight. A deep, shaky sigh escaped her.

Kit took a breath and said: 'There's more.'

'What?' Bianca murmured.

'Honey – Tito was never your brother.'

She looked up at him. 'I know, I was adopted. Mama always said I was special because she chose me from an orphanage. I've always known he wasn't my blood brother, but—'

'Bianca, there was no orphanage. You weren't adopted.'

Now she was frowning at him. 'I don't understand.'

He took her hand, led her over to the bed, sat down there with her. 'Before he died, Michael Ward told a friend of his about something that had been preying on his mind for years. It used to wake him up in the night, give him nightmares. In the end he felt like he had to tell somebody or he'd go mad.' Kit paused, took a breath. 'He said it broke his son, Gabe, because he was there when it happened, and afterwards he couldn't live with the guilt. He took to drugs, to drink – anything to wipe out the memory. And Michael was so disgusted that Gabe had been a part of it that he split with him, kicked him out of the house, when he was only nineteen.'

'I don't understand,' said Bianca. 'What does this have to do with me being adopted?'

'You weren't adopted, Bianca. Tito *took* you. You were stolen to order,' said Kit.

'But . . . what . . . ?' she asked. Then she shook her head. 'No, don't be silly. I was adopted.'

'No, you weren't. Bella wanted a daughter, but she couldn't have one by normal means and she was too old to adopt. That only made the wanting worse. She craved a daughter like a druggie craves his next hit. So Tito went out and got her one. He got her you.'

For a moment Bianca was too stunned to speak.

'Bianca—'

'No! What are you saying . . . ?'

'Bianca.' Kit was holding her hand very tightly in his. 'Honey, Tito . . . well, he went on a trip with Gabe, searching until he found a couple with a little daughter, a three-year-old child. I'm sorry, but he slaughtered the parents, and took the daughter home. You—'

Bianca surged to her feet. She whirled and stared down at him. 'No!' she said firmly.

Kit stood up too. 'It's the truth. It's what happened. You've been lied to all your life. I'm sorry.'

'You want me to hate him,' she said.

Kit shook his head.

Bianca started to cry. 'Not Tito,' she sobbed. 'He wouldn't . . .'

Kit pulled her to him and held her tight. 'He would. He did.'

'No!' She tried to pull away. Kit held on until she gave up struggling. 'He wouldn't,' she said more quietly.

'Jesus, I'm sorry,' Kit murmured against her hair as she shook with the force of her tears. He was hurting her, and it killed him to do that. 'You were stolen from your parents. Kidnapped. Taken because Bella Danieri wanted a girl. And your attachment to Tito . . . I'm so sorry, Bianca. It was him who snatched you away from your family, and your strong feelings for him, the way you've always loved him . . . it's all wrong. It's like that thing kidnappers' victims develop.'

'I can't believe this,' said Bianca.

'Believe it. It's true.'

She stood up, walked away from him, arms clasped around her, as if to keep out a chill. She was shaking her head slowly. He kept quiet, let her take it in. Poor little mare, this must be a hell of a shock.

Finally Bianca turned back to face him.

'You think that Tito killed my real parents?' she said

quietly. 'Then why don't I remember? Why don't I remember anything about . . .' Into her mind came the image of Tito, her beloved Tito – and the blonde smiling woman, and a strong arm, a man's arm, and the blade of grass, the bead of blood slipping down its edge. What did it all mean?

'Maybe it was so bad that you blanked it,' said Kit. 'People do that sometimes. In wartime and when people have been through something terrible, I've heard that can happen. It's like it's so bad, their mind just can't take it in.'

The blood slipping down the edge of the grass, staining green to brown . . .

'So it was all lies? My whole life is nothing but a lie? You're saying that they tricked me, deprived me of what I should have had, my own family, my real family, not them?' asked Bianca.

'I'm sorry,' said Kit.

107

'He's late,' said Vittore, sitting in the back of the car with Ruby beside him and Fabio on her other side. It was five minutes past midnight.

'Maybe he won't show up,' said Fabio. That wouldn't surprise him, Miller calling their bluff. He glanced at Ruby. Not a mark on her. Not yet. A shame, really. She was a good-looking woman and whether or not Miller played ball she was going to be dead meat within the hour.

They were in the abandoned skeleton of an old rope-making factory off a deserted side street in Clerkenwell. Miller had been told to bring Bianca there to exchange, or else . . .

Now Vittore was getting seriously annoyed. That fucking *schifosa* Miller. Vittore had six of his people spread out around the factory, all packing guns, all ready for the action to start should Miller try anything crafty. No way was that bastard getting his mother back alive. He would pay, *all* of them would pay for what he'd done. And once he had Bianca back, he would sort her out, make her toe the line. Make sure that she never again brought such shame upon the family name. She would be punished for her transgressions. And when he'd seen to all this, got even with Miller, dealt with Bianca, *then* he would address the Fabio problem. Fabio – the cheating conniving little cunt – had to go.

Fabio was twitching, snapping his fingers, humming under his breath, sweating and shooting anxious looks across at Vittore. He knew that Vittore planned on killing him. Maybe even tonight. After all, this exchange would make good cover. Fabio could find himself hit in 'accidental' crossfire; such a shame, Vittore would say, his little brother, how sad. But in reality, he would be pleased.

Between them, Ruby was silent, trying to make herself invisible. She stared ahead, drained of hope. Kit wouldn't come for her. She knew that. *They* didn't know it yet, but soon they would. And when they did, she knew they would kill her. Dump her body on her son's doorstep, saying, *Look, you bastard, this is your mother and she's dead. We warned you and now look what you've made us do.*

Her head jerked up. She could hear the rumble of an engine. She looked out through the windscreen to where the blue-white glare of the Danieris' headlights were illuminating the grim interior of the empty factory; the rust-bitten metal supports, the wet gleam of moisture, sodden leaves and old beer cans on the concrete floor where they'd been washed in by the rain and wind over the years and never swept away, because no one ever came here.

There was another car crawling towards the car they sat in, its headlights sweeping around in a blinding arc. It came to a halt about twenty paces away, its engine still running. Ruby blinked, unable to see anything but the white tunnel cast by the glare of two clashing sets of headlights. Her heart was beating so hard and so fast that she thought she was going to faint.

Kit . . . ? Jesus, could it really be him?

'Well not before fucking time!' said Vittore.

Roughly he flung open the car door, grabbed Ruby by the arm and dragged her out after him.

108

Kit was in the back of the other car with Bianca; Rob was at the wheel with Fats riding shotgun. They watched the bulky shape of Vittore emerge, then Fabio and the two minders. Vittore was holding Ruby by the arm, pulling her along to the front of his car where the light washed over them both, turning them into black silhouettes. But Kit recognized the outline of his mother. She was tall like him, and slender. There was no mistaking her.

He glanced at Bianca as Rob came and opened the door for him, mindful of his weak left arm. Kit got out, easing Bianca out beside him. He kept a tight grip on her with his right hand. Daisy had wanted to come too, but Kit had said no way. There would be too many bodies littering up the place as it was, without her adding to it. He'd given her another job to do.

Vittore and Ruby were at the front of the car now, standing ready. Vittore was smiling. He had the place well covered, and Miller was unarmed, the twat. None of Miller's people would get out of here alive tonight, he promised himself that.

Kit and Bianca were ready too.

'Send Bianca over!' yelled Vittore, and his voice echoed around the place like a ghost-whisper. *Send, send, send . . .*

'Ruby first!' shouted back Kit.

'On the count of three, we both let them go. OK?' said Vittore.

'Kay, 'kay, 'kay . . .

'OK!' said Kit.

Rob watched his boss and thought, *Fuck, he's going to do it. It's all going to be all right.*

He'd had his doubts. But now, Kit was coming good.

'One!' shouted Vittore.

Kit tensed. Shot a quick look at Bianca.

'Two!'

Rob, glancing all around, saw sudden movement at the far edge of the factory floor. *What the f—?*

'*Three!*'

Vittore gave Ruby a shove forward, and she stumbled then straightened and started walking toward Kit. Kit let go of Bianca, and she started walking too. They had each taken three steps when Vittore took a gun out of his pocket and aimed it between Ruby's shoulder blades.

Kit had already primed Bianca. *If I yell 'down', hit the floor.*

'Down! Get down!' Kit yelled, reaching inside the concealing sling on his left arm, and pulling out his gun.

Ruby flung herself onto the dirty wet concrete. Vittore's shot nearly deafened her as it zinged over her head, narrowly missing her.

Bianca went down too, very fast.

Kit lifted the gun and shot Vittore straight between the eyes. A perfect plum-coloured hole appeared there, and blood streamed down over Vittore's shocked face. He flew backwards, the force of the blast spinning him around. He lay across the bonnet like a stretched-out sacrifice. Both Vittore's minders and Fabio dived for cover behind the open car doors.

A bullet whizzed past Kit's ear like a buzzing insect and he turned.

'Look out!' shouted Rob, and took a shot at the shadowy figure running to their left. It let out a yell, and collapsed to the ground.

109

Fabio drew his gun and squatted behind the sparse cover of the car door and wondered what the hell was going on. Vittore had taken a shot to the head and was dead. *Vittore was dead.*

All Fabio cared about was making sure he didn't end up the same way. He squinted into the darkness, wondering what could have happened to the six armed heavies they had dotted around the place. Where were they, off taking a piss or something?

He crawled up into the car, scooted over until he was behind the wheel. Peeked up through the windscreen and saw Vittore's face right there against the glass, blood all over the place, saw his brother's eyes staring back at him yet seeing nothing.

Jesus . . .

Shaking, he got his foot down onto the pedals and slammed the car into reverse. The big limo shot backwards, knocking over one of the other boys, spilling Vittore's dead body off and onto the floor as Fabio spun the wheel. All the doors were open and swinging back and forth. He threw the car into first and floored the accelerator, knocking another man off his feet as he roared across the rubbish-strewn factory floor and out, free, into the night.

110

The tall Danieri heavy with the knife-scarred left cheek was laid out cursing and groaning on the factory floor where the car had hit him, but the other boy had got off more lightly and was crouching beside his dead boss, pulling out a gun, ready to come on all action hero.

'Don't bother,' said Thomas Knox, moving out of the shadows and pushing the muzzle of his gun hard up against the Italian's meaty head. He hauled the man to his feet.

'Get rid of that,' he ordered.

The Italian tossed his gun aside.

'Hands on your head. Quickly.'

As Kit watched, people started emerging from the shadows. His own men, and some of Knox's too, pushing in front of them six heavies with their hands on their heads: Vittore's crew. They came into the headlights and saw their boss laid out there, dead. One of them went over to the moaning scar-face on the floor, helped him back to his feet. His leg was all askew, obviously broken, and as he came upright he let out a yell of pain.

Fats and Rob went over to where the man that Rob had shot lay. He was sprawled out, clutching at his bloody ankle, snarling and writhing like a rabid dog.

'Gabe bloody Ward,' breathed Rob, staring down at him.

Gabe looked up at him and spat.

'That's not nice,' said Rob, and kicked him hard in the ribs.

Gabe howled.

They were still unsure whether Gabe had killed Michael Ward – his own father – but if he was, then maybe it would serve the scum right if he had to go on living with the guilt of it for the rest of his drug-laden days.

'Get up,' snapped Rob.

Fats grabbed the back of Gabe's jacket and threw him onto his feet.

'Bastard!' yelled Gabe, sobbing with pain and trying to keep his weight off the injured ankle.

'Walk,' commanded Rob, and shoved him hard. 'Go on. Fuck off out of it.'

Gabe fell down again, then crawled. Fats came after him at a run and Gabe whimpered with fear and scrambled to his feet. He limped away.

'I ever see that backstabbing bastard again, that's it,' said Rob. 'He's dead.'

'Do it now,' urged Fats.

Rob looked speculatively at Gabe's retreating back. Pictured the drug dens and the grasping women and the pimps beating him up and the general fucking miserable seedy hopelessness of the life that Gabe would live. It was no more than he deserved. A quick end? Nah. That would be too good for the likes of him. And if anyone should have the honour of finishing the little waster, it should be Kit. And maybe he'd do it, too – one day. But not right now. It could wait.

111

Kit was helping Bianca to her feet.

'You all right?' he asked, pulling her upright.

'Yes . . .' She was staring at the dead form of her brother Vittore. Only he wasn't her brother at all. And if he'd got her back . . . he would have punished her. Maybe even killed her when she defied him – and she would have.

'God, Mama is going to be . . .' She couldn't finish the words. She was shaking too much.

Mama had lost her favourite, and she would be beyond grief, beyond consolation. Bianca hated the thought of Mama's pain – but then she thought of all that Kit had told her. Her *real* mother was lying in an unmarked grave somewhere, murdered by Tito. Mama Bella had stolen her from that woman, snatched her true mother's happiness away without a care, claimed it selfishly for her own.

Rob and Fats came over to where they were standing.

'Look after her,' Kit said to Rob, who nodded and took Bianca's arm.

They watched as Kit went to where Ruby was sitting on the ground. Thomas Knox was standing over her.

'She OK?' Kit asked him.

'I'm fine,' said Ruby. She felt so choked up she could barely get the words out.

He'd come for her.

She couldn't believe it, but he had. Her son, the son she had never thought would return her love, had come here to save her.

'She's a bit shaken up,' said Thomas. He looked at Ruby for long moments, then at Kit. 'You can take it from here?' he asked.

'Thanks. Yeah,' said Kit, and held out his good hand.

Thomas shook it, briefly. Then he turned and merged into the darkness. Minutes later he was gone, taking his men with him.

'Come on,' said Kit, and gently got Ruby back to her feet. 'You OK?'

'I'm fine,' she said, and now, seeing the concern for her right there in his eyes, she was fine, she really was. At last.

112

Fabio found Mama in the kitchen as usual. A real Italian mama, his old mother was, always cooking up the ricotta ravioli, the *cozze gratinate e fagiolini*, the *cestini di patate con salsiccia e casizolu*.

Now here she was, and he had to compose himself, break the bad news to her. He had to compose himself not because he was grief-stricken but because he felt like laughing out loud. This was delicious, this was as good as Mama's food, this thing he had to tell her.

Her favourite boy was dead.

And funnier than that, *better* than that, was the fact that all that she had left of her family now was him. Fabio, the one who had always been such a disappointment to her, the one she had always pushed away, the one who should have been the girl, but wasn't. Years and years he had endured the fact that his mother tolerated him, that she'd never loved him. She had loved big, ebullient Tito. She had adored that dull dead bastard Vittore. And Bianca! Oh, how she had fawned over that little cow, who was in fact a traitor to her own family, to the Danieris, preferring to get herself fucked by Miller than be true to her own kin.

'Mama . . .' Fabio said gravely, while inside he could feel laughter bubbling up, almost overwhelming him. He was about to deliver the worst news of this woman's entire life, and he felt overwhelmed with sheer joy because at last, *at last*, he'd won. 'Mama, I have bad news. Terrible news – I'm sorry.'

Bella's face froze. She sank down into a chair, clutched at the table as if to steady herself.

'What is it?' she asked, wide-eyed. 'Oh, Fabby, what's happened?'

'I am afraid that Vittore is dead,' said Fabio, thinking of screwing Maria, who he firmly believed was dead, bricked up in the cellar now – and thank Christ he hadn't gone the same way.

And then he simply couldn't help himself. The laughter exploded out of him as if suppressed for a whole lifetime. He laughed until his sides ached, while his mother sat there and stared at him in abject shock and horror. Presently he staggered to his feet, left the room, went out into the cold night and got back into the car, still laughing, feeling lighter than he had in years.

He drove to the club – once called Tito's, then Vito's. First thing tomorrow he was going to have a new sign put up proclaiming it Fabio's. He parked, went inside. Ignoring the hostesses and the patrons he made his way upstairs to the room where once Tito's sex palace had been installed, and then Vittore's dull little room of beiges and browns and ochres. *Dull, dull, dull!*

Fabio swiped the mustard-coloured cushions off the Habitat sofa and onto the floor. He was still laughing, he couldn't stop laughing. It was over, it was all over at last. Everything was his now. He went to the drinks tray and poured himself a triple whisky, then moved into the centre of the room and shouted it out loud.

'*All hail King Fabio!*'

And then he raised his glass in a toast to himself, the survivor, the least likely to succeed. And look, just *look* at what had happened: he'd done it, walked past two graves to do it. Three, counting poor stupid Maria. Just look at the huge favour Miller had done him tonight; he ought to go over there and *kiss* that fucker.

'To me!' he roared out happily, and he drank the whisky down in one gigantic hit.

113

'You think Fabio's going to come up against us again?' Rob asked Kit as they sat in Kit's living room.

Rob didn't like loose ends. Vittore was done for, but there was still Fabio. And Gabe. Rob couldn't help wondering whether he'd been right in thinking the guy was such a loser that the worst punishment would be to let him live. He only hoped he wouldn't have cause to regret the decision to let him go.

'Why should Fabio bother?' asked Kit. He had the sling off now, his left arm was getting stronger. 'Bianca says he always hated Vittore and despised her, what should he care if she's out of the family fold and Vittore's dead as toast?'

'Never did like that little tit,' said Rob.

'Let it go,' said Kit.

There'd been pieces in the paper about gangland violence, shots heard late at night and a businessman called Vittore Danieri and some of his employees had vanished, seemingly without trace.

'How's your mum doing?' asked Rob.

Kit glanced at his watch. 'I'm just off to see her. Come if you want.'

Rob shook his head.

'Daisy's with her,' said Kit.

'Dunno.' Over these past weeks Rob had felt himself

getting on far too well with Daisy. Maybe it was time to step back from that. She was a posh bolshy cow, there was no doubt about that. She'd always want to be in charge.

'Ah, come on.'

'What are you two deliberating about?' asked Bianca, coming in from the hall and sitting down next to Kit.

Rob watched them, thinking what a striking couple they made. Bianca so pale, Kit dark like his mum. Kit kissed her cheek, grabbed her hand and held on.

'Rob's scared of Daisy,' he told her, sending a smile up at his number one man.

'Scared? In what way?' Bianca looked puzzled. There were big dark shadows under her eyes and a strained thinness to her lips. Rob thought that the news about the Danieris, the stark facts about her real family, the knowledge that it was Kit who had finished Tito – all that had eaten into her and was hurting her still.

'Scared in the way that he finds her fucking irresistible,' said Kit.

'I didn't say that,' said Rob.

'You didn't have to.' Kit looked at Bianca. 'You going to be OK here on your own for an hour or so?'

He worried about her. She'd had some terrible shocks and upsets, and while she seemed to have taken it all with her customary nerve, he wondered what the true impact of it all was going to be. Somewhere out there, maybe she still had real family, people who had been missing her for years. And he suspected that she still felt something for Bella Danieri, who was now mourning her favourite son. Bianca must be in turmoil.

'I'll be fine,' she told him. 'You two go, I'm going to have a snooze.'

114

When they got out to Ruby's place, it was to find an excited Daisy waving the Roy Orbison LP around and asking when the twins and Jody could come back, everything was all right now, wasn't it?

Rob wasn't sure about that. And he was winded by seeing Daisy again. Every time, the shock of her physical impact on him damned near took his breath away, but still he resisted it. What else could he do? It would be a bloody disaster, he knew it.

Kit was smirking at him. The bastard knew Rob had the hots for his sister. 'Soon,' he told Daisy.

'And we nearly forgot about this,' she said. 'Didn't we?'

'What, the handwriting?'

'Of course the handwriting. Kit, you know about this, don't you?'

Kit nodded. 'I do.'

They went into the sitting room where Ruby was shuffling through a box of magazines and cards. She looked up, saw Kit and Rob there with Daisy, smiled and stood up.

This time it wasn't her who opened her arms hopefully. This time was different. Kit came straight over to her and hugged her, hard. It hurt his shoulder a bit, but he didn't care.

'You OK?' he asked, thinking that he could have lost her, never got the chance to make it up. This woman – his mother – had talked him back to life. She had proved her devotion, when he hadn't even truly been there to see it.

'Absolutely fine,' said Ruby, hugging him and trying not to cry. He'd come for her, rescued her. Her son. Her beloved boy.

'Good. What's all this then?' Kit cleared his throat and indicated the box. He saw birthday greetings, Christmas wishes, Valentines . . .

'We thought maybe Mum night recognize the writing on the LP sleeve,' said Daisy.

'I don't know,' said Ruby. 'I don't think so. I'm going through my old cards to see if I could match it up to anything.'

'You and Michael did share contacts for quite a while,' said Kit.

'Yes, we did.' Ruby sat down again, picked up a handful of the cards. 'Stupid to keep them all really. Just clutter. Old things, old memories. Look at this . . .'

She pulled out a dog-eared copy of *London Life*. The date on its tattered cover was May 1941 and there were three women depicted there, dressed in lingerie and gas masks.

'They're Windmill Theatre showgirls,' she said. 'The one in the centre's Vi – my friend who's now Lady Albermarle. She was *so* glamorous. She was everything I ever wanted to be.'

Ruby put the magazine aside and thumbed through the cards.

'I really don't think I'm going to find anything here,' she said. She'd been looking for nearly an hour now, comparing the writing on the record sleeve to the jottings in the box. Privately she thought it was a waste of time, but she was doing it to please Daisy, who seemed to be chewing at this thing like a dog with a bone, determined to solve the riddle of Michael's death.

Ruby was becoming more philosophical now. She didn't think the mystery would ever be resolved, that they would eventually be forced to let it go, let him rest. It was silly to—

'Oh,' she said suddenly.

'What?' asked Kit.

Ruby's eyes were moving between the record sleeve and a Christmas card. There was a fat red robin on the front of it, and *Season's Greetings* printed in glittery script.

'Look,' she said, and put the card in his hands.

Daisy hurried over with the LP sleeve. They stood there and stared at it. Ruby looked up at Kit, her eyes anxious.

'You know that my brother Charlie was killed in a hit-and-run not long after he got out of jail? After he'd done time for the mail-van robbery?'

Kit nodded.

'Thomas Knox told me Michael was behind the hit-and-run. And that would fit. Charlie was trying to intimidate me, and Michael didn't like it.'

'You think this matches?' Kit was peering closely at the two sets of handwriting.

'It's close. Don't you think?'

It *was* close.

And it fitted, too.

Ruby knew that Betsy had always loved Charlie best; Joe was second choice. And if somehow she had found out that Michael was behind Charlie's death, couldn't she have targeted him? Seduced him, perhaps, and lured him to the place where he was killed?

I'm Still in Love with You.

Ruby shuddered. Yes, it could be Betsy. But it could also

be Joe. Charlie was his brother, after all. Perhaps Joe and Betsy had colluded over this, arranged Michael's downfall between them.

'You'll just talk to them, won't you?' she asked anxiously. 'He's . . .'

Dying.

'. . . He's very ill.'

Kit and Rob exchanged a look. 'We'll go easy,' said Kit.

After they'd left, Ruby sat there on her own and thought about what an individual thing handwriting was. Graphologists could tell a person's entire personality, just by the way they slanted letters and added loops. She sorted through a few more cards, thinking that she ought to toss this old stuff out. Look to the future, forget the past. She'd even put Thomas's card in here, the one he'd sent her after Michael's death. She thought she'd thrown that away . . .

Suddenly she saw it, and jumped as if someone had shot her. She dropped the box of cards and they fell to the floor. She bent down and with shaking fingers picked up the one that had caught her eye. She stared at it.

Couldn't believe it.

But there it was.

115

Rob dropped Kit back at his house because Kit was worried about leaving Bianca on her own for too long. Rob thought he was right to worry, she was a highly strung girl and she'd had some very hard knocks.

'We can take care of this,' he assured his boss. In the back of his own mind, he still suspected Gabe at work in this, somewhere. 'Let us go in first, suss out what's been going on. Maybe Ruby's mistaken. Maybe the writing's similar but not quite the same. Who knows?'

Because Kit was concerned about Bianca, he agreed to Rob's plan. He stood on the kerb for a moment, watching the car pull away, wondering how Rob and Daisy would get on in Chigwell. When he went indoors, he found that Bianca was gone.

'Joe and Betsy Darke – they're your uncle and aunt,' said Rob on the way out to Chigwell.

'Yes, but I've never been acquainted with them.'

'Your uncle's not well,' said Rob.

'I know.' Daisy shot a look at him. 'It seems Ruby and Betsy fell out a long time ago. And Joe took his wife's side, as you would. So there was an estrangement there, and it's never been resolved. Not my fault, or Kit's. Nothing to do with us.'

'Your aunt Betsy's a man-eater, Daise. Kit and me, we had a laugh about it after we came out here, but now I'm thinking it's not very funny. Your uncle knew what a loose tart she was, he saw her swanning half-naked around the house, chatting up the builders, and he resented it, poor old bastard. We guessed she'd be knocking off someone, but Michael? I thought he had better taste.'

Daisy was silent. She had a horrible image in her mind, of Michael in an alleyway, dead, his head shot away. Uncle Joe might be ill, too weak to do the job himself, but he still had plenty of criminal connections. If Betsy *had* been having an affair with Michael, then it would have been a simple matter for Joe to hire in help to kill his rival and – bonus – the man who had offed his brother Charlie. Or for Betsy to pull in a few favours and organize it in revenge for Charlie's death.

'Well, here we are.'

Rob pulled in beside the gateway of the Chigwell house. It looked quiet in there today, the house sitting serenely in its lush two acres, the gates shut, no builders, nothing. He got out and pressed the intercom. Waited.

He glanced back at Daisy in the car. Shrugged.

He pressed again. He could hear a dog barking in the distance, and wondered if it was Prince. Maybe Betsy was out, maybe she'd left Joe in the conservatory dozing, and the dog on guard. But peering up there, he could see her car was on the drive. You didn't just 'pop to the neigh-bours' round here. This was a classy enclave, people kept themselves to themselves.

Rob moved away from the intercom and started walking along beside the five-foot wall that skirted the property. He heard Daisy get out of the car behind him, and slam the door.

'What are you doing?' she asked.

'You think Joe's told Betsy he rubbed Michael out? Poor git's on his way to the pearly gates, confession's good for the soul. Maybe she's realized we've finally made the connection with the pair of them, or suspects we have, and is keeping a low profile?' he wondered aloud.

'We need to be careful here,' said Daisy.

'Meaning?'

'This could be either one of them. Joe or Betsy. If she was pursuing Michael, giving him gifts like the LP—'

'And the ring.'

'And that, yes. Maybe Michael was on his way to meet her when he died. Maybe that call from Joe was some sort of confrontation. Or a trap.'

'Well, we'll soon find out.'

Rob was approaching an accessible section of the wall. He glanced left and right, saw all was quiet, and heaved himself up and over.

116

'This is crazy,' said Daisy as they walked across the closely cut lawn to the house.

She'd scrambled over the wall after Rob, despite his moaning that she ought to keep the fuck out of this, wait in the car.

So here they were, approaching the house, and the barking was getting louder.

'What if the police are watching the place? What if the alarm's on?' she asked him, panting as she tried to keep up with the length of his stride.

'Easy. These people are your relatives. You were concerned when they didn't answer the intercom, you decided to come in. And the alarm? I checked it all out last time I was here. You only got to say what a nice place this is to Betsy and she gives you *all* the details. They don't bother setting the alarm, and it's a piss-poor single system anyway.'

'What?' asked Daisy.

'Christ, Daise, there are some big gaps in your education. It means you only have to cut the phone lines to the house and it's out of action. Plus, there are no movement sensors, either inside the house or out here.'

'You're so clever,' mocked Daisy.

'You get clever in this game, Daise, or you get dead.'

'That's a very big dog barking in there,' said Daisy.

'I know, I've seen it.'

They were at the front door now. Rob rang the doorbell. He leaned on the button for about a minute. Stood back. There was no answer. No movement. Only Prince, barking frantically.

'Let's go round the back,' he said, and Daisy trailed after him. They stood on the patio and looked in the kitchen window. Prince lunged up at the window, barking, snarling, smearing the glass with hot breath and saliva.

'Kitchen door's shut,' said Rob, peering in past the maddened animal. 'He's trapped in the kitchen, can't get out. That's good. Looks like all the refitting's been done, so the builders won't be in today.'

'Please tell me you're not going to break in,' said Daisy.

Rob looked over his shoulder at the big wooden bulk of the outside pool house. If he ever made a fortune like Joe so clearly had, he promised himself he would have the pool inside the house, not outside, save all that shivering your bare-naked arse off running between the house and the pool.

'Let's look in there first,' he said, and set off.

Daisy followed Rob through the double doors at the end of the pool house. It was humid in here, super-heated, all the windows that looked out onto the gardens were densely misted. Instantly she felt sweat break out on her skin. There were a couple of blue-padded sun beds at the far end of the pool, and they could hear the pump working next door. The water shimmered pale blue, lit by underwater lamps, throwing hypnotic dancing shapes up onto the wooden beams over their heads.

'What the f . . .' Rob said, his voice echoing as he moved ahead of her.

Daisy looked at what had caught Rob's attention. There

was a wizened old man sitting on the edge of the pool. He was wearing a navy-blue dressing gown and she could see striped pyjamas underneath, buttoned up to the neck. His scrawny legs were dangling in the water, so that the bottoms of his pyjamas and the trailing hem of the dressing gown were floating, sodden. His bony feet were bare.

He looked up as the two of them entered the pool house.

'Mr Darke? Joe . . . ?' said Rob.

Joe gave a ghastly death's-head smile. His skin was paper-white, pulled tight over the skull beneath. Only his brown eyes had any life left in them.

'You. I know you,' he said weakly, wheezing the words out, then giving a long, gurgling cough.

Rob moved closer. 'Yeah, I came out here before to see you. I was with Kit. Your nephew.'

'That's right.' Joe nodded, his head waggling around on his thin neck.

'Rob . . .' Daisy was looking at the pool.

Rob hunkered down beside Joe. He indicated Daisy. 'This is Daisy. Kit's sister. Your niece.'

Joe's eyes went to Daisy. She didn't even glance at him. Her eyes were wide open with shock.

'Rob . . .' she said, more urgently. She kicked off her shoes.

Rob turned his head, looked at what Daisy was staring at, down in the depths. *Jesus, wasn't that . . . ?*

'Fuck,' he muttered.

'*Don't!*' said Joe as Daisy threw off her cardigan. She froze there, arrested by the sharpness of his tone.

'But that's . . . she's . . .' Daisy blurted out in panic, staring fixedly down at the woman lying at the bottom of the pool.

'That's Betsy.' Joe gave a breathy, rasping laugh that was almost a sob. 'And the cow's dead.'

117

Daisy stood transfixed. Down there in the blue-shimmering pool, Betsy's streaked blonde hair was billowing softly around her head. Her eyes were half-open, glaring as she lay in a death lock with the red oxygen cylinder, its tubing coiled tight around her throat. Her skin was suffused with angry purple blotches where the tube had cut into her windpipe. Betsy was wearing a spangled pink bikini and a matching coverall. Even in death, she was flashily attired, with her pearly-pink-painted toes and fingernails, and masses of silver jewellery.

Starting to shake, Daisy turned shocked eyes upon her uncle.

He gazed right back at her. 'She was a fuckin' tart,' he said weakly, struggling to draw in breath and get the words out. 'No bloody good. I wanted to do that for years, put an end to her fuckin' rubbish. So when she came out here yesterday for her swim I . . .' he paused, coughed, then hitched in a struggling breath, '. . . I followed. Carried the fuckin' bottle with me, sodding thing weighs a ton. She laughed when she saw me come in with it. Asked me what the hell I thought I was . . . was doing. She soon found out though.'

Neither Daisy nor Rob said a word.

'I been sitting here ever since. Didn't have the bloody

strength left to move.' Joe coughed again; it was a horrible, guttural sound.

Rob looked at Daisy. She had one hand clamped over her mouth and she was trembling. She wasn't used to this sort of shit. He thought of the writing on the card – Betsy's writing – matching the writing on the LP sleeve. Or did it? Was Ruby certain about that?

Not that it mattered a toss now. If Betsy *had* bedded Michael – among he guessed maybe a thousand others – then she'd paid the price as far as Joe was concerned. And if Joe had ordered Michael's execution, well, the man was finished himself now. He was *this* close to death, any fool could see that.

'I been sitting here, looking at her down there in the water. I loved her, you know. She didn't love me though. For her, it was . . . always Charlie.' Joe hitched in a long, painful breath and looked at Rob. 'So here's what I want you to do. I want you both to go, and what I'm going to do is this: I'm going to lean forward a bit, I think I can do that, and get into the water. I'm weak as gnat's piss, but I can manage that, I reckon. Finish this whole fuckin' thing off. OK?'

Rob stared at the man and thought of the police, cells, prison hospitals. This was Kit and Daisy's uncle. Slowly, he nodded.

'We can't!' said Daisy to Rob, understanding that Joe was talking about drowning himself. He'd never have the strength to get out of the water, once he got in there.

Rob looked steadily at Joe. Then he turned away, looked at Daisy.

'Put your shoes on, Daise,' he said, and walked over to where she stood.

'We *can't*,' she said again, almost pleadingly.

Rob took her arm. 'We can,' he said gently. 'It's the kindest thing, Daise. You know it is. Come on. Let's go.'

118

They went back to Rob's flat out near Holborn. Rob was worried about Daisy; she was shivering hard, her teeth chattering. She said nothing all the way there. Once inside his flat, he pushed a brandy into her hand.

'Come on, drink it up.'

He downed one himself, too. It hadn't been the best of days.

Daisy threw back the brandy with a shudder.

'God, that was awful,' she moaned.

'Bathroom's through there, go and have a nice hot shower.' Rob was peeling off his jacket. 'Don't think about it, Daise. I know it's sad, but shit happens. He was suffering and now he's out of it. They both are. Try and think of it like that.'

Daisy went into the bathroom. Rob made his way through to the bedroom and found a robe that one of his girlfriends had left in the closet, in case Daisy needed it.

He went back into the living room and drank down another brandy. Now he could hear sobbing coming from the bathroom, over the background roar of the shower.

Oh, for fuck's sake.

He stood listening to it for a minute. Then he went over to the closed door.

He knocked. 'Daise? You all right in there?'

'Fine,' she said in a tearful voice.

And then it started again – the crying. He hated her crying. He grasped the handle and pushed the door open. Steam billowed around him. The noise of the shower was suddenly louder, and her gasping sobs were louder too.

'Daise . . .' he said, going over to the shower cubicle.

And all the while he was thinking, *Mate, what the fuck are you doing . . . ?*

He opened the door, and there she was. More beautiful than he ever could have guessed at, her skin pinkened by the hot water, her naked body all hot luscious curves and her face a mask of tragedy, her blue, blue eyes reddened by tears.

She saw him there, and froze.

'Daise . . .' he murmured.

'Rob . . .'

'Jesus, Daise, there's no way *around* you, is there?' he said, and quickly threw off his clothes and stepped under the hot soothing spray with her, pulling her into his arms, pressing his naked body tight against hers, knowing that this was precisely what he had been wanting to do for a long, long time.

'It's just so sad,' she mumbled against his shoulder. 'That poor man, and that's my uncle, and I never even knew him. He killed her. That's so terrible. And they've got children, I don't know them either. And they're orphans now. It's . . . horrible.'

'Daise . . .' Rob was kissing her hair, burrowing his face into her throat.

'And the dog!' Daisy stiffened. 'Oh God, the dog's going to starve in there, no one knows he's shut in the kitchen!'

'Fuck's sake, Daise, I'll phone the RSPCA from a phone box later on, say I'm one of the neighbours and I can hear him barking. Don't worry.'

Daisy slipped her arms around him, cuddled in close. 'It was awful,' she muttered.

'I know,' he said, smoothing her hair back from her eyes, kissing her salty cheeks.

'Oh God, Rob,' she said, and their mouths met, and that was it. He gave up, gave in. There was nothing else he could do. 'I'm such a mess,' she murmured against his lips. 'I cry at anything, and I've got this temper . . .'

'It's your hormones, after having the kids. My sister was the same. You can't help it.'

'And my breasts leak milk all the time, it's embarrassing . . .'

Rob took Daisy's breasts in his hands. He didn't give a toss whether they leaked or not, they were delicious, fabulous, deeply erotic.

'They're gorgeous. You're gorgeous,' he said, and kissed her again, and couldn't wait a moment longer. He lifted her, slipped his cock easily inside her. Nothing had ever felt so good.

'Oh God – Rob!' she cried out as he filled her.

He'd been fighting this for so long, but now he was lost and he didn't care. He made love to her, right there in the shower. And it was better than he could ever have dreamed it would be.

119

Ruby phoned the London place first, but there was no answer. So she called the other house and told them she was on her way. She wrote a note for Daisy and placed it in their usual spot for messages, on the hall table. As she passed the mirror she saw her strained reflection there and thought back to that day when she took the phone call from Bella, and all that had happened since.

Blood will flow . . .

Maybe this would be an end to it.

She went upstairs and packed the essentials in her small overnight bag and got one of Kit's boys to drive her to the railway station, where she got the train to Oxford. From there, she took a taxi out to Albemarle House, way out in the Oxfordshire countryside among a vast patchwork of fields and huge stretches of open country.

Finally the house loomed up, very tall, constructed in the sixteenth century, boasting a massive long gallery and a priest's hole, a knot garden and a ha-ha. The home of Lord and Lady Albermarle.

Vi was expecting her. She opened the front door herself, a broad smile of welcome fixed to her face. She looked the same as always – polished, well groomed, her red bob sleek, her fingernails red, a mist of Devon Violets all around her.

'Rubes! Well, this is a bit of a surprise. I'd have been

back in town next week, you didn't have to come all this way. What's happened? Where's the fire?' she asked with a laugh. 'Let me take your coat. An overnight bag! Are you staying in Oxford?'

Ruby nodded.

'No, you must stay here. No arguments!'

'I had to speak to you,' said Ruby, letting Vi take her coat, stepping into the cavernous hallway with its walnut wood panelling and its vast array of hunting trophies.

A myriad of dead deer stared accusingly down at her from the walls. There was no fire in the big stone fireplace today. It felt cold in here, and as usual the place smelled faintly musty. In the winter, it was a freezing house to live in, Vi had told her. Thick cardies and hot water bottles were the order of the day. Good job the aristocracy were tough, she always joked.

'What, it couldn't wait?' asked Vi, leading the way over to the drawing room.

'It couldn't wait,' Ruby confirmed.

They went inside. The drawing room was decked out in damask pink with faded tapestries on the walls. Two hard-backed couches were pulled up in front of the empty fireplace. Vi indicated that Ruby should sit down, and gratefully she did.

'So!' said Vi brightly, sitting opposite. 'To what do I owe the pleasure? You sounded a bit grim on the phone.'

Ruby eyed her friend steadily. 'I felt a bit grim.'

'Oh dear. Troubles?'

'Some, yes.'

'Come on then, what's up? That's what I'm here for.'

That's what I'm here for. It was so ironic, that statement, that it made Ruby want to laugh. Or cry. She reached into her bag, drew out the record sleeve.

'What's this?' asked Vi, leaning forward, all interest.

'Here. Have a look,' said Ruby, and handed it over to her.

Vi kept her face amazingly straight as she looked at the writing on the sleeve: *I'm Still in Love with You.*

Then she looked up at her dearest, oldest friend, her face puzzled. 'So? What are you showing me this for?'

'Because I'd like the truth,' said Ruby. 'Also, because that's your handwriting.'

120

'What . . . ?' Vi was looking from the writing on the sleeve to Ruby's face. 'I don't know what you mean, Rubes.'

'At first I thought it was Betsy's. You went to the same school as her and me, but you were a couple of years above us. And they were very keen on us all having that uniform super-neat writing in those days, weren't they? There was a left-handed girl in our class and they used to tie her hand behind her back to force her to write with her other hand. So everyone came out of class with this same neat, well-formed writing. Although I believe that left-handed girl came out with a nervous stutter too. My writing's similar to yours, to Betsy's. But not quite the same; my loops are bigger. Yours and Betsy's are *very* alike, I think that's a family thing. That's what confused me at first. But now I can see it. That's not Betsy's writing at all. It's yours.'

Vi's smile had vanished. 'I don't know—'

'It *is* your writing, isn't it, Vi?' asked Ruby, her voice hard.

Vi looked up at Ruby's face. She swallowed, then nodded.

'That was in Michael's record collection.'

'Rubes . . .' Vi was shaking her head.

'You gave it to him.' Ruby was staring at Vi as if she had never seen her before.

Vi was notorious – and it had always struck Ruby as

amusing, a friend's foible – for chasing men, for being seen out on the town with her young, handsome 'walkers' while her elderly husband stayed here on his estate. It didn't strike her as funny any more.

'Rubes, please . . .'

'*You gave it to him,*' said Ruby forcefully, cutting across Vi's feeble words.

Now Vi's face became set, mutinous. 'All right. OK. I *did* give it to him.'

Ruby took a breath. Vi might as well have stabbed her in the heart.

'Why?' she asked quietly. 'Why would you do that?'

Vi's eyes slipped away from Ruby's. She shrugged. 'Michael was . . . well, I found him very attractive. *You* did, why shouldn't I? And I suggested to him that he and I . . . well, just a fling, you know? A little bit of fun.'

'Oh God.' Ruby stared at Vi's face. 'You're not even his type,' she said dazedly.

Michael's taste in women had always been for the dark, the exotic. Like his Italian-born wife Sheila; like Ruby herself. He hadn't cared for blondes, or redheads.

'Don't look at me like that. You've no idea what it's like, married to . . .' Her voice trailed away.

'He was with *me*, Vi.'

'Weren't you the lucky one,' she snapped. Her eyes, still beautiful, emerald green, flashed into Ruby's. 'He was absolutely bloody devoted to you, of course.'

'I thought so,' said Ruby. She leaned over and snatched the record sleeve back off Vi.

'It started out as a bit of fun, Ruby,' said Vi almost pleadingly, spreading her hands as if in supplication. 'I wish I could tell you that he chased me. That would salve my conscience quite a lot. But the truth? The truth is I pursued him. I had to know: could I get him? I could usually get any man I wanted, but could I get him when he already had you?'

'You bitch,' muttered Ruby.

'You *know* I'm a bitch. You've always known it.' Vi swallowed and then went on more calmly: 'But the game soon got serious. I *wanted* him. I fell in love with him. Michael wasn't a toy like my usual boys. You've seen them: pretty little things, thick as pigshit. But Michael was a *man*, a real man, he was dangerous and alluring. I wanted him so much. Showered him with gifts – like that.' She nodded at the record sleeve.

'Go on,' said Ruby numbly.

Vi gave an awkward laugh. 'I suppose you think it's all a bit sordid, don't you? I gave him bigger things too. Expensive things.'

'The Krugerrand ring, inscribed *I'm Still in Love with You*. That was you too?'

'Oh, you saw that?'

'He had it with him on the day he died.'

Vi's mouth twisted. 'I'd given it to him a couple of days earlier. And no doubt he would have returned that, too, if he'd had the time. I wonder why he didn't return the record? Not that it matters, not any more. Because his time ran out, didn't it.'

Ruby said nothing.

'He wouldn't cave in. He sent so many of my gifts back. Rejected them, and me. I became desperate. What can I tell you? I'm a bored, rich woman with too much time on my hands and I started to pursue him like my life depended on it. Then I followed him one night when he was getting into his car. I was wearing a fur coat, nothing underneath it. I was *desperate*, Ruby. That writing on the record sleeve? That inscription on the ring? It was the absolute truth. I *was* still in love with him. And . . . I wanted to prove I could have him.'

Ruby's face looked as if it had turned to stone.

'And did you?' she asked.

Vi nodded, biting her lip, eyes downcast. 'Just that once. One night! And the minute it was over, he said, *Enough. Never again. Keep out of my way.*'

Ruby was listening, taking it all in. Michael had betrayed her. Thomas had been telling her the truth. Someone had seen Vi, in the priceless blue mink Anthony had given her for their first wedding anniversary, follow Michael to his car.

Just once and under extreme provocation, she thought.

But once was enough. Once was still a betrayal. And with her friend, of all people.

'You know me, Rubes.' Now Vi was smiling again, but the smile was sad and tired. 'Never could follow the rules, could I? Having had a taste, I wanted more. I kept running after him, he kept pushing me away. He really loved you, Rubes. Really and truly. He didn't want me. He never did. And that's why he died, in the end. Poor Michael.'

121

Ruby was very still, watching her friend – her *friend*! – as she talked about Michael's death.

'Oh, Rubes, please don't look at me like that. I adored him. I loved him *so much*,' Vi moaned.

Ruby was startled to see that Vi's eyes were full of tears.

'And I wanted to know I could still do it, Rubes, do you see? That I still had it, like I had it back at the Windmill all those years ago, that I could call any man to my side with nothing more than a glance . . .'

Ruby felt faintly sick, sitting here looking at Vi now. A woman who had everything in the world, and still wanted that little bit more. Even her friend's man. Just to prove that she could.

Ruby took a breath. It was cold in here, but she felt hot, almost dizzy with the shock of what Vi was telling her. All the way here she had been hoping, praying, that she'd got it wrong, that she was mistaken. But now she knew she hadn't, and it killed her. Vi was her best friend in all the world. And she had betrayed her.

'Was it you that killed him?' she asked in a breathless whisper. This was crazy, disgusting, and the worst part of all was Michael's death. Over this.

Vi's mouth dropped open. '*Me?*' she almost laughed, but there were tears making tracks down her cheeks now, real tears of grief and remorse. 'God, no. No! How can you think that?'

'Violet?' It was a man's voice, quavering, uncertain.

They both turned towards the door; they'd been so deep in conversation that they hadn't heard it open. Now Anthony stood there and as they watched he shuffled into the room and came over to where the two women were sitting.

The last time Ruby had seen him was in the autumn of the previous year when she and Michael had been here for a shooting party that ended in tragedy. In that short space of time, Anthony seemed to have aged even more. His white hair was too long, and stuck out in cowlicks. His face was a network of wrinkles, dried up as an old riverbed. His eyes were anxious. He was wearing an old food-stained waistcoat, red cord trousers, carpet slippers. He was leaning on a stick.

Vi stood up, quickly wiping away her tears as he approached, his eyes first on her and then on Ruby.

'Darling, what is it?' he asked, his eyes going back to his wife. 'You look upset.'

Vi forced a smile. 'It's nothing. Just reminiscing. Sad old days, all that.'

Anthony nodded and his eyes went back to Ruby. Now they held some of their old asperity. 'Can't have my girl upset, you know,' he told her.

Ruby felt the words clang around her brain like a bell. Somehow, she managed to summon a smile for him. 'No. Of course not,' she said.

Now he was slipping a trembling arm around Vi. Ruby saw the flinch away, saw this little tableau being acted out in front of her; ancient, mouldering Anthony, still protective of his wife – and Vi, repulsed by his touch, still feeling herself young, trying to prove that she could be the eternal Windmill Girl.

'So long as we all *understand* that,' he said, and there was an expression in his eyes that chilled Ruby to the marrow.

She swallowed. 'We do,' she said. 'Of course we do.'

'Good.' Anthony lunged in, kissed his wife's face.

Doesn't he see how she strains away from him? wondered Ruby.

Probably he did. And he ignored it.

He gave Ruby a curt nod, then walked to the door, opened it, and was gone.

122

The instant Anthony was out of the room, Vi wiped her cheek where he had kissed her. Her eyes were fixed to the floor.

'Were you very upset when Michael rejected you?' asked Ruby into the stone-hard silence of the room.

Vi cast a despairing glance at Ruby's face. She almost collapsed back into her chair, then buried her face in her hands. 'Rubes . . .' she muttered. 'I'm so sorry, I never wanted this . . .'

'*Were you?*' hissed Ruby, cutting across Vi's words.

'I never wanted you to know, I wanted you to let it go. A gang thing – couldn't you have just accepted that it was a gang thing, left it at that?'

Ruby surged to her feet and stood over Vi. She shrank back. Ruby looked mad enough to hit her.

'*Were you?*' she demanded.

Vi's eyes were full of fear. Then she nodded. 'Yes, I was upset. I was *devastated*. One night wasn't enough. Not with him. But he was having none of it. He loved *you*, Ruby, not me, never me.'

Ruby started pacing up and down, her hand over her mouth. She felt like she was going to throw up, or punch Vi in the face. She came back to where Vi sat and looked down at her.

'Anthony's very protective of you,' she said.

Vi nodded, sheet-white.

'It was him, wasn't it? It was him who killed Michael, because he'd rejected you, upset you. Anthony was used to your little affairs, all the young men, but this one was different. You cared about this one. It hurt you when Michael pushed you away. What happened, Vi? Did you cry to Anthony about it? Was that how it happened?'

'Oh Jesus . . .' sobbed Vi. 'I'm so sorry . . .'

'Was it Anthony?' pressed Ruby. She leaned down, grabbed Vi's arm and shook her, hard. 'Was it?'

'No, it—' Wincing, Vi wrenched her arm free. Her eyes when they met Ruby's were imploring. 'Ruby, I'm sorry – you have to believe that. Anthony . . . yes, it's true. I told Anthony about what happened. I know this must be hard for you to understand, but I often told him about the boys I went with. It amused him. He couldn't . . . he hasn't been able to do a damned thing in the bedroom for a long time. And thank God for that, I couldn't stand him pawing over me. But he liked to hear about my "little adventures" as he called them.'

'So you told him about Michael,' said Ruby.

Vi nodded, swallowed. Wiped her eyes again.

'I was distraught. Hurt. Furious. I told Anthony how Michael had pushed me away. And he so hates to see me upset.' She looked up at Ruby. 'He didn't do it himself.'

'So who did it?' Ruby's heart was pounding so hard it frightened her.

'Oh, Rubes . . .' groaned Vi.

Ruby grabbed a hank of that shiny red hair and pulled Vi's head back. She brought her face down very close to this woman who had been her friend.

'*Who did it?*' she spat.

'I don't know. Anthony doesn't, either.'

'*What?*'

'It's true,' said Vi, grimacing with pain. 'One of the casual workers who used to be on the estate was told to meet someone in a pub in London, pay them to do it. Someone unknown. And that's how it happened. So I don't know who did it. There's no way of knowing. But Anthony told me it had been "taken care of". I knew what that meant. I was half pleased about it – isn't that awful? Michael had hurt me so much. And I was horrified too. Horrified at what I'd done to you. And so, so sad. When I knew he was dead, I . . . well, all I could do was support you. Or try to.'

Ruby let go of Vi's hair as the words sank in. They would never know who did it. But an over-indulgent semi-senile old man had as good as pulled the trigger. And Vi had been with her at Michael's funeral, playing the good, caring friend. When all along she had been *totally* responsible for this disaster.

'You complete and utter cow,' said Ruby, and hit Vi very hard across the face.

Vi didn't even cry out. Her head snapped sideways. Ruby, starting to sob, hit her again. And again. Then she stumbled back and sat down hard, unable to stand any longer. At last, at long last, she knew what had happened to the man she'd loved. But this was no tidy solution. A stranger had been paid to carry out Lord Albermarle's wishes. That was all she knew. All she would ever know.

Ruby stared at Vi; her cheeks were reddened from the blows Ruby had inflicted on her. Her eyes were puffy with tears. She looked what she was: a sad middle-aged woman trying to cling to her youth. And in doing so, she'd wreaked devastation.

Ruby staggered to her feet, picked up the record sleeve, put it back in her bag.

'I'd like to phone for a taxi,' she said as steadily as she could.

'Yes,' said Vi, sniffing, trying to compose herself. 'Rubes, I'm so—'

'*Save it*,' snapped Ruby. She went over to the phone and made the call to the taxi company who had brought her out here. Then she sat down and in silence she waited for the cab to arrive.

'Rubes . . .' said Vi pleadingly after a minute or two.

'Shut up,' said Ruby, and Vi did.

Within five minutes, the taxi drew up outside, and Ruby left.

She knew she would never see Vi again.

123

'Maybe there's a way we can trace the son of a bitch who did it,' said Kit when Ruby got back and explained what Vi had told her.

They were all – Kit, Rob, Daisy and Ruby – at Ruby's house in Marlow. It was the day after she'd taken off for Oxford, leaving a note for Daisy.

'You shouldn't have done that,' Daisy complained.

'I had to. I couldn't wait for you all to come back. I needed to see her, face to face, to know what was going on.'

'It must have been horrible for you. And it could have been dangerous,' said Daisy.

Ruby thought that Daisy was probably right; it could have been a risk, going there. Thinking of it now, of Vi sitting there trying to justify the chain of events she had set in motion, made Ruby feel nauseous. But she was glad she had confronted her. Now she felt a weight had been lifted. At last she knew what had happened to Michael.

'Daise is right. You shouldn't have done that, you should have left it to me,' Kit told her. 'Anything could have happened to you.'

'But it didn't,' said Ruby.

'It's all been such a nightmare,' said Daisy. She'd told her mother what happened at the Chigwell house, the horror they'd stumbled across.

Ruby was still trying to take it all in. Her brother Joe was dead, and Betsy too. And Vi? Well, she might as well be dead – she *was* dead, to Ruby. Overwhelmed by sadness, her eyes drifted back to Kit. She could see that he was suffering, and her heart went out to him. Bianca had gone, without a word. He'd searched so hard for her, but he couldn't find her.

Then she looked at Daisy, and Rob – and she saw how his eyes followed Daisy when she left the room and came back in with Jody, each of the women carrying a baby. Daisy was like the cat with the cream, having her twins home, and every time she looked at Rob she lit up like a Christmas tree.

'What happened,' she asked Kit, 'about Reg?'

Kit was taking his nephew Matthew from Daisy, bouncing him in his arms. Matthew was laughing.

'Dunno. We haven't caught up with him yet.' Kit shot a look at Rob.

No need to let Ruby know they'd found Reg in the flat over the garage at Ruby's place, dead from an overdose. And no way of knowing what tricks Vittore had pulled – blackmail, money, who knew? – to turn a faithful old soul like Reg against the people who'd been like family to him for so many years. At least he'd had the decency to top himself before either Kit or Rob had to do the job for him.

'Jeez, what you feeding this kid, Daise?' Kit asked her. 'He weighs a ton.'

Kit came over to Ruby and put baby Matthew down into her arms. Ruby rocked the baby soothingly and smiled up at her son. Kit smiled back at her. In this room, right now, were the people she loved best in all the world. The riddle of Michael's death was solved. Despite her sorrow for all that was lost, she felt at peace. Almost.

There was still one thing left to sort out.

124

'You know what shocks me?' said Thomas Knox to Ruby when he opened the door of his Hampstead house to her next day.

'Hello to you too,' said Ruby. She was wearing a coat and carrying a bottle of Cristal champagne. It was freezing out here on the doorstep. Summer in England. It was pissing down.

'You know what absolutely *floors* me?' he asked, leaning against the door and staring at her.

'No,' said Ruby. 'Go on then. What?'

'That you actually believed I could rub out my old mate.'

'I didn't know you. I still don't. My toes are cold.'

'You hungry?'

'No.'

'OK.'

'You said I was on my own. That you wouldn't help me, or Kit,' said Ruby, feeling a little breathless.

'I know I did.'

'So . . . ?' Ruby leaned in until she was nose to nose with him.

'I lied,' said Thomas, and pulled her inside and kissed her.

★

An hour later, most of the champagne had been drunk and they were in the heated luxury of the pool, swimming naked.

'Forgiven me yet?' asked Ruby, floating; this felt like paradise.

'Dunno,' said Thomas. 'So you found out who did it in the end,' he said.

'We found out who was behind it.'

'Kit going to let it rest there?'

'I doubt it. So, am I forgiven?'

'Still dunno.'

'You want me to beg? On my knees?'

'That could be interesting.'

'You've got a sadistic streak.'

'You love it.'

'Hm,' said Ruby, as he pulled her into his arms. 'I think I might be falling in love with you,' she murmured against his mouth, gazing into those stony blue eyes.

'You *think*?'

'Maybe.'

'Well, let me persuade you . . .'

125

It was Sunday lunch at Rob's family home. Rob's dad had already settled in front of the telly with his beer, and Rob's two married older sisters were on the sofa, chatting and doing their nails. His two teenage brothers were play-fighting, bouncing around the living room like they were on speed.

'Careful!' cautioned Dad, peering around them at the screen.

Of course they didn't take a blind bit of notice. They romped up and down the hallway, up and down the stairs, making a bloody row.

Rob assembled them all, asked Dad to turn down the telly, called Mum in from the kitchen. The table was already set.

'What is it? This ruddy dinner won't cook itself,' said his mum, red in the face and undoing her apron in a hurry.

'Just a quick word,' said Rob. He glanced at his watch. 'I'm off to get her. We'll be back in under an hour. Now the thing is, *no one laughs at her posh voice*. All right?'

'We wouldn't do that,' said Mum, but the boys were already doing shrug-shouldered impressions of Ted Heath laughing.

'I mean it,' said Rob, giving them a stern look.

'Hmph,' said Dad.

The family Sunday lunch. Always a nightmare. And now

he was going to thrust Daisy into this madhouse, the poor cow.

He drove over and collected her from Ruby's place. She looked terrific, as always. Gorgeous. They kissed on the doorstep. Ruby was out, visiting a friend, Daisy said, then she'd be having Kit over for dinner this evening.

Daisy was ecstatic at how well Kit and Ruby were getting on now.

'Yeah, well, it shook him, nearly losing her like that,' said Rob when Daisy enthused about it. 'Woke him up, I think. Made him see the light. Made him see what a prize prat he was being.'

He drove them back to his parents' house. Took her inside.

'Hello!' she said, beaming around at them all.

'It's like a fuckin' royal visit,' said one of the boys, and Dad cuffed him.

'Hello, Daisy,' said Rob's dad, standing up and holding out a hand. 'Come on in.'

And much to Rob's surprise, it was all right. It really was.

126

November 1975

It was a day much like the one on which Michael Ward had died a year ago. Two thirty in the afternoon and already the sky was a darkening purple-grey bowl over their heads. It was drizzling, and there was a cold wind blowing. Browning leaves were drifting down from the silver birches and the oaks around the perimeter of the graveyard, forming a mushy uneven carpet on the tussocks of grass around the graves.

Kit had parked the Bentley at the cemetery gates and together he and Ruby had walked slowly over to Michael's final resting place beneath the yew tree. The headstone was large, black granite inlaid with gold, and elaborately carved; Kit had chosen it, paid for it.

Here Lies Michael Ward
Much Loved, Much Missed
1917–1974

While Kit looked on, Ruby emptied the dying flowers from the urn, refreshed the water from the tap beside the gate, and arranged the new red roses on the grave. Then she stood up and slipped her arm through Kit's. He didn't flinch away, not any more.

'A whole fucking year,' said Kit with a sigh.

Ruby squeezed his arm. 'He meant such a lot to you,' she said. 'I know that.'

Kit looked at her. She almost thought there was a glint of tears in his eyes. He'd lost so much, her poor nameless boy. Michael, Gilda, Bianca . . .

'He was my dad, you know. My *true* dad. Not that fucker Cornelius.'

'We both loved him.'

Ruby thought about how much Michael had meant to her. There had been just one betrayal, with Vi, with a woman who pursued him fanatically, put it right there on a plate. Foisted it in his face, the bitch. Maybe she wouldn't have forgiven him for that if he'd still been alive, but he was dead, the victim of one woman's mad obsession, so what the hell, what difference did any of it make now?

'Kit?'

'Hm?' He was staring at the gravestone.

'Have you really forgiven me? Truly? Completely?'

Kit looked up and his eyes met hers. He heaved a sharp sigh.

'You know what? For the longest time, I couldn't. I tried. For Michael, I tried. But I couldn't do it. And then I was shot. And Rob told me about how you sat there beside me all the time, even though you were exhausted, wrung out, you sat there and talked to me, willing me back to life. And I could hear you. It was a fucking frightening place to be, but I could hear your voice and . . . well, it made it bearable somehow.'

Tears slipped down Ruby's face as she recalled how awful it had been, fearing he would die. Kit squeezed her arm.

'Hey, don't cry. Everything's fine now. You and me, we're OK. All right?'

Ruby nodded, smiling through her tears.

'Perhaps she'll come back,' said Ruby, sniffing. 'Bianca, I mean.'

She knew that was his dearest wish, but she was torn over it, wanting his happiness but fearful of his choices. Really, she was glad Bianca was gone. The girl had hurt him, nearly killed him.

Kit stared at his mother's face. Ruby was being kind, trying to give him a little hope, but he had none, not any more. Ah shit, Bianca! He'd searched for her so hard, he'd nearly gone crazy looking for her. He'd had word out on the street, find her, *find* her. But no one did. He'd gone to the Danieri house. He didn't give a fuck if he ran into Fabio there, but as it happened he didn't. There was no cream Morgan on the drive, no sign of Bianca. The old woman was there, Bella, and she came to the front door when he rang the bell.

'Is Bianca here?' he asked her flat-out.

And what had struck him as weird was that Bella didn't answer. Eyes blank, she turned and shuffled across the hall and into the kitchen, then sat down at the table. Kit followed. Somewhere in the building '*Nessun Dorma*' was playing on a stereo. The kitchen was dirty, disorderly. Everywhere there was dust and mess. The place felt cold, and there was a faint smell, sour and unpleasant, hanging in the frigid air as he crossed the hall – like something nasty had crawled behind a wall and died.

'Have you seen Vittore?' she asked him.

Kit looked at Bella more closely. *Shit, she's off her head*, he thought.

'I told them blood would flow. I *warned* them,' she said,

thin lips trembling. 'Sometimes I think I see her, you know. In the hall.'

'Who?' he asked. 'Bianca? Is she here?'

'No, I mean the slut . . . that *slut* who took my boy . . .'

Kit left her sitting there and searched the house, top to bottom.

No Bianca.

After that he drove down to Dante's, but the place was boarded up, the car park empty except for a few desolate fliers swirling along the ground in the fresh sea breeze.

In the end, he gave up, admitted to himself that this was it; she was gone for good. He had killed Tito, and owned up to it; here was his punishment. He'd lost the love of his life.

Ruby thought that it was all past. None of it mattered any more. All done – like poor Joe, like Betsy, like her friendship with Vi.

Time to let it go.

She had her son back now, *truly* back, and her daughter, and the twins. There was the question of what would become of Nadine and Billy, Joe and Betsy's orphaned children. She had already stepped in, conferred with the boarding school they attended so that their schooling went on without interruption. She'd had them with her in Marlow during the summer holidays, and kept in regular contact with them over the autumn term. Now she was determined to see to Christmas for them, to make sure they were cared for.

And there was Thomas, of course. She had lost a friend but gained a lover. Life could be good again. It *would* be. She was determined about that. And finally she was ready to voice what she had been thinking about for the past few weeks.

'I'm considering selling the business,' she said.

Kit looked at her in surprise. 'Really?'

Ruby nodded. 'I reckon it's time for a new challenge,' she said. 'I'd hoped Daisy might follow me into it, take it over one day, but that was just wishful thinking. I've no idea what she'll do, but it's certainly not that.'

'Maybe she'll marry Rob,' said Kit with a faint smile.

'That would be wonderful. I love Rob.'

Kit shrugged. 'It's a good business. A *big* business. You sure you'd want to give it all up?'

'I could do something different,' she said.

'Such as?'

'Sail the world. Hike across the Pyrenees. Anything.'

'You hate boats. And hiking?' He looked down at her elegant court shoes. 'I don't think so, Mum.'

Mum, thought Ruby. The sweetest word in the whole English language. She smiled up at him. Her son, who'd come through for her when she was sure he would not. She loved him so much.

'I'll see,' she said, thinking that the world held all sorts of possibilities now that she had her family united once more.

'Let's get on home,' said Kit, and together they turned and walked back to the gate as the darkness of the winter's afternoon gathered around them.

127

Life went on.

Kit carried on running his firm, with Rob at his side, watching his back. Traders, shopkeepers, restaurant owners, paid him to keep them safe from thugs, and he did. His boys collected on loans, broke a leg or two on the late-payers – this was after all a business, not a fucking charity.

Time went on.

General Franco died, and so did Graham Hill the famous racing driver, in a light aircraft he was piloting. The Australian Prime Minister was sacked and the Queen opened the North Sea oil pipeline.

Winter deepened and hardened its grip, and soon it was December: Christmas Eve. Kit had presents to buy for Daisy and Ruby and the kids. Along with most of the rest of the population of London, he'd been up and down Oxford Street, which was twinkling with a million festive lights.

Finished at last, knackered after jostling through the crowds, he drove back home, parked up, got the presents out of the boot and locked the Bentley. He was halfway across the pavement in the rain when he saw someone sitting on the steps leading up to his front door. He stopped walking and stood, immobile, staring up at the small white shape huddled there. His heart was in his mouth.

'Bianca?' he said.

It couldn't be her. He'd lost her, she'd vanished from his life, and he had come to terms with that. He wasn't going to get her back. The shock of all he'd told her had been too much for her. But now . . .

She was here.

Her head lifted. Their eyes met and held. Slowly she stood up, walked down a step or two. He dropped the bags and she almost fell into his arms.

'Jesus, Bianca . . .' he moaned, and kissed her over and over again. Feverishly, she responded. Nothing was said for long moments, then Kit eased her away from him. 'Where have you been?' he demanded.

'Oh – here and there,' she said, with a small sad smile.

'You just left. Vanished without a fucking word.'

'I had to think. I had to be alone for a while.'

'Are you all right, you crazy cow?'

'I'm fine. I needed to think about everything. I was . . . confused.'

Kit nodded slowly. Of course the poor little bitch had been confused. Her world had been thrown into chaos.

'I thought I might have some real family out there, some-where,' she said. 'That I might be able to find them. But I can't remember them. I've tried, so hard. But I can't. How am I ever going to know if I can't remember anything?'

'You haven't been to see . . .' He'd been about to say *your mother*. But Bella Danieri wasn't Bianca's mother. As for her real family – who knew?

'I haven't seen *her*,' said Bianca.

Kit was silent.

'I hate her,' said Bianca. 'I hate them all. They snatched my past away. Robbed me of everything. Lied to me.'

'Even Tito?' asked Kit.

'Yes. Even him.' Her eyes were hard. 'Him more than any of them. You know Fabio's in charge now?'

It was cold out here and the drizzle was starting to turn to sleet.

'Now Vittore's out of the way? Yeah. I know. What will you do?' he asked her.

'Tito taught me to be camorristi,' said Bianca. 'That's what I am. Fabio's going to hear about it.'

Kit stared at her. 'I'll help. If you want.'

Bianca's eyes softened as they looked into his. 'I want that very much,' she said, and they kissed again, standing there in the pouring rain, neither one of them caring in the least that they were getting wet.

EPILOGUE

Ruby was crossing the hall at the Marlow house when the newspaper came through the front door. She went over and picked it up, and took it through to the kitchen. Pouring coffee from the cafetière into a mug, aware of happy chattering coming from upstairs where Daisy and Jody were getting the twins up and ready for the day, she thumbed through, glancing at the headlines, not paying anything very close attention. And then she saw it.

Tragic Accident

> The bodies of Lord Anthony and Lady Violet Albermarle were discovered yesterday evening in the lake at Albermarle House. Both were pronounced dead at the scene. It is believed that they were fishing from a small boat and that it overturned and both sadly drowned.

Ruby sat there for a long time, her heart pounding as she stared at the newspaper.

Oh, Kit, you had to make someone pay, didn't you, she thought.

Then she heard Daisy, a gurgling baby in her arms, coming down the stairs. She closed the paper and slipped it quickly into the bin. She'd lost her oldest and dearest friend, but she knew that she wouldn't be shedding any tears.

Not now.

Not ever.